THE LINES

ALSO BY MATT BROLLY

Detective Louise Blackwell series:

The Crossing

The Descent

The Gorge

The Mark

The Pier

The Bridge

The Solstice

Lynch and Rose series:

The Controller

The Railroad

DCI Lambert series:

Dead Eyed

Dead Lucky

Dead Embers

Dead Time

Dead Water

Standalone novels:

Zero

The Running Girls

The Alliance

THE LINES

MATT BROLLY

THOMAS & MERCER

Published by Thomas & Mercer, Seattle

www.apub.com

EU Product Safety contact:
Amazon Publishing, Amazon Media EU S.à r.l.
38, avenue John F. Kennedy, L-1855 Luxembourg
amazonpublishing-gpsr@amazon.com

ISBN-13: 9781662520419
eISBN: 9781662520426

Cover design by Tom Sanderson
Cover image: © elbud © Peter Turner Photography
© Anna Mente / Shutterstock; © Tim Robinson / ArcAngel

Printed in the United States of America

For Hamish

Prologue

Marlon Tomlinson missed his mother. He missed his father too, but in particular his mother. If she were here, she would have known what to do. At least, she would be able to tell him what was happening. But she was dead, as was his father, and Marlon guessed he would be too, soon.

It had started about a year ago. He'd met them outside a pub in Camborne where he'd just got a kicking from a couple of his old school acquaintances. It happened now and again. Marlon was a loner who didn't know how to fit in with others. This made him a target, especially late at night when people had drunk too much. The newcomers had asked him if he was OK, bought him a kebab, and shared a joint with him. Before he knew it his house – the house his parents had left for him – had been taken over.

It was fine to begin with. They'd treated him as a friend; one of the gang. There had been a seemingly unending supply of drugs and drink, and it had been good to share the house with people again. But gradually that had changed. It had become a twenty-four-hour party place, the drugs and alcohol just the start of it. Soon they'd sent him out on the streets, dealing for them. If he complained, he was beaten, or locked away in his house. By the time he realised he was being used, it was too late.

He'd tried to get help, and that, he presumed, had been his undoing. It was why he was lying in the hull of the boat, his hands and feet tied, his mouth gagged, as the craft sped over the swell, lifting him into the air before crashing him back down.

Marlon didn't fight his binds. Even if he could free himself, what could he do? He could hear their baying on deck, the inane laughter drifting over the sound of the gulls, the roar of the waves, and the constant drone of the engine which eventually cut out as the boat came to rest.

He closed his eyes as the boat drifted. The swell felt gentle beneath him and Marlon was wondering if he'd already died, and if his mother was going to appear to take him away, when his eyes were assaulted by a bright light as two men joined him in the hold and lifted him to his feet.

'Come on, son,' said one of them.

He didn't know either man – he was sure he'd never seen them at any of the endless get-togethers that happened at his house. They seemed more serious than the people he was used to dealing with. Everything about their actions suggested they were just doing their job, and had no consideration for what Marlon was going through.

It was night, the only illumination a weak spotlight glowing down on the water. The men placed him on the side of the boat, holding on to him so he remained balanced.

A third man appeared – older, bigger, his eyes dark and unblinking. 'Do you know who I am?' he asked.

Marlon shook his head and the man continued staring, as if he could see Marlon's soul. 'I didn't mean to,' said Marlon, his voice brittle as the sound drifted away.

He'd never met the man, but he knew that he had to be in charge. Marlon should never have gone to the police. The warnings had been there all along, but he'd succumbed to a moment of madness, a first moment of bravery in a life of cowardice. He'd run out of the house, gone to the local police station . . . and found they were closed. He'd never thought about whether the police took days off, and he'd sat outside for a few minutes before heading back home.

But someone must have known what he'd done. Two days later, he'd been grabbed off the street by people he'd never seen in his life. They'd put a bag over his head, dumped him in a van and taken him somewhere he didn't know. By the time they removed the bag, he was on the boat.

'You don't need to explain anything to me,' said the boss man. 'That's not why you're here. There are always casualties, Marlon, and today you're one of them.'

The man had an almost hypnotic voice, and the way he spoke made everything sound reasonable. Marlon gazed at the rippling water, searching for an end to the sea's depth in the gloom, and discovered that he was crying. 'Please, no, I promise. I did everything you told me to do.'

'But I have never asked anything of you,' said the man, nodding to his two colleagues.

'We're doing it here?' said one of them. 'We're not that far from shore.'

'I am well aware of that. Untie him.'

Marlon struck out as he was untied, punching and kicking at his captors who wrapped giant hands around him until he was subdued. They lowered him into the sea, the rush of the water taking his breath away.

The biting water stung his skin, the salt stinging his eyes, as he bobbed below the surface and back up again, his lungs on fire.

Marlon didn't know how to swim. Despite living by the sea all his life, no one had ever shown him how. He tried to keep afloat but his limbs were all but useless in the swell of water. He glanced at the boat where only one of them, the boss man, was watching, arms folded, as if bored by the situation. Marlon wondered if this was a test or maybe a warning, praying that at any moment they would send over a life buoy for him, but as he began to sink into the depths of the sea he understood this was going to be his resting place.

But his body had other ideas. It thrashed at the water, pulling him back up for one last gulp of air, one final glimpse of the man on the boat, before the acid-like water rushed his lungs, his chest and body feeling as if it were about to explode, his limbs tensing to rigidity, as he was finally swallowed by the sea.

Chapter One

Liam Kilshaw was running late, which added to his nervousness as he dashed through the hushed streets of St Ives to the bar where he'd arranged to meet Millie. He could taste the salt in the air, the day's humidity causing him to break into a sweat as he climbed the steps to the gastro pub, straightening his clothes before stepping inside.

He wasn't used to being nervous, and inside he scoured the room for his date.

'Liam?'

'Hi, Millie,' said Liam, turning to the woman who happened to be his nine-year-old's schoolteacher. 'You haven't been here too long, have you?'

Millie smiled. 'I've been admiring the view.'

'Shall we get a drink?'

'Sure. I got us a table by the window.'

'Sorry I'm late.'

Millie smiled again but a quick look at his watch told Liam he had been nearly thirty minutes late, and he noticed a curt smile cross Millie's face as they approached the table. 'I imagine George gets a tardy mark if he's ever this late for school?' he said, waiting for Millie to take a seat first.

'He's never this late,' said Millie, her raised eyebrows suggesting that Liam was forgiven for now.

He'd been attracted to Millie from the moment he'd seen her. That was on George's first day back in school, last September. Her appeal was obvious – he'd noted more than one of the dads staring her way – but there had been something about the way she'd held herself – demonstrating to both the children and their parents that she was in charge – that had made her stand out.

Yet it had taken nearly nine months for this date to be arranged. For that, Liam had his ex – George's mum – to thank. Kim had set up the date having bumped into Millie at the local supermarket. And ever since he'd been told that Millie had said yes, Liam had felt nervous.

It wasn't like he had ever been short of female attention. He was six foot two, with a perfectly hairless scalp – a result of childhood alopecia – which had earned him numerous nicknames. His mother used to say that God had blessed him with extra good looks as compensation for a childhood without hair, and he'd grown into himself as an adult. He was an ex-marine and Special Boat Service – SBS – operative, and still had the same muscular physique now he was in the police. Yet despite the admiration that often came his way, it had been a long time since he'd experienced a connection with anyone. He had a tendency to keep people at arm's length, but had promised himself – and Kim – that he would try harder this time.

'So what were you teaching them today?' he asked, feeling the question was inadequate as his pager went off, buzzing across the table.

A tightness ran through Liam's chest, and he took in a deep breath through his nose.

'What's that?' said Millie, glancing at the pager that was still buzzing.

The tightness had spread and, for a second, he wasn't able to move his body. 'I'm on call with the lifeboat tonight. I should have said, but we are so nearby . . .' he said.

If Millie was angry, she didn't show it. She stood up before Liam did. 'Don't be silly. You go, I'll settle up here,' she said, her eyes not leaving his.

Liam rooted in his pocket for his phone. 'We're so near, I can't really let them down.'

'Go, you don't have to explain.'

'I don't have any cash,' he said, squirming as he got to his feet. 'I've really messed this up, haven't I?'

Millie held his gaze. 'I've had better first dates,' she said, pausing. 'How about you get the next one?'

A siren rang out as Liam sprinted the short distance to the lifeboat station on the wharf. Although the call would have gone out to around twenty volunteers, and the boat could only take seven of them, time was of the essence, and being so close he had felt compelled to respond.

Yet, as the station approached, he felt the familiar pain return to his chest and he was forced to stop to catch his breath by the sea wall. He could hear the water lapping at the shore, the boat already being prepared in the lifeboat station.

The sea had been Liam's life for as long as he could remember. In fact, he couldn't remember a time when he hadn't been able to swim. He must have had lessons, but his earliest memories were of him in the water – riding waves, or racing with his father to shore on boogie boards. Such was his affinity with the water that he'd followed his father into a career in the navy as a marine, progressing to join the SBS, before everything had changed.

Liam placed his forefinger to his thumb, controlling his breathing as memories of his last deployment played through his mind. He'd been deep within the Indian Ocean as part of an ongoing operation when his breathing apparatus had failed. He often suffered nightmares of his slow ascent where he'd suffered decompression sickness, and the panic of those last moments, the unbelievable tension in his body as he came within seconds of drowning, were never far from his thoughts, especially this close to the water.

He arrived at the station to see the coxswain, Miles Fischer, had beaten him to it. Fischer was the director of operations, and now that Liam was there, would skipper the team that night. Like Liam, Fischer was ex-navy. He was thirty years older, and with his rugged silver-grey beard looked every part the salty sea skipper. 'You're running late, Liam,' he said.

'Don't worry about me,' said Liam, as they rushed into the centre and changed into their drysuits.

'Are you sure you're OK? You look a little peaky.' Fischer was the only one of the team who knew about Liam's past. He'd made the final decision to allow Liam to join as a volunteer. In fact, Fischer had been the one who suggested Liam sign up and use the time on the water as a kind of exposure therapy.

Ever since his honourable discharge, Liam's affinity with the sea had been overtaken by fear. He could have taken the easy option and moved inland somewhere. But the sea was an ingrained part of Liam's life. And although it now scared him, he found his life was emptier without it. 'I'm fine.'

Fischer stared hard at him. Liam had been an active member of the crew for the last six months. During his time in the SBS, he'd experienced things on the open sea – hostile encounters, rescues in gale force conditions, and covert operations like the one that had almost got him killed – that none of the other volunteers had. Yet every time the lifeboat was launched, he was forced to hide the terror running through his blood.

At last Fischer nodded, and with the rest of the team assembled, the boat was launched. Fischer was at the helm, Liam one of the deck crew along with two crew virgins – Wayne 'Mouse' Mainwood and Billy Rowson – both good lads who had been volunteering for the last few months. The water was choppy, the boat skimming through the waves as they headed into St Ives Bay towards Godrevy Island with its active lighthouse, close to where the call had come in.

'Suspected body in the water, sir,' said Billy Rowson, who was coordinating the radio. 'Call came from air-sea rescue who happened to be in the area on training activities.'

'You don't need to call me sir,' said Liam, who could see the chopper in the distance as Fischer kept the throttle of the boat at max, the vessel cutting through the waves, at times seemingly flying through the air, until he stopped the engines as they arrived at the coordinates.

The chopper hovered overhead, its spotlights illuminating the swell as the bowman shone the boat's lights on to the undulating water. Holding the grabrail, Liam shone his torch into the water, searching for the body. It was all too easy to imagine himself falling overboard, and he felt his hand ache from the grip he had on the rail as he wondered, like he'd done on every call since joining, what the hell he was doing here.

'Body in the water.'

Liam forced himself to loosen his grip as he glanced towards Billy who had made the call.

'Show me,' said Fischer.

'It's there, Commander,' said Billy, pointing out to the floating body which was face down in the sea.

Fischer glanced at Liam, and the pair shared a smile. 'I'm the coxswain, son, not the commander. You been watching too much James Bond?' he asked, deepening the lilt of his already deep Cornish accent, making the young lad blush.

'Sorry, sir,' said Billy.

A call was put in to the coastguard before any attempt was made to retrieve the body. Photographs were taken of it before boathooks were used to gently pull it to the side of the boat.

'Body net, Liam,' said Fischer, as two of the crew kept the body in place.

The pressure still in his chest, Liam deployed the body net over the corpse with Billy's help. He refused to show his fear to the other crew members, but it was taking all of his mental strength to remain in place as they lifted the body on to the boat, ensuring it was kept as horizontal as possible.

A body bag had been placed at the front of the boat, and the corpse was lowered gently on to it. Liam's role as a detective sergeant was secondary to his role as a volunteer as far as the lifeboat station was concerned, but when on board he was always expected to deal with the dead. He instructed everyone to keep clear of the body, and told Fischer they were ready to head back to shore.

The coxswain gave him a little nod, as if telling him he'd done well, and Liam was momentarily able to forget his fears as he shone his torch on the body.

The deceased was male – late teens or early twenties. How and why his body had found itself out at sea was a question for another day, but Liam noted the red marks on the man's wrists. He was shoeless, and as Liam lifted his sodden trousers he saw another set of marks around the man's ankles. The autopsy would tell them more, but it wasn't the first time he'd seen these marks on a body found at sea. Earlier in the year, the corpse of Eleanor Cooper had been discovered close to shore in Sennen with nearly identical wounds that indicated she'd been zip-tied at her wrists and ankles.

The official cause of death had been death by drowning, but Liam and his colleagues were convinced there was more to it than that. During their investigation, they had discovered Eleanor had been selling drugs in the Penzance area and the suspicion was that she'd fallen foul of one of the county lines gangs working in the area.

As Fischer started the engine and they headed back towards the lifeboat station, Liam wondered if this fresh body was another victim of the gang and what the young man's crime had been for him to be treated in such a manner.

Chapter Two

Peter Britten took a final swig of the mud-coloured beer and slammed his glass down on the bar counter. No one looked at him, or said goodbye as he left the premises. He'd been going to the pub since he was a teenager, when it had been a proper pub. He could still recall the sense of community, the hierarchy of old and young, when the generations shared the property as a meeting place, a hub of the community for all.

His dad had bought him his first beer here, when Peter was sixteen. Peter wondered what the old man would think of the place now, with its sterile interior and sky-high prices which prevented most locals from visiting – these days, it only attracted tourists and the upcountry lot who had their second houses in the area.

Peter was only in the bar because it was better than being at home, and as he walked the darkened roads towards the dunes, he shuddered at the thought of what was waiting for him.

They had moved in six months ago. The first – a young woman called Stacey – had stopped him on the beach one day when he'd been walking his gundog, Spot, God rest his soul. She'd been enchanting – petting Spot, and showing more interest in Peter than he'd received from a woman since the few romps he'd had as a young man. Peter wasn't completely stupid – he knew he was no match for Stacey, would never have been, even in his pomp, and he was old enough to be her grandfather – but the attention had been gratifying. He'd begun to look forward to seeing her on his walks. And, slowly, he'd begun to consider her a friend. Which he knew was pretty far from the truth.

He stopped by the church to take a piss. It wasn't the one where his parents were buried so he didn't care. The wind was up and beyond the dunes the water was rabid. He could hear it striking the shore, breaking on the rocks. Peter had always marvelled at the sea's power – it had been the one constant in his life. In his more fanciful moments, usually after a skinful of drink, he would fantasise about being carried away by the tide. Sometimes he would be in a boat, sailing towards the horizon, at other times he imagined the water carrying his body far away. He sucked in a breath, picturing in his mind's eye the sea's raging quality as he moved on to the coast path, the hum of the overhead pylons accompanying him as he laboured his way back.

After one of their many walks, Stacey had asked him to the local bar for a drink. Like a fool Peter had said yes.

Peter's parents had been relatively well off. They had left him a good sum, managed by someone upcountry who sent him a monthly stipend, which he used mainly in the local bars. He still recalled the look of surprise on the face of the local landlord when he'd walked in with Stacey that day. Peter was no stranger to company but he'd never been anywhere with someone like Stacey, and for thirty minutes or so it had been the best time of his life. And then Stacey had introduced him to the others.

Peter had never been quick-witted – his teachers had used phrases such as 'not the sharpest tool in the toolbox' to describe him – but he'd sensed something was off about them from the beginning. The young men had lacked Stacey's charm and warmth, but he'd continued drinking with them. He wound up accompanying them on a pub crawl through Hayle and, to a certain extent, had enjoyed their hospitality.

But that was when it had all gone wrong.

Peter wasn't sure how it had happened. One minute they were offering him a way to make money – selling hash to his friends in the fishing community and beyond – and the next he'd messed up, losing some of the drugs they'd given him. Peter had found himself in debt, and to repay that debt, some of the gang had moved in, and they'd never moved out.

He could see them now. The lights were on in the farmhouse and they'd built a fire outside. His father would be turning in his grave at the very thought of his property being treated this way. It was like living in a never-ending party, and Peter hung his head low as he walked the path back to the house.

'Here he is,' said one of the crew, a weaselly-looking man who went by the nickname of Midge, who along with Stacey and another man by the name of Gary, was a permanent fixture at the house. 'What have you got for us?'

Peter fumbled in his pockets for the remaining cash and hashish.

'Fuckin' hell, Peter, what have you been doing all night? You want to pay off your debt, you're going to have to work a lot harder than this. Go and get me a beer.'

Peter didn't really understand how much he owed the gang, or even really how he'd accrued the debt. It didn't seem to matter how much he brought them, they always wanted more. He'd considered trying to get help, but Midge had shown him pictures of what happened to those who didn't do what they were told, and Peter didn't want to think about those poor people again – their faces messed up, limbs broken at impossible angles. He didn't meet the man's eyes as he went inside and fetched him his beer. As at the bar, he was all but invisible. Gary's colleagues were spilled out in front of the fire, drinking and smoking as if they were on holiday.

'Give us one of those, Petey,' said a lump of muscle they called Perky, whose body was intwined with Stacey.

Peter wanted to throw the bottle of beer at the man's head. But the last time he'd tried that they'd made him sleep outside for three nights. Instead, he did what he was told, managing to catch Stacey's eye – the young woman having the decency at least to look away – before heading outside to give Midge his drink.

'Important visitor coming tomorrow evening, Peter. I need you to get this place looking good. As good as this shit-hole can look, anyway,' said Midge, laughing to himself as he took the beer from him. 'Well?'

Peter stood in the dim glow of the outside fire staring at the man, as Midge brushed his greasy hair from his forehead. He got confused sometimes and didn't know what the man was asking.

'Jesus Christ,' said Midge, shaking his head. 'Get yourself a beer then get to your room. You can have a lie-in tomorrow. We'll probably not be up till about nine. Make sure breakfast is ready.'

Chapter Three

DCI Tom Hargreaves had recruited Liam to the CID three years ago. Hargreaves was in his early fifties and had been in his role for over a decade. He had a much softer approach to management than Liam had encountered during his time in the navy and it had taken some getting used to. Hargreaves was more a colleague than a boss – less inclined to bark orders than to listen for constructive feedback.

Obeying orders had been one aspect of his life as a marine and an SBS operative that Liam didn't miss, but leaving that world still weighed heavily on him. The decision hadn't really been his to make. After the incident in the Indian Ocean he'd gone through rehabilitation, but it soon became clear that he no longer had the mental aptitude for operations. He was a trained soldier, a marine specialist who was effectively scared of water, and although he was given an honourable discharge with a reasonable payout, the sense of failure still lingered.

It was the morning after the second body had been found, and Hargreaves had invited Liam into his office first thing. Liam had already briefed his superior on the marks he'd noted on the deceased whose identity they'd yet to confirm.

'We're going to have to go through some paperwork before we get you to work on this investigation,' said Hargreaves, one eye on his laptop as he spoke.

Liam hadn't arrived home until the early hours and had to stifle a yawn. 'Why's that, boss?'

'With you finding the body as a volunteer, it could create a conflict of interest.'

Liam smiled, the gesture his mum always said could light up any room. 'Seriously?'

Hargreaves sighed, a familiar weariness to the sound. 'Precautionary but best to sign it off as soon as we can.'

Liam understood, even if he didn't like it. He'd encountered more red tape in the police than he'd ever experienced in the navy – where on missions he'd routinely been engaged in fire fights – and it only seemed to get worse. 'I was first at the scene, even if I was volunteering. I'd really like to work on this one.'

'I have you down, but I need clearance. I'll let you know when.'

Liam had to hold his tongue. He was sure there was a link between the corpse in the water and the Eleanor Cooper case. More than that – after lifting the body out of the ocean, he felt responsible for the victim. 'I'd like to attend the autopsy though, guv.'

Hargreaves shook his head. Whether it was because of the equitable way he'd always treated him, or the disciplined respect for authority instilled in him from his time in service, Liam didn't argue his case further.

'Maya can do it,' Hargreaves said. 'For now, work through the old case on Eleanor Cooper in preparation for when we get an ID on this guy.'

Liam thanked the DCI and left the office. Maya was DI Maya Trent, Liam's direct superior. Five years Liam's junior, she was a career officer on the graduate fast-track scheme. She was highly analytical, and often masterminded operations from head office. He caught up with her in the CID's open-plan office where she was at her desk drinking coffee. 'Hargreaves is forbidding me to attend the autopsy on the victim we fished out of the sea last night,' he told her.

Maya raised her eyebrows. Out of everyone in the team, it was Maya he had the strongest bond with. She was like a sister. She had a dry wit, and never took herself too seriously – a quality that helped put her team at ease. 'Forbidding?' she said.

'Because I was on the boat that found him.'

'Meaning?'

Liam feigned a grimace. 'He would like you to attend the autopsy.'

Maya glared at him as if this new information was his fault. 'Why do you have to go messing around on boats?' she said, shaking her head.

'Don't know, boss. Guess it's just in my blood.'

He spent the morning as requested, reacquainting himself with the suspicious death of Eleanor Cooper. He uploaded photos to his phone from the woman's autopsy – zooming in on the ligature marks to her wrists and ankles. Aged sixty-three, Eleanor had been something of a loner who'd lived all but off grid in a village outside Redruth. When they'd turned up at her isolated house after her body had been discovered at sea, they'd found it trashed, full of discarded alcohol bottles and general rubbish. It was believed that Eleanor had been cuckooed – cuckooing being the term used when gangs took over the properties of vulnerable people in local areas to help distribute drugs – and that the gang had left shortly before her body was found at sea. Liam and the team had been unable to track anyone who had been living there with Eleanor. The most they'd been able to do was to bring in local, small-time dealers, but no one was willing to talk.

Liam scrolled through the images once more, imagining the elderly woman being bound and gagged in her own house and wondering what she'd had to endure before her death.

Hargreaves gave him clearance to work on the new investigation later in the afternoon. The body from last night had now been identified as Marlon Tomlinson – a nineteen-year-old from the Phillack area of Hayle.

Heading off the A30 into Hayle nearly an hour later, Liam received a call from his ex, Kim.

'Hi – everything alright?' he asked, as he inched forwards along New Road towards Newlyn.

Liam had been serving with the SBS when he'd found out Kim was pregnant. He'd made it back once, before the birth, but after that he hadn't seen George until he was four months old. And that was when Kim had told him she'd found someone else – George's now step-dad, Mark.

Liam had tried to remain a constant in George's life, but those early years away on deployment had caused something of a rift in their relationship which he was still trying to catch up on.

He'd always been grateful that Kim had remained so open to him being part of George's life, but it was unusual for her to be calling. 'I just picked George up from school,' she said.

'What's going on? Is he OK?'

'I spoke to Miss Foster . . .'

'Oh, Jesus. This is all a bit weird, Kim. My ex calling me about my date with my son's teacher? It sounds like an episode from one of those dreadful daytime programmes.'

'She said you bailed on your date.'

'I didn't bail.'

'You left after ten minutes.'

'There was a lifeboat shout.'

Kim stayed silent. She was one of the few people in his life who knew the full reason for him leaving the SBS. 'I couldn't turn it down,' he said, hearing the pleading in his voice.

'We both know that's not true. Someone else could have taken your place. This woman likes you, for some strange reason. Why would you sabotage that before you'd even given it a chance? Actually, no need to answer that.'

Liam rubbed his hand over his hairless scalp, feeling the occasional bump and fissure of old scars. He knew that – despite their continued friendship – Kim still blamed him for their relationship failing. He was aware that his work back then had meant he'd spent months away from her at a time, so he couldn't blame her for feeling that way. 'I'll call Millie, I promise.'

'That's all I ask. Can you take George to cricket practice this Thursday?'

'It would be my honour,' said Liam, hanging up as he arrived at Marlon Tomlinson's house, close to the dunes in Phillack. He walked along a narrow drive overgrown with weeds and vines until he reached the detached property, which had already been checked out earlier by the local police. At first sight, the building looked derelict. The windows were covered from the inside by faded newspapers, the blossoming weeds threatening to engulf the house whole. As far as Liam was aware, Marlon had lived alone, but he still knocked on the front door and checked the back of the house when there was no answer. When he was satisfied no one was home, he called headquarters. With Marlon dead, and no one else registered at the house, Liam was granted access to enter the building.

He had an enforcer – the name for the battering ram used by the police – in the boot of the car, but there was no need. The front door gave as Liam kicked hard at the lock, the hinges cracked and warped.

Liam called out as he stepped through the threshold over a mound of unopened mail, the air fetid.

He was currently renting in St Ives, a tiny one-bedroom apartment that ate hard into his wages, and would have loved to live in a place like this, despite the deep care and attention it needed to get it back to a habitable state.

Liam followed his nose, his eyes watering as he entered the living room. Covering his mouth, he looked around the mess and decay. The room was littered with half-eaten food, takeaway boxes, overflowing ashtrays and more empty bottles of spirits than a pub would get through in a year. To top it off, it seemed Marlon, or whoever had been staying there, had started using the place as a toilet. In one corner, flies and insects swarmed over a mound of what appeared to be human excrement, while the carpet was clearly sodden with urine.

Liam stepped carefully around the mess, opening a window before moving around the rest of the house where the same story played out. It had been a similar scene at Eleanor Cooper's house but this took things to a new level. By the time he'd gone through all the rooms, he was in no doubt that more than one person had been living there. The bedrooms were lined with numerous single mattresses and sleeping bags. It was possible that squatters had moved in, but all the classic signs of a cuckooed house were present, and he imagined the human waste downstairs was most likely a parting gift from the gang who had used the place.

Maya called and updated him on the findings of the autopsy. The cause of death was the same as it had been for Eleanor Cooper: death by drowning. Like Eleanor, Marlon's body was noticeably malnourished, and the pathologist confirmed that the marks around the man's wrists and ankles had been most likely due to zip-tie restraints, although there didn't seem to be any signs of long-term captivity or physical abuse. It was agreed that the CSI team should attend Marlon's house to search for forensic evidence that could link the two investigations.

Liam waited for them to arrive before driving to St Ives, where he joined the volunteers at the lifeboat house, helping with maintenance on the boats. He was pleased to see the two young lads from last night were volunteering again, and he teased Billy by calling him Commander, before speaking alone with Miles Fischer.

'Thanks for last night,' Liam said, his pulse spiking at the memory of being at sea. He understood Fischer was slowly pushing him, helping him face his fear in his own way.

'You did well, Liam.'

'We have a name for the body we found last night.'

'Another suicide?'

'Not sure at the moment.'

'You think it could be drug related?' asked Fischer who was scrubbing the hull of the boat. The ops director was no stranger to the drug problem that had swamped the county in recent years. Occasionally, the lifeboat crews had to deal with the fallout of smuggling in the area and often worked with the police in dealing with suspicious boats and packages.

'Could be,' said Liam, not able to share any police information.

'See those lesions on his wrists and ankles?'

'We noted them.'

'Same as that woman we found a few months back. Another drowning victim. Seems like a hell of a coincidence to me.'

It did to Liam as well but he didn't comment. Cuckooing had become an endemic issue these last few years in the county. The lines gangs targeted vulnerable individuals often battling addiction or mental-health issues, and took over their homes as a low-profile base of operations. The dealers moved in with deceptive ease, befriending the victims or offering them small loans before outnumbering them and taking over. Victims rarely reported the takeovers due to fear of retribution. By the time any complaints were made and all the legal obstacles were overcome, the gangs had generally disappeared and moved on to someone else.

If Marlon and Eleanor had been embroiled in the county lines system, the thing that puzzled Liam was the manner in which the pair had died. Violence in all its grotesque forms went hand in hand with the work of the county lines. It was a multi-million-pound enterprise, and numerous homicides were linked to the operation every year.

However, this felt different. Although the gangs were ruthless, they didn't like drawing attention to themselves. Disposing of the victims in this identical way seemed like some sort of oversight. It was as if whoever was responsible either hadn't learnt from the attempt to dispose of Eleanor Cooper's body out to sea, or had intended the bodies to be found, perhaps as some form of statement or warning. At this point, Liam thought that the gangs must be sending out some message, but who could it be meant for?

The lifeboat team invited him to the bar after the clean-up but Liam declined. All he could think about was Marlon Tomlinson's lifeless body, and the squalid conditions he'd been living in. He had no doubt that Marlon and Eleanor's deaths were linked, and that meant somewhere out there someone else was probably going through the same thing they'd endured.

In many ways, police work wasn't much different to being in the armed forces. In the SBS, the rule of law had been less clear cut. There were legalities to follow, but those in the wrong could be dealt with by force. It frustrated Liam that the county gangs could get away with so much, and that there was so much process he had to follow to bring them to justice. But essentially, he was in the same role. Two people in the county had died in horrific circumstances, and he would do everything in his power not to let it happen to anyone else.

He walked along the sea wall, and stopped to watch the waves dancing into shore, the tide at its highest point of the day. After a childhood spent surfing those waves – and those in the surrounding area – on an almost daily basis, it was disheartening that he couldn't recollect the last time he'd taken a board out, and the very thought made his body tense up. He hadn't been out on a board since leaving the SBS, and it dismayed him to think what his younger self would have to say about the situation.

He thought back to better times, to the last summer before he'd joined the marines, when he'd spent every day at the beach with Kim. It reminded him, as he walked the steep incline home, about what she'd said earlier regarding his date with Millie. It still felt a little odd that the mother of his child was trying to set him up with someone else, but he wondered if she had a point. When his relationship with Kim had broken down, Liam had blamed her. As far as he could see, he'd been doing his duty fighting abroad and risking his life. What he hadn't appreciated at the time was how single-minded he'd been. It hadn't been his absence that had caused a rift in their relationship, it had been the distance between them that had remained whenever he returned. He could admit now that back then he'd been preoccupied. His work for the marines and SBS had consumed him, and he guessed the same could be said about his work for the police now.

Dwelling on Kim's advice, he decided to call Millie to see if he could rectify the mess he'd made of their date.

'You left in a hurry last night,' she said, after they'd gone through the niceties.

'It was nothing you said, I promise,' said Liam, wondering if he'd said the right thing as he walked the steps to the front door of his flat.

'Was everything OK? On the boat, I mean?'

A short stab of pain ran across Liam's chest as he pictured himself reaching for Marlon's corpse, the endless depth of the sea inches away from him. 'It was fine. How was school? My son behaving himself?' he asked, trying to change the subject.

'Two fights, and a poor young girl fainted in assembly. All go.'

'Bloody hell, I know George is a handful . . .'

'Thankfully, your son wasn't involved. Anyway, the fights aren't a regular occurrence, thank goodness. I think the heatwave is getting to everyone.'

Liam nodded to himself, as the line went silent. 'Listen, I'm a bit busy on a new investigation at the moment, but I don't have George this weekend, so it would be great to meet up if you're free? I promise I won't be on lifeboat duty,' he said, before the pause in conversation became too much. He was surprised by the burst of adrenaline through his system, and the way he could hear his heart beating. He was rarely stressed by any encounter, and wondered why such an innocuous question was making him act this way.

'I'm away on Saturday, but could do something Sunday, if that works?'

'Sounds great,' said Liam, his thoughts already returning to the investigation as he said goodnight.

Chapter Four

Even now, knowing his oxygen tank was near depletion, Liam loved his second world, surrounded by water, freed from weight, wrapped in a comforting silence. It was something he could never fully explain to those not like him. Where many would feel trapped, or threatened, so deep beneath the sea, Liam had an almost reverential love of the water. It was here he found some form of clarity to the chaos above. He was alone with his breathing, weightless in the thick fluidity of the sea. Or he would have been, if it wasn't for the occasional words filtering into his headset.

The SIB – soft inflatable boat – was somewhere above, but his headtorch wasn't strong enough to see its shadow on the water's surface. 'Running low,' he said again, touching the rebreather system that recycled his exhaled breath, ensuring minimal bubbles and sound.

There was no response. 'Come in,' said Liam, as his rebreather malfunctioned.

They had trained for this eventuality many times over, and Liam had seen it happen in operation before, but it had never happened to him.

Don't panic.

Two words he may as well have got tattooed on his chest. Panic killed but it was hard to remain calm when your only source of life had just been taken away from you. He pushed at the rebreather, his breathing laboured, as he was thrown through the currents, the lack of oxygen affecting his thinking until he remembered to switch to the bail-out cylinder.

'Come in,' he said, not recognising his own voice within his headset, as he began his ascent, and things took on a surreal quality. He was there but not there, his nerves and joints on fire when his vision blurred, the vastness of the ocean spinning him seemingly in all directions. A distant part of him knew he was suffering from decompression sickness. This was it, the realisation of the distant fear he shared with his colleagues, that one day he would die in the water he loved so much. His training told him to make an emergency stop, to fight against the buoyancy urging him upwards, but he couldn't stop, his body a pressure cabin as he rushed to the surface and woke screaming, breathless in his bedroom.

◆ ◆ ◆

The dream stayed with Liam as he headed on to the A30 early that morning. The nightmares were a constant in his life but last night's had been particularly vivid, no doubt triggered by his recent work with the lifeboat. The decompression sickness he'd suffered following a failure of his breathing apparatus in the Indian Ocean hadn't left any lasting physical damage, but sometimes Liam wondered if the legacy of his fear of water was worse.

Quickly, he touched the challenge coin he wore as a pendant beneath his shirt, guilty for thinking in such terms as he remembered his two comrades who had lost their lives that night.

He could still feel the coin, cold against his chest, when he arrived at headquarters, running late.

'Thought you must have had the day off,' said Maya, before he'd even had time to pour himself some coffee. 'When you're ready, join us in the incident room.'

Liam sighed and poured the coffee. Maya was only teasing him. She knew as well as anyone the hours he put into his work. He followed her into the small incident room where photographs of Eleanor Cooper and Marlon Tomlinson took centre stage on the crime board.

Maya explained in detail the results from the previous day's autopsy, and the similarities between the two deaths. 'Two suspicious deaths by drowning is enough for me to believe these cases are related. Add to that the ligature marks and we're definitely on to something.'

Liam presented his findings from the search of Marlon's house, having skimmed through the report from CSI. 'The next couple of days will be all about finding out who Marlon Tomlinson was. Interviewing anyone who knew him in whatever capacity. It seems he had people staying with him. Let's find out who they were, and where the hell they are now.'

'I take it – from what Liam discovered at the house – that this is another case of cuckooing?' asked Jack Lawson, the youngest member of the team.

'There was never any formal proof of that in the Eleanor Cooper case,' said Maya. 'Maybe that is an angle we need to explore further. Why don't you look further into this, Liam? I've already spoken to Whitfield this morning. Good for you to have a chat with him about developing issues in the drug trade in that whole Penzance area.'

DI Paul Whitfield worked for Major Crimes. He was an old-style copper, and Liam didn't see eye to eye with him. 'Will do, boss,' he said, with a sigh.

'Good, let's get going,' said Maya, wrapping things up.

Liam got a refill of coffee before he went to find DI Whitfield.

Eventually, he tracked the DI down in a separate section of CID. Major Crimes was a specialised unit within CID, and Liam's team often worked together with them. The headquarters in Bodmin wasn't a huge place, so he knew everyone on the team well enough to exchange some nods of acknowledgment as he walked over to Whitfield's desk.

The DI was on a call. He lifted his hand towards Liam as he finished off, and then took a quick look at his computer after hanging up, before finally giving Liam his attention. 'Ah, Monk,' he said, with a little smile, as if he'd just come up with the nickname. 'Maya said you would be coming over. Take a seat, then.'

Liam didn't mind the nickname. He'd embraced it as a child – adopting it to take the power away from the bullies who had tried to weaponise it. Not many of his colleagues used the nickname nowadays and he always introduced himself as Liam.

Whitfield had only got wind of the nickname during a drunken leaving party, back when Liam had been new to CID. He'd used the moniker ever since – Liam sure that Whitfield was only doing so as a way to bring him down.

It was a tactic he'd seen in the navy, too. One of the training staff on the SBS course had taken great enjoyment in ridiculing Liam for his appearance, coming up with every name under the sun for his hairless scalp. But that had been for training purposes – to put Liam under the same gruelling conditions he would experience should he be taken hostage during engagement, which subsequently happened. Whitfield used the nickname because he thought it gave him some power over him, and Liam had long ago stopped respecting the man because of it.

'I've been looking at the Marlon Tomlinson file. Not a hundred per cent sure why you guys are looking into this and not us,' said Whitfield, as Liam sat down.

'I was first on scene,' said Liam.

'Accidentally,' said Whitfield, unbuttoning the top of his shirt, which looked a size too small. 'From what Maya says, there could be a link between this and the Eleanor Cooper death. We could be looking at a double murder.'

Liam shrugged. He was not about to get into a debate with the DI about which department should have the investigation. 'I went to Tomlinson's house yesterday. We'll be conducting interviews today, but from what I've seen it looks as if he definitely had some people staying with him. Ever come across him before?'

'Marlon Tomlinson? No. As you know, there are a number of small-time dealers in that area. Couple of bigger outfits working out of Camborne and Penzance, but he isn't on our radar.'

Liam knew the area well, but the dealer landscape changed with the wind. 'Who controls Hayle at the moment?' he asked.

'Depends what you're after I guess. Mainly small fry out there. There isn't that much trade, and not enough to warrant out and out war. To be honest, we don't give it that much attention. Camborne and Penzance are the biggies for us down that way. St Ives can be interesting in the summer, as you know.'

'Who would you suggest leaning on?'

'Look at you,' said Whitfield, undoing another shirt button despite the air conditioning working at full pelt. 'Tell you what, give Martin Sloan a squeeze. If Tomlinson was a user, Sloan may well have supplied him.'

Relatively speaking, St Ives was a small place, and there weren't many people Liam didn't know. He'd never had a reason to officially talk to Martin Sloan before, but he'd spoken to him in the past before he'd become police. Sloan had been a constant figure in the town since Liam's teens. If he was involved, that was definitely not good news.

'Thanks, Paul,' said Liam, getting to his feet.

'No problem. One thing though, might be best to get your hair cut before you go. You know, make a good impression,' said Whitfield, chuckling to himself as he spun around on his office chair.

◆ ◆ ◆

Liam was back in St Ives before midday, parking less than a mile from his own flat as he took the short walk to Martin Sloan's house.

DI Whitfield had called Sloan 'small time', but that wasn't the full story. Sloan was thirty years Liam's senior, and Liam had known of him ever since he'd been at school. In a town as small as St Ives, there were people of notoriety and Sloan was one of the faces Liam had been told not to mess with since he'd frequented the local bars when he was in sixth form. At the time, Liam hadn't been planning a future in the police. He'd dabbled in drugs – though his main vice had been copious pints of lager after playing rugby on a Saturday afternoon. He'd never dealt with Sloan face to face, but it was an open secret that the man was still dealing in the area.

Liam was wearing light trousers and a short-sleeved shirt, but he still felt the heat as he walked up Bedford Road to the top of the town. Such was the unpredictable weather patterns in the county, it was more than feasible to expect the good weather to fade. No doubt there were a couple of weeks of rain to come when the schools broke for summer and the town was swarmed with tourists.

Dark red curtains were drawn in the ground-floor flat where Sloan lived so it was impossible to gauge any movement within. Liam walked the stone path to the door and rang the bell, a dog barking in response. A few seconds later, the door was slowly prised open, a man with long black hair and a full beard answering. 'What?' he said, before he recognised Liam. 'Mr Kilshaw, this is an unexpected honour.' Sloan looked him up and down.

'Mr Sloan. It's DS Kilshaw nowadays.'

Sloan opened the door further and bent down to hold the collar of his dog, an elderly rottweiler. 'How are you with dogs, DS Kilshaw?' he said, tilting his head as he smiled.

'How is your dog with humans?'

'He loves them, don't you, boy?' said Sloan, letting go of the dog who sniffed Liam before moving back inside the flat. 'What can I do you for, Liam?'

The use of Liam's first name surprised him, though the fact that Sloan knew it wasn't a surprise. Aside from his stints in the navy, Liam had spent his whole life in the area and, with his height and distinctive look, was well known to everyone. 'I'd like to ask you some questions about a recent suspicious death. May I come in?'

Sloan smiled, holding his ground. 'I always thought it was a shame when you joined the police, Liam. Must be a bit of a comedown after being a marine.'

Liam glanced at the faded tattoos on the man's forearms. 'You served, didn't you?'

'As a matter of fact, I did. Light infantry,' said Sloan, his eyes never leaving Liam's.

'Small world.'

'I remember you as a boy. Outside centre at the rugby?' said Sloan, sneaking a look at Liam's hairless head as if that explained everything.

'May I come in, Mr Sloan?'

'Not today, Liam. But happy to help as much as I can.'

Liam sighed and loaded a photograph of Marlon Tomlinson on to his phone. 'You know this man?'

Sloan frowned, a furrow of lines appearing on his forehead and around the sides of his eyes. 'Scruffy fella. Can't say I recognise him.'

'Take a closer look. I believe he drinks a lot in the area. Hayle especially.'

'Can't say I leave St Ives that much any more. Sorry I can't help.'

'That's Marlon Tomlinson. His body was found out to sea a couple of nights ago.'

Sloan shook his head. 'And?'

'We believe Mr Tomlinson may have been involved with some local drug gangs,' said Liam, not prepared to play along with the pretence any more.

Sloan held his gaze. He looked slightly amused, as if a little surprised that Liam had asked the question. 'And what makes you think I know anything about that?'

Liam tried to keep the questioning pleasant. 'Let's not play these games, Martin. We both know there isn't much you don't know about what goes on around here.'

'You flatter me.'

Liam showed Sloan the photo again. 'Take another look.'

Sloan barely glanced at the screen. 'Where did this guy live?'

'Phillack.'

'I'm not sure what you've heard about me, DS Kilshaw, but even if what you've heard is true, I live in St Ives. As I said, I hardly, if ever, bother going to Hayle.'

Liam sighed. 'If you change your mind,' he said, handing Sloan a card with his phone number on it. 'Two suspicious deaths so close to one another is going to bring a lot of heat to the area. Never hurts to cooperate.'

Sloan turned the card over in his hand. Liam noted that his fingernails were long and well-manicured. 'How is your mother?' Sloan asked.

Liam's mother had severe dementia, and was a resident at a local nursing home. Liam's relationship with her was fractured. After his father had died, her mental health had collapsed and she had succumbed to numerous addictions, her care for Liam becoming secondary.

Liam didn't react. He had no idea how Sloan knew about his mother, and wasn't about to get into a discussion with him, though the question seemed genuine.

'I knew your old man. We were at school together. Tough bastard.'

Liam looked Sloan up and down. He wasn't sure if the man was testing him, or simply trying to get on his good side. Liam's father had died in action when Liam was eight years old. He could hardly remember the man – his memories confused by the faded photographs and videos he'd been shown of his father while growing up. Liam guessed his dad would be a similar age to Sloan if he was still alive, but wasn't about to ask the drug dealer for any more information about their relationship. 'I doubt my father would have had anything to do with you, Sloan. Think on,' Liam said, glancing at the card in the man's hands before moving off.

The mention of his parents had shaken Liam in a way he hadn't anticipated, no doubt as Sloan had intended. Liam stood outside the dealer's house, replaying the conversation in his head, wondering how he could have handled it better when he heard footsteps on the pavement opposite.

He looked over to see his some-time CHIS – covert human intelligence source – Justin Blake staring at him. Blake lived over towards Praa Sands, and had helped Liam over a spate of house burglaries in Penzance last year. It wasn't a huge coincidence to see him in St Ives, dressed in shorts and a surfing T-shirt, but going by his expression it was as if he'd been caught doing something he shouldn't. 'Everything OK, Justin?' said Liam, moving towards him.

Blake froze, staring at Liam as if he were an apparition, before turning and fleeing down the Stennack steps.

Chapter Five

One of the downsides to living in St Ives were the steep inclines in and out of the centre. With its narrow streets and lack of land, parking was limited towards the waterfront, and a number of car parks had been created on the outskirts of the town. As a child, Liam had never minded the descent, but the ascent following a day on the beach had been a different matter.

Not much had changed as an adult, but he was relieved that Justin Blake had chosen to take the Stennack steps down towards town rather than going uphill to flee the scene.

Liam had no idea why the informant was there, and why he'd looked so spooked. He called after him as he sprinted down the stone steps, Blake's speed and agility taking him by surprise. 'This is stupid, Justin, I have your address. Just stop so we can talk.'

Blake had been the first informer on Liam's books in CID. At the time he'd genuinely thought he was doing Blake a favour. The man had been on a path leading to jail time, and working with Liam had changed that. He'd managed to get free from the entanglements of a local drug gang, and get help for his addictions. Unfortunately, there hadn't been the funding for Liam to keep helping Blake after that. He'd put in the odd call to the man, just to check in. But once Liam moved on to Bodmin, contact had been lost. Even from this brief glimpse, it looked like Blake might have returned to his old habits.

Blake ignored him, sprinting directly across Trelawney Road. Liam groaned and followed, increasing his pace until he was almost in touching distance. 'If I have to tackle you, I will arrest you,' he said, his breathing laboured as Blake finally came to a stop.

Liam was taking no chances and placed his hand on the man's back as Blake dropped on his haunches and tried to get his breath back. Blake was in his thirties, stick thin with a wiry strength which had seen him get into the odd bar fight back in Penzance. 'What the hell is going on, Justin?' said Liam, trying to control his own breathing.

'Sorry, Mr Kilshaw, I didn't know it was you,' said Blake, head bent.

'You just decided to up and run for no reason?' said Liam.

'Something like that, Mr Kilshaw.'

Liam let out a breath. The sun had burst through the morning clouds and he felt its rays on his scalp. He guided Blake to a side street, relieved to be in the shadows. 'What are you doing in St Ives?'

'Just a bit of sightseeing.'

'Sightseeing? Come on, Justin.'

'What, Mr Kilshaw?'

'You holding?'

'No.'

'Shall I check?'

Blake tensed. Liam feared he was about to make another run for it. 'That won't be necessary.'

'Then tell me what you're doing here.'

Blake swayed on the spot. His skin was rough and pocked. His eyes had deep shadows beneath them – ageing him by at least a decade. 'Things are a bit strange at the moment, aren't they?' he said.

'In what way, Justin?'

'I heard about Marlon.'

'Marlon Tomlinson? You knew him?'

'I knew of him.'

'He didn't drink down your way, did he?'

'Camborne and Hayle mostly, I think, but I'd occasionally see him in Penzance. Nice lad.'

'What do you know about his death, Justin?'

Blake took a step back, so he was standing under the glare of the sun. 'Nothing, Mr Kilshaw, I swear.'

'Then why are you here, outside Martin Sloan's house? You buying?'

Blake shook his head. 'I'm not a grass. I don't know anything about Sloan.'

You are a grass, thought Liam, but he didn't say anything. 'Two people are dead. You need to tell me what you know, or you can speak to me back at headquarters.'

Blake looked around him, either searching for an escape route or to check he wasn't being overheard. 'OK, I may be here to score. But not from Sloan. I don't even know him.'

'Long way for you to come?'

'As I said, it's all a bit crazy down my way. You see . . .'

'Just spit it out, Justin, for crying out loud.'

'I used to get my stuff from Marlon. Well, not him exactly, from the people he was working for.'

'I see,' said Liam, thinking about the mattresses he'd discovered at Marlon's house. 'And they're not around any more?'

'No, not that I'm aware of. So, I may have been here trying to find some stuff, if you know what I mean. But not from Mr Sloan, you understand?'

'I understand perfectly, Justin. But I need something from you.'

'We don't have that agreement any more, Mr Kilshaw.'

'I didn't realise we had severed ties, Justin. Shall we start by me searching you? Or shall I just go and visit Mr Sloan and ask if he's seen you today?'

Blake stood, open mouthed. 'Whoa – no need for that now, is there, Mr Kilshaw?'

'Some names. Now.'

Blake hung his head. 'This can't get back to me,' he mumbled.

'We never met. Names.'

'I only know them by the first names. Young lads. Cockneys, I think – well, most of them. Gary and Midge were the guys I spoke to.'

'Gary and Midge?' said Liam, incredulous. 'That's all you got?'

'It's not as if we got into big conversations or anything. I must say, I didn't like them. Nasty guys, right mean streak. Gave this guy a right pasting one day outside the Dolphin.'

'And what was their connection to Marlon?'

'I saw him with them a few times. Didn't really treat him very well, though I did see them buy him drinks. I think they were staying with him?'

'And where are they, Justin?'

'I don't know, Mr Kilshaw. As I said, that's not why I'm here.'

Liam grilled him some more. Justin gave him brief descriptions of the men, but it soon became clear he'd given him all the information he could. 'I need you to keep your ears open for me, Justin, do you understand? Soon as you spot Gary or Midge, you let me know, OK?'

Blake coughed. Sighing, Liam produced a twenty-pound note from his wallet. 'Five more of these if you spot them, OK, Justin?' he said, holding on to the note as Blake grabbed at it. 'OK?'

Blake nodded and Liam released his grip on the cash.

As Liam drove to Hayle, he called Maya and relayed his run-ins with Sloan and Blake. 'I'll see what we have on file for a Gary and a Midge,' said Maya, a hint of humour in her voice.

'Don't shoot the messenger, just telling you what I've been told.'

'When are you back in?'

'I'm going to visit some of Marlon's old haunts, see if anyone is willing to talk about him and the men he was hanging around with.'

'See if you can find Midge?'

'Something like that.'

'Listen, you might want to get back a little sooner. Hargreaves has told me we may have a visitor later this afternoon from Major Crimes in the Met. Seems they have taken some interest in Marlon's death and want to speak to us.'

'Sounds ominous. Do we have a time in mind?'

'4.30 p.m.'

'I'll do what I can,' said Liam, hanging up.

The tide was high as he drove alongside the Hayle estuary, a ray of light bisecting the water that was a haven for birdwatchers. He parked next to the viaduct, and stopped in a few local haunts trying to find any locals he knew who could shed some light on Marlon Tomlinson.

He'd grown accustomed to the looks that came his way. People either knew him as a copper, or would sneak a look at his head as if they'd never seen a bald man before. He drove along the Commercial Road towards the Copperhouse area of town, stopping every now and then to question shop owners and landlords, before heading out along the coast towards Gwithian. It was the same answer everywhere he went. A few people knew Marlon, but no one was talking about any drug gang in the area. Liam wasn't sure if it was ignorance or fear, but he would retrace his steps later that evening when the bars would be a bit busier.

He headed back to Bodmin, replaying the conversations with both Sloan and Justin in his head. Although Sloan was a known drug dealer, he was too clever to be caught holding anything himself. That made Liam question why Justin had been prepared to go to the man directly. He thought about Sloan's understandable reticence to talk about the threat of any drug gangs in his area, and despite himself couldn't shake the casual way Sloan had talked about Liam's parents, as if they were close family friends.

The loss of his father was something Liam was still coming to terms with. Even though he'd passed when Liam was so young, the direction of Liam's whole life felt like it had been determined by his death. It didn't take much analysing to understand that he'd gone into the marines because of his father – though whether that was out of tribute or as an underlying desire to somehow correct the wrongs that had brought about his father's death, he wasn't sure. He had no way of knowing what his father would have thought about Liam's discharge from the SBS, the botched operation that had almost cost him his life, or his subsequent decision to join the police.

He would have asked his mother, but her memories were no more detailed. She'd taken to drink and drugs hard after her husband died. When Liam was in his twenties, she'd suffered a life-changing stroke that had incapacitated her, resulting in severe brain damage. She still had the occasional lucid moment; as though her real self were buried somewhere deep within the shell of her body. But for the most part it was like talking to a ghost.

Liam resented many things that had happened in his life, but the fact that his only living parent had all but abandoned him when his father had died, and was now inaccessible and didn't recognise him, felt like the biggest injustice.

He presumed the negative thoughts were a response from the other night on the lifeboat, and as he arrived back in Bodmin he took a few minutes to rest in the car, using the breathing and mind exercises he'd been shown by the counsellor assigned to him after his accident, before leaving.

'Liam. I was wondering if I would bump into you.'

He turned to see the slight figure of a woman from his past – Grace Hartley. They'd been in police training together and had dated for nine months. They'd split after Liam had accepted a position in Cornwall, and Grace had taken a role in London.

'Grace,' he said, his mind working overtime trying to piece together why she would be here before it dawned on him. 'Don't tell me, you're the hotshot officer from the Met come to save us bumbling locals.'

Grace gave him a quick hug, Liam unable to avoid the familiar scent of her perfume which brought back a hundred memories. 'That's right,' she said, smiling as she looked him up and down. 'DI Grace Hartley at your service.'

Chapter Six

Liam walked Grace to the entrance of the station. Their split six years ago had been amicable enough but they hadn't kept in contact. They'd known at the time that things between them were unlikely to progress. Their career paths had been chosen, and they'd decided just to enjoy the time they had together. But Liam had often wondered if he could have made more of an effort at the end. He'd suspected that Grace would have continued the relationship if he'd shown some commitment, and seeing her now, he wondered if he'd made a mistake letting things end so easily.

'When did this happen?' he asked, as they walked up the steps.

'What?'

'You being a DI. That is an outrageous movement through the ranks,' Liam said, feigning shock.

'Hardly, Sergeant,' said Grace with a wink, as Liam buzzed them through.

'Did you know you would be seeing me today? You must have known I'm working on the Tomlinson investigation.'

'Oh, I knew alright. Thought it would be a nice surprise for you.'

'Well, it's certainly that,' said Liam, walking her to the arrivals desk. 'Dave here will sort you out. See you upstairs.'

Liam stopped in the canteen for a coffee before heading up to CID. It had been surreal seeing Grace after all this time, and he had no idea how it would be working with her if it came to that.

Maya caught up with him as he was walking over to CID. 'The Met officer is here. Meeting room six.'

'Saw her in reception. I know her – we did the foundation course together.'

'What's she like?'

Liam thought back to the time he'd spent with Grace. She was a Londoner through and through, and the thought of moving to Cornwall had not appealed to her at all. Liam had considered moving to London and trying his luck in the Met, but he could never have lived so far from George. 'She's made it to DI before I did, so she must be superhuman,' he said, deciding now wasn't the best time to tell Maya about his and Grace's former relationship, in case Grace didn't want it to be public knowledge.

'Or competent,' said Maya, deadpan, as they entered CID and walked over to the interview room, where Grace was already in conversation with DCI Hargreaves and DI Whitfield.

Hargreaves started the meeting, introducing Grace to Liam and Maya. Grace got to her feet, loading a small presentation which played out on the white screen. 'For the last two years I have been involved in an ongoing investigation into a multinational organised crime operation. Project Gamma is a cross-border operation that includes work with Interpol and investigative departments throughout Europe. We believe the organised crime group currently at work in this area originated in Georgia. The investigation is particularly challenging, as the group work together in individual cells. In the UK alone, we believe we have uncovered six separate cells with links to the OCG. We have been making inroads into these cells, one in particular that works out of London. Over the last eight months, they have been extending the scope of their operation through the use of county lines. One such line we believe exists in Cornwall,' she said.

'And you think this group is related to the deaths of Eleanor Cooper and Marlon Tomlinson?' asked Liam.

'That, I'm not sure about; it isn't really my remit. What I would say is that if such deaths are related to the OCG, then such behaviour is uncharacteristic. We have seen numerous homicides throughout Europe attributed to them, but never in this manner. I understand both these local victims were not involved in the drug trade?'

'From what I have ascertained so far about Marlon Tomlinson, I believe he was a victim of cuckooing – as was Eleanor,' said Liam.

'That's exactly my point. It seems totally out of character for the OCG to kill these people, especially in such a showy way. It only serves to draw unwanted attention towards them.'

'Maybe it was rival gangs?' said DI Whitfield, who had been surprisingly quiet.

'That is definitely a possibility, but with all due respect that is a question for another day. The reason I am here is that we have intel about a significant drug delivery in Cornwall in the next week or so. We believe the cells in the county have been working well, and that Cornwall is seen as a good option for expansion.'

'Do we know where exactly they plan to deliver, or where it is coming from?'

'The shipment – at least this part of it – is coming from Portugal. Where they want to deliver is still not clear, but our UCO believes they will find out soon. What troubles us most is the intel we have that the group plan to bring fentanyl into the county.'

Fentanyl was a synthetic opioid which had caused a major drug epidemic in the States. Fifty times more potent than heroin, it had been a long-term concern for law enforcement agencies in the UK.

Liam exchanged looks with Maya. 'What exactly has this to do with us?' asked Maya.

Grace pressed a key on her laptop, twelve mugshots appearing on the screen. 'These are known operatives of the London cell of the OCG. We believe all of them are working, one way or another, on a county lines operation connected to Cornwall.'

'Do you have names for these people?' asked Liam.

'Yes.'

'Any of them go by the name of Gary or Midge?' he asked, thinking about the names Justin had mentioned.

Grace hesitated, and Liam could tell the names meant something to her. She placed her hand to her mouth, a gesture Liam remembered from their time together, and pressed a few more keys. 'Gary French and Malcolm "Midge" Ure. How do you know of them?' she said.

'That explains the Midge,' said Liam. 'Their names came up today. A CHIS of mine told me they were involved with Marlon Tomlinson.'

'This is what I was afraid of,' said Grace.

'What exactly are you afraid of?' asked Maya.

Grace placed her hand to her mouth again. 'I'm here to ask for some cooperation. Intercepting this drug-smuggling ring could be pivotal in unravelling the whole OCG operation. This isn't a small thing.'

'What exactly are you saying?' asked Maya.

'We would like to ask that until the operation is over, you refrain from speaking to any of these twelve people.'

Maya appeared amused, but her tone was anything but. 'This is potentially an active murder investigation,' she said, unable to hide the incredulity in her voice. 'Tom?'

DCI Hargreaves looked torn. No doubt he was feeling pressure from senior officers, otherwise Grace wouldn't have been in his station making such demands. 'For now, all we are asking is that we refrain from bringing any of these twelve in for questioning.'

'Or to question them at all,' said Grace, interjecting.

Hargreaves sucked in a breath. 'Yes, thank you, DI Hartley, I think we all understand that,' he said, raising his voice slightly and reaffirming his authority. 'I know this is not ideal, but once the sting on the smuggling scenario is exhausted, we would hope to bring in all these twelve people and we can then interrogate them about Marlon Tomlinson and Eleanor Cooper.'

'But we don't know when that will be?' asked Liam.

Hargreaves looked over at Grace. 'Not yet – but we are sure it will happen any day.'

'You're quiet,' Maya said to DI Whitfield, who was watching the conversation with a wry smile.

'Needs must. Sounds like a huge investigation to me. Gary and Midge can wait as far as I can see.'

Liam thought about the chaos of Marlon Tomlinson's house. Everything pointed to the fact that the county lines gang had cuckooed him and taken over his life before eventually killing him, and Gary and Midge were the closest link he had to finding out who was responsible. He was used to taking orders, had been taking them ever since he'd joined the navy aged eighteen. Orders had almost got him killed, but one thing he'd learnt both in and out of the armed forces were that orders were not very easy to disobey without huge ramifications. 'There must be limits on this,' he said, as he sensed Maya simmering in anger next to him.

'Obviously, any risk to life then you can bring them in,' said Hargreaves.

'You'll get to speak to them, Liam, I promise. Just give us a few days,' said Grace, receiving a stern look from Maya.

'If that's all,' said Hargreaves, getting to his feet and signalling an end to the meeting.

Maya and Whitfield followed Hargreaves out; Liam remained in his seat to talk to Grace. 'You could have warned me about the involvement of the OCG before you shared it with everyone,' he said, after making sure no one was in earshot.

'Where would the fun be in that?' Grace smiled, and once again he was transported to the time they had spent together. It had been something of a honeymoon romance. They'd still been in the first stages of a relationship when their enforced break had come about after their training course ended. He thought back to his conversation with Kim from the day before, and her suggestion that he was prone to sabotaging relationships.

'So are you roughing it with us locals until this is done?'

'Sure am – they've got me staying at the finest Premier Inn they could find.'

Liam nodded, matching her smile. 'Best get back to work, Inspector Hartley.'

'It was good to see you again, DS Kilshaw,' said Grace, watching him leave.

Chapter Seven

Liam spent the rest of the afternoon searching through the files on Gary French and Malcolm Ure supplied by the Met. If he wasn't allowed to bring them in for questioning – not that he knew their location at present – then there was no harm in finding out as much about them as possible for when the time came.

The pair had been under the Met's surveillance for a number of years in conjunction with their ongoing investigation into the OCG. They appeared to be an intrinsic part of the drugs operation, and it was suspected they were heading up one of the lines' cells in Cornwall.

He understood Grace was looking at the bigger picture, but Liam couldn't forget the recent memory of fishing Marlon's body out of the water. He needed to find those responsible before it happened again, and his mind was still preoccupied as he arrived at a local bar in St Ives later that night where he'd agreed to meet up with Fischer and the rest of the lifeboat crew.

It was a strong turnout, the occasion nothing more than a few games of pool in a bar close to the station. Fischer was great at organising these get-togethers for the volunteers, and it helped cement what was already a strong community. They all threw in a tenner to the kitty, and Fischer ordered some drinks. It had already been predetermined which of them would respond to any calls, and those eight, Fischer included, were on soft drinks.

Liam helped dole out the order, and the first players smacked open the first frame of pool as Liam took a seat at the bar with Fischer. The ex-marine had been the operations director of the lifeboat station since before Liam had signed up for the navy, and this was his domain. He seemed to be available 24/7 to manage the crews. Liam didn't know how they would cope should he wish to retire one day.

Liam winced as he took the initial sip of his cider.

'How's work?' asked Fischer, sipping on a glass of tonic water. The man must have been in his mid-sixties, but Liam wouldn't want to get in a confrontation with him. He was an inch taller than Liam's six two, and standing in the narrow confines of the bar it felt like he was almost as broad.

'Same old.'

'They let you work on that body we found?'

'Marlon Tomlinson? Yes, eventually.'

'Yeah, I read about him in the news. Sad way to go. Not suicide though?' Fischer had a wonderful Cornish lilt to his voice that Liam could have listened to all evening, and probably would if the boat wasn't called out.

'Case is open on that one.'

Fischer nodded, before shouting out, 'No more for you, Woody,' to one of their colleagues who'd just missed an open black ball on the table.

Liam couldn't share any of the details of the investigation, even though Fischer was the perfect man to talk to. He had an encyclopaedic knowledge of people in the town. He was always there, speaking to the locals every day, as much part of St Ives as the lifeboat station itself. 'Ran into Martin Sloan today,' Liam said, bending the truth regarding his meeting with the town's resident dealer.

'That fucking degenerate, what did he want?'

'You know he was in the forces?' said Liam, for now suppressing the anger he'd felt when Sloan had asked him about his parents.

'Army, they'd let anyone in.'

'That's true,' said Liam, clinking his glass with Fischer.

'You ask him about this Marlon Tomlinson guy, then?' Fischer asked. His lips curled into a smile, which Liam matched.

'Can't discuss that,' Liam said, taking a drink of his cider, which was starting to go down easier. 'Why, should I?'

'You know better than me, Detective Liam. What I've been hearing, this Marlon guy was big into his drugs, and used to come to St Ives sometimes to get them. Can't say I ever saw him though, but we both know who controls all that rubbish in this town.'

Liam thought back to his encounter with his ex-informer, Justin Blake. Maybe it was worth getting Martin Sloan in for a more official chat, he thought, while the sound of sixteen pagers went off at once. 'Be safe,' he said, bumping fists with Fischer, and eight of the volunteers fled the pub as if they were being chased by some invisible force.

He had one final drink before making the steep trek back to his flat. It never felt right staying out when he knew his colleagues were at sea, risking their lives. He pictured Fischer now, leading the team – and was thankful for their sake that the waters were calm.

As he reached the fire station on Higher Stennack, he received a text. The number wasn't in his contacts. He saw it was from Grace, asking him if he wanted to meet up for a drink.

He stared at the message, and wondered why she was leaving it so late to ask him. Maybe she'd just finished for the day, or maybe she was lonely on her first night in Cornwall. It had been good to see her, but seeing her out of work felt like a complication he wasn't prepared for at the moment.

Sorry, on lifeboat duty tonight, he replied.

He watched the three dots on his screen as Grace started to type, before the screen went blank.

As he ran down Porthmeor Hill towards the beach the following morning, his watch ticking over to 6 a.m., Liam regretted the two ciders he'd had last night. He felt sluggish now, stepping on to the sand, his body slow and lethargic as he moved in time with the operetta of seagulls on the shore's edge, the Tate St Ives building foreboding above him as he went into a sprint to shake the tiredness away, only to stop twenty seconds later, his lungs fit to burst.

Bent on his haunches, he looked out at the sea; the waves tumbling into shore as if issuing him a challenge. Part of him wanted to accept them and run into the breakers, but the very thought brought him out in a cold sweat. He knew the fear was baseless in the literal sense. He was an extremely able swimmer and there was little risk of a rip tide. But his mind had overall control, and even as he thought about a swim it reminded of him what had happened with the Special Boat Service. In the end, he was forced to look away.

He stopped in at the care home on the way back to his house. It wasn't his day to visit, but the staff greeted him in their usual welcoming way, and he took the stairs to where his mum lived, ignoring the smell of the place which always reminded him of being at school.

She was in bed, watching television – as she was every time he visited. He guessed it must have been Martin Sloan's mention of her, and his dad, that had made him want to visit.

'Hi Mum,' he said.

His mum glanced away from the screen, looking him up and down, before returning her attention to the moving pictures. 'Who are you?' she said.

◆ ◆ ◆

Liam spent the morning in Hayle. Grace had warned him off talking to members of the OCG, but he was still dealing with a suspicious death, and there were people he could talk to about Marlon Tomlinson to at least gain some idea about his life, and maybe even his death. Lots of people seemed to have known who Marlon was, but no one had had any direct interaction with him beyond late-night drinks.

After speaking to a couple of Marlon's old school friends, a pattern began to emerge. Marlon had been something of a recluse as a teenager. In and out of trouble, he had kept himself to himself and didn't have any close friends to speak of. No one really knew the impact Marlon's parents dying had had on the young man, and no one seemed to have kept up to date on his life since then.

At lunch, Liam stopped in at an old bar close to the Towans Beach in Hayle. He received the usual glances from staff and customers who recognised him, and strangers checked out his distinct look. He ordered a sandwich from the landlord, before showing the picture of Marlon to everyone there.

'I knew Marlon,' said one of the old boys, nursing a half of bitter in one of the nooks. 'I was at school with his granddad, don't you know.'

Liam sat down. 'What's your name, sir?'

'James Ward.'

'When did you last see Marlon, Mr Ward?'

'I don't get out that much. Can't afford to any more with the prices they charge nowadays. Only out today because it's my birthday.'

The man's hands were shaking as he lifted the drink to his lips. Liam guessed he was a similar age to his mother. 'Do you have a family?' he asked, wanting to stay on track but saddened that the man was all alone on his birthday.

'Boy and girl. Both live upcountry and can't blame them for that. They sent me a card, and the girl will call me tonight. Maybe the boy will too. The way of the world, isn't it?'

Liam took in a deep breath. 'It must have been hard on Marlon, losing his parents?'

'He used to mention them now and again, you know, when he'd had a bit too much to drink.'

Liam thought they must have made a strange pair, Mr Ward in his seventies and Marlon in his late teens, sitting together in the pub, sharing their woes.

'He seemed to be hanging out with some odd folk these last few months?' asked Liam, thinking about the snapshots of Gary and Midge that Grace had shown them.

'Strange times. I don't know one person in here,' said Mr Ward, looking around the pub. 'Time was, you could come here and know everyone. Too many people come and go now. No one ever stays in one place long enough to get to know them. I saw Marlon a couple of times of late, but I struggled to get any sense from him. He was always so pissed.' Mr Ward chuckled at this. 'He would chat to anyone when he was like that. Problem was, the people talking to him were usually laughing at him. I felt sorry for him. Wish I could have helped him more.'

'When did you last see him?'

'A few weeks ago. He was with a group of people I'd never seen before so I left him alone.'

Liam showed him the photos of Gary and Midge, but Mr Ward couldn't remember seeing them. Liam bought the man a pint, and wished him a happy birthday before standing to leave.

'Funny thing is, I saw the same people the other day in the Copperhouse.'

'The same people who were with Marlon?'

'Yes. They were with an old drinking buddy of mine, Peter. Peter Britten. Lives over Gwithian way. Pissed as a newt as always. Some strange fellas hanging out with him. Definitely from upcountry but I'm no good with faces. Sorry.'

Liam took the address and was about to pay the place a visit when Grace called. 'How was the lifeboat?' she asked.

'Didn't need to go out in the end,' said Liam, feeling guilty for his lie.

There was a pause, and Liam wondered if Grace already knew he'd been lying, before she said, 'I need you back in headquarters. We think the drug run is happening tonight.'

Chapter Eight

Liam sat in the second of two surveillance vans that were parked close to Prussia Cove on Mount's Bay on the south coast. He was with Maya and two colleagues from Major Crimes, DI Whitfield and DCI Hargreaves in van number one with Grace.

It was 11 p.m. and they'd been here for over four hours. Maya's unsmiling face was glued to the screen in front of her, her attitude suggesting she felt the same way he did – that they were bit players invited out of necessity or politeness.

It was true this wasn't their investigation – Grace was handling a cross-organisation behemoth which included input from the marine unit, border force and the coastguard. But with the investigations into Eleanor Cooper and Marlon Tomlinson still ongoing, he would have hoped to have more of a say.

Grace had been tipped that a drop would be made sometime that evening and it had become a waiting game. The most important aspect now was for their presence not to be detected. They had two boats offshore, licensed fishing trawlers, carrying teams who could get to the scene within minutes, as well as eyes on the shoreline from other departments. Various footage played on the screens in the vans, each showing different viewpoints of the murky ocean, which was being pitted with rain heralding an oncoming storm.

It was this storm that was causing Grace most consternation. Liam listened to her on his headphones as she coordinated with the other team leaders, a hint of disquiet in her voice as updates of the storm came in from the coastguard. He could tell she was worried this could stop the operation taking place that evening, throwing everything into disarray, but it seemed everything was still going to plan as one of the lookouts from the cliff edge signalled a sighting of two RIBs – rigid inflatable boats – heading into shore.

'Where the hell have they come from?' asked Grace, as the marine unit sent their own RIBs after them.

Liam watched the scene play out on the screens. Joining the marine unit should have been the natural option for him after leaving the navy, and if it hadn't been for the incident with the SBS, he imagined he would be out there now with them.

A distant part of him was envious of the marine unit officers on the RIBs, rushing after the would-be smugglers. Nothing in his life had ever been as exciting as being on deployment – speeding along on a boat with his colleagues, adrenaline rushing almost unbearably through his bloodstream, heading towards an encounter that could end his life.

But no sooner had the thought entered his head than his memory turned to those frantic moments beneath the Indian Ocean and he had to look away, hoping no one noticed the slight tremor in his hands as he fought the tightness in his chest, and took in long breaths until his breathing was back to normal. He had truly faced death in that moment, and the reality of it had been sobering.

'You OK?' mouthed Maya, as he looked back at the screens.

Liam nodded, feeling the weight of the challenge coin against his chest. The waves had picked up, visibility becoming poor, and the marine unit's boats were forced to slow.

'They're turning away from shore,' came the panicked call from one of the spotters on the coast.

'What do you mean?' said Grace, the drone footage showing the two smuggler RIBS retreating in semi-circles back out to sea, each going in different directions.

Liam had seen it happen often before, but even he was surprised at the virulent nature of the storm which engulfed the area in a matter of minutes, making the drone footage obsolete.

The vans headed towards the cove, rain battering their exteriors as Grace made frantic calls to the other team leaders, but it was all in vain. It seemed certain that the smugglers had been tipped off, most likely by their own spotters, and their two RIBs had disappeared from sight.

Liam and Maya joined the rest of the team outside by the cove, the swirling wind battering them with a mixture of seawater and rain. Grace was staring out towards the sea, but visibility was so poor that it was impossible to see much beyond the swirling waves. Liam heard her make some frantic calls, as she coordinated with the marine unit. He shared her frustration as she ripped her headphones off. Liam knew the RIBs had a potential range of up to three hundred miles, and with the storm worsening it would be impossible to track them.

'We've lost sight of them. I'm calling it,' said Grace, catching Liam's eye before returning to the van.

The mood at headquarters the next day was muted. Everyone was sleep deprived, and their moods matched the gloomy weather.

Grace gave the assembled team a debrief on the situation, her usual enthusiasm restrained. Neither of the RIBs from last night had been located, and there had been no sighting of a 'mothership', the term used for the larger vessel where the RIBs may have set out from.

'Is it possible they had a second destination in mind, and were using the storm to their advantage?' asked Maya.

'That's if they knew we were watching them,' said Liam.

'We need to keep our ears to the ground. If fentanyl is hitting the streets, we will soon know about it,' said Grace.

'Check your sources, from the lowest street seller upwards. If this gets out there in the quantities suggested, then the impact could be unimaginable,' said DCI Hargreaves.

Like the rest of them, the DCI was clearly suffering from lack of sleep – but Liam could also see something had hardened in the man. His eyes were narrow, and his jaw clenched as he spoke. His tone was more aggressive than Liam had ever heard from him. He wondered what pressure Hargreaves was receiving from higher up the chain, and what long-term impact this would have on all of them.

'What about the members of the OCG? Are we free to question them now?' said Liam.

Grace went to speak but Hargreaves beat her to it. 'We need to know if the fentanyl is on our streets. We need to know where it is being stored, and who is distributing it. Everyone is in play as far as I'm concerned.'

Liam could see Grace wanted to interject, but Hargreaves was the most senior officer in the room. She wasn't about to embarrass herself by risking an argument. No doubt, it would be a dispute that would linger in the background but for now he had the permission to speak to Gary and Midge, the two men who may have infiltrated Marlon Tomlinson's house, and had most likely been responsible for his death.

All he had to do now was find them.

◆ ◆ ◆

Liam told Maya about the address he'd been given yesterday for Peter Britten in Gwithian, and she decided to join him on the journey. 'So, are you going to spill the beans?' she asked, as they approached the Chiverton Cross roundabout which led on to the A30.

Liam jumped in his seat, opening his eyes to the sight of a giant white wind turbine on the hill to his left. 'Must have dozed off there. What was that?'

'Don't play dumb, Liam.'

Liam straightened himself up, chuckling to himself. 'What is it you're asking?'

'You're going to make me say it?'

Liam had an inkling but wasn't going to make it easy on her. 'I have to, as I have no idea what you're on about.'

Maya sighed. 'DI Grace Hartley is an attractive woman, don't you think?'

Liam smiled. 'Don't worry, Maya, you'll always be my favourite DI. You know that.'

'I didn't say she was more attractive than me, did I?'

'No, you didn't.'

'So?'

'So what?'

'So help me God, I will pull this car over. It may not be obvious to everyone else, but everyone else is not me. I see you both. Those quick glances, those knowing smiles.'

Liam was grinning – he enjoyed that they could still tease one another despite Maya effectively being his boss. 'I am finding this line of questioning unprofessional.'

'Bullshit. Tell me.'

'OK, OK, you win, as always. We used to date. Happy?'

'Tell me more,' said Maya, grinning.

Liam told her about his previous relationship with Grace, and their eventual split.

'Do you regret not taking it further with her?'

'I did for a while. But I couldn't have hacked it in London – and she is very career minded, as you may have noticed.'

'Anything going on between you two now?'

'DI Trent, I am shocked you would ask me such a personal question.'

'Just be careful, Liam, that's all I'm saying. I'm not sure I trust that woman.'

Liam looked at Maya. The grin had disappeared from her face and he realised she was being serious. 'Noted,' he said. 'Actually . . .'

'Actually?'

'I did go on a date the other night.'

Maya did a pretend double take. 'A date? Do tell.'

'Now, don't laugh, but it was with George's schoolteacher.'

Maya laughed.

'I said don't laugh.'

'Oh come on, this is priceless. How did it go?'

'Not great. That was the night we found Marlon Tomlinson's body,' said Liam, a shiver running through him as he recalled his proximity to the open sea that night. 'But she has agreed to a second date.'

'My God, she must like you. Well, I am intrigued to see how this love triangle progresses.'

'There is no love triangle,' said Liam, laughing as he blocked out the thought that she might be on to something.

Maya pulled up outside a rusted gate blocking their route into the driveway of Peter Britten's house.

Liam got out of the car and checked the gate, which was falling off its hinges in the brick wall surrounding the old farmhouse. There was no bell, so he opened the gate and walked down the driveway while Maya parked up.

It was humid but the sky was a steely grey colour, last night's storm yet to fully dissipate. 'Who gave you this tip?' asked Maya, joining him outside the farmhouse.

From the outside it looked dilapidated. Chipped paint fell from the front door, and there were cracks in the upstairs windows. Even from the low vantage point, Liam could see a number of tiles missing from the roof.

'Some old guy in a bar,' said Liam, answering her question.

'Shouldn't have asked. Do the honours then.'

Liam stepped over a line of ants spilling along the weed-strewn pathway and rapped his knuckles against the wooden door, as Maya peered through the dirty white net curtains covering the downstairs windows.

'I'm getting the same vibe I got from Marlon Tomlinson's house,' said Liam, surprised to hear the front door opening.

A young woman, early twenties at most, stood in the doorway. She was wearing a T-shirt that stretched to her knees, a shot of purple hair darting from the middle of her scalp, the rest of which was as hairless as Liam's. She blinked at the daylight, as if she'd just woken up. 'Yes?'

'DS Kilshaw and DI Trent,' said Liam, displaying his warrant card. 'Is Mr Britten in?'

The woman yawned. 'Uncle Peter? No, he's out at the moment.'

'Do you know where?'

'Pub, probably,' said the woman, taking a great interest in Maya, who was still looking through the windows.

'And you are?'

'His niece.'

Liam decided to play and gave her his best smile. 'And your name?'

The young woman was still squinting. Her skin was almost translucent; Liam noted the cobra tattoo inching up her forearm and under the sleeve of her T-shirt.

'Stacey.'

'Stacey . . .'

'Stacey Smith.'

'When are you expecting your uncle back, Stacey Smith?'

'Probably when the pubs close. What exactly is it you want with him?'

'We're investigating the death of this man. Marlon Tomlinson,' said Liam, showing her a photo of the victim on his phone.

Stacey nodded. 'What has this to do with my uncle?'

'May we come in?' asked Liam. 'I would love to use the loo if that's possible.'

Stacey blocked the entrance of the door. 'It's on the blink, and the place is a mess.'

'Anyone else in there with you?' asked Liam, trying to keep the conversation light.

'I really don't understand what this is about. If you want to speak to my uncle, then I'm sure you'll find him in the local. But if you don't mind, I'm going back to bed. And I don't think you should be looking through the windows. This is private property,' said Stacey.

Maya put her hands up and walked away.

Back at the car, Liam checked the list of the twelve OCG members Grace believed were working in the area. There were three women on the list, none of whom were a match for Stacey Smith.

They drove to the first of four local bars in the area but there was no sign of Peter Britten in any of them. Liam didn't have to ask Maya the question. There was no way they were going to get a search warrant for the house. The fact that Peter Britten had a niece staying with him was more than a plausible explanation for the 'strange folk' Mr Ward had seen Peter hanging around with.

Liam made a note to visit Peter again as he suggested they head into St Ives. He wanted to speak to a suspected drug dealer he knew about the possibility of a shipment of fentanyl arriving in Cornwall.

Chapter Nine

Peter had heard the policeman at the door, and had listened in on the effortless lies Stacey had told the man. He'd wanted to scream, to run to the door and tell the policeman these people were not wanted in his home, but he lacked both the energy and the ability to move. Midge had descended on him as soon as the knock on the door had come, his arm around Peter's throat, his sour-smelling hand over his mouth.

Peter remained in the seat, too scared to move, as Gary, Midge and his pretend niece, Stacey, discussed the situation.

'We're going to have to leave,' said Stacey.

'You want to tell him that, because I don't. He's already pissed at what happened last night,' said Midge, who was walking around the living room in nothing but his underpants.

Peter had no idea who 'he' was, or why he was so pissed off. All Peter wanted was to sit in the corner and hope he was invisible. But Midge had other ideas.

'This is your fault, old man,' he said, as he walked over to Peter, his hands clenched into fists.

'Leave him alone,' said Stacey, grabbing Midge's arm as it swung back. 'He doesn't know what's going on.'

'He knows a lot more than he lets on,' said Midge, staring hard at Peter before finally sitting back down.

Stacey bent before Peter. The light that peeked through the net curtains caught the top of her strange purple hair. 'You haven't been talking to anyone, have you, Peter?' she asked.

Peter didn't know what to say. He couldn't remember what had happened an hour ago, let alone anything from much further in the past.

His mind was a collection of snippets of memories. The strongest were the ones of his parents. Farming with his father, making shortbread with his mother. He didn't understand why that had changed. His memory had been fuzzy for years now. People had come and gone in his life. His solicitor, the carer who used to come to the house, the cleaner who worked once a month when the carer had stopped coming, and then Stacey.

She was his strongest memory from recent times. He could still see her on the beach, with her funny hair and the sunshine in her eyes. He had no idea when that memory was from, however, and had already forgotten the question she'd just asked him.

'Peter, who have you been speaking to?' asked the one called Gary, his words loud and elongated as if he were speaking to a child who was hard of hearing.

Peter shook his head, his mouth hanging open.

'We're going to have to take him in,' he said.

'We can't do that,' said Stacey.

'That copper sounded like he meant business,' Gary said. 'He'll be back – and I'm not sitting this guy on a full-time basis.'

'Let's just move. We can take the stuff. We have another house over in Penzance,' said Stacey.

The words filled Peter with dread. He wanted the two men gone, but he needed Stacey to stay. She was his protector. She fed him, nursed him when he came back sick from the pub. He didn't know if he would survive without her in his world.

'We're moving alright, as soon as it gets dark, but we're taking him with us,' said Gary.

Stacey appeared alarmed, glancing at Peter as if he were in danger. 'But you know what happened last time,' she said.

'Not my problem,' said Gary. 'Now, let's get everything ready to move. Leave nothing behind that suggests we were ever here.'

Chapter Ten

Maya dropped Liam at the train station car park in St Ives, having been recalled to an incident in Camborne. It left Liam without a car but she promised to pick him up later.

Liam made the short walk along the coast, until he arrived at the lifeboat station. Inside, Fischer was working on one of the boats: the larger Shannon-class all-weather boat – the Annie Wilkinson – they'd been on the night they found Marlon Tomlinson. Liam would have gone in to speak to him, but he would have ended up being roped into helping.

At the front, the water was in, some of the local fishermen touting for trips on their tourist expeditions around the bay, despite the swell of water being rougher than it had been these last couple of weeks. Liam walked along the wharf, past the galleries and ice-cream parlours, and did a loop around Fore Street with its collection of quaint shops before heading up the town to Sloan's address.

With no reply, Liam headed back into town, stopping at all the local bars and cafés, only to find Martin Sloan in his last port of call – the Lifeboat Inn, the bar opposite the lifeboat house.

Sloan was having a coffee with the publican, Joseph Baines. Baines had once barred Liam from the premises following an altercation on his eighteenth birthday. The ban had been lifted soon after, Liam learning his lesson. It was still a place he frequented often.

Sloan's giant rottweiler – which with its greying fur and slow, drawn-out movements must have been older than any dog of that breed Liam had ever encountered – lifted its large head as Liam entered the pub. It sniffed the air, and satisfied that Liam was no direct threat, lowered it again on to the stone floor.

As Liam approached, the landlord moved away from his conversation with Sloan and all but skipped to the end of the bar. 'What brings you here?' he asked, scratching his ragged silver-brown beard.

'How's business, Joe?' asked Liam, glancing at Sloan, who had moved to a booth at the side of the all but empty bar.

'Not too bad, but it will be better when the schools break up. What can I get you?'

'Coffee. I'll take it with Mr Sloan over there.'

'All these years we never speak, and now twice in a few days,' said Sloan, as Liam sat down opposite.

'You're such scintillating company, Mr Sloan.'

Sloan tipped his hat to him. 'I saw you again yesterday. Over Porthmeor way. Visiting your mother?'

Liam didn't react. He doubted Sloan was just being polite, and wondered at the coincidence of Sloan having been near the care home so early in the morning.

'Where were you last night, Martin?' asked Liam, no longer in the mood for politeness.

Sloan raised his eyebrows and sipped at his drink. The landlord placed a coffee in front of Liam.

'Last night?' Sloan said, once the landlord had moved away. 'Let me think. Now my memory isn't what it once was. You'll know all about that I suppose with your poor mum and that.'

Liam didn't know why Sloan was trying to provoke him. Admittedly, it was pissing Liam off that he kept mentioning his mother and it could be that was his intention. 'Answer the question.'

'What time?'

'6 p.m. onwards.'

'I was over at the Sloop until about half nine. Then I walked home.'

'Anyone verify that?'

'Everyone in the Sloop.'

The Sloop was a bar on the other side of the harbour, popular with locals. 'And at home?'

'Home alone, DS Kilshaw, what can I say.'

Liam doubted Sloan had any direct involvement in last night's events, but it didn't mean he hadn't had a part to play. Liam had always considered Sloan to be low level. He was a necessary evil – the kind of small-time dealer the police turned a blind eye to most of the time. But that didn't mean he didn't know what was going on. Liam decided to be direct, to see if he could catch the man out.

'What have you heard about a fentanyl shipment?'

It was slight, but Liam still caught the indecision in the previously unflappable features of the local dealer.

Nothing in the files hinted at Sloan having interest in class A drugs, let alone fentanyl. Liam had always known him as the guy you knew who could get pot, but he never carried it himself. Fear of a wave of synthesised opioids had recently become a big concern UK wide. There was a massive undertaking to prevent a replica of what was happening in the States occurring over here. A man like Sloan would understand the risk of getting involved in that kind of business.

'You know I don't do any of that shit,' Sloan said, ceding some of his power for the first time.

'I don't know what you do or don't do, Martin. I do know that there was supposed to be a shipment of fentanyl dropping on the south coast early this morning and your only alibi is that you were in a pub until 9.30 p.m.'

Sloan straightened his back, taking off his hat and running his fingers through his long, thinning hair. 'What is it you want?'

'I want to know what happened to Marlon Tomlinson. You said you know who he is.'

Sloan went silent, as if considering the request. He'd denied he knew the man personally the other day but it was clear the last thing he wanted to do was get involved in a fentanyl ring. 'I've seen him around. Came as a surprise when you found his body. Did you know him before then?'

'I'm asking the questions.'

'OK.'

'Did you ever supply Marlon Tomlinson with drugs?'

Sloan laughed at the directness. 'Oh yeah, sure.'

'You know DI Whitfield from Major Crimes, Martin? Because he knows you. I'm just trying to find out what happened to Marlon. But Whitfield? He wants nothing more than to bring you down. Maybe you're not involved in this fentanyl thing, but you're involved in something. You might think your operation is cleaner than clean, but try to make some money with a full team down here for the next nine months watching your every move.'

The indecision returned to Sloan's eyes and Liam saw him for what he truly was, a low life who just did what he could to get by. He preyed on those less intelligent than him to help shift his goods but he didn't have the fight to move any higher up the chain. 'I heard that he was hanging with some London types.'

'Competitors?' asked Liam, showing him the photographs of Midge and Gary from his phone.

'I don't know what you're talking about, DS Kilshaw.' Sloan's voice had dropped to a whisper, and he handed the phone back to Liam. 'What I heard is that they were shifting brown and they were serious players, part of a much bigger group that seems to be taking over Cornwall.'

'You think they were responsible for Marlon's death?'

Sloan shrugged. 'Why kill him? Why bring that sort of heat? Doesn't make sense to me. My guess is he offed himself. Wouldn't be the first suicide you'd fished out of the sea, would it?'

He was right about that. Liam had been on board the lifeboat to bring in someone who had taken their own life too many times to count. In part, he blamed the urban legend that drowning was a peaceful way to die.

Liam's experience – and the regular nightmares that followed – pointed to the truth. Slowly suffocating beneath the pressure of the water was a terrifying ordeal. Whether voluntary or not, the body would naturally go into survival mode. Experienced as he'd been at deep sea and scuba diving, Liam had been unable to fight the panic that night when his gear had malfunctioned. The fight to survive had been all consuming, and he could still recall the sensation of lungs desperate for air as if he were back there now. His hand went involuntarily to his chest, and he caught Sloan looking at him before he removed it.

Even with the ligature marks on Marlon's wrists and ankles, he may still have bought the idea that the man had taken his own life if it hadn't been for Eleanor Cooper. 'We both know it wasn't suicide. Look, I don't want to get you involved in this, Martin, but if you know something, you need to tell me now.'

'As I said, I heard he was hanging out with some London guys.' The surety had disappeared from Sloan's voice. 'That's all I know, I swear. I don't recognise any of those photos you showed me. If they're active in St Ives, then I haven't seen them.'

Liam wasn't sure if he believed that, but for now it was enough to know he had spooked the small-time dealer. Sloan was demonstrating he wasn't about to snitch on anyone, even if they were rivals. But Liam was convinced that if someone came between Sloan and his livelihood, he would give them up – ally or foe – if it meant saving himself.

'One last thing, you know a guy by the name of Peter Britten? Over Gwithian way?'

'That I do not, Scout's honour,' said Sloan, with a sardonic salute.

Liam stood, deciding he wouldn't push it for now. 'I'd keep my head down if I was you, Martin,' he said, leaving the pub.

The sun had returned with a vengeance, and he cursed himself for not bringing any sunglasses as he crossed the road to the lifeboat station. He was disappointed to see that Fischer was no longer there as he would have liked to ask him if he'd heard anything about last night's drugs run.

He met Maya in the car park by the train station, overlooking the aquamarine waters of Carbis Bay. From the safety of the car park, the waters looked inviting. But Liam didn't dwell on the view. Instead, he climbed into the passenger side.

Maya was speeding away before he had time to fasten his seat belt.

'What's the rush?' he asked.

'Your girlfriend's been busy. We think those boats may have made shore yesterday. There were reports of a boat were seen in the water at four in the morning, over in Portreath. We're closest, at least we will be if we hurry up.'

'She's not my girlfriend.'

'Whatever you say, Romeo. Buckle up,' said Maya, switching on her integrated lights as she headed on to the A3074 out of St Ives.

Chapter Eleven

Liam and Maya arrived in the small fishing port of Portreath twenty minutes later. Like so many places in Cornwall, Liam had spent a good part of his youth surfing here. It didn't always have the best waves, but Liam loved the bay, which was surrounded on both sides by high cliffs.

They drove around the back of the town and parked in the car park next to the harbour. The tide was out so the inlet was a deluge of mud, the air ripe with the smell of seaweed.

'Where are these boats then?' asked Liam.

'Through here,' said Maya, walking towards the entrance of the Waterfront Inn.

A slim, well-dressed man raised his hand in greeting as they entered the main bar area, as if he knew them.

'Sean Thornley?' asked Maya, walking over as the man got to his feet.

'Pleased to meet you. I thought you must be police . . . by the look of you, I suppose,' said Thornley with a nervous laugh.

'I'll take that as a compliment, I guess. Please, take a seat,' said Maya.

Liam remained silent and sat down after Thornley.

'You live in Cornwall?' asked Maya.

'No, no,' said Thornley, as if the idea was ludicrous. 'I'm in Truro on business, and I have a friend who lives here. I was staying with her last night.'

Maya checked her notes. 'You told our team you were on the beach at 5.30 a.m.? Was your friend with you then?'

'No, no, she was still in bed.' Thornley blushed. 'I mean, she was still asleep. I'm a bit of a fitness freak so I was up early for a morning run. That was when I saw the boats.'

'Where did you see them?' asked Liam.

'I was running up Tregea Hill. Well, I'd got to the top and was looking down on the bay. I think it's called Western Cove? It was light by that point and I saw them coming to shore. Didn't think much of it really until I saw them drag the boats on to the beach, and they started unloading some packages. Jenny told me not to get involved, but I had to wonder what they were doing. And when I spoke to your colleagues, I was told to wait here to speak to you.'

'You took some pictures?' asked Maya.

'Yes, yes,' said Thornley, a slight tremor in his voice as he handed over his phone.

Maya scrolled through the images on the phone. They had been taken from a great distance, but were clear enough to show two RIBs pulling up to the beach. Liam counted eight figures, three on each boat and two collecting the packages. 'Did you see how many packages came off the boat?' asked Liam.

'Sorry, no. I got a bit spooked when I thought about what they could be doing. If I'm honest, I wanted to get out of there as quick as possible.'

'Did you think they were going to sprint up the cliff to get you?' asked Liam, receiving a look from Maya.

'Not exactly, no,' said Thornley, taken aback.

'You did the right thing, Mr Thornley, and thank you for contacting us. Could you email me these images in hi-res?' asked Maya, who was still frowning at Liam.

Grace and Whitfield arrived as Maya was sorting out the images on their phones. Despite the late night she'd had, Liam had to concede that his ex was looking great. He explained the feedback Thornley had given them.

'Did he see where they took the packages after they were delivered?' asked Grace.

'No. It's a very steep climb from Western Cove. There is a pathway from that part of the beach that leads to a few detached properties. Someone could have seen something from there,' said Liam.

'OK. Let me speak to Mr Thornley. You seem to know the area, so could you go over there and question the locals?'

'You're the boss,' said Liam, glancing at Whitfield as Grace's lips curled into a half-smile.

◆ ◆ ◆

Maya drove Liam over to the properties, a mixture of traditional Cornish cottages and more modern houses, overlooking the bay.

Unsurprisingly, it proved to be a wasted journey, none of the residents having been up that early to have seen anything.

'You ever think like we're working someone else's case for them?' asked Liam, as they headed back to headquarters.

'That's not very team-spirited of you, DS Kilshaw,' said Maya. 'Trouble in paradise?'

Liam tried his best not to smile. 'You really are going to milk this Grace thing for all it's worth, aren't you?'

'What can I say? I love to see you squirm.'

Liam came close to telling his colleague about Grace's invitation the other evening but decided against it. 'What about you? Still seeing that dentist?'

Maya turned to him and flashed him a toothy smile. 'Let's say we're still friends with benefits.'

'You'll have to give me her number. Could do with a check-up.'

'Not a chance in hell,' said Maya. 'So what did your drug dealer have to tell you?'

Liam updated her on his meeting with Sloan. 'I don't think he's involved directly. But he did admit to knowing Marlon Tomlinson.'

'If he's not linked to the OCG he might fear he'll be squeezed out if they take hold. Maybe we could push that angle, see if he will help us.'

'Maybe, though I think shifting fentanyl will be a step too far for him. Selling weed to tourists and locals he's known for ages seems to be his thing. He just wants to keep his nose clean.'

'What better way than working for us?'

Liam nodded, though he doubted he could recruit Sloan as a CHIS. Although the man had given him some information during their last conversation, there was an icy side to him, reflected in the way he'd kept mentioning Liam's parents.

Back at headquarters in Bodmin, Liam and Maya joined the afternoon briefing in the incident room. The priority seemed to be the sighting of the boats near Portreath, but Liam was keen to explore what had happened at Peter Britten's house and his run-in with 'Stacey Smith'. He shivered as he recalled retrieving Marlon Tomlinson's body from the water, and reiterated – for those in the team who couldn't see the connection – the parallels between Marlon and Peter.

'Despite their age differences, we are looking at two lone men with no living family. If the lines gang had taken over Marlon's house, I am sure they could have done the same to Peter's,' he said.

He spent the afternoon searching databases and social media for details on Stacey Smith but came up blank. He phoned around all the local bars in the Hayle area about Peter Britten, but there were no recent sightings of the man.

He glanced at the crime board with its images of Marlon and Eleanor, and the smaller images of the twelve suspected members of the OCG. The deaths were still being seen as suspicious, but it felt to him as if the investigation into them was a distant second to the suspected fentanyl ring, despite the high probability that the cases were linked.

Unable to find more information on Britten's recent activities, Liam turned his attention to arrests relating to county lines operations during the last six months in Cornwall. It was a large database to work from, consisting of arrests both by Liam's team and Whitfield's Major Crimes team. The targeting of minors, and those with mental-health issues, by the OCGs made the investigations that much harder. Naturally, the gangs had no interest in the people they recruited beyond their ability to help shift gear. The people they targeted were disposable and easily replaced. They were also easily scared and confused, which meant – even if they were caught with enough drugs to warrant a charge of possession with intent to distribute – the evidence they were able to provide against those in charge was limited at best.

It was after 6 p.m. when Grace called him in for a meeting with Major Crimes and the rest of CID.

Tiredness was still evident in everyone's features following last night's events. Like his colleagues, Liam wanted to go home and make up for lost sleep, but instead he forced himself to listen as Grace informed them that new intelligence suggested a large batch of fentanyl had entered the county, and that they should be targeting all their sources to get it off the streets as soon as they could.

DCI Hargreaves couldn't hide his alarm. 'I can't overstate the seriousness of this situation. As you know, it's been a long-term fear and not only for us. This is a nationwide concern and we will have eyes on us from all the other constabularies. If the OCGs can infiltrate Cornwall with this shit, then they'll see it as a green light. We cannot let that happen,' he said.

'I have two colleagues joining us from London tomorrow,' said Grace, before sharing details of a number of failed raids that had taken place in the city that day.

'And those twelve?' asked Liam, glancing at the members of the OCG he'd previously been told not to speak to.

'If you find them, bring them in. We have enough on each of them to detain them at the very least.'

It was another hour before he managed to leave. As he climbed into his car, he wondered how he was going to make the journey home without falling asleep when there was a knock on the window. Liam buzzed down the window. 'DI Hartley,' he said.

Grace gave him the same intent look she used to give him when they were together, her eyes focusing on him as if he were the only person in the world. 'Hungry?' she asked.

Liam ran his hand over his scalp, his finger rubbing against the scar he'd received on his last military operation for the SBS. 'I am, but . . .'

Grace began shaking her head. She was smiling but Liam wasn't sure it had yet reached her eyes. 'You're not going to turn me down again, are you?'

'I need to get home.'

'It's only dinner, Liam. Don't get ahead of yourself.'

Liam smiled. Grace had told him many times in the past how his smile could unravel her, and he wondered if it still had the same effect. 'No one is getting ahead of themselves. You may remember you kept us up all night?'

'That's not the first time I've done that to you, is it?'

There was an awkward moment of silence. Liam wanted to say something along the lines that it could never happen again, but he couldn't deny his attraction to her. He'd told himself the last time they'd started seeing each other that it was never going to be a long-term thing, but their split had been difficult. He wasn't sure what she wanted from him this time, if she even wanted to rekindle what they'd had together, but he didn't want to go through that again.

He thought about Millie. Even though they'd only gone on one date, he didn't want to risk sullying any possible relationship with the memory of a night of catch-up sex with his ex-girlfriend. 'Maybe next time,' he said.

'If there is a next time,' said Grace, walking away before Liam had time to buzz the window back up.

Chapter Twelve

On Thursday, Liam finished work early to pick George up from school.

As he stood in shade at the back of the playground behind the mound, he was aware of the glances of the other parents waiting to pick up their children. With his distinctive look, and his role in the police, most people knew who he was – even if this was a rare appearance for him in the schoolyard.

Kim usually did all the pick-ups and drop-offs, so he wasn't on speaking terms with the majority of parents. It was a club he was happy not to be a part of as he watched them gather in groups, overhearing the conversations about homework and plans for the summer, only to disperse as the bell rang out and children began leaving their classes.

Liam inched through the mob as the door to George's classroom opened. He was looking forward to seeing his son, but couldn't deny the hope that he would get to see Millie too and was disappointed when he saw one of the teaching assistants leading the children out.

He edged nearer, pleased to catch sight of George in conversation with a couple of his classmates. The boy seemed to have no shortage of friends, and it was great to see him acting so carefree. Liam lifted his hand up as George looked at the throng of parents, a tiny smile breaking out when he spotted Liam looming over everyone.

George walked over and gave him a quick hug. Liam didn't know how long the boy would be open to such public displays of affection and hugged his son tight as Millie stepped through the door of the classroom. 'How was your day?' he asked, sneaking a quick look at Millie, who was in conversation with one of George's classmates.

'Usual. We got cricket now?'

'Sure do,' said Liam, catching Millie's eye, the teacher giving him a quick smile before returning to her work.

Liam took George to the seafront for some food before his cricket practice. The wharf was packed, tourists battling along the narrow road as seagulls swarmed about, every now and then lunging at anyone foolish enough to be openly carrying some ice cream. The tide was in, a mass of yellow and red self-drive motorboats bobbing on the water. Liam thought how he'd love to take George out on one. But he couldn't risk the PTSD striking when alone with his son on the water.

They stopped at a café on the front, doing their best to drown out the sound of an evangelist who had hooked up an amplifier and was preaching to the tourists and residents alike.

It felt like a special treat getting this extra time with George, and he promised himself not to think about the investigation as George devoured a tuna melt panini. Liam couldn't deny the stab of melancholy as he ordered George some dessert. He loved spending time with him, but it always reminded him of what he'd lost; what he'd thrown away by being absent. It made him think of his own father, how he'd been absent for different reasons. Liam often wondered if he'd sabotaged things with Kim on purpose. Yes, they'd been young and he'd been away on duty, but he could have done more to keep the relationship together. He didn't blame her for leaving him, and setting herself up with someone else, but maybe if he hadn't been so scared of committing, or facing up to a life in a normal family, then he wouldn't be in this situation, snatching fleeting moments with his son.

Dessert finished, he drove George to cricket. He told himself that he should be thankful that the boy was in his life. He might not be a full-time dad, but George still had him in his life and that was the important thing. George was happy and well adjusted. He had two loving homes unaffected by Liam's upbringing, and that was all that mattered.

'I'm going to the Scilly Isles,' said George, the statement coming out of nowhere, as was often the case with the boy.

'Really, when?'

'End of term with the school. We're going sailing.'

A shiver ran down Liam, as a familiar pain crossed his chest. He parked up and stretched out his arms, trying not to let George see his concern. 'Sailing?' he said.

'Yes, there's this big boat and we'll all get a chance to try out the different parts of sailing.'

Liam took a deep breath. The last thing he wanted to do was to pass on his insecurities to his son, but all he could think about was a sailing boat overcrowded with children sinking into the depths of the ocean. 'That sounds great,' he said, mustering a smile which he managed to keep on his face until George had left the car and joined up with his cricket mates.

◆ ◆ ◆

The rest of the week was spent interviewing every existing and former informant possible about the distribution of fentanyl in the local area. The goal was to find whatever had been smuggled into Portreath the other evening.

By Friday evening they were no nearer to getting a result. Liam had spoken to everyone he could think of, but there wasn't even a whisper that any shipment of fentanyl had reached the shores. If the county lines gangs were planning to launch the drug then they were being very careful about it, which was making everyone's job that little bit harder.

Liam knew that finding more information about Marlon Tomlinson would aid the investigation. Every time he questioned anyone about the drug, he mentioned Marlon. He refused to believe the man's death was an accident or of his own choosing.

But the more Liam looked into Marlon's life, the more he came to see that Marlon had lived on the fringes of society. People knew of him – and this often meant that they bought drugs from him – but no one really knew him. Marlon hadn't had friends, at least none that would come forward, and increasingly the picture being painted of his short life was a bleak one.

On Friday morning, Grace informed Liam that she was going back to London for the weekend. He may have misinterpreted her, but it sounded like a chance for him to ask her to stay. And maybe if he hadn't been meeting with Millie on Sunday, he would have done just that. As it was, he mumbled something about having to work for the lifeboat crew and there was an awkward period of silence before Grace walked away without a response.

Saturday afternoon, Liam sat on the veranda of a local bar, drinking coffee alongside Fischer. They'd spent the morning draining the hydraulic fluid from the SLARS – the Shannon Launch and recovery system – the Annie Wilkinson anchored out to sea. The tide was high, the surface of the water glass-like as sunlight darted across it. Liam found himself sitting in silence as he drank his coffee, the lifeboat chief not in the best of moods, staring out towards the sea.

Liam was already counting down the time until tomorrow afternoon's date with Millie and wasn't going to let Fischer put him in a bad mood. 'What's got to you?'

'I don't know. People.'

'That's cryptic,' said Liam.

'Looks like we're going to lose some of our budget next year.'

'I see.' The lifeboat station existed solely through charitable donations and the whole enterprise was run on a shoestring budget. 'We'll make do. We always do.'

Fischer grimaced, lifting his hand to order another drink from the teenage waitress. Although Liam had known Fischer ever since returning to Cornwall, he still didn't know much about the man on a personal level. He'd been amazing and helped Liam face his fear and his ongoing struggle with the water, but this was probably the most emoting he'd seen from him, though he was certainly capable of a mood swing – usually from genteel to highly agitated and angry when things were not going to plan on the boat. As far as Liam knew, Fischer lived alone in Lelant. He'd once been married but that had ended during his time in the navy. Beyond that, and the shared stories of action in the marines, and latterly their time on the lifeboat, Liam didn't know him at all.

'Saw you talking to that old bastard, Sloan, again,' said Fischer, as the new coffees arrived.

Liam recalled seeing Fischer that day in the lifeboat house. 'Can't talk about that.'

'You be careful with that one. And don't believe a word he says to you.'

'I'll bear that in mind,' said Liam, as their pagers went off in unison.

◆ ◆ ◆

Liam was surprised that three other volunteers were already at the station before he and Fischer had even paid their bill. Then, within minutes of their arrival, they had a full crew complement ready to launch. A familiar buzz of anticipation came over Liam as he dressed into his drysuit and the smaller boat – the Charlotte Mae – was launched into the still waters of St Ives Harbour.

It sounded like a routine call – two surfers caught in a rip tide over at Gwithian – but the crew were experienced enough to know there was no such thing as routine when it came to the sea. The last time Liam had been on duty was the callout that led to retrieving Marlon Tomlinson from the water, and Liam considered the possibility that they would come across a similar situation this time around. It was harder being on the smaller boat, the water that much closer, and he concentrated on his breathing as they journeyed across St Ives Bay, towards Godrevy Island with its active lighthouse. Liam understood he was progressing all the time. This time last year, he wouldn't have even been able to step aboard a boat. But it still dismayed him that all he could think about as they sped through the glorious scenery, the pristine sea surrounded by stretches of golden sand, was being caught in the depths of the ocean.

Fischer eased the throttle as they identified two bobbing heads in the water. Liam looked over the side of the boat to see two teenage boys holding on to their boogie boards for dear life. Despite the warm weather, and the seeming calmness of the sea, there were areas of the beaches on the surrounding coasts that had vicious undercurrents. It seemed the boys had been caught by such a rip tide and had been unable to pull themselves back in. 'It's all right now,' he said, exchanging looks with Fischer, who nodded in response.

Liam tried to control his shaking hands as he harnessed himself to the side of the boat before sending a life ring to the pair. He reminded himself that he was probably the strongest swimmer here, that he was surrounded by rescue professionals, and this was likely the safest he would ever be out at sea, but it didn't stop his fears. He double-checked his own harness before reaching over to grab one of the boys, flinching slightly as water splashed on his face. With the help of the crew, he pulled the boy on to the boat, but his friend had started panicking. He had hold of the life ring but was splashing wildly in the water as if he feared he was about to sink.

It was too much for Liam. He was back at that last night with the SBS, fighting his own panic, the break of the water seemingly out of reach.

Before he knew it, Fischer was next to him. 'You're OK. Give me your hand. The ring will keep you afloat,' said the coxswain to the boy, easing Liam out of the way.

Liam snapped back to reality. He looked around, worried he'd been caught out, but the crew's focus was on the body still in the water. Fischer was leaning over, his grip on the boy who with some wild kicking propelled himself forward enough that he could be pulled to safety, along with their boards.

A colleague wrapped the boys in thermal blankets. Fischer started the engine and turned back towards shore. Relief spread through the crew. Liam saw it in the relaxed shoulders of his colleagues, the concerned faces now smiling as they motored back towards the harbour. Liam shared their relief, but his body was full of tension. Fischer had stepped in seamlessly during the rescue, but he must have noticed Liam panic, and that meant it was more than possible that others had too.

'Don't worry about it,' said Fischer later, after the boat had been returned and the crew dismissed.

'Don't worry about it? I could have cost someone's life.'

'That's why we go out as a crew. You think you're the only one who's frozen on a job? It happens. And no one noticed.' He stopped for a moment, fixed Liam's eyes with his. 'We both knew this wouldn't be easy but you're making great strides. When we first talked about this, you could barely be near the sea. Now look at you. We'll just be more careful next time, give you more of an ancillary position on the boat. You're going to get through this, I promise.'

Liam accepted the reassurance, but his unease followed him into his dreams that night, as he experienced the familiar nightmare before waking up as if his lungs were on fire in the middle of the night. He thought he'd moved past this stage. After the SBS incident, he'd been forced to attend weekly meetings with a navy psychologist, Dr Bennett. It was her he'd opened up to about the nightmares. They'd worked through numerous scenarios in their time together, and she'd helped him develop the coping strategies that eventually enabled him step aboard the lifeboat years later.

The nightmares had always been there but of late they had worsened. It was no stretch to put that down to the deaths of Marlon Tomlinson and Eleanor Cooper. They had drowned when Liam had survived, and he wondered if he would ever fully be able to function out at sea again, or if he should just give up the volunteering, move further inland, and try to put it all behind him.

But no sooner had the thought crossed his mind than he dismissed it. Knowing he would never get back to sleep, Liam changed into running gear and headed into town and the beach in the early morning. Complicated as his relationship was with the water, he always wanted to be near it.

Running along the beach, a calmness returned to him and he began to focus on the recent investigations. He thought about the marks found on Marlon Tomlinson's wrists and ankles, and pictured him sinking into the water unable to propel himself back to the surface, and had to fight the image from his earlier nightmare, the metres of water above him as his dream self struggled for air.

At some point, his run morphed into a sprint and he stopped by the rocks and bent over his knees, his breath ragged. He was seeing Millie later – and he didn't want to be in this state when did. He wasn't sure what was coming over him, and reluctant as he felt to do so he wondered if it was time to seek out counselling again.

That evening, he was on the verge of telling Millie about the dreams and his fear of the water, but decided it was too early. He didn't want to frighten her off, and although he was enjoying being with her he wasn't sure if he was ready for any kind of commitment at the moment.

Instead, he shared some details about his time in the SBS and how it had led to his split with Kim.

Millie watched him closely as he spoke. 'You were very young,' she said.

'Maybe,' said Liam, thinking that he hadn't been too young to be involved in military operations where people had lost their lives. 'I just hope George remains well adjusted. He is well adjusted, isn't he?' he asked, with mock fear.

Millie chuckled. 'You're not asking for a personal report on your child out of school, are you?'

Liam smiled, his hands held up. 'Never crossed my mind.'

Millie told him about her own upbringing and her affinity for the sea. She'd been surfing in Gwithian yesterday, and talked about the waves with an almost evangelical glee. 'We should go out sometime. If you think you can keep up with me?'

For the briefest of seconds, Liam forgot about his fear. He pictured catching some waves with Millie, thinking how nothing in the world at that moment sounded better, before reality hit home and he realised that part of his life was probably gone for good. He smiled instead of answering. 'Dessert?'

Mille shook her head, a slightly confused look on her face, as if she'd missed something, while Liam asked for the bill.

They walked back towards the centre along Fore Street, neither speaking, both content to be in the other's company. They were turning the corner into Ayr Lane when Liam spotted Fischer and another member from the team, Alan Thompson, leaving a local bar. Liam stopped and introduced Millie, ignoring the knowing look on Fischer's face before walking Millie back to her house share on Bedford Road.

Liam felt like a giddy teenager as they stood outside the terraced house. Things were happening quicker than he'd anticipated. Since he'd started dating again, he'd had a number of one-night stands which he'd regretted the day after. He didn't want to rush things with Millie, and as she took out her front door keys he hung back.

'So,' she said, her face lighting up as she smiled at him, clearly as nervous as he was.

'So, I've had a great evening,' said Liam, but before he could finish the sentence, Millie leaned in to kiss him.

Chapter Thirteen

Peter began panicking as they put the bag over his head. They had to restrain him. As Stacey tried to keep him calm by holding his hand, the bigger of the two men, Gary, put him in a headlock as the cloth covering was pulled down over his face.

'It won't be for long. Just until we move you,' said Stacey, her voice a distant whisper, but Peter couldn't be calm. He thrashed with his arms and legs until they were bound, and all he could do was wriggle about like a worm.

This was the worst thing they had ever done to him. He didn't like the way they had taken over the house, or the constant demands they made on him, but they had never really hurt him before – beyond the occasional drunken smack from the larger one. Peter struggled to think beyond the present time he was in. He rarely thought of the past, apart from daydreams about being with his mum and dad again, and the future he could rarely anticipate. He'd never really thought about what their long-term intentions were, but now that he was restrained it began to dawn on him that this could be it.

Stacey's words drifted towards him. 'We're just going to take you somewhere safer,' she said.

Peter was exhausted and he stopped moving. 'But this is my home. Where else can I go?'

'Everything will be OK. I'm sure you'll be allowed to come back here soon.'

Peter wasn't sure if he heard one of the men laugh as he was lifted to his feet and carried out of the house. He could hear seagulls, and the heat of the sun through his covering. He closed his eyes, which made it feel like he didn't have a bag over his head, and allowed himself to be placed inside some sort of van. At least, he assumed it was a van from the sound of the engine. Stacey was still with him, cooing soft words, as the engine growled further into life and they moved away.

Peter wished he had a drink. He was rarely sober; sobriety made him ill. He was nauseous now, his head thumping time with the laboured movement of the vehicle as it drove over an uneven road.

'We should have run this by him. He is going to be fucking livid.' Peter recognised the voice of the subordinate man called Midge.

'He'd be a lot more livid if that copper returns and finds us in the house. Not worth the risk,' said Gary.

'If you say so.'

The words were muffled, but even in his weakened state Peter heard the fear in both men's voices. It was only Stacey who sounded calm. She still held his hand, and it was enough to stop Peter panicking as the van stopped.

'He's here.'

'I can see that. Wait there.'

Peter kept his eyes closed, Stacey stroking his hand as Gary left the van.

'You think this is a good idea?' said Midge.

'Not my decision, is it?' said Stacey. 'But we need to get this thing off him, he doesn't like it.'

Peter didn't much care for the way they talked about him as if he wasn't there but he was used to it. It had happened all his life.

He saw it wherever he went, people speaking behind their hands or openly in front of him. He was clearly not invisible, but it often felt that way. He jumped as he heard the van door slide open.

'Boss wants to see him now.'

'Come on, Peter, it will be OK,' said Stacey.

He was pulled from the van, his legs kicking in the air as if he were falling from a cliff, and they carried him away.

Chapter Fourteen

Liam's drive to work that Monday morning was one of his better journeys. He didn't mind the grey clouds and occasional drops of rain despite it being early July. And although Marlon Tomlinson's death and the county lines problems were not far from his mind, he was able to put them to the periphery.

He'd spent the night at Millie's – the only downside being he had to leave earlier than he'd have liked so he could get home and change. The endorphins were clearly still alive in his system, as he could feel himself smiling as he arrived and parked at headquarters, and although he wasn't complaining he took a minute to refocus before heading up to CID.

If it hadn't been for DCI Hargreaves calling a department meeting, he would have worked from home that morning. There were still a number of people he needed to speak to in the St Ives and Hayle area, and he planned to take a second look at Peter Britten's place to see if the house owner was back, or if his niece was still holding the fort.

The meeting was as dry as Liam had expected, Hargreaves running through the priorities for the coming week which still had as its main focus the locating and recovery of the shipment of fentanyl that had supposedly hit the county last week.

After assigning tasks, Hargreaves handed the meeting over to Grace, who hadn't spoken to Liam since his arrival that morning. 'There have been some developments with the OCG,' she said, getting to her feet, and loading a picture on to the white screen behind her.

'Gregory Moore. Long-time involvement and suspected member of the OCG. We've been tracing his movements for the last two years. Lots of flights to Tunisia, Morocco, and Portugal.'

Grace pressed a key and a second picture of the man appeared. This time he was lying in a pool of blood, a bullet hole to his head. 'Found dead in his hallway Sunday afternoon in Selsdon, south-east London. Looks like a professional hit. Two to the chest, one to the head. Although we can't rule out this being the action of a rival gang, we believe it could possibly be an "in-house" hit.'

'They're killing their own?' asked Maya.

'That's the intelligence we're getting. It seems Mr Moore was pivotal in the arrival of fentanyl to our shores. Even though it now looks like this was a success, we believe Moore paid the price for the scuppered drop.'

'They think he was a grass?' said Whitfield.

'No, but someone had to get the blame for us being ready for the shipment,' said Grace, who looked slightly embarrassed, no doubt reliving the botched operation from the other night in her head.

'Where's the information coming from?'

'I can't share that, but I'm sure you can put two and two together,' said Grace, alluding to the information that had supposedly come from a UCO.

'And what does this mean for us?' asked Liam.

Grace barely made eye contact. 'We aren't sure. It's a big step to take out someone so senior. There will potentially be fallout. We're not sure exactly what that will be. A possible outcome we are hearing is that the planned drop of fentanyl in Cornwall could be changed to another county, one where there is less heat for the OCG. Obviously, that will be great for here but it's just hearsay for the moment. We have to do whatever we can to prevent them getting this in great numbers to the streets. Once it starts, it is going to take a Herculean effort to stop the momentum. So, for now, we continue the work we did last week.'

◆ ◆ ◆

The dead gang member, Gregory Moore, wasn't one of the twelve members believed to have been working in the Cornwall area, but Liam still read the notes before heading back south towards Hayle. As Grace suggested, the hit had been professional in nature – Moore was gunned down as he opened the front door of his house.

Liam wouldn't have been surprised if the killer had military training. He'd met many criminals and service personnel who talked a good game, but executing someone in cold blood took a remorseless nature that was rare. The military was often where such people began their careers. Liam had known colleagues he'd been glad to have on his side but would never have liked to come up against.

He was thinking about one such person, a former colleague, Ethan Mitchell, as he stopped at the bar where he'd met the elderly gent, Mr Ward, the other day. Mitchell had been in the SAS and had worked with Liam during a joint operation. Mitchell, then a sniper, had killed three gunmen during the operation in Somalia, effectively saving Liam's life. Liam had spoken to him about it afterwards. The enormity of what the man had done hadn't seemed to register with his colleague. The men he'd killed had simply been dangerous enemies, and in Mitchell's eyes it had been either them or his colleagues. Liam wondered if Moore's killer had the same outlook, and what that meant for anyone who came up against the organised crime group from now on.

Mr Ward was sitting alone in the lounge, nursing another half of bitter. 'Couldn't keep away?' he said, raising his glass as Liam sat down opposite.

'I need your help again,' said Liam. 'I went to Mr Britten's house the other day, but he wasn't in. I was wondering if you'd seen him of late.'

'Not since that last time – the one I mentioned.'

'Do you happen to know if he has a niece?'

Mr Ward thought about the question, pausing so long that Liam worried he'd forgotten what he'd been asked. 'I don't honestly know. His parents died when he was in his twenties. Quite wealthy. People thought Peter was a fool . . . and probably still do. But no one ever questioned how he could gallivant around all day, buying himself drinks all the time. He's smart.' Mr Ward pointed to his head. 'Not in the traditional sense, and he probably drank most of those smarts away these last few years, but he was smart enough to invest that money. Smart enough so he didn't have to spend another day working. But as for a niece? I'll be honest, I haven't got a straight word out of that man for decades, but he never mentioned a niece.'

Liam thanked Mr Ward, bought him another drink, and took the short drive to Peter Britten's house, parking up and battling his way along the pathway with its overgrown weeds. The gateway was open, as was the annexed garage where it appeared a motor vehicle had been stored. He knocked on the door but this time there was no answer, so he stepped into the garage.

A faint aroma of petrol filled the enclosed area. Liam still didn't know much about Peter, but was under the distinct impression that the man was a habitual drunk, and therefore never in a position to drive.

Liam tried a second door in the garage which presumably led to the house. It was locked so he gave a gentle shove but it still didn't budge. Retreating outside, he walked the perimeter of the house. Every window on the ground floor was obscured with either newspaper taped to the panes, or by dirty net curtains. Liam peered inside as best as he could but couldn't see much. He considered calling headquarters but there was no way he would be given permission to break into the house. To do so he would have to fear for the safety of someone's life, and it was hard to justify that on the basis that the garage door was open and no one was home.

He wrote a short note on the back of his card for Peter, which he posted through the rattling letter box. He wondered where the young, spiky-haired woman – Stacey Smith, if that was her real name – who'd claimed to be Peter's niece was. He should have taken her phone number. It wasn't the first semi-deserted property he'd visited since he'd joined CID but something about the situation felt off to him. But for now, all he could do was keep returning until he managed to speak to the owner.

Heading towards the car, he heard the sound of another vehicle in the area. Upping his pace, he reached the car in time to see a white transit van driving away down the lane. He called for the driver to stop but they either hadn't heard, or were ignoring him.

Liam ran to the car and started the engine. At the end of the lane he had a decision to make, and five minutes after turning left he understood that he'd probably made the wrong one. It wasn't ideal but it wasn't a completely wasted situation.

He had the number plate of the van, and he recognised the man who'd been driving.

Chapter Fifteen

Peter wasn't taken to meet Stacey's boss. Instead, they dumped him inside a small room, his wrists and ankles tied, the hood thankfully taken from his face. The room was something of a storage cupboard. Inches away, but infuriatingly out of reach, were two boxes each filled to the brim with vodka. How he would love a drink now. Drinking helped blur the world, and that was the way Peter liked to view it.

Instead, he was made to wait and listen as a man dressed down Stacey and her friends as if they were no higher on the food chain than Peter. Although that gave him a little thrill – especially when he heard Gary whimper in complaint – it did make him fear what would happen to him.

'You need to go back,' said the boss man.

'But that's why we got out. The copper was asking all these questions,' said Gary.

'And now what do you think is going to happen? He's going to see the place is empty, and he will come back again . . . and if the place is still empty, he is going to start to worry about him in there. If you'd just stayed where you were, none of this would have happened. The copper will be talking to everyone in the area. But as long as Stacey's story is convincing, what's it going to matter? Now get back there now, all of you.'

Peter braced himself and sure enough the door swung open and Midge shoved the hood on him, Peter howling in complaint as he felt his neck muscles strain.

'Hurry the fuck up,' said Midge, hauling Peter to his feet, and dragging him back to the van.

They drove in near silence – faster this time – with no words of encouragement from Stacey as the van swerved from one corner to the next.

'What the hell is that?' said Midge, as the van slowed some time later.

'That's the copper's car,' said Gary. Even from beneath his hood, Peter heard the indecision in Gary's voice. It felt too soon to wonder if this was all over, but surely if the policeman saw them, he would search the van. Even Gary and Midge wouldn't be so stupid as to do something to a man of law, would they?

Before the thought had time to register, the question was answered for him. 'Get the hell out of here. Now,' screamed Gary, as Midge swung the van around, sending Peter sprawling to the side of the vehicle, knocking his head and making everything go fuzzy.

'He saw us, he saw us,' said Midge, in such a high-pitched voice that at first Peter thought it was Stacey's.

Peter spent the next few minutes on the floor of the van as Midge sped along the country lanes even faster than before. Peter prepared himself for the inevitable crash. Maybe it was better this way. It wasn't as if he'd ever really liked his life and surely death was better than the way things had been these last few months, being a prisoner in his own house. He only hoped that any crash took Gary and Midge, and spared poor Stacey. Peter knew she was as much a victim as he was, and it was such a terrible shame that she was involved.

'The copper's at the house,' said Gary, his voice barely audible above the sound of the engine.

No one else spoke so Peter presumed he was on one of the phones the three were so obsessed with.

'OK,' said Gary, after a pause. 'He wants us to go to the house in Penzance.'

'How did he sound?' said Midge.

'How did he sound? I'll tell you how he fucking sounded. Like he wanted to kill someone,' said Gary. 'No more talking, let's get there. And Stacey, stop that useless prick rolling around in the back. He's giving me a headache.'

Chapter Sixteen

Liam met with up with Maya next to the viaduct in Hayle. He bought coffees from the local bakery and they drank them outside their cars, and waited for the emergency search warrant to be granted. He'd spent the last hour driving around on the off-chance of spotting the white van he'd seen at Peter Britten's house, and what patrol cars they had in the area were doing the same.

'You sure it was them?' asked Maya, who was leaning against her car. With her shades on, and a cool summer suit, she looked like a fashion model posing for the cameras. Not that Liam would ever tell her as such.

'Gary French, and Malcolm "Midge" Ure, clear as day. And they must have recognised me from the other day when I visited the house.' The number plates had been confirmed as fake and that, combined with the fact that Peter Britten had to be considered a vulnerable person, meant the warrant would hopefully be granted without any fuss.

They finished their coffees and headed back to Britten's place where two patrol cars were waiting for them. Liam was a little surprised that Grace wasn't there. Gary and Midge were two of the twelve OCGs members she had been targeting and locating them could help unravel everything.

It was another thirty minutes before they were given the all-clear, and Maya instructed one of the uniformed officers to use the enforcer to break down the front door.

Liam was the first through the threshold, warning anyone inside that he was entering the building. He moved from room to room, half expecting to find Peter's corpse in each new space.

It seemed evident that it hadn't been just Peter and his so-called niece who were staying in the building. There were four bedrooms, each with unmade beds, and enough debris – takeaway boxes, liquor bottles, cans of lager and cider, ashtrays filled to the brim, dirty dishes and coffee cups – to suggest that Gary and Midge had definitely been residing here alongside Peter and his 'niece'. It was an obvious reminder of the state they'd found Marlon Tomlinson's house in, and the immediate concern now was Peter Britten's safety.

The house was searched top to bottom but no drugs were found on the premises. 'Begs the question why they were returning,' said Maya, as they searched through the garage together. 'I guess we can't dismiss the possibility that they may have killed Peter and disposed of his body. It would follow on from what happened to Marlon Tomlinson and Eleanor Cooper.'

'Then why return? It doesn't look like they left any drugs here, and Peter isn't here,' said Liam.

'Maybe they were here to pick him up and got spooked by seeing you.'

'I hope so. That would at least mean Peter is somewhere in the area. I might as well make a swing around the local bars and check if there have been any sightings of Peter or the van. Unless you need me here.'

Maya shook her head, and Liam headed to the bar where he'd met with James Ward earlier that day. The old man had left at lunchtime according to the student worker behind the bar who hadn't seen Peter Britten in the last few days.

Despite the re-emergence of the sunny weather, everywhere was dead. Without the full hit of the school summer holiday, bars and restaurants struggled during the day. For most establishments, business survival centred around utilising the peak season for all its worth and everything in between presented more of a struggle to break even.

Liam saw the same familiar faces, chatted to the bar staff and restaurant owners. Peter Britten was a familiar figure in Hayle but no one had seen him in the last three days. A few recognised the description of Stacey Smith, and responded to the photographs of Gary French and Malcolm Ure, but no one knew anything about them. Liam kicked himself for not following up more after he'd visited the house that first time as he made his way back to the viaduct.

He wondered what would have happened if he'd insisted on looking around the house the first time he'd visited. The OCGs involved in the county lines operations were not scared of getting weaponised. More than one raid had resulted in guns being recovered, and it seemed highly likely that Gary and Midge had been waiting inside Peter's house the last time he'd come calling.

What still puzzled him was what the lines gang wanted with Peter. And why they had seemingly killed both Eleanor and Marlon but so far left him alive?

The traditional method of cuckooing involved taking over someone's house and using it as a base to aid distribution of drugs. People had gone missing in similar situations before – and Liam understood that after his visit the gang might have been worried there would be more heat on them – but why, as seemed likely, had they taken Peter with them? It was hard to come up with any other conclusion except that if they didn't find him, they would soon be pulling Peter's corpse from the water.

Maya was leaning against the hood of her car again, sipping another coffee as if she hadn't moved since the last time they'd been there. He wondered what she made of Grace and the involvement of the Met. Liam had learnt these last three years that Maya tended to keep things very much to herself, and would only reveal how she was feeling about any given situation when she was ready and on her own terms. 'Any luck?' she asked, disposing of the coffee cup.

'Nothing, you?'

'Nope.'

'What next?'

'Let's get back, plenty of CCTV footage to spool through. That van must have gone somewhere.'

'Joy of joys,' said Liam, climbing into his car.

He'd reached the roundabout at Chiverton Cross when a call came through from a duty sergeant he used to work with during his time on probation in Penzance.

'Hi, Ted,' he said, crossing the roundabout and pulling into the petrol station.

'DS Kilshaw – how is life in the big leagues?'

'You know how it is – fast cars and fast women, that sort of thing.'

'I bet it is. Bit of a strange one here. We arrested an IC1 male, intoxication in a public place. Completely out of it in Market Place, could barely get a word out of him. Two things. One, we've found some pills on him we don't quite recognise. About to send them off for analysing but wondered if you wanted a quick look first considering the work you're doing at the moment.'

'You heard about that, did you?'

'Your fame proceeds you, young man.'

'And second?' asked Liam.

'Said delinquent has just come to, and when questioned says he only wants to speak to a certain DS Liam Kilshaw.'

'Now we get to the crux of the situation. What's the name?'

'Justin Blake,' said Ted.

Liam thought back to the other day and his chase down the Stennack steps to catch up with Blake. 'Christ, what's he up to now? OK, leave it with me, should be there in the next thirty minutes,' he said, rejoining the roundabout and heading back the way he'd just come.

Chapter Seventeen

Liam never tired of the sight of St Michael's Mount, the glistening water brushing against the sea wall. He headed into Penzance, driving down by the harbour and up Alverton Road to the police station.

'The prodigal son returns, and blesses us with his presence,' said Ted Fletcher, the duty sergeant who had called him.

'Ted. How are things in the front end?'

'Same as ever. I see you're still follicly challenged.'

Liam ran his hand over his scalp. 'Same as ever. Right, where are these pills?'

Ted showed him through to the evidence locker, entering details on to a keypad and pulling on some protective gloves before taking out a small baggie of green-coloured pills.

Liam placed on his own gloves before inspecting the baggie. 'Did Blake tell you what these were?'

'Nope. When we asked him, that's when he asked to speak to you, though he was alert enough to claim they were for personal use only. Whatever they are, they must be quite potent. The arresting officers said he was like a walking zombie. As for the personal use, we've counted twenty-two pills. I think this Mr Blake could be a dealer making the classic mistake of using his own goods.'

'He's a registered CHIS,' said Liam. 'I ran into him a couple of days back in St Ives.'

'That would explain why he wants to speak to you. Shall I get him ready?'

'Please.'

Liam went to the kitchen area and made himself a cup of instant coffee. The station was working with a skeleton crew, and Ted appeared to be the only officer in situ other than a pair of community officers.

'Ready for you. Centre court, interview room one.'

'Big leagues. Thanks, Ted.'

Blake didn't make eye contact as Liam entered the room. 'Justin, how are you?' said Liam, sitting down opposite.

The informant appeared to be wearing the same clothes as the last time he'd seen him, the T-shirt the same surfing brand and washed-out colour. Blake grunted as Liam went through the preliminaries of informing Blake of the charges against him, and his right to legal representation, which he declined with a wave of his hand and another grunt.

'For the tape, the suspect has signalled he doesn't want legal representation at this time. You wanted to see me, Justin?'

'They want to put me in front of the magistrates,' said Blake, lifting his head, the bags beneath his eyes dark and heavy, almost as if he'd been in a fight.

'I've read the report, Justin. It's not looking good for you. I'm afraid Market Place isn't your personal toilet.'

Blake grinned.

'And as for these pills. Looks like possession with intent is going to be easy to prove. Where did you get them?'

'Personal use.'

'Listen, Justin, I have a lot going on at the moment, as you probably know. You're the one who asked me to come here. If you're not going to give me some pertinent information then I'll be adding wasting police time to the charges. Now tell me, where did you get the pills from?'

'Don't know his name. Big guy. Huge guy. Definitely local. Cornish, at least.'

Liam stood up. 'Haven't got time for this, sorry.'

'OK, OK. His name is Adams. Possibly Connor Adams, I don't know.'

'And he sold you these pills?'

Blake was still too wasted to fake a response, shrugging his shoulders.

'He gave them to you?' asked Liam.

'Freebie. I told you: personal use. How long have you known me, Mr Kilshaw? I may be stupid, but I'm not stupid enough to start dealing.'

'Well, that's not quite true – you have a record for dealing hash.'

'Come on, Mr Kilshaw, that was years ago. I know my place.'

Liam was close to believing him. He was sure Blake still sold the occasional bit of weed but this was a different league. 'Let's say I believe you. Why would someone give you a bag of pills for free?'

'Why do you think?' said Blake, the pleading tone vaporising.

'First hit is free type of thing?' said Liam.

'I was supposed to give a few of these out. See what the feedback was. Didn't expect to have the effect it did on me. The last thing I want is to get into trouble, you know that.'

'I know I had to chase you through half of St Ives the other day. We're going to find out but you need to tell me what these pills are now,' said Liam, already knowing and fearing the answer.

'Opioids.'

'Specifically?'

'I think they're fentanyl,' said Blake, lowering his eyes in defeat.

◆ ◆ ◆

The pills collected from Justin Blake came back from the lab as a match for the sample of fentanyl that Grace had brought with her from London. Liam had an e-fit of Connor Adams. If Blake was to be believed, the man was in his fifties, over six feet tall, and seventeen to eighteen stone, though there was no immediate match on their databases.

'Good work, DS Kilshaw,' said Grace, when Liam was back in Bodmin later that day.

They were alone in the incident room, Liam adding Adams' e-fit to the crime board. 'Thank you, ma'am,' he said, nodding his head and smiling.

'Bet that feels weird to say.'

'Doesn't it just?'

After all but ignoring him in the morning's briefing, Grace's mood towards him seemed to have thawed. Liam wondered what would have happened had Grace reappeared in his life a few weeks ago, before he'd gone out with Millie. 'I thought you'd be back to London with the death of Gregory Moore.'

'I'm afraid you're stuck with me for a bit longer. Perhaps a lot longer, now we know fentanyl is on the street.'

'I guess we'll be getting some more of your lot down here now.'

'Quite possibly but I'm sure we can work together in a spirit of cooperation.'

Liam thought he detected a hidden meaning to Grace's words, but didn't ask her to elaborate. It was odd that she was back in his life, but he was already getting used to it. He had fond memories of their time together. It had made splitting up that much harder, but he was sure they'd made the right decision. They'd both been embarking on the start of their careers, and a long-distance relationship would never have worked. He wondered if things could work out between them now, dismissing the idea immediately as he recalled last night with Millie. 'What's next?'

'Your boss has given me permission for overtime for everyone. We need to find Connor Adams, and get these pills off the streets before they take hold.'

◆ ◆ ◆

Grace was true to her word. A couple of hours later, it felt like every copper in Cornwall was in headquarters. Grace was working with DCI Hargreaves, DI Whitfield, Maya and other senior officers on the uniformed side to manage the night's activity.

A coordinated raid was to take place in the areas of Hayle, St Ives, Camborne, and Penzance. Every known user and dealer, however minor, was to be targeted and if necessary searched, and all known drug spots were to be under surveillance. 'I want these pills off our streets with immediate effect,' said Hargreaves, glancing at Grace as he spoke.

Duties were handed out. Liam took the lead in the St Ives area, his first port of call another conversation with Martin Sloan. He managed to find a spot in the railway station car park and took the Pednolva Walk to the lifeboat station in time to see the D-class being launched. As he was working, he didn't have his pager with him so hadn't been notified.

He stepped into the lifeboat house where the rest of the volunteers were watching the boat's progress, one of them in contact by radio. 'What's the shout?' asked Liam, as the boat jumped over the waves.

'Mechanical failure on a pleasure craft four miles out,' said Billy Rowson, the young lad whose first voyage had been fishing Marlon Tomlinson out of the water.

Liam considered asking him if he'd seen any little green pills for sale in the area but decided it would be unfair in the current situation. 'I'm in town and on my phone if you need any help,' he said, and there was a general murmur of approval as he left the station and crossed the road to the Lifeboat Inn.

He ordered a sparkling water from the barman, another twenty-something whose face was adorned with a mixture of colourful tattoos and piercings. 'Is Joe in?' he asked.

'Just popped out. Should be back in about thirty,' said the man, before turning to serve another customer.

Looking the way he did meant Liam wasn't an ideal candidate for undercover work. Grace used to call him a distinguished-looking dude, which had been another way of saying he stuck out in a crowd. He still wasn't sure if she'd been complimenting him or not.

It was early evening but there were a few groups of young people out. St Ives wasn't his beat, but he knew lots of the people in the bar and they knew him. He decided to make a quick circuit of the place, exchanging brief hellos, and mentioning the possibility of fentanyl being on the streets as he shared the e-fit image of Connor Adams. Part of him wondered if he was making a mistake, as if he were advertising the product for the drug dealers. All he could do was remind everyone he spoke to of the epidemic in America, and trust they had more sense than to start taking the opioid.

The lifeboat was out of sight as he left the bar. He was glad to see the water was calm, and wished the crew safe travels as he heard his name called out. He turned around to see Millie arm in arm with another woman outside the amusement arcades. 'We were just talking about you,' she said, as Liam walked over. 'This is my friend, Becca. She works with me in the school.'

Liam smiled and nodded. He recalled seeing the teaching assistant in the playground when he'd collected George the week before. 'Are you two allowed out on a school night?'

'Research purposes,' said Becca, who appeared to be blushing.

'We're about to research the drinks in the pub, if you fancied joining us?'. asked Millie.

At that moment, there was nothing more Liam would have liked to do. Even with everything that was going on, Millie had remained foremost in his mind, and his late night and long day was taking its toll on him. 'I would love to, but I'm on duty.'

'Oh, what's going on?' asked Becca.

'That would be telling.'

Millie looked at Becca, who made her excuses. 'Lovely to meet you, handsome policeman,' she said, giggling as she stumbled off towards the Lifeboat Inn.

'You need to keep an eye on her,' said Liam.

'I need to keep an eye on you,' said Millie, moving towards him.

'Hey, not in public, I have a reputation,' said Liam.

'Oh shut up,' said Millie, hugging him.

Liam hugged her back, still surprised by his strength of feeling towards her. 'Still on for Friday?' he asked.

'You betcha.'

'Don't get arrested,' Liam called after Millie, as she walked away.

She shrugged before turning, and smiled at him. 'I'll do my best,' she said, and then disappeared inside after her friend.

Liam continued along the wharf, trying to get his mind back on work. He recalled the dishevelled state of Justin Blake in Penzance, and wondered if Eleanor Cooper and Marlon Tomlinson had got themselves mixed up in fentanyl prior to their deaths. He thought too of Peter Britten. It wasn't much of a stretch to picture the lifeboat crew returning having fished the old man's body out of the sea. With the threat of fentanyl now being on the streets, the recent deaths and Peter Britten's disappearance, it was as if the county was on the precipice of unravelling.

He walked up Alexandra Road and knocked on Martin Sloan's door on North Terrace. The two recent exchanges with the man were still fresh in his memory, in particular the way the drug dealer had insisted on mentioning Liam's parents. He peered through the window when there was no answer, the lights in the downstairs room switched off. A vision of Sloan bound and gagged flashed in his mind, but a premonition wasn't enough to allow him into the house. It was more than feasible that Sloan had heard about Blake's arrest for possession and was lying low, but for now all Liam could do was continue asking questions around the seaside town.

Maya called for an update, and they shared similar stories: there was no further sign of fentanyl being available for sale, although it was still early. Liam called around a few more bars, trying to locate Sloan, before making the short journey over to Penzance.

He parked down by the harbour and stopped in every bar he came along on the way towards Market Place at the top of the town. He recognised plain-clothes officers in most of the bars who would be waiting for any hint of dealing. It was feasible that Blake was the only current source of the drug, but he doubted that Connor Adams would be stupid enough to give sole responsibility for handing out free samples to a degenerate like him.

He met Maya in a bar in Market Place, along from the cinema. She was sitting with Jack Lawson, who looked uncomfortable as they pretended to be on a date. The pair were a mismatch – the young detective a few leagues out of reach of Maya.

'You can take off now,' said Maya, as Liam arrived. 'Try to find out what you can about this house party and report back.' Jack nodded and left.

'Think I'm a bit old for a house party,' said Liam, taking his seat.

'You and me both. We've heard more than one mention of a late-night gathering, but no address yet.'

'Exciting, reminds me of going to raves.'

'That was before your time, wasn't it?'

Liam shrugged. 'We had our raves, don't you worry about that. Though never on a Monday night . . .'

'What can I say? New generation. We party when we want.'

◆ ◆ ◆

The location for the party came in around 11.30 p.m. as the pubs were kicking out. The gathering was to take place in a house close to Penlee Park. Four of the plain-clothes officers working the town that evening had been given invites of a sort. Maya and Liam waited together in Maya's car a street down from the gathering. Patrol cars and riot vans were put on standby.

Maya called Grace as they waited. They received occasional text messages from the officers inside the house. Grace was currently in Camborne, tracking another sighting of fentanyl from one of the town's bars, and updated her that four people had been arrested so far for possession.

It was sombre news. Sometimes it felt like the county couldn't catch a break, and the last thing it needed was a fentanyl problem. 'At least we've made the arrests,' said Maya. 'Time to stop it in its tracks.'

'Maybe,' said Liam, but they both knew that four arrests meant there were others either carrying or supplying the drug in the area, and something as addictive as the synthetic opioid could take hold of a community within a matter of weeks.

'Got something,' said Maya, starting the car before they had a chance to discuss further.

Liam took Maya's phone as she sped towards the house. The message on the phone said: At least one dealer operating in here – giving things out for free.

'Tell them to hold tight and call for backup. I want the front and back of the house locked down.'

Liam did as instructed, Maya driving to outside the property where they waited for backup to arrive before storming the party.

Uniformed officers went in first, after Maya had sent one team to the rear. The officers inside had been told to watch the bathrooms to stop people flushing the drugs, and by the time Maya and Liam walked in three arrests had been made.

Liam knew things could have been a lot worse. None of the partygoers had started panicking, or had tried to leave the building. Officers were busy arranging people into different rooms where they could be processed, the instructions from headquarters being that every trace of fentanyl be recovered.

One of the plain-clothes officers brought over a bag of green pills to show Maya. 'David Beresford, known dealer. Says he was giving them away so it's not dealing, apparently,' he said.

'We'll let the magistrates decide that tomorrow morning,' said Maya, as the culprit was taken from the house.

Liam followed Maya into the kitchen area where a group of women were being questioned by two female uniformed officers. He was about to ask Maya how many pills she thought were in the bag when he caught sight of one of the women and his heart sank. Staring at him, clearly wasted beyond words, was Becca, the friend Millie had introduced him to earlier that evening.

Chapter Eighteen

Liam pulled Becca to the side, making sure he was in view of other officers as he did so. He needed to make sure this was all above board. 'What the hell are you doing here?' he said.

'Oh look, it's the handsome policeman. You know how I remember you?' Becca was slurring, struggling to keep her balance.

'My bald head?'

'No,' she said, pretending to be outraged. 'Well, maybe – yes.'

'Is Millie with you?' asked Liam, fearing the answer.

'No, no. She stayed back in St Ives.'

Liam let out a breath. Millie being at the party wouldn't necessarily have been the end of the world, but it would have added some unneeded complications to his life. 'Don't you have work tomorrow?' he asked, as Becca slumped against a wall.

'I'm a part-time teaching assistant. No work tomorrow.'

Liam signalled to one of the uniformed officers. 'Please could we get her processed as soon as possible?' he asked. He hoped Becca wasn't carrying any of the pills but it was out of his hands now. 'Let me know when she's ready to go.'

'You know her?' asked the uniformed officer.

'Not really. Friend of a friend, but I'd like to make sure she gets home safely.'

Six arrests were made from the party, though the focus was on two men who had been supplying fentanyl for free. They were detained and taken for questioning at Penzance nick the following morning.

The party crowd began to filter out. Each attendee was handed a leaflet on opioid addiction at DCI Hargreaves' request. Devoid of people and music, the house looked rundown. Wallpaper flaked from the walls, the carpets were stained and the lack of furniture suggested no one actually lived there.

'Sir. Rebecca Wilson. No drugs on her. She's free to go,' said the uniformed officer, returning with Becca, who appeared to be coming down.

'How are you feeling?' asked Liam.

'Shitty.'

'Give me your address, I'll get you a taxi.'

He waited with her outside for the taxi to arrive. It was a cloudless night, the sky pitted with blinking stars. 'How did you find out about the party?' he asked, as Becca sat on the pavement.

'Some other friends joined me after Millie went home. It was all the talk.'

'You try any of those pills?' asked Liam.

'I already told your colleagues.'

'I know, but you're telling me now.'

Becca looked up at him. 'I tried one. What the hell, you know?'

Liam nodded. Becca was a few years younger than him and Millie so he guessed he shouldn't be surprised that she would take something at a party. 'I would take a look at the leaflet you were given. There are some horrors from the States about the stuff you took. Very easy to get hooked.'

'The way I'm feeling, I'll never take anything again.'

Liam laughed. 'That's good then, but you're definitely not to go anywhere near the school tomorrow. You understand?'

Becca nodded, her eyes downcast.

'Right, let's get you up. Your taxi has arrived.'

Liam visited his mother the following morning before heading to Penzance. She wasn't responsive, one of the carers telling him she'd taken a turn for the worse the previous evening and had to be sedated. He watched her sleeping for a while – captured by her laborious breathing and prematurely aged skin.

He wasn't sure why he made these weekly pilgrimages. He supposed she was as much a victim as any drunk or drug addict. He shouldn't blame her for the way she'd treated him. She'd taken his father's death as badly as would be expected, and oblivion was her only way out. That it had such an impact on Liam was neither here nor there. He'd needed her, and she'd failed him, but her addictions were at least partly to blame. The irony that the drugs she may have once taken recreationally were now being used to medicate her was not lost on him. Maybe that was why he visited her every week, or maybe it was the ingrained obligation society deemed necessary.

She wheezed. For a second it, was as if she'd stopped breathing. As if her breath had caught then become lost. Not for the first time, he considered what her death would mean to him, and he worried what it said about him that the idea only filled him with relief.

As if in response, she let out an extended breath. Liam took that as a sign to leave, not bothering to say goodbye as he exited the room.

Millie texted him as he was getting into his car:

Just heard about Becca. I'm so sorry. Thank you for putting her in a taxi.

No problem. I'm just glad you weren't there, he replied.

Too old for house parties. See you Friday?

Can't wait.

He took the back roads to Penzance, via Halsetown. Fine mist rolled over the farmland. The tide was low in the town, and he glimpsed the breaking surf in the distance before heading inland to the station.

Coordinated interviews were taking place in three stations that morning following last night's arrests. Maya and Liam were interviewing the dealers found at the house party, DI Whitfield was in Camborne, and Grace was interviewing two suspects back in Bodmin.

Ted was there to greet him as he walked through the station. 'Nice to have some action for once,' he said, as Liam headed upstairs where Maya was waiting for him.

'Just need to ask, before we get started,' she said, handing over a coffee. 'That woman you put in a taxi last night. She isn't this new one you've been seeing?'

'New one?' said Liam, feigning outrage.

Maya raised her eyebrows, not commenting further.

'No, she isn't my new one. A friend of a friend from St Ives. We went through all the procedures.'

'She has a record, you know.'

'Bloody hell, you checked.'

'Needed to make sure, Liam, that's all.'

'I only met her for the first time yesterday, but thanks for trusting me.'

Maya frowned. 'It's nothing to do with trust. We have checked everyone we interviewed.'

'Even so.'

'You don't want to know what's on her record?'

'Enlighten me.'

'Drunk and disorderly. Two cautions. She was lucky.'

'Jesus! Lock her away.'

'Thought you should know.'

'Thank you, DI Trent,' said Liam, heading towards the interview room. He wasn't sure why Maya's questions had irritated him, and put it down to the minimal hours he'd slept of late.

'Everything OK?' asked Maya, stopping him before he entered the interview room. 'I wasn't checking up on you. You know that, don't you?'

Liam nodded. 'I'm fine,' he said, opening the door to the first interview of the day with David Beresford, the dealer they'd arrested last night. The goal was to locate the supplier, though Liam hadn't given up hope of a link to Marlon Tomlinson's death, and the missing Peter Britten.

Beresford was all smiles – which was a surprise considering his record and the fact that he'd been holding over a hundred pills of fentanyl. In his late thirties, Beresford had pocked skin and thinning hair which aged him a good decade more. He was represented by a duty solicitor Liam knew well – Sally Watson – who gave him a quick smile as he sat down opposite.

They went through the usual preamble. Maya reiterated the charge of possession with intent.

'I told you, I wasn't selling them,' said Beresford, before he'd even been asked a question.

Liam noted the exasperation in the solicitor's eyes at her client's outburst. The fact that Beresford claimed not to have been charging for the pills was irrelevant as far as the law was concerned, a point his solicitor had no doubt told him, and one Maya reminded him of. 'We're looking at a custodial sentence, David. Quite likely a long one, with your record and what you were distributing.'

'This is bullshit, man, I told you I wasn't selling anything,' said Beresford, still not getting the point.

Liam gave the solicitor a consoling look. 'Listen, you can still help yourself here. I get what you're saying – that you didn't take any money. What we need to know is who gave you the pills in the first place.'

Beresford leaned back in his chair. 'I'm not a grass.'

'Thing is, Dave, you've got yourself into something a little bit bigger than you may have thought. You know either of these men?' asked Liam, showing him photographs of Marlon Tomlinson and Peter Britten.

'He's the guy who drowned. Saw that in *The Cornishman*, so what?' said Beresford, pointing to the photograph of Marlon.

'How about this man?' asked Maya, showing the e-fit Blake had given them yesterday of Connor Adams.

Beresford shook his head. 'Nope.'

'Come on, Dave. We're giving you an opportunity here. As you say, you weren't taking any money, you didn't know what the pills were. Tell us who gave them to you, and we can see what we can do,' said Liam.

Beresford jutted out his lower jaw. He looked at his solicitor who nodded. 'Never met the guy before. Cornish lad. In his twenties maybe. Blond hair. I know, narrows it down. He seemed to know who I was. Said he was working for someone and this was a sample. Told me to share with some of my clients . . . people I know, I mean.'

'And you took a bag of pills off him, no questions asked?'

Beresford looked at his solicitor again. 'Gave me some money, didn't he. What was I supposed to do?'

◆ ◆ ◆

By the time the interviews finished that afternoon, they had three suspects claiming to have been given pills to distribute in lieu of payment. None of them had been willing to divulge details of the person who'd paid them beyond vague, generic descriptions – white male, average height, late twenties/early thirties.

Each had been quizzed over Marlon Tomlinson, Peter Britten and shown images of the e-fit Justin Blake had created of Connor Adams, as well as photos of the twelve members of the OCG. Again, they had refused to identify anyone.

Back at headquarters, Liam and the team tried to make sense of what was happening. Free samples were a common enough practice among new dealers trying to get a foothold in a market. The cost of production for fentanyl was relatively low, so it seemed like a logical step for a new or existing player to make. And as successful as the previous evening's raids had been, there was no way they would have caught everyone who had been given the pills. In America, the epidemic had been started by an unscrupulous pharmaceutical company pushing the pills on to doctors and their patients who had subsequently become addicted. The OCG were clearly taking a different approach, but with the same possible outcome.

Grace talked through the operations taking place back in London following the death of the OCG member Gregory Moore, while DCI Hargreaves promised more overtime to crack down on the spread of the drug. How this all linked in with Marlon Tomlinson's death and Peter Britten's disappearance seemed to be a side issue for both of them, and it seemed for now that it was up to Liam's team to work through those cases.

Maya stayed at headquarters as Liam went south, visiting first Marlon Tomlinson's house, and then Peter Britten's. The similarities between the properties and the men were striking, despite the difference of over fifty years between the pair. They had both lived alone in secluded properties, and were known around town, although they didn't seem to have any close friends.

Liam walked through the squalor of Peter's house once more, wondering how the old man had got caught up with the drug-dealing OCG. As he searched through the old belongings in the main bedroom, he wondered what it had been like these last few weeks for the man with the cuckoos in the house, and if Peter had been fearful for his life.

Birdsong and the chime of crickets filled the air as Liam returned outside and walked over to his car. Liam's shift had ended but he felt too frustrated to stop working. He knew the chances were high that something had already happened to Peter, but if there was an opportunity to save the man's life then he wasn't going to stop.

He set off to St Ives, deciding he would try again to speak to Martin Sloan who he'd been unable to find last night. He passed the A30 and was turning to Camborne when his phone rang, a number he didn't recognise appearing on screen.

'DS Kilshaw.'

'Oh hi, DS Kilshaw. Can you hear me? This is Anna Tuttle. We spoke the other day.'

Liam recalled the name; the woman owned one of the coastal properties in Portreath where the RIBs possibly belonging to the drug smugglers had been spotted. The line was poor. It sounded as if she was out in the wilds, wind blowing down the speaker. 'I can hear you. How can I help?'

'The boats you mentioned the other day? I think I may have found them.'

Chapter Nineteen

Liam called Maya as he made the short trip towards Portreath. Anna Tuttle claimed to have photographic evidence of an abandoned boat at Ralph's Cupboard – a collapsed cave system near to Portreath, now a very narrow inlet next to Western Cove, where they had been the other day searching for the drug-smuggling boats.

'You ever heard of this place?' she asked, as Liam sped through the country lanes.

'I went there once. You wouldn't want to go on foot. Huge drop and it's very tidal. We used to kayak out that way as kids. It's like being in your own secluded paradise but the tide is low, and you wouldn't want to get caught there.'

'Is it feasible that the smugglers could have used it?'

'I think there are some stories that it was once a place for smugglers to store their goods. But we're talking olden times here. Wouldn't make much sense to me to use it as a place to bring drugs in, as there would be no easy place to get them to land. Maybe they panicked that night and used it as a hiding place?'

'Take a look and let me know. Your girlfriend had to rush back to London, and Hargreaves has gone home so I'll need something more concrete to get them involved.'

Liam was about to protest – the words 'she's not my girlfriend' stuck in his throat – as Maya ended the call. He laughed to himself as he continued on the A30 to Hayle, and along the coast to Portreath. He didn't have his integrated lights on, stuck driving twenty-five miles an hour behind a string of cars. To his left, the Atlantic Ocean stretched out in all its glory. Despite his accident in the SBS, and his constant proximity to it, the sight of the rolling waves never ceased to enthral him. A part of him missed being able to explore its depths, but the very thought made him catch his breath, a pressure building in his chest. He looked away, using his breathing exercises to regain his composure, as the slow car in front of the line finally pulled over and he was able to increase his speed.

He pulled into Carvannel Farm, where Anna Tuttle had agreed to meet him. A slender woman, wearing a three-quarter-length wetsuit, was standing next to an Audi estate with a kayak tied to its roof. Liam parked up alongside, recognising the woman from the other day.

'Miss Tuttle, thanks for calling me,' said Liam, getting out of the car. The wind had picked up, and he took out a lightweight jacket from the back seat.

Anna looked breathless, her tied-back hair still damp. 'Thank you for coming. I called as soon as I got a signal.'

'You were kayaking alone out there?'

'Calm sea today. I set out from Portreath. That is where I called you from. Here,' she said, handing him her phone.

Liam pressed Play on the video, which showed the approach to Ralph's Cupboard through the inlet.

'Headcam,' said Anna, as Liam peered closely at the screen. 'I record all my trips.'

Liam watched the front of the boat slice through the hazy green-coloured water, reminding him of similar journeys he'd made in his teens. He could hear Anna's breathing as she manoeuvred the kayak through the water, her actions more intense as she breached the threshold into the small cove.

'What the hell?' she said on the recording as the cove came more clearly into view, revealing a small stretch of sand, the water slowly creeping in. Behind was the sheer rock cliff stretching hundreds of feet upwards, but Anna's attention was elsewhere. The video feed went out of focus, a screeching noise coming from the phone until the scene reappeared.

'I took off my helmet,' said Anna, who was standing behind Liam watching the footage. 'So I could record the scene better.'

The camera was pointed at a dull-grey boat – a RIB, like the ones spotted off the coast the other night. It appeared to be marooned on the rocks, covered in a grey tarpaulin which was stretched over the top of the boat.

Anna had zoomed in the camera and was paddling nearer. 'See there,' she said, pointing to a large black object next to the boat.

'An anchor,' said Liam.

'One of two,' said Anna.

The video stopped a few seconds later. 'Sorry I wanted to get the hell out of there. After what you said the other day, I had no idea what was in that boat. It seems strange to have abandoned it, and the fact that it was anchored made me think someone was coming back for it.'

They walked through the brittle long grass peppered with wildflowers until they were at the edge of the cliff. The tide was in, water filling the space where the sand had been in Anna's video. From their vantage point they couldn't see the boat. Liam got to his knees and crawled through the bracken until he was at the edge of the cliff. Heights didn't bother him – but neither had depths until his accident. He peered over, the sheer drop punctuated by occasional jags of rock, beneath which he made out the shape of the covered boat bobbing in the sea close to the cave entrance.

◆ ◆ ◆

Liam checked the tidal times before calling Maya. 'The next low tide is 6.52 a.m.'

'Is there any way of getting to the boat before then?' she asked.

'Not easily. We could try to get a boat out there but it is a huge risk to recover something that should essentially be there tomorrow morning. That boat isn't going anywhere.'

'OK, I'll make some calls. Any boat we send, I'd like you to be on board. You OK with that?'

Liam hesitated. It was one thing being on the lifeboat, surrounded by professionals – and more importantly Fischer, who knew what Liam was going through. But he wasn't sure if he was ready to be on a boat without that sort of backup.

The details of his discharge were in his file, but the full extent of his PTSD wasn't known by anyone in the police. The incident had happened when he'd been working for the SBS, so much of it was classified. He'd passed the police psych evaluations with ease, and although he'd mentioned a newfound aversion to water, he'd managed to hide the full extent of his condition.

'Of course,' he said, after a pause, hearing the doubt in his voice.

'In the meantime, I think we need to send someone to take your place to watch over the boat until the morning.'

'Christ, you're going to be popular,' said Liam.

'Not me, you. I'll call the marine unit. You get on to uniform and get someone out where you are. Then get some sleep.'

'Thanks, boss, knew I could count on you.'

Liam thanked Anna for her help and walked her back to the car before arranging for a replacement cover who would arrive an hour later. He made a quick detour to Martin Sloan's house in St Ives – the dealer once again not home – before returning to his flat. A message had arrived from Maya telling him to get to Penzance for

4.30 a.m. to be on board one of the two police boats she'd arranged to visit Ralph's Cupboard.

◆ ◆ ◆

Liam wasn't surprised that he had another nightmare. Going on the lifeboat was one thing – the trips were spontaneous, his mind not having time to worry about potential risks – but knowing in advance was a different matter. It gave his mind time to dwell. The journey from Penzance to Ralph's Cupboard was about as low risk as it got, especially in comparison to his operations for the SBS where water safety was one of multiple considerations, but it wasn't without risk and that was enough for his subconscious to latch on to.

He woke in a sweat, his chest constricted as if he'd momentarily stopped breathing. It was 2.30 a.m. and there seemed little point going back to sleep when there was a good chance he would be propelled into another underwater nightmare.

He made some coffee and sat on the veranda, looking down on the sleeping St Ives. He'd been thinking for a long time now how good it would be to share the view with someone. It made him think of Millie, and how well the other night had gone. Their relationship had only just begun, and so much could go wrong. She hadn't even visited his flat, let alone had to wake him from a nightmare in the middle of the night. But he'd already warned her about the possibility of his nightmares when he'd stayed over; something Grace had only found out two months in when he'd woken from sleep in a panic, unable to breathe.

The thought triggered a physical reaction. He pictured himself on the marine unit boat succumbing to panic in front of his colleagues.

He'd managed to separate his past and present for so long, he didn't want to risk everyone seeing him so vulnerable. But the fear was about more than that. The very idea of making the trip without the safety net of Fischer and the lifeboat team, and the idea of being so close to the depths of the sea, filled him with terror.

Noting his breathing was laboured and his pulse was racing, Liam sat back in the chair and concentrated on his exercises. He used the cognitive behavioural therapy techniques he'd been taught, giving himself positive reinforcement and visualising an alternative scenario where the boat trip was a success and he was safe.

He continued the techniques as he drove through the darkened streets towards Penzance, though the lure of calling in sick was strong. He reminded himself that he'd joined the lifeboat crew as a form of exposure therapy, and that this was a natural next step. The risks were minimal to non-existent, and more than that he owed it to Marlon and Eleanor.

He called the uniformed officer tasked with watching the boat as he passed through Gulval – the sullen response suggesting that a night of watching a boat bob on the water from a cliff edge had not been what the officer had dreamed about when he'd wanted to join the police.

It was still dark when he pulled into the harbour twenty minutes later. 'You came to see me off,' he said, surprised to see Maya waiting for him.

'I wasn't going to let you have all the fun, was I?'

'You're coming on the boat?'

'I've got my sea legs.'

A wave of relief washed over him. Maya didn't know the extent of his PTSD, but he trusted her implicitly. Just having her on board would make the trip easier. 'If you say so,' he said. 'It could get a bit choppy.'

'I've sailed around the Isles of Scilly, I'll have you know. Going out on a powerboat is child's play.'

Liam thought about George's upcoming sailing trip, and took in a deep breath which he held for as long as possible before releasing it as they walked together down the jetty to the waiting boat.

They set off at 5.30 a.m., the lights on the first boat guiding them out of the harbour and into the waiting waters, passing Land's End and then heading north-east along the coast. It was a different sensation to being on the lifeboat, which in most circumstances was an emergency call. Yet there was an underlying sense of tension in the crew, and Liam specifically, as they hit the open sea. Thankfully, Maya was happy to stay inside the cabin as they picked up speed, the boat choppy in the increased waves, which gave Liam an extra protection between him and the sea.

'You OK? You look a bit peaky,' he asked Maya, trying to deflect his own fears.

'I'll peaky you,' said Maya, taking a drink of coffee from her thermos. 'Must be like old times for you.'

'Put me in a drysuit, with a sub-machine gun, and turn off the lights, then we'd be talking. This is like a cruise.'

'Very sorry, GI Joe.'

'He was in the army.'

'Sorry . . . captain?'

'Not quite, but better.'

The sun began to rise as they passed St Ives, Godrevy Island coming into view. 'Could have picked me up here,' said Liam, the vast spread of the sea a gleaming carpet pierced by splinters of light from the morning sun.

They left the cabin as they passed Portreath, a fine mist of sea spray brushing against Liam's skin as he edged along the deck, Maya behind him, her thermos flask still in her hand. The boat was slowing down. It was not quite low tide but the waters at the breach were calm enough to allow the two police boats through to the cove. Liam looked up and caught sight of the shadowy figured he presumed was the lookout officer at the top of the cliff.

The PC had completed his task, the grey RIB with its tarpaulin cover where it was yesterday, anchored in the shallow water. The captain of Liam's boat killed the engines as it floated toward the RIB. The crew pulled the port side of the RIB over and secured the boats side to side before anchoring.

Liam did his best to control his breathing as the engine cut. The sea was perfectly calm, and he told himself that even if he were to fall into the water there was no danger to him. It was enough to lower his pulse, but he still felt a tremor rush through him as he moved to the side of the boat. 'Let's see what's underneath, shall we?' he said, tensing his arm.

Maya recorded him as he began to open the covering of the abandoned RIB.

He supposed what he'd really expected to see was an empty boat beneath the covering, or maybe some unused supplies. There was an outside chance that, in their rush, the OCG may have left some of the smuggled drugs behind but that seemed unlikely.

What he hadn't expected to see as he pulled open the tarpaulin was the sight of a human hand. 'Shit, did you see that?' he said to Maya, dropping the covering back down.

'Yes. Wait, let's get a second recording before we go any further,' said Maya, instructing an officer on the other police boat to record as Liam pulled up the tarpaulin once more on the RIB.

For the next few moments, his fear of the water became secondary. Whatever he'd imagined seeing beneath the tarpaulin, it wasn't this.

Lifting the tarpaulin again, Liam saw that the hand belonged to the deceased body of a man he'd seen on the list of the twelve OCG gang members.

But he wasn't alone.

By the time Liam – with the help of his colleagues – had fully removed the tarpaulin, he'd revealed five more people all huddled together, all bound by their hands and ankles.

All dead.

Chapter Twenty

After the grisly scene of the six corpses – all redundantly bound by wrist and ankle – had been photographed and filmed, it was decided the best course of action was to tow the RIB to the harbour in Hayle, given that the one in Portreath was too narrow to easily accommodate the two police boats.

The crew placed the tarpaulin over the bodies, and made sure the connections were secure enough for the police boat to tow the speedboat. They moved the short distance along the coastline, a trio of boats with a terrible secret, watched by the walkers on the cliffs and the sun seekers on the beach. A pair of surfers, sitting on their boards, waiting for the swell to grow, waved to them as they motored away. Liam nodded, his back tight against the cabin wall, wondering what the pair would think at some later point when they realised what they'd witnessed – what grotesque train of boats had passed by them, almost close enough to touch.

A cordoned-off area had been set up in the car park alongside Hayle Harbour, the blue lights of the emergency services acting as homing beacons. The three boats moored against the harbour wall, their arrival unnoticed by a lone fisherman on the shore who gazed out towards the horizon, seemingly oblivious to the procession behind him.

The RIB was manoeuvred out of the water and rested on plinths so the waiting team of crime scene investigators, with their white jumpsuits and masks, could examine the contents.

Liam kept his composure as he and Maya left their boat. It was a relief being back on dry land, where they were greeted by DCI Hargreaves and Grace. 'Your girlfriend couldn't stay away, could she?' said Maya, under her breath.

'Sir, ma'am,' said Liam to Hargreaves and Grace, ignoring the comment.

'We've set up a coordinating point through here,' said Hargreaves, pointing to the white tent erected in the car park.

They moved inside, the interior strangely cold despite the numerous bodies exhaling hot air. Maya connected her phone to the larger screen of a tablet computer where she played out the video she'd recorded on the boat.

'All six of them were bound?' asked Grace, as the footage of the bloated corpses played out on the screen.

'My guess is they were each drowned, before being dragged on to the boat.'

Hargreaves squirmed. 'But why?'

No one had a clear answer for that particular question. Liam had been considering it ever since he'd pulled back the tarpaulin to reveal the first body. It felt like much more than a simple gangland hit. Someone had gone to the trouble not only of binding the ankles and wrists of the six victims, but to drown them, and then retrieve the bodies and arrange them on the boat in an unholy collage as if they wanted them to be found.

'A show of power? A warning?' said Grace, as she studied the photographs of the six victims.

It was certainly both of those things, but the personal nature of the killings couldn't be ignored and the parallels between the deaths of Marlon Tomlinson and Eleanor Cooper were unmistakable, although the two earlier victims hadn't been bound when their bodies were recovered.

'The deceased were all members of the OCG?' asked Liam.

Grace reeled off the six names, which didn't include either Gary French or Malcolm Ure, as if she'd been rehearsing them. 'With Gregory Moore dead as well, that's seven members of the OCG gone in a matter of days.'

'Surely it's a rival gang?' said Maya.

'That or infighting,' said Grace.

Both theories were plausible but Liam wondered if something else was happening. The six floating corpses taken in isolation, or even with Gregory Moore's death, would suggest the killings were gang related. But that didn't explain Eleanor Cooper's or Marlon Tomlinson's deaths. It seemed to him that the killer was taking a perverse pleasure in the ritual of drowning their victims, and was about to air his viewpoint when one of the CSIs walked over.

The CSI took off her mask, revealing the face of Tina Madeley, who Liam had once had a drunken kiss with during a Christmas party. Maya had been there that evening, and he felt her eyes bore into him as Tina spoke, all business.

'It's no great leap of deduction to believe the six were drowned. Their hair and clothes are damp, and there are signs of a foam cone in at least three of the victims' windpipes which again suggests drowning. We'll need to wait for the autopsies but I would suggest it is a good working theory.'

'They were tied up when they were drowned?' asked Liam.

'Hard to know either way, but seems logical, doesn't it?'

Liam nodded, Tina walking back to the CSIs who were still working through the boat.

'She doesn't like you, does she?' said Maya, as they walked outside.

'What are you talking about? We had a drunken kiss, so what?'

'She was expecting a phone call.'

'Says who?'

'I have my sources.'

'I'm not sure I like the way you are integrating yourself into my love life,' said Liam, squinting into the early afternoon sun.

'Someone needs to look out for you.'

'Maybe, but I'm not sure that person is you.'

He thought about Millie. He was looking forward to seeing her on Friday – with the added bonus of seeing George on Saturday morning. Both would provide an antidote to the horrors he'd seen that morning, and the grim reality of the investigation as a whole.

On his way back to headquarters, he stopped first at Marlon Tomlinson's old place, and then Peter Britten's. He wasn't sure what he'd hoped to find, perhaps a remaining member of the OCG returning to the scene of the crime, but both homes were desolate. He took another walk through Peter's house, searching for something he'd missed. The place was still full of detritus, but it had a ghostly feel, as if no one had lived there for months.

When Liam had first pulled back the tarpaulin on the boat, he'd half expected to find Peter Britten's corpse. It had been a relief to discover that he wasn't one of the fallen crew, but it didn't make what had happened to him any clearer. If the killer or killers had Peter in captivity, why hadn't he been on that boat? They hadn't previously demonstrated any reluctance to kill cuckooed victims, so why keep him alive?

As he left the house, he considered returning to St Ives to speak to Martin Sloan. He still hadn't managed to see the dealer since the crackdown on the fentanyl distribution and wanted to see the man face to face to gauge his reaction to this latest event.

But there was no time for that. The investigation into the bodies found in Ralph's Cupboard was a major investigation – Hargreaves wanted everyone in Bodmin.

Liam spent another hour getting back. A few colleagues from the lifeboat crew sent him messages, asking about the incident at Ralph's Cupboard. He ignored them for now, willing to let the rumours grow in the knowledge that no one would predict what had actually happened.

By late afternoon, CID had become one giant incident room. Hargreaves had decided the best way to move forward was to appoint different senior investigating officers for the various crimes. DI Whitfield was appointed SIO on the six bodies found in Ralph's Cupboard. He was to work alongside Grace, who was the acting SIO on the Gregory Moore murder in London.

Liam understood why Major Crimes had been appointed for the six bodies, but shared Maya's anger that she hadn't been chosen as SIO. It was their investigations that had led to the bodies being found, and Maya's continued appointment as SIO on the Marlon Tomlinson suspicious death and the missing Peter Britten case was of little comfort to either of them, or the rest of the team.

'Remember, these investigations are all linked. I'm only dividing these roles to make managing them easier. Our goal is to find out who is responsible for these deaths, and what their links to the introduction of fentanyl on our streets is,' said Hargreaves, ending the briefing without asking for questions.

The appointment of SIOs didn't really matter in the long run. As Hargreaves suggested, they were all one team working towards one goal. It felt like a slight on Liam's team, but it was soon forgotten as DI Whitfield, Grace and Maya led a second briefing into next steps.

With Maya's backup, Liam insisted that their team take responsibility for following up the recent arrests in Penzance. Connor Adams, the man who had supposedly provided Justin Blake and the others with the fentanyl for free distribution, was the number one target, and it was agreed that Liam's team continue their interviews with those involved.

Back in CID, Liam shared plans to speak to Justin Blake and David Beresford again, both men having been released on remand, subject to a home confinement curfew, as well as locating Martin Sloan who was still conspicuous by his absence.

As part of the crackdown the rest of the team would work through the usual lists of informants, known drug users, and ex-convicts in the area. There were already a number of suspected cuckoo sites in the area which needed to be checked, and Liam hadn't given up hope that one of them might contain Peter Britten.

Although it wasn't his direct current remit, Liam looked through the case notes on the six men he'd found that morning at Ralph's Cupboard. He knew this would now take precedence, but he needed to know why Eleanor Cooper and Marlon Tomlinson had been drawn into this situation. Death had been a constant in his life from his father dying, through his time in the armed forces, and into the police and lifeboat volunteering. He'd seen more than six people killed during ops with the SBS, but knew the sight of the six men huddled in the boat that morning would live with him forever. If he could find those responsible, then surely he could find justice for Eleanor and Marlon too.

Liam had found that during his time as an operative, he'd wearily grown to accept death as part of the natural order. He'd seen some atrocities, particularly during his missions for the SBS, which had been difficult to accept. But he'd soon learnt that during times of war and conflict, accepting death was the only way to deal with it. He'd had a job to do, as had his colleagues, and part of that was understanding that your life was on the line. At the time, it had felt like a fair contract. He would risk his life, in order to be able to take a life if absolutely necessary. It hadn't made it any easier, and he'd probably yet to come to terms with the friends he'd lost in the line of duty, but there was at least an explanation he could hold on to, a reason why his colleagues had given their lives.

And that wasn't something he could say about the six men in the boat. From what he could see in their files, they were all career criminals. Like Gregory Moore, they would have known the risks when they got involved in the county lines operations, and it wasn't as if Liam had any remorse for their passing. No doubt, they had inflicted misery on others, and were each possibly involved in the deaths of Eleanor Cooper and Marlon Tomlinson. But did they deserve to die in the manner they had? Liam supposed that wasn't really the question he should ask, but he couldn't help but picture the six men being tied before being lowered into the sea. He wondered what had gone through their minds. Maybe they'd thought – or hoped – that it was all a test, and that when it was over, they would be released.

It was all too easy for Liam to empathise. He didn't even need to close his eyes to picture himself beneath the sea, the unbearable pressure building on him. Whatever the crimes of the six men on the boat, he couldn't wish that upon them.

The uneasiness remained with him for the rest of the afternoon. It was dark before he left the office. Exhaustion overwhelmed him as he drove back towards St Ives, thankful that the roads were all but empty. It had been such a long day it was hard to reconcile that earlier that morning he'd been driving to Penzance to catch the boat out to Ralph's Cupboard. As he parked up, and wondered what delights his subconscious had in store for him that night, his buzzer went off. His key was hovering by the front door, and he considered ignoring the call. There were enough people on standby that the boat would easily be manned, but with everything that had happened of late, he felt he needed to be on board.

He fought the gruesome images of the bodies they'd found that morning, as he sprinted down the hill towards the station. He caught up with Wayne Mainwood, the young lad also known as Mouse, leaving the Queens Hotel bar. 'You haven't been drinking, Wayne, have you?' he asked, as they ran in tandem down the final slope of Lifeboat Hill.

'Of course not,' said Wayne, pushing past him through the doors where Fischer and the others were changing into their suits.

Liam was the last member of the crew to sprint down on to the beach where the boat had already been towed out to the water because of the late tide. As he approached the sea, more fired up than ever, he made out the shape of a rottweiler dog in the distance over towards the Sloop.

'Everything OK?' called Wayne, who was running alongside him.

Liam nodded, catching what appeared to be the outline of Martin Sloan in the lights outside the pub. He swore to himself, upping his pace towards the boat, hoping the dealer would still be there when he returned.

Chapter Twenty-One

The callout was for two people who'd left their yacht on a dinghy to view the night sky, only for the dinghy's outboard motor to run out of fuel. It was a frustrating job. The crew found the boat drifting towards Hayle, close to the Bar – the perilous sandbar at the mouth of the Hayle estuary – and managed to tow it back to the yacht. The two occupants were contrite. Liam reminded himself that everyone made mistakes and he was there to serve along with the rest of the team. The most important thing was everyone was safe, including him.

As the boat motored back to the station, his mind was elsewhere. He declined Fischer's offer of a drink, changing in a rush and heading alone over to first the Lifeboat Inn, then the Sloop, in search of Martin Sloan. It was a relief to know the man was still in the area, but although he had been in the second bar that night, there was no sign of him in the town, and if he was home, he was not answering the door.

Liam wondered if Sloan was staying elsewhere for a time, possibly to avoid police attention. As he walked back up the hill to his flat, he noted Millie had texted, asking how his day had been. The message buoyed his spirits which were low, in part from the mess the investigation seemed to have become, and his extended period without sleep. He sent her a quick reply back at the flat, before undressing and collapsing on to his bed.

Sleep refused to come. His mind was too busy unravelling all that had happened that day. He tried not to think about it, but he wondered where Peter Britten was at that very moment, and if the woman who had claimed to be his niece was with him. With the members of the OCG dying, it was hard to know who was the most in danger. It was possible that Gary French and Malcolm 'Midge' Ure, along with Stacey, were involved in the recent killings, but they could also be considered potential victims.

He must have slept at some point, his eyes creeping open and glancing in dismay to his phone to see that it was only 5.30 a.m. He wouldn't be able to return to sleep. His body had reprogrammed itself to wake at this horrendous time and wouldn't allow it. After a quick protein shake, he put on his running gear and headed into town.

It was a joy to have the beach to himself, and he savoured the loose sand beneath his feet, and the taste of sea salt in the air. Even the morning operetta from the seagulls was a joy as he ran up on to the wharf towards the lifeboat station.

He stopped to get his breath, watching the shimmering water in the distance. It was hard to fathom that this time yesterday he had been in Penzance waiting to board the boat for Ralph's Cupboard. So much seemed to have happened since then. He looked through the windows at the Annie Wilkinson lifeboat that had been cleaned and serviced since last night, fighting the anger about the stupid couple who had potentially risked lives, before breaking into a jog the rest of the way home.

◆ ◆ ◆

Liam called Maya and told her he would be staying in the region that day instead of heading back to headquarters in Bodmin. He breakfasted at home, drinking more coffee than usual, and then drove into town where he spent another fruitless hour trying to locate Martin Sloan. After that, he travelled towards Penzance – diverting to the address he had for his one-time informer, Justin Blake, who was under house arrest out towards Praa Sands on the south coast.

It was a wonder Blake wasn't under a custodial sentence, but Liam hoped to play that to his advantage. He was sure Blake was withholding something, and was confident that he could still be key in finding the man who had supplied the fentanyl the other night.

Liam drove along the A394 before heading inland. He loved the remoteness of the area, driving past a local garage with a sign and petrol pump that could have come straight out of the fifties, before heading further out to Blake's address.

The last time he'd worked with Blake as his CHIS, the man had lived in the Carnewas Estate to the east of the town centre in Penzance. The estate had been part of Liam's beat during his two-year probationary period, and it had been an eye opener for him, dealing with domestic abuse cases, burglary and the odd drug raid, among other delights. It was a surprise to find him now living so far away from the town. Liam parked outside a small bungalow surrounded by desolate farmland, and heard the dull thud of drill music as he reached Blake's front door. It was 10 a.m., which meant that the noise would be loud enough to constitute being a nuisance had there been anyone in the vicinity to hear it.

The noise of the music was insufferable as Liam banged on the door, the noise diminishing but still loud enough to be obtrusive. A young woman, possibly a teenager, dressed only in a T-shirt highlighting how unhealthily thin she was, opened the door and stared at him.

'DS Kilshaw. Is Justin there, please?' said Liam.

It took a few seconds for the question to register, the young woman staring open mouthed at him before turning around and shouting out Blake's name.

Liam took it as an invitation. He followed her inside, where he could feel the walls vibrating from the relentless noise.

He found Blake strewn across an armchair – one body of five in the living room. The belt around his waist was undone as were the top two buttons of his jeans. Liam walked over to the elaborate stereo equipment stacked five sections high and after a bit of trying managed to turn the thing off.

The silence was abrupt. Liam lowered his eyes, the remnants of the sound ringing in his ears as Blake looked over at him as if he were dreaming. Liam wondered if any of the five semi-comatose bodies in the flat had taken fentanyl.

'What have you got yourself into here, Justin? You did read the conditions of your house arrest, didn't you?'

'DS Kilshaw,' said Blake, buttoning up his jeans and belt and, with an unsteady push from the chair, getting to his feet.

The others paid Liam no heed, the lack of music seemingly not having registered with them. 'We both know there's enough here for me to take you in, Justin. You shouldn't be involved in this. What were you thinking?' Liam hadn't read the specific terms, but knew drug use would be prohibited.

'Through here,' said Blake, barging past him, his body odour so ripe that Liam had to turn away.

The skinny woman who'd answered the door was in the kitchen nursing a tea, the same faraway look on her face as Liam followed Blake into the room.

'Give us a sec, Kat,' said Blake, pouring himself some water.

The woman looked Liam up and down as if disgusted by his presence before she left the room.

'Tea?' said Blake.

Liam looked around at the black mould creeping up the walls and shook his head. 'When did you last see Martin Sloan?' he asked, as Blake switched on the kettle.

Blake frowned, the question catching him by surprise. 'That other day – when I saw you.'

'So you're telling me he had nothing at all to do with what went down with the fentanyl?'

'I told you then and I'm telling you now. I've been locked up here, for God's sake – when would I have seen him?'

'What about those wasters in there?' said Liam, raising his voice. 'You want to see something, Justin?' he said, getting in Blake's face and showing the man his phone.

He was surprised by the high-pitched squeal that escaped Blake's lips when he viewed the photograph of the six men found at Ralph's Cupboard the previous day.

'What the hell are you showing me?' said Blake, handing the phone back with shaking hands.

'Six dead people found yesterday. Hands and feet bound before being drowned. Their only connection? The shipment of fentanyl dropped on our shores. You ever come close to drowning, Justin? I have and it's not something I would wish on my worst enemy. The tightness and panic, it's unimaginable. You want to end up like that? Because I'd say it's a fifty-fifty chance the way you're going.'

He was coming on strong, but felt like it was the only way to drive the message home.

'What is it you want me to say?'

'I want to know where the guy you said gave you the fentanyl, Connor Adams, is, and where Martin Sloan is as well.'

'Don't want much, do you?' said Blake, regaining his composure.

'Remember that gang you helped put away, Justin?'

Blake looked around, frowning.

'Well, they're nothing compared to this mob. Not even bit players. I don't know how much more I need to show you. Those six on the boat? Seasoned drug dealers. Experienced, big time. What do you think the people who did that to them will do to you?'

Liam could see the possibilities were dawning on Blake. He was like an open book, his eyes darting upwards as if he were picturing his demise in the recesses of his mind. 'I don't know what to tell you.'

'Tell me where I can find Connor Adams, and/or Martin Sloan.'

'I don't know where they are,' said Blake, raising his voice before cowering away.

'You need to give me something, Justin, or I'm taking you in and you know what that will mean.'

Blake looked on the verge of tears. 'There may be something I forgot to mention the other day.'

'Go on.'

'Someone may have pointed me to Connor Adams. Told me he had some gear he wanted shifting. I had no idea what it was, honest.'

'Who introduced you?'

'A guy I know round your way. Young lad, Wayne.'

'Wayne?'

'Don't know his surname. They call him Mouse.'

Liam moved towards Blake. 'Are you shitting me, Justin?'

'Straight up, I saw him that same day I saw you.'

Liam shook his head. 'You better not be messing with me.'

'I swear.'

'This the guy?' said Liam, finding a photo of his fellow volunteer at the lifeboat house, Wayne 'Mouse' Mainwood.

'That's him,' said Blake, drool falling down the side of his mouth. 'Straight up.'

Chapter Twenty-Two

Peter couldn't remember the last time he'd been out of the flat. For that matter, he couldn't remember the last time any of them had been outside. Others came and went, but Gary, Midge and Stacey were a constant presence.

They were at the top of some mid-rise building on a housing estate. From what his captors had said, Peter believed they were somewhere near Penzance. Peter could see the building opposite the small, locked window in his store cupboard room, and had concluded they were four of five flights up. Too high to consider an escape – high enough that a fall would be fatal.

For now, he didn't care. Bar the odd expletive thrown his way, and the occasional smack across the cheek from Midge when he was in a mood, they had left him to his own devices. They'd even let him crack into the stash of vodka in the storeroom that doubled up as his sleeping quarters. It was that which was keeping him alive. Peter laughed at that particular irony, taking another swig and spilling some of the clear liquid down his already soiled front.

'Fuck sake,' said Midge, glancing over at him, his eyes laden with disgust.

'We've bigger problems than him,' said Gary, who'd barely uttered a word since driving away from the policeman.

They were sitting in the open-plan living room which was also a kitchen and dining room. It was Peter and the three of them, Gary having just sent one of their runners away with a small package of drugs.

Gary passed his phone first to Midge then Stacey. 'Six dead,' he said, Stacey unable to hide her fear as she looked at the phone and began to tremble.

'Where did you get that photograph?' asked Midge.

'Don't you mind that. They're all our members,' said Gary.

'How do you know that?' asked Stacey, handing the phone back to him.

Gary glared at her, and though Peter had never seen him hit her he thought he was about to. 'What's with all the questions? I've been in contact with one of the other cells, if you need to know. Everyone in that fucking boat is one of ours.'

Peter tried to retreat into himself. He pulled his arms and legs into his chest and tried to hold his breath, knowing any movement could spark a moment of violence from Gary or Midge.

'What does the boss say?' asked Midge, his voice almost apologetic.

Gary frowned. 'We're to keep going. There should be another shipment coming shortly.'

'When will that be?' asked Stacey. 'I'm going crazy cooped up in here.'

'Better that than dead in a boat, don't you think?' said Midge.

'Stop the goddamn bickering. We'll be lucky to get out of this alive ourselves if things don't improve. Whoever killed those men has already started distributing. We need to get a stranglehold in this area before it's too late. So we'll wait for the new shipment and start using our network.'

'But what about this rival gang?'

'Boss thinks they're small time who got lucky with the boat. He isn't happy but he says another cell will be sent to the county. For now, we just need to keep doing what we're doing.'

'And him?' said Midge, looking over to Peter.

Gary stared through Peter as if he wasn't there, as if he were looking at a ghost. Part of Peter just wanted it over, only the half-full crate of vodka in the storeroom currently giving him a reason to live.

Gary sighed. 'He's all but useless, but for now the boss wants us to keep him alive.'

Chapter Twenty-Three

Wayne 'Mouse' Mainwood had been a volunteer for the lifeboat station for the last six months. He had made his maiden voyage on the night they recovered Marlon Tomlinson's body. He was in his early twenties, and – as far as Liam could remember – worked as a builder for a firm in Redruth. Liam didn't know Mouse very well, but had helped with his training when he'd seemed pleasant enough and open to learning. It had never crossed Liam's mind that he could be involved with drug dealing, but for all his faults Justin Blake rarely gave bad information.

Liam had a number for Wayne in his phone, but he'd never called him before and didn't want to scare the man off. He spoke to Maya as he returned to St Ives, updating her on his meeting with Blake, and had to wait for twenty minutes in the station car park before a space became available.

The water was in, and lapped against the rocks by Pednolva Walk. The schools had yet to kick out but the wharf had the feel of summer to it, tourists milling on the seafront eating ice creams and pasties, trying their best to avoid the diving seagulls.

Liam waved to Rob Mills, an old fisherman he'd known since he was a child who now ran half-day cruises around the bay, as he unlocked the door to the lifeboat house. He could smell the sea on the lifeboat as he stepped inside despite it having been washed and scrubbed since the last shout. He touched the hull, and nodded in appreciation to the boat before moving into the office.

He didn't have much to do with the admin side of things, but knew everyone's details were kept both on the station's decrepit computer, with its bulky monitor that looked like something out of the nineties, and in the equally dated filing system which was his first port of call. At least the metal casing was arranged well, and he found the personnel drawer easily enough.

'Can I help you?'

The drawer still open, Liam turned around to see the grinning face of Fischer looking over. He was wearing shorts and a vest, his old navy tattoos decorating his still-muscular arms. 'Jesus Christ, Fischer. You move like a cat burglar.'

'It's called stealth, DS Kilshaw. What are you doing snooping around here?'

Liam had the file for Wayne open in front of him. He memorised the man's address before shutting it. 'It's an I-could-tell-you-but-I'd-have-to-kill-you type of situation.'

Fischer nodded and sat behind the desk, as Liam closed the filing drawer. 'You off sunbathing or something?' Liam asked, sitting opposite him.

'Getting my pre-tan on,' said Fischer, in a poor imitation of an American accent.

'String vests are not in vogue, Fischer.'

'Fuck you, it's not string.'

'But it is a vest.'

'When you've got shoulders like mine, you get away with it.'

To be fair, for a man in his sixties he carried it well. Liam would have liked to question him about Wayne Mainwood, but couldn't risk it until he'd caught up with the young lad. 'You hear about Ralph's Cupboard?'

'I did call, but presumed you were busy.'

The six deaths were national news, DCI Hargreaves having made a fleeting appearance on television last night. 'I was the one to find them. All a bit weird. They almost looked serene, all huddled together like that,' said Liam, wondering where that thought had come from.

'Nasty business. Glad we weren't called out for that.'

'So where are you getting your tan on?'

'Meeting up with Nick in a minute. Not on call today so thought we'd get a few sunny beers in. Guess you can't join us?'

'Not today,' said Liam, as Fischer got to his feet. 'I'll lock up. Don't fall in the harbour.'

'You got it, boss.'

Liam waited until he saw Fischer meet with Nick, another of the lifeboat's stalwarts. He locked up as the pair headed towards the Sloop. The sky was cloudless. On such a glorious day, Liam envied his friends' freedom. He promised himself he would drop in for a beer later that evening should he have the time.

The address he'd memorised for Wayne Mainwood was out towards St Erth. It was only a short distance from St Ives, and he took the back roads towards Hayle. The last thing he wanted to do was have to arrest someone in the lifeboat team, but he couldn't see how Wayne would be able to explain away what Blake had told him. At best, Liam hoped he could point him towards the supplier Connor Adams. But, either way, it seemed unlikely he could allow Wayne to continue volunteering at the station.

Liam parked on a side road and headed on foot to the address, which was situated within dense woodland. He knew the properties in the area didn't come cheap, so he imagined Wayne still lived with his parents. The ground was dry, and the air was ripe with the smell of fox piss. Liam rubbed his eyes, realising too late that it was hay-fever season and he'd yet to buy any spray.

The house was secluded in a little patch of land in the corner of the woods. As Liam approached, he was reminded of the Brothers Grimm book he'd had as a child, the house where Wayne lived enclosed by drooping trees and high hedges.

It wasn't the best place to be alone, but he didn't see any need to call for backup at this stage. From a safe distance he checked for movement behind the darkened windows but couldn't see any so decided to move to the rear of the property, wanting to be sure of any potential exits before confronting Wayne directly.

Liam shook the gate at the rear fence which opened directly on to a pathway into the woods. He jammed a rock up against the gate which would make it harder to open should Wayne decide to run, before returning to the front of the house where he saw some movement.

Crouching down, he hid behind a tree as he watched Martin Sloan's elderly rottweiler walk one full circuit of the front garden before all but collapsing in a heap. 'So this is where you've been hiding,' Liam said to himself, marvelling at how Sloan's dog was still alive, its body movements slow and laborious.

He had no issue confronting Sloan and Wayne at the same time but with recent events, the sensible move was to call it in.

'You happy to wait there while we get backup? I'd hate to find you bobbing around in the sea,' said Maya.

'Happy to wait here as long as it takes, but I don't think I have anything to worry about.'

'Let's play it safe. I'll speak to the local plod and see if we can get someone there quick.'

It was another twenty minutes before he got the nod. Finally, two officers traipsed through the woods to join him. 'Not conspicuous at all,' he said, looking at their uniforms. 'Right, one of you at the back, the other wait here.'

The dog was still in the garden as Liam walked up to the front door. It lifted its head with speed but must have recognised him, dropping back to the ground immediately. Liam knocked on the door, avoiding the camera doorbell which he covered up with his hand. Leaning his ear to the door, he heard voices before a silhouetted figure in the small window of the door walked towards him.

The door creaked open, the face of Liam's colleague peering through the gap. 'Liam,' he said, appearing genuinely surprised to see him.

'Hello, Wayne. Can I come in?'

'I'm a little busy at present, looking after my mum, you know?'

'It's police business, Wayne.'

Even in the gloom, Liam saw the colour drain from the young man's cheeks and movement from behind the door. 'Do not move,' he said, stepping into the house to find Martin Sloan making a run for it through the back garden.

Wayne sat on the bare wooden staircase as Liam radioed to his colleague.

'Got him,' came the message not long after, the uniformed officer marching the drug dealer back to the front of the house.

He moved Wayne and Sloan into the living room and instructed the two uniformed officers to join them. 'Are your bodycams on?' he asked, both nodding. 'OK, let's focus on Martin and Wayne here, shall we?'

The living room reminded Liam of the waiting room at his mother's care home. It had deep maroon carpets, flowered wallpaper and sofas straight out of the sixties. He could almost taste the dust in the air. 'Where are your parents, Wayne?'

'Dead. Yours?' said Wayne, finding some confidence in the company of Sloan who chuckled.

'You think this is funny. Accomplices to murder?'

Sloan frowned, Wayne returning to his earlier colour of ghost-white. 'Don, could you take Mr Sloan next door? I'd like to ask Wayne some questions alone,' said Liam, who had planned to split the pair up immediately to unsettle Wayne. 'Of course, I'm happy to make this formal. I can arrest you now and bring you both in for questioning. I think we already have enough to get a warrant to search both your properties. Isn't that right, Don?'

'Definitely, sir,' said the PC, hauling Sloan to his feet and out of the room. The other officer followed.

'You know this man?' said Liam, showing Wayne a picture of Connor Adams.

'No.'

Liam swiped to a picture of Justin Blake. 'How about him?'

Wayne tried to hide it but the recognition was evident in the narrowing of his eyes.

'Let me help you, Wayne. You've got yourself caught up in something, but I can get you out of it. I know you know Justin Blake. You need to tell me where I can find him,' said Liam, pointing to the image of Adams.

'Never met him.'

Liam shuffled closer to the man. He was little more than a kid, his lineless skin and large blue eyes betraying his relative innocence. There was no way he was the mastermind behind everything that was going on, but he was risking everything on the back of the actions of other people. 'How long have we known each other, Wayne. Over six months now? All that training you went through.'

'So what?'

'You can drop the hard-man persona with me, OK? You're a good lad. I've seen you work at the station, and you handled yourself well that other evening on the shout. I can understand why you would get attracted to Sloan and his activities. Fast, easy money. But, here, see what fast, easy money gets you.' Liam showed him the images of the bodies found at Ralph's Cupboard. 'These are the people you're involved with, and those six dead people are way up higher on the chain than you. At least they were. They were bound by their ankles and wrists before being placed in the water. God knows how long they were there, held under before being brought up for some air. You want to go out that way?'

Wayne tried to keep his composure. He looked back at Liam as if he could out-stare him, but Liam could see the slight contractions of his facial muscles as if the young man were picturing himself slowly drowning. 'I don't know what you're talking about.'

'You introduced Justin Blake to Connor Adams. Adams gave Blake a batch of fentanyl to distribute. More people are going to die, and we're not just talking drug dealers here.'

'I can't,' said Wayne.

'I told you, we'll protect you.'

'I'm not saying nothing.'

Liam sighed. 'You're making a mistake. How is he involved?' he asked, nodding towards the other room where Sloan was waiting.

'He's not.'

'One last chance, Wayne. Tell me what you know and I'll protect you. As soon as I take you in, that's you done. You'll end up with a record, and could easily end up in prison.'

Wayne lowered his head. 'I can't,' he said.

Chapter Twenty-Four

Liam instructed one of the uniformed officers to watch over Wayne while he spoke with Martin Sloan. It was clear Wayne was terrified of something, which wasn't surprising considering the deaths surrounding the county lines operation. Wayne's involvement with the lifeboat was a complication he didn't want to consider at present, as he sat opposite Sloan in the kitchen area, Sloan's dog lifting his head up as he walked in.

'You're a difficult man to find at the moment,' said Liam.

Sloan looked like he'd aged a few years since the investigation had started – his beard more unkempt, the lines surrounding his eyes and, on his forehead, deeper, as if carved into his flesh. 'I've been around.'

'Not at home.'

Sloan shrugged. 'What do you want?'

'I want some answers, Martin. I know you're involved in all this. The next thing will be for me to take you in and formally charge you.'

Sloan chuckled, looking at the other uniformed officer before looking back at Liam. 'With what?'

'Resisting arrest for one. Here, take a look at this,' he said, once more showing the images of the corpses found at Ralph's Cupboard.

Sloan's response was all but unreadable. A narrowing of the eyes, a parting of the lips. 'I don't even like the sea.'

'Why are you here, Martin? What's your link to Wayne?'

'He owed me a favour and I needed a little break.'

'A break from the hustle and bustle of St Ives?'

'Something like that.'

'You know why I'm here?'

'Desperation.'

Liam ignored the self-congratulatory smile on the drug dealer's face. 'I had a lovely conversation with Justin Blake. You know Justin, don't you?'

Sloan sucked in a breath, frowning. 'No.'

'We both know that's bullshit. Justin has been caught distributing fentanyl, did you know that?'

Sloan's body tensed, his frown hardening. 'It's got nothing to do with me what that fucking grass is up to.'

'Maybe, maybe not, but it's not looking great for you. Who is Connor Adams?'

Sloan sat back in his chair, as if surprised by the question. 'Who?'

Liam showed him the e-fit image they had of Adams. Sloan barely looked before dismissing it. 'Never seen him before in my life.'

'You know what happens next, Martin, don't you? You get arrested and your life gets turned upside down. You'll be considered a viable suspect in the deaths of those men on the boat, and if we can link you to Marlon Tomlinson and Peter Britten, which I'm sure we can, you'll risk going down for them.'

'What can I tell you? I do not know who that man is.'

They sat for some time in silence. Liam knew Sloan was lying – he just needed to know why. 'What are you scared of, Martin?' he asked, the smile never leaving Sloan's face throughout.

'Darkness, my thoughts, sea snakes.'

Liam allowed himself to laugh. 'I'm glad you find this all so funny. Let's see if you're still smiling back in Bodmin. Martin Sloan, I am arresting you—'

'Saw your mum the other day,' said Sloan, interrupting.

Liam caught his breath. 'Go next door,' he said to the uniformed officer, who reluctantly obeyed. 'What the hell are you talking about, Sloan?' he said, once they were alone.

'Our little chat the other day had me reminiscing. Not the woman she once was, is she?'

Liam was thirty years Sloan's junior. He could reach out and punch him in the throat, deny all knowledge when his colleagues returned, and he doubted Sloan would be able to respond. But he knew from the growing smirk on Sloan's face that it was exactly what he wanted him to do. 'She would probably say something similar about you.'

'If she could speak. You know we slept together, don't you? Not recently, obviously – that would be hideous – but when we were younger.'

Liam's heart was thumping in his chest. He didn't know why Sloan's provocation was having such an effect on him, but he needed to control his emotions. 'You think you can change any of this, Martin? You really think you can get to me.'

'It was OK,' said Sloan, ignoring him. 'Had better, had worse. One thing that did make it exciting though . . .'

Liam got to his feet.

'The thought that your dad could return at any time.'

Liam moved towards him. He wasn't sure what he was about to do, but was glad when he heard the kitchen door open.

'DS Kilshaw,' came a distant voice.

Liam glared at Sloan, who was still smirking, before turning to see Maya standing in the doorway. A wave of relief came over him, as he realised he'd probably been on the verge of doing something stupid. 'I was just about to read Mr Sloan his rights,' he said.

'Good. Don't let me stop you,' said Maya.

◆ ◆ ◆

'Everything OK?' she asked, when they were outside the house.

'Yes, why?'

'You'd asked to speak to Martin Sloan alone after he'd said something about your mother.'

'Oh, you heard about that. It's nothing. I thought I could get more out of him alone, that's all.'

Maya nodded, moving off to help supervise Sloan and Wayne as they were taken to the waiting patrol cars.

Liam took a deep breath, rubbing his itchy eyes. He had no idea if Sloan had been telling the truth and wasn't sure why he cared. His mother had failed him since he was a boy, so it shouldn't have come as much of a surprise that she'd cheated on his father. Maybe it was the idea that she'd done so with a low life like Sloan that bothered him so much, and the fact that the man now had one up on him. He couldn't hide his anger, as he imagined Sloan visiting his mother at the care home.

He called the home as he drove back to Bodmin to discuss the matter, insisting to be put through to one of the managers.

'Mr Kilshaw, this is Janice Linklater.'

'Janice, has anyone been to see my mother in the last few weeks?'

'I'll need to check the records but I'm 99.9 per cent sure no one has. You're the only one who visits her.'

Liam's anger was momentarily appeased by that sad fact. 'Please check,' he said. 'I can hold.'

What friends his mother may have had over the years had been slowly whittled down by her addictions. No doubt there had been sympathy for her to begin with, but that had only lasted for so long. Liam had been young but he'd understood there were different versions of his mother, and had noted the way others looked at her when she'd been drinking.

Janice returned to the call. 'I have checked our records, and spoken to the staff. No one other than you has visited Mrs Kilshaw.'

Liam ended the call without response, his knuckles white as he gripped the steering wheel. Either Sloan had been lying to him, or he had paid one of the care home staff off. Either was plausible.

◆ ◆ ◆

Back at the station it was decided that with Liam being a member of the lifeboat crew, it would be best for DCI Hargreaves and Grace to take over the interviews with Wayne and Sloan, Liam and Maya watching from behind a two-way mirror.

The contrast in the two men was obvious. Wayne looked like the scared child he was. Sloan wore his smile as a mask throughout. Both men stuck to their stories about not knowing Connor Adams, although Wayne looked like he was about to break on a couple of occasions.

Following a search of both their properties, both men were released without charge much to Liam's frustration. 'Nothing we can really charge them on, is there?' said Grace, as the various teams met late in the afternoon. 'We have the flimsiest connection between Wayne Mainwood and Connor Adams, and as far as I can see nothing whatsoever to hold Martin Sloan on.'

Liam knew she was right but still had to stop himself arguing the point. He wanted a raid on Martin Sloan's house, wanted to turn his life upside down like he'd promised, but that wasn't going to happen and he had to consider why he wanted it to happen.

DCI Hargreaves called Liam and Grace into his office after the debrief, and for a second Liam thought he was going to mention something about their past relationship. 'Wanted to speak to you on your own, Liam,' said Hargreaves, glancing at Grace.

'One thing came up from the interviews,' said Grace, taking over.

Liam wasn't sure what was happening, but felt like he was about to be ambushed. 'Wayne Mainwood,' she said. 'He volunteers at the lifeboat station in St Ives. The same one where you volunteer.'

'We all know that.'

'It's just that with his potential involvement, and the fact that there is a powerboat at the station, we think it prudent if we question all the volunteers who work out of there.'

'You really think that's necessary?' asked Liam, thinking about how Fischer and some of the others would respond.

'We do,' said Grace, as if she spoke for her superior. 'And I'm afraid you will have to suspend your role with them until this is all resolved.'

Chapter Twenty-Five

Liam sat by his mother's bedside the following morning. He'd spent the last hour examining the care home's CCTV footage after the manager had reaffirmed her belief that Martin Sloan had never been to the home, let alone visited Liam's mother. In the end, he'd had to request all the footage since the last time he'd visited, though he had no idea when he would have time to analyse it.

'Did he come to see you?' he asked his mother.

Her eyes were open but she wasn't responsive. She stared blankly ahead, Liam wondering what was going on behind her eyes. 'Did you even know him?' he said out loud, more for his own benefit than in expectation of an answer.

Over the years, he'd come to terms with the way his mother had behaved after his dad died. It was wrong that she hadn't been there for him, but her husband's death had triggered something within her that she couldn't fight.

What he couldn't accept was that his mother had had an affair with anyone – let alone Martin Sloan – when his father was still alive. For Liam, that would be the greater betrayal.

Of course, he'd seen it during his time in the armed forces. The nature of the work, especially in the SBS, meant many months away from home. Never a positive thing for any relationship. Such was the camaraderie between his colleagues that they would share the times when girlfriends and wives had left them. In many ways, it helped bring the group together, instilling an us-against-them mentality. But he'd never blamed Kim for leaving him after George was born.

But the thought of that having happened to his father – the idea that his mother may even have been with Sloan on the day his father died in conflict – enraged him in a way he was struggling to handle.

He stared at his mother's wizened face, at her brittle, paper-thin skin, at the welts and growths, at the deep grooves around her eyes, and told her that if he ever found out it was true then he would no longer visit.

She blinked, her lips parting, and for one surreal moment he thought she was going to say something, before she closed her eyes and lay back on her pillow.

After exchanging muted goodbyes with the care manager, Liam walked into town, fighting the urge to visit Martin Sloan's house. Another confrontation with the drug dealer would be counterproductive at this stage. Instead, he stopped at the Lifeboat Inn, bought a coffee and took it to the front of the bar where he had a perfect view of the lifeboat station opposite.

Grace had decided the lifeboat house would be the perfect place to conduct interviews with the volunteers and, after calling Fischer last night, had managed to get most of the group to agree to attend throughout the day.

She was already on scene with Maya. Liam could see them through the windows as he approached the building. They were talking to Fischer and Nick, who'd opened up the house for them. Fischer had called Liam last night, presumably to ask what was going on, but Liam had declined the call. He'd sent a quick message saying he couldn't get involved, receiving a curt 'understood' in response. Maybe it was guilt, or a voyeuristic curiosity, that was making him watch. He was still coming to terms with Wayne Mainwood being involved, even if they only had Justin Blake's say-so for that at the moment.

Twenty minutes later Nick left the building, followed by Fischer not long after. The pair headed in opposite directions – Nick towards the Sloop bar at the other end of the wharf, and Fischer presumably back towards the railway station car park.

Liam drank up and headed to his car, which he'd parked in the long-stay car park off Clodgy View. He decided to make a quick visit to Peter Britten's place in Gwithian, recalling how when he'd pulled back the tarpaulin on the boat in Ralph's Cupboard, it had been Peter he'd expected to see.

He did a sweep of the place, knowing as he did it was all but redundant. The house and surrounding area had been searched. Whoever had taken Peter had already made the mistake of returning once and they weren't about to do the same thing again.

From the back of the house, the land swept down towards the dunes. It was such an idyllic sight, the pastel hues desolate and peaceful. Liam wondered if Peter would ever get to see such sights again, and took one final tour of the perimeter when a call came in from Penzance.

Thirty minutes later he was in the Carnewas Estate, where officers had been conducting a number of random searches which were taking place countywide.

'This is Jess Watson, sir. We found her in possession of this,' said one of the uniformed officers, PC David Bradshaw, holding out a small baggie with seven pills inside. Jess looked like she was in her late teens. Her hair was matted in tight, black curls, her skin awash with acne.

Liam took the bag, examining the pills which looked identical to the fentanyl previously recovered. 'Where did you get this from, Jess?' he asked.

'Found it,' she said.

Liam sighed. 'We have any idea who distributes around here?' he said, taking the uniformed officer to the side.

'You know how it is, sir. There are faces we know. We do the odd raid. You put them away, new faces appear.'

'Jess, did you hear about those people found in the boat over by Portreath?' he asked.

Jess scowled. 'Yeah, so what?'

Liam dangled the bag in front of her. 'So they were involved in this stuff. You want to be part of something like that?'

'I told you, I found it.'

'You know what it is?'

Jess shrugged.

'It's a class A drug and is illegal to possess without prescription.'

Liam watched the realisation dawn on the young woman. 'I didn't know. I wouldn't have taken it if I did. It was free, I didn't buy.'

'Tell me where you got it and we'll see if we can make this just a caution for you,' said Liam.

Jess looked incredulous, glancing from Liam to the uniformed officer, and around the estate. 'I don't know. Some scrag-end teenage boy.'

'What does he look like?' asked the officer.

'Pig ugly.'

'We need a bit more than that, Jess,' said Liam.

'I don't know. He was white, spotty, black spiky hair. Always hanging around this place,' said Jess.

'That doesn't really narrow it down, does it?' said PC Bradshaw.

'I don't know, he had one of those things on his face. It's not just spots,' said Jess.

'A scar?' asked the officer.

'If you say so.'

'I think I know who she means. One of the runners on the estate, Jason Mills. Has a scar on the right side of his face.'

'Was that who sold you the pills, Jess?' asked Liam.

'Never said I bought them.'

'I'm getting tired of this, Jess. I've already told you this is an arrestable offence. Who did you buy these pills from?'

Jess contorted her features until it appeared that she was snarling. 'The lad with the scar, OK?' she shouted. 'But I don't know his name.'

Hargreaves had been explicit that everyone caught in possession of fentanyl was to be charged. Liam arranged for another officer to take Jess in, and told them that due to her cooperation she should be let off with a caution, before walking to the estate with PC Bradshaw.

'Takes me back,' said Liam, entering one of the communal buildings.

'Lives at home with his mum,' said Bradshaw, as the lift arrived on the top of three floors.

Liam let out a breath. 'How old is he?'

'Twenties.'

'Christ, nothing changes, does it?' said Liam, knocking on the front door.

A woman in jogging bottoms and a white vest answered. 'What?' she said, after looking them both up and down.

'Is Jason in, Maude?' asked Bradshaw.

'No. Who's this?'

'DS Kilshaw. It's very important we speak to Jason.'

Maude squinted as she glanced at Liam's head before looking him in the eye. 'He's not here, is he. Try down there. Probably getting up to no good as usual.'

'We need to check,' said Bradshaw.

'No way,' said Maude, folding her arms.

Liam stepped in front of the PC. 'Either that, or we get a warrant to search your place. If that happens, and he's in there, then it won't only be Jason that's in trouble, do you understand?'

He caught movement behind the door, and was about to force his way in when a man fitting Jason's description came to the door. 'It's OK, Mum,' said the man, who didn't look old enough to be out of school, the right side of his face darkened with a maroon-coloured scar.

'Jason Mills?' said Liam, as the man stepped out into the corridor.

'Yes, what of it?'

'I am arresting you on suspicion of selling class A drugs,' said Liam, nodding to Bradshaw to cuff their suspect before continuing to caution him.

Liam called Maya as he drove the short distance to Penzance station. 'Finished interrogating my fellow volunteers?' he asked.

'Pretty much. Talkative bunch, especially when it came to you.'

'Jesus, what have they said?'

'Suspect–police confidentiality.'

'Is that so?'

'Yes.'

'Then none of you want to know about the arrest I just made of someone selling fentanyl on the streets of Penzance?'

'Look at you. Spill the beans then, DS Kilshaw.'

Liam updated her on Jason Mills' arrest, Maya in turn sharing the news that the majority of the team at the lifeboat station had been interviewed without charge. 'Looks like that kid you interviewed, Wayne the Mouse or whatever, will be rejoining your team as well – we haven't made a charge.'

'We'll see about that,' said Liam, making a note to speak to Fischer later as he arrived at Penzance police station.

'Just so we're clear, you don't work here any more,' said Ted, as Liam walked through reception.

'Can't keep away from your smiling face. Where's my suspect?'

'Interview room two. Being watched over by the ever-observant PC Bradshaw.'

Liam thanked Ted, and poured himself a coffee before joining Bradshaw and Jason Mills in the interview room. After checking that Mills knew his rights, and that he had waived his right to legal representation, he began speaking to him.

'Jason, we have a witness who will testify that you sold them eight fentanyl tablets, which I'm sure you know are class A.'

'Never sold anyone anything,' said Jason. He maintained eye contact, and had a steely determination to him, but Liam saw the vulnerability behind his eyes.

'What do we have? Some cautions for possession, a suspended conviction for possession with intent. Seems you're going up in the world. You'll be pleased to know that selling class A drugs, whether money was exchanged or not, coupled with this record, will see you do a stretch. Fancy that, Jase? You might think the people you hang round with are tough, but wait until you spend some time at His Majesty's pleasure.'

'Prove it.'

'I already can. We have the drugs and the person you sold them to. That will be enough.'

Jason squinted, the scar on his cheek flushing red. Liam wondered if the boy had been bullied for his appearance as a child, like he had for his alopecia. The mark wasn't unsightly, and probably made his appearance more interesting, but children didn't always care about that. 'Not so sure that's true.'

'PC Bradshaw has advised you to get a solicitor in. You still have that option. They'll tell you what I'm telling you.'

'What do you want?' said Jason.

'Simple. Tell us who gave them to you to supply and we don't need to look into this further.'

Jason scratched his head. 'I can't.'

'We know the usual crew you hang around with. I presume they're involved?'

Jason's scar flushed red again.

'It's not them?'

'There's not been much food around of late. Some guy approached me, paid me to hand them out to the usual suspects and then said I could start selling them.'

'Is all your crew selling them?'

'It's complicated,' said Jason.

'I'm sure we can work it out if we try.'

Jason shook his head, and Liam worried that he was about to clam up before he said, 'The people we work with now are from upcountry. London. It's just that they haven't been around this last week or so. None of us are sure what the hell is going on.'

Liam showed him the e-fit of Connor Adams. 'This the guy who sold them to you?'

Jason scratched his cheek, as if the flushed scar was burning him. 'Yes.'

'You know him?'

Jason interlocked his fingers. 'He can't know it came from me.'

'No one will know it's from you, I promise,' said Liam.

'I don't think he realises but I do know him.'

'Connor Adams?' said Liam.

Jason smiled. 'That's what he called himself . . . but it's not his name.'

Chapter Twenty-Six

Peter's father had been a man of few words, but Peter had always known the old man had loved him. They would go on long, rambling walks together, and his father would point out the names of the various plants, trees, flowers and wildlife they would see. Always the name, nothing else. Sea holly, thrift, red fescue, skylark, adder, sand martin.

Peter had learnt the names through repetition, and even now could recall everything his father had ever shared with him. Nowadays, he presumed things were passed on in a different fashion – by computers, phones, and whatnot that Peter didn't understand. He missed the old ways. Not because he thought they were any better, but because they reminded him of those happy times with his parents.

Not that he had anyone to pass what knowledge he had to. It was never said, but deep down Peter knew his parents never had any expectation for him in those matters. Peter hadn't much talked to girls when he was a teenager, and they hadn't much talked to him. And nothing had changed as he got older. He'd probably spoken more to the young woman holding him in custody, Stacey, than he had any other woman. That made him sad, but not as sad as thinking about his parents.

He wondered what his dad would make of him now. He doubted the man had ever set foot in a building such as this, with its curious mixture of ugly concrete and uglier decor. He doubted his father would have put up with everything that Peter had gone through. He would have probably taken out his shotgun the first time he'd laid eyes on Gary and Midge and scared them off his land. But it was too late for that.

'I need to get out of here,' said Midge, as Gary arrived back in the flat with supplies.

'Place is crawling with cops. I had to dodge them just to get back here. Make us some lunch, Peter,' said Gary, dumping two bags of groceries on the table.

'What's the latest?' said Stacey.

She was such a funny-looking thing, with her strange, coloured hair and tattoos. And she was always so nice to him that Peter often forgot she was the reason he was here in the first place.

'We're pulling out,' said Gary, grabbing a can of lager from the fridge.

'What?' said Midge.

'If it hasn't escaped your attention, things aren't going well for us at the moment. They want us to return and regroup.'

'What the hell does that mean?' said Midge, following the other man's lead by opening a beer.

'They're going to collect us tomorrow morning.'

'You think that's on the level?'

Peter buttered some bread, noting the way Stacey's eyes moved from man to man as she waited for them to answer.

'What the hell do you mean by that?' said Gary, downing his can and opening another in a seamless motion that made Peter's stomach rumble.

'I mean, people are dying left, right and centre. What if we're next?'

'Don't be so paranoid. Why would they kill us?'

'Um, we've failed setting up a line for them. You know what they're capable of.'

'It's hardly our fault though, is it? Can't sell what we don't have, can we?'

Stacey helped Peter make the sandwiches, which were eaten in silence. When the others were fed, he retreated to the corner of the room with his spoils, sneaking a can of lager in the process. He hated the silence more than anything. They were usually a prelude to Gary losing his temper, the result of which was usually focused on Peter.

'What's going to happen to him?' asked Midge, pointing at Peter as if he wasn't in the room.

'Nothing.'

'But he's seen our faces.'

'So what? You want to do something to him? He's an incoherent drunk. Even if he could remember what we look like, he wouldn't be able to describe us.'

'And this is coming from up top?' said Midge.

'Don't you worry yourself about it,' said Gary, shooting Peter a look before returning to his sandwich.

'I need to go out,' said Stacey, after they'd all finished their sandwiches and Peter had tidied up.

'No one is going out,' said Gary.

'I need to,' said Stacey, insistent. Peter had rarely heard her raise her voice, and noted Gary and Midge looking at one another in surprise.

'I already told you, the place is crawling with pigs. And they will know your face.'

'I'll put a hat on, but I'm going out.'

Gary stood and walked to the door. Peter was still trying to process the earlier conversation about him. Gary had said he was going to be left alone, but hadn't sounded that convincing.

'Get out of my way,' said Stacey.

'Orders are we stay here until they are ready for us.'

'I need something.'

'What?' said Gary.

'Jesus Christ, you want me to spell it out for you? I am on my period,' said Stacey, elongating every word. 'I need to buy some tampons.'

'Wondered why you were so grumpy,' said Gary, sharing a chuckle with Midge. 'Why didn't you say so?' He opened the door for her. 'Back in half an hour.'

Stacey barged past him. 'I'll be back when I'm good and ready,' she said.

Chapter Twenty-Seven

Liam called Maya again as he left Penzance station.

'You can't leave me alone, can you?'

'I have an alias for Connor Adams. Edward Turnbull. The suspect I was interviewing ID'd him. Claims to have known him from when he lived in south Cornwall – Looe, specifically.'

'Remembered him how?'

'Used to be his rugby coach, if you can believe that.'

'Small world. Let me have a look for you.'

'I'll start heading to Looe now just in case.'

Liam entered Looe into his satnav, and was dismayed but not surprised to find it was nearly an eighty-minute journey from Penzance. Jason had been adamant that the drug dealer going by the name of Connor Adams was his old rugby coach, Edward Turnbull. Liam knew from his own experience playing junior sports the impact coaches could make on your life, and how they were ingrained in your memory, even if, as Jason claimed, he hadn't seen Turnbull since he was eleven.

As for Turnbull not recognising Jason, that seemed plausible. Liam hadn't seen pictures of Jason as a kid but he imagined the transformation into the skinny, acne-scarred adult he'd become had not been a pleasant one.

'Got him,' said Maya, calling as he reached the roundabout at Redruth. 'Expired DBS from ten years ago obtained from the RFU. No record. I'll text through the last address we have for him.'

If Adams and Turnbull were the same person – and Turnbull had been doing his best to hide his identification – then finding him could unravel anything. Liam also understood it could be nothing, but he was still feeling buoyed as he arrived in Looe ninety minutes later.

It was another glorious, cloudless day that always put Liam in mind of the endless summers of his childhood. Cornwall was like nowhere else when it was sunny, and the calm waters by the harbour looked so inviting that Liam promised himself he would take a boogie board down to the beach with George this weekend if time allowed it.

A brief vision of his accident – the distant surface of the water out of reach – flashed in his memory. His chest constricted as if a harness had been placed around him. He took in some deep breaths, and centred himself in his current situation as he made a circle with his index finger and thumb.

He called in his location as he arrived at the address they had for Turnbull a mile out from the centre of Looe. It was a well-maintained terrace property, a porcelain seagull attached to the front door with the number twenty-six painted beneath it.

A woman in a bright yellow bikini answered the door. She smiled as Liam ensured he maintained eye contact. 'DS Kilshaw,' he said, showing her his warrant card.

'Sorry, I was out the back sunbathing. How can I help you?' said the woman, still smiling, seemingly unbothered by being all but undressed.

'I'm trying to locate Edward Turnbull. We have this as an address for him.'

The woman pursed her lips and shook her head. 'We're here on an Airbnb but the owners don't go by that name. You're very welcome to come in and have a look. Just me and some friends,' said the woman, looking Liam up and down, smiling as she looked at his gleaming skull.

Liam thanked her, and took details of the homeowners before leaving. He hadn't quite expected Turnbull to answer the door himself, but it was still a little disheartening to feel like he was so close and yet so far from finding the man.

He parked at the end of the street and managed to get through to one of the homeowners on first try. They confirmed they had owned the property for six years, and had purchased it off a couple called the Fosters who'd been moving to Wales. Liam called the information in, Maya updating him that further searches on Turnbull hadn't been fruitful. The last time they had a tax or national insurance record for the man was around the same time the DBS was issued.

Liam called into the local rugby club where Turnbull had supposedly coached a young Jason Mills. It was a weekday but the bar was open, Liam managing to speak to Vic Boswell, the president of the club. 'Of course I remember Turny,' said the president, a burly man in his sixties who was drinking down a pint of lager like it was water. 'You couldn't really forget him.'

'When did you last see him?'

'Must be a good ten years now. Not much of a steady Eddie, our Turny. Odd-jobs man, labourer, that sort of thing. He'd been in the army as a young 'un and didn't know what to do with himself when he came out. Hell of a number eight. He liked coaching the kids but he was a bit unpredictable.'

'In what way?' said Liam, paying the barman as Boswell ordered himself another pint.

'Nothing too serious. Liked a drink, Turny did, if you know what I mean. We couldn't ever let him lead a session as we were never sure if he would turn up.'

'Sounds like a great role model for kids,' said Liam.

Boswell squinted, this time sipping at his lager. 'He was never drunk around them, if that's what you're getting at.'

'Where did he go, ten years ago when you last saw him?'

'Heard he got a building gig, upcountry.'

'London?'

'That's what he said. Never seen him since.'

Liam spent the rest of the day speaking to former colleagues and acquaintances of Turnbull. The consensus seemed to be the same. Turnbull was well meaning but disorganised, which was partly explained by his love of drinking. No one mentioned any violent tendencies, and every time Liam brought up the matter of drugs he was met with blank faces.

It felt like a wasted day as he explained the situation to everyone at the late afternoon debrief.

'At least we know he's been to London. Could be that's how he got involved working with the OCG,' said Grace.

'The small-time dealer, Jason Mills, who identified Turnbull, says he wasn't acting for the usual group they deal with so we could be looking at a rival gang.'

'Would go to explain why we found six dead drug dealers in that boat,' said DCI Hargreaves, surprising him by adding, 'Good work, Liam.'

It wasn't until Liam heard what everyone else had to say that he understood the compliment. It seemed he had been the only one to make any inroads into the investigation in the last twenty-four hours, aside from a couple more arrests for fentanyl possession in Camborne.

Overall, it wasn't the best way to end the week. Although he was meeting Millie later that evening, and seeing George tomorrow, he still felt deflated driving back to St Ives. He wanted justice for Marlon and Eleanor – but at present all his focus was on finding Peter Britten.

He thought about the stories he'd been told about Peter by the old guy, Mr Ward, in the pub. How he was a loner, a long-time orphan riddled with addictions. It was impossible not to see the parallels with his own mother, but Liam also had to concede that he wasn't entirely dissimilar to Peter Britten.

OK, Liam had managed to keep any addictions at bay – but he was nearly thirty and lived alone in a cramped flat in his childhood town. He loved the area, and had friends and family he spent time with, but in many ways he was as alone as it seemed Peter had been all his life.

He went for a run to clear his head and expel all the negative thoughts. He reminded himself that he still had George, and was seeing Millie later that night. It didn't hamper his desire to find Peter, but it helped him to focus on the fact that his future was in his own hands.

Back at the flat, he had to rush his shower to get to the Lifeboat Inn to meet Millie.

'Nice of you to make it,' said Millie, as he walked through the door, his body coated with a fresh layer of sweat from his brisk walk into town. He was about to come back with a witty response when he noticed Millie wasn't alone.

'Hi, Liam,' said Becca.

'We got you a lager,' said Millie. 'Becca wanted to say a quick hello, didn't you?'

They took their drinks to the corner of the bar where Becca apologised for the other night. 'I'm so sorry if I embarrassed you. I'm afraid I got a bit pissed and decided to party on a bit longer than I'd anticipated.'

Liam took a long drink of lager which tasted like nectar after his long day. 'You did nothing wrong. At least, not on purpose. I think that's the case?' he said, raising his eyebrows.

'Thanks for getting me a taxi,' said Becca, getting to her feet.

'Drinks were on Becca,' said Millie.

'Thank you,' said Liam, as Becca left with a sheepish smile. 'You didn't have to arrange that,' he said, once she was gone.

'All her idea. She was mortified when she saw me.'

'We've all been young.'

'Some of us still are, Granddad,' said Millie, finishing her drink. 'Where shall we go now?'

They bought a bottle of red wine from the off-licence and took it to Porthmeor Beach. Night was falling, and Millie snuggled close to him as the temperature dropped slightly. For a time, it was like nothing else mattered. Liam had all but forgotten the frustrations of the investigation, his mind wrapped up in the moment: the sound of Millie's breathing and the feel of the coarse sand beneath his fingers.

'How does this compare to living in Bristol?' he asked her.

'Should have made the move years before. I know it is clichéd, but there's something about being next to the sea. It feels like I belong here,' said Millie, giggling as she took a swig from the bottle.

Liam took in a deep breath of the sea air. 'You were teaching the same age group when you were there?'

'Bit younger. Year Two. Bit of a different experience. I was teaching in quite a deprived area. I see some kids here who aren't very well off, but back there . . .' Millie drifted to silence, her gaze going out to the distant light of a container ship towards the horizon as she reached for his hand.

'Back there?'

'Those poor kids. I started a breakfast club. Funded by the teachers. Some of those children would come to school and they would be starving or wearing clothes they'd been wearing for weeks. It wasn't always the parents' fault, but many of them didn't seem able to care. I still feel guilty now for leaving them but I was at my wit's end. The system was broken, if it was ever in place to begin with. We all did our best, but there was no support.'

Liam held her hand tighter. She didn't need his reassurances, she just needed him to listen. 'Do you ever hear from your old colleagues?'

'They've all moved on, except for the head. She's still there, working away, trying to change things. It's her that I feel I really let down, but she was the one who encouraged me to leave and set up things here. She was originally from Cornwall funnily enough.'

'Not Mrs McGuire?' asked Liam, feigning fear.

'One of your former teachers?'

'The worst. You know, she didn't pick me for the school choir when I was nine.'

'Can you sing?' asked Millie, smiling.

'I can sing.'

'But can you sing well?'

Liam took the bottle of wine he'd yet to drink from and pretended it was a microphone. His mind was trying to come up with a tune, when Millie took the bottle from him. 'I'll take your word for it,' she said. 'Let's go back to my place.'

◆ ◆ ◆

Liam lay next to Millie as she slept, struggling to fall asleep himself. After all his self-pity earlier, he'd found himself in a perfect situation but still couldn't fully relax.

He'd already warned Millie he suffered the occasional nightmare – alluding to something that had happened in the SBS, but leaving out the details – but he wondered if that was what was keeping him awake. If he hadn't said anything, perhaps he wouldn't have been so afraid of an incident occurring.

If he'd been at home, he would have left and gone for a walk or run, but he didn't want to wake her and was instead left to work through the investigation in his head.

Soon his tiredness crept up on him, and thoughts of Edward Turnbull giving away fentanyl on the streets of Penzance merged with distorted images of Martin Sloan hiding out in the woods, and the six corpses floating in the cove of Ralph's Cupboard, as Liam found himself beneath the water, struggling for air.

A distant part of him knew it was a dream but that didn't stop the panic. He could feel the ice-cold water, the unbearable weight in his chest, and the useless flailing of his limbs as he searched for the surface. Even within his nightmare, he recalled similar nightmares from his childhood. Then, he'd been trapped in bed fighting against an invisible force while he tried to make his way to his parents' bedroom, the air thick and relentless, holding him in place as he tried to drag his body across the landing.

'Liam? Liam?'

He heard the voice from afar, a hand dipping into the water, and he swam towards it. 'Liam,' it said. He opened his eyes and found he was sitting bolt upright in Millie's bed.

'I think you may have been having one of the nightmares you mentioned,' she said, her eyes full of concern.

'I think you might be right,' said Liam, forcing a smile, his body coated in a layer of sweat. 'I hope I didn't scare you.'

'Of course not. Are you OK? You don't look great, if you don't mind me saying.'

Liam glanced at his phone. It was 4.23 a.m. 'I don't mind you saying,' he said.

'Come here,' she said, holding out her arms.

'I'm a bit clammy.'

'I don't care about that,' said Millie, grabbing him into her arms where he stayed until the morning, when they were both woken by the sound of his phone ringing.

Chapter Twenty-Eight

As soon as Stacey left, Peter retreated to the box room, where he took a deep drink from the looted bottle of vodka. He knew something significant had just taken place, but didn't understand what Stacey's departure – and the way she'd ignored Gary's instructions – truly meant.

But he did know that Gary wasn't happy – that the way he'd laughed at Stacey as she left had been a deception of its own. More than that, he understood that Gary would soon need an outlet for his humiliation, and that Peter would be the number one target.

He spent an indeterminate time sampling the vodka, which tasted like water. It wasn't his drink of choice but he'd built a tolerance for it these last few days. All it did now was serve to keep him on the same level. Holding one of the bottles, he glanced through the grainy windowpane and the promise of freedom beyond its barrier. He peered down, wondering if there was enough vodka in the room to deaden the pain of falling from such a height, when he heard noise from within the flat.

After taking another swig of the flavourless drink, Peter found himself crawling to the storeroom door, which he inched open. Stacey had returned, and Peter was awash with relief. Why, he wasn't sure. It was her fault he was in this place, that his life had been turned upside down. But of the three, she was the only one to ever utter a kind word to him, to treat him with something approaching humanity. And if what Gary said was true, that they were all going to leave the area at some point soon, then Peter knew he needed Stacey to be there if he had any chance of surviving.

'Where the hell have you been?' said Gary, clearly drunk.

'I told you. I needed to get some things.'

'That was two hours ago.'

Confused, Peter glanced at the window where the world had darkened without him noticing.

'You're not my keeper, Gary,' said Stacey. She was about to move past him when Gary reached out and grabbed her.

Peter held his breath as he watched Gary and Stacey locked into position, Midge frozen to the spot only yards away, his mouth wide open like a caricature.

'Let go of me,' said Stacey, her voice calm.

'Not until you tell me where you've been.'

The movement was so swift that Peter thought he may have imagined it. Stacey's hands appeared to move independently of the rest of her body. Peter caught the reflection of the kitchen light on the shaft of metal in her hand before it disappeared numerous times into the flesh of Gary's body, blood spraying, then bubbling like oil from his neck as he slumped to the ground.

Midge was still standing motionless, his mouth now formed into a bigger O, as Stacey moved towards him like a ballerina. It was as though she were floating across the linoleum on the kitchen floor, moving in wondrous slow motion, and Peter thought he'd never seen anything more beautiful in his life until she planted the knife perfectly into the side of Midge's neck.

Still stunned, Midge remained upright, eyes wide as if he were still contemplating what was happening. Then Stacey withdrew the knife and Midge's blood began making patterns on the wall.

Peter crawled back into his room. The vodka may have tasted like water but he couldn't get it down his throat quick enough. He closed his eyes, picturing the beach with his parents, wishing to God they were still alive, or that he was already dead, when he felt warm flesh on his arm.

'We have to go, Peter,' said Stacey.

She wasn't smiling, but she didn't appear to be angry. If Peter hadn't known it was impossible, he would have said this wasn't the same person he knew standing before him. She'd morphed into someone else. Somehow she was taller, older even, as she grabbed his hand and pulled him to his feet. 'I just need you to hold on to this for me,' she said, thrusting the used knife into his hand, and pressing his palm into the handle before taking it back. It was only then Peter noticed she was wearing thin latex gloves like they sometimes wore in the crime shows on TV.

'Thank you,' she said.

Peter stood there and closed his eyes. Both men had been dispatched quickly, so he hoped Stacey would show him the same mercy.

'What are you doing? We need to go,' she said.

Peter opened one eye, and then the next. 'You're not going to kill me?' he asked, or thought he did, his words slurred and lost as they left his mouth.

He saw the indecision in her eyes, and thought that it was probably a mistake on her part.

'You're coming with me,' she said, her voice different, more assured and powerful than he'd heard before.

Peter picked up another bottle of vodka from the cardboard box, and followed her out of the flat.

Chapter Twenty-Nine

The call had been anonymous – a male voice on the other end of Liam's phone, giving an address for the Carnewas Estate in Penzance where he had arrested Jason Mills the day before.

Liam eased himself away from Millie, kissing her on the cheek before changing into last night's clothes. Millie frowned. 'You have to go now?' she asked, looking at her phone.

He hadn't been in a serious relationship since he'd been with Grace, so not since he'd joined the police. He knew all the clichés about how difficult it was being with a copper, and had experienced something similar with Kim when in the navy. Then he would be away on duty for weeks, and even months, at a time, but he'd already let Millie down once on their first date and was loathe to do so again, especially after last night.

'It's no problem, but it's so early,' said Millie, as if reading his mind.

'I promise this doesn't happen very often, but I need to go,' said Liam. He called a cab back to his place where he got straight into his car and drove into Penzance, phoning Kim as he drove to tell her he wouldn't be able to take George today.

'He's going to be so upset,' said Kim, her voice a mixture of anger and disappointment, Liam unsure which one bothered him the most.

'Can I speak to him?'

'No, I'll break the news to him.'

'I'll try my best to pick him up later. I just can't say when.'

'Don't bother, we have plans,' said Kim, hanging up.

Liam felt a hollow pang in his stomach. It didn't happen very often, but he hated letting George down. It wasn't the type of thing that was easily explained to a child. It wasn't as if he could say he was busy trying to find the people who had drowned six men in a boat, and to locate another missing person who was in danger. He pictured the sadness on George's face as he was told the news by his mum, and promised himself he would make it up to the boy; he was grateful that he'd at least had the chance to spend some time with him on the previous Thursday.

He'd handed his card out to over a dozen people the other day, so there was a good chance the call was a hoax. If it was, he'd have been better off picking up George. But there had been something in the caller's voice – a hint of panic, or disbelief – which made Liam think it was worth looking into.

Despite the early hour, the sun was bright, and he was glad of the spare pair of sunglasses he always kept in the car. He thought about last night, how he'd opened himself up to Millie about his nightmares, realising he didn't regret one minute of it. He presumed the nightmares were triggered by his recent investigative work, in particular the gruesome discovery at Ralph's Cupboard of the six bodies. He tried not to think of the victims being drowned, how their panic must have been exacerbated by being bound and not able to move.

'It's too early for this,' he said, arriving at the estate and leaving the car.

Sand rubbed against his feet, a memento from last night's visit to the beach, the grains scratching his soles as he climbed the steps to the address he'd been given. It was a picturesque view, the ocean just about visible in the distance, and he wondered what price such flats would command had they been built for private purchase, and a little bit more love and attention been given to them.

A few steps down the corridor, he could see the door of the address was ajar. He stopped and looked about him, for a second fearing this was a set-up, before moving down the terrace.

'Hello,' he said, knocking on the door, then prising it open with his foot.

When no answer came, he called in his location and withdrew his extendable baton. He knocked on the door again. 'Police,' he said, moving into the hallway, a smell, hideously familiar, coppery and undefinable, coming to him as he made his way towards the living room and opened the door.

It took him a couple of seconds to adjust to what he saw, a blast of deep black-red assaulting his eyes before he alighted on the sight of two dead bodies. He scanned the room, poised for attack as he shouted, 'Police, is anyone here?'

When there was no answer, he alerted headquarters to what he could see, before moving to the first of the bodies. He didn't need to check for a heartbeat, the lifeless eyes of Gary French staring back at him, on closer examination his body littered with stab wounds.

Trying not to contaminate the scene any further, he moved towards the second body of Malcolm 'Midge' Ure. His eyes were closed, the same litany of wounds on his body.

But when Liam checked the man's wrists, he found there was a very weak pulse.

◆ ◆ ◆

Liam did what he could to keep Malcolm Ure alive as he waited for the paramedics to arrive. In the corner, Gary French's corpse watched them dispassionately, his body a human pin cushion.

'Stay with me,' said Liam, wondering as he kept his finger to the dying man's pulse who had done this and why this had happened. Had it been a fight between the two drug dealers, or had someone been sent in to dispatch the pair, as had happened to Gregory Moore in London?

At the moment, Liam didn't think it was the latter. Both men had numerous knife wounds, which didn't corelate with the professional nature of the hit on Moore or the personalised, methodical drownings that had taken place. The violence in the flat had been frenzied and unplanned, and – as proven by the fact that Ure was still alive – less than professional in its undertaking.

So had the two men fought each other? That too seemed doubtful. Knife fights were usually ended by the first incision. It wasn't like a fist fight when blows were exchanged. So where did that leave them? A third person who had attacked both men? Liam would have liked to think that it was Peter making a bid for freedom, but whoever had done this had done it before, even if only from a training viewpoint. That meant one person he'd yet to consider. The woman who called herself Stacey and had claimed to be Peter's niece.

'Police,' came the call from outside the flat, disturbing Liam from his thoughts.

'Paramedics only,' called Liam, as one of the responders stepped through the door.

A team of two paramedics took over, questioning him before placing an oxygen mask on to Ure's mouth. 'Everyone not a paramedic out of this crime scene,' said Liam, checking the other rooms before leaving the building and waiting for the CSI to arrive.

Liam was surprised to see Grace was one of the first on scene. 'Thought you were back in London?' he asked.

'Couldn't keep away. Who called this in, Liam?' Grace was dressed in more casual clothes than she usually wore to work, tight-fitting jeans and a thin blouse, her hair untied. He noted some of the other officers looking her way, and couldn't deny an old stab of attraction to her.

'Unknown number called me direct. I've given out lots of cards these last few days. They gave the address and hung up.'

'Recognise the voice?'

'Male, Cornish. That was it. What's the news from London? Has this come as a surprise?'

'It's a surprise to me. There'll be no one left from the OCG the way things are going.'

'Then your little Cornwall adventure will be over.'

'Will you miss me?' said Grace, holding eye contact.

Liam couldn't tell if she was being serious or not. It felt like they had unfinished business between them. Had they met a few years later or had both lived in the same town then things could have been different. Or maybe he was kidding himself, and some subconscious part of him had welcomed the chance not to have to commit. It was a familiar pattern, and one he had to wonder if he was destined to repeat.

He was stuck for a second, unable to form a reply, and was glad when Maya arrived and interrupted them. 'They're taking the survivor to the hospital. Very weak vitals,' she said.

Like Grace, Maya was dressed in her civvies. She looked as tired as he felt. The three of them stood aside as the paramedics carried Malcolm Ure outside. The man was on a ventilator, his injuries having been patched up. It looked doubtful he would survive the trip to the hospital, let alone be fit enough to speak to them about what had happened.

Once he was out of sight, they made plans for next steps which included door-to-door interviews of everyone in the building and the surrounding estate. 'I'll go through my list from the other day. See if I can narrow down who could have called me.'

'Good idea,' said Maya. 'Isn't that guy you arrested from this estate? Jason Mills?'

'Neighbouring building. I'll go speak to him now,' said Liam, taking a final look inside the flat, where all he could see was the white-coated CSIs moving like ghosts in the red-splattered room.

◆ ◆ ◆

Jason Mills' mother, Maude, answered the door – as she had the last time Liam was there. Her son had been released under caution which, considering the current circumstances, should have been considered a break for the young man. A feeling evidently not shared by his mother.

'What the hell do you want?' she said, the veins on her neck rigid like little steel bars.

'Maude,' said Liam. 'Is Jason in, please?'

'He's told you all he's going to tell you.'

'There has been another incident. He's not in trouble, but I need to speak to him.'

Maude stared at him as if doing so would make him disappear. 'Jason,' she shouted, not once looking away.

Jason appeared a minute later. He was wearing jogging bottoms and a stained T-shirt, the colour of which matched his flushed face. 'What now?' he said to Liam, his shoulders slumping.

'I need to speak to you privately.'

'Oh don't mind me, I only live here,' said Maude, offering a final withering look before storming off down the corridor.

'You found him then?' said Jason, looking down both sides of the corridor.

'Who, Edward Turnbull? Not yet, but your tip was a good one, so thanks for that. I received a call early this morning, giving me an address. The building opposite.'

Jason shook his head. 'Not me.'

'You know who was living opposite you, Jason?'

'Not really. People tend to keep themselves to themselves around here.'

'At least two known members of an organised crime group we have been monitoring. Most likely the people who have been supplying the drugs for this estate.'

'That's above my pay grade, DS Kilshaw.'

'Maybe so, but surely you would have seen them?'

'I see lots of things around here, and I tend to ignore them for my own good.'

'So you didn't make that call?'

'What bloody call? Why, what's happened?'

'There was an incident. An attack.'

Jason held out his hands. 'Not my scene, man, you know that. I'm all for the quiet life.'

'Anyone you know who could have called me?'

'I don't want to do your job for you, DS Kilshaw, but have you tried the neighbours?'

'Thanks, Jase, great idea,' said Liam, not hiding his sarcasm. 'Any busybodies on the estate? Anyone always in someone else's business?'

'You could try that pervert over there,' said Jason, nodding behind him.

Liam didn't turn around. 'Which pervert are we talking about?'

'Guy called Henry Brooks. Big, ugly lump. Always on his phone, taking pictures and stuff. Had the shit kicked out of him a few times, but he keeps at it. Weirdo.'

Liam checked his notes from his last visit, confirming he'd given someone with that name his card. 'OK, thanks for now,' he said. 'If you think of anything else?'

He didn't look over as he walked down the corridor, not wanting to alert Henry Brooks that he'd been spotted. His notes stated that Brooks hadn't seen any fentanyl being distributed on the estate, and the man hadn't made any mention of taking photos as Jason claimed, but Liam recalled he had a Cornish accent and thought it could have been him who'd rung earlier.

'Any luck?' asked Maya, as he reached the car park.

'Possible lead. It would be nice if someone could live on the ground floor, though,' said Liam.

'CSI have found a knife. Looks like the murder weapon.'

It was surprising that the killer wouldn't have had the forethought to dispose of the murder weapon but there were many possible explanations for it being at the scene. 'Let's hope we get something from it. Back in a bit,' said Liam, walking over to the other building.

Purposely, he hadn't once looked towards the man Jason Mills had claimed had been watching him. The last thing he wanted was to spook him away, and he didn't fancy having to chase anyone. He'd made a quick note of Henry Brooks' address. He was one floor lower than the flat where the incident had taken place, the view from his terrace overlooking the whole estate.

Liam was about to enter the stairwell when out stepped Henry Brooks. 'Been looking for me, have you?' said the man, his accent an almost impenetrable Cornish.

'Mr Brooks? Yes, I was coming to see you as a matter of fact.'

'I could tell. Thought I'd save you the trip.'

'You were the one who called me?'

'That I was.'

'Why didn't you give me your name?'

'Thought it didn't matter at the time. Anyways, I needed to get back to filming.'

'Filming?' asked Liam.

'That's right. Knew something weird was going on. Thought you'd like to see who left and where they went.'

Chapter Thirty

Liam studied the grainy image on Henry Brooks' phone before taking it to Maya and Grace. The three of them watched the recording together, while Brooks stood behind them with a permanent smile on his face, as if he were the hero in his own particular story.

The time of the recording said 4.20 a.m. Liam had yet to ask Brooks what he'd been doing up recording at that time, and why he'd waited another two hours to call him. A light was on in the flat where the two OCG members had been discovered, and now the front door was opening. The footage showed two people leaving the apartment: a tall, slender woman and a much older man who was struggling with his balance. The woman had hold of the man's hand, dragging him along like an unruly toddler.

'You have any close-up images of these two?' asked Liam.

Brooks shook his head, the smile still on his face.

The scene cut to the car park. A black Volkswagen van – its plates not visible, the engine running – sat in the middle, fumes trickling from the exhaust as the man and woman reappeared. The back door of the van opened, the elderly man being snatched from within before the woman climbed in and the van drove off.

'Do you know who these two people are?' asked Grace.

'I've been watching that place,' said Brooks, pointing up to the flat where the CSI were still working. 'Always some weird stuff going on up there. It's been empty for ages, then out of nowhere lights are on all the time.'

'Do you think this is something you could have mentioned the other day?' asked Liam.

'Lots of strange things go on around here. You only need to look,' said Brooks.

'That doesn't answer my question, Mr Brooks.'

'I didn't know that was what you were looking for,' said Brooks. 'I could have told you ten other weird things about this place, but I didn't think you would listen.'

'I think we'll have to sit you down and go through everything you know,' said Liam, Brooks smiling in return.

Liam nodded to one of the uniformed officers to take Brooks away. 'I can't be sure but that looks like Stacey Smith. Same build, and spiky hair.'

'And that was Peter Britten, being dragged along?' asked Maya.

'I hope so. It would at least mean he is still alive.'

It was Saturday, but Liam had already written the weekend off. He called Kim to try to speak to George, but his call went straight through to voicemail. He sent a text, apologising again, before heading to the Royal Cornwall Hospital Treliske in Truro, where Malcolm Ure had been taken.

There was already a police presence at the hospital, one of the uniformed officers from Truro nick informing him that Ure was undergoing emergency surgery.

Liam thought back to the multiple wounds they'd found on the man. It was a wonder he'd left the apartment still breathing. As frenzied as the attack appeared to have been, he couldn't believe the attacker would have purposely left Ure alive. The wounds inflicted on the two men looked random, wild and reckless, and he was sure only chance had kept one of them alive.

It felt like an oversight by the killer, the first real mistake Liam had seen in the investigation so far. It was obviously a different MO to the other killings as well, though that didn't mean it wasn't the same person behind the deaths. He thought about the video footage Henry Brooks had taken, the outline of the spiky-haired woman dragging the elderly man from the flat, and grew more concerned that the biggest mistake made so far had been his failing to apprehend the woman who'd called herself Stacey when he'd had the chance.

With Ure still undergoing surgery, Liam bought himself a coffee and walked the antiseptic corridors of the hospital. It was pointless blaming himself for not arresting Stacey when he'd had no grounds to do so, but it still stung that she could have been responsible for what had happened to Gary French and Malcolm Ure, and for the missing Peter Britten. The only consolation was that she was definitely not working alone. The video footage suggested there had been at least two others waiting in the black van – the driver, and whoever had dragged Peter inside, and Liam had to question if Edward Turnbull had been one of them.

As he completed a full circuit of the ground floor, Liam's thoughts once more turned to Peter Britten. Of late, there appeared to be a change of tack. The first two dead bodies – Eleanor Cooper and Marlon Tomlinson – had seemingly been victims of the county lines, but since then there had been eight further murders, and one as yet attempted murder, all of whom had been members of the OCG.

Ordering another coffee, Liam thought how righteous it would be if Peter was somehow behind the killings, that he was taking revenge for the two victims who'd gone before him, but knew that was fanciful thinking.

Yet, the fact Peter was still alive seemed like an anomaly. Coupled with the possibility that Malcolm Ure – should he survive the emergency operation – could help their investigation, this gave Liam fresh hope.

Waiting in the hospital felt like a waste of time, but Liam needed to be close by when Ure finally came out of surgery. He informed one of the response officers that he was stepping out for a time and made what was becoming a common ritual of driving to Peter Britten's house in Gwithian.

His lifeboat beeper went off as he drove along the harbour wall in Penzance. He'd forgotten he was on call that day, but there were enough volunteers on standby that he wouldn't be missed. As seemed to be the case every time the boat went out nowadays, he wondered if they were on their way to find another dead body. Maybe another boat had been discovered with the other half of the OCG, tied and gagged, dipped in the water to be drowned, only to be fished out again for show.

At Peter's house, he sent a text to Fischer asking him for an update when the callout was over. Walking through the threshold at Peter's house once more, it was impossible not to imagine the old man being the one fished out of the sea today. His only hope was that Stacey had already had the option to eliminate him, and that for one reason or another they still needed or wanted the man alive.

As he walked through the oddly cold rooms, he was again reminded that he'd met Stacey here. He may have been able to stop everything that subsequently happened if he'd been more forceful, or insisted that he was allowed entry into the house. What if Peter had been inside that day, being watched on by the two members of the OCG?

The thought made him wonder if Stacey had been the ringleader from the beginning, or whether something had happened to make her turn on her colleagues.

Liam walked the perimeter of Peter's garden, the relative peace and quiet giving him time to think. No doubt Grace would blame the latest deaths on some kind of bitter feud between competing county lines gangs, but Liam wasn't so sure if there was a different explanation.

First the tortured ritual of binding then drowning the victims, then the frenzied brutality of the stabbing attack on Gary French and Malcolm Ure. There was no specific pattern to the mode of killings, but each had its own distinct hallmark as if two people, each with their own peculiar taste in killing, were working in tandem.

The thought remained with him as he returned to the hospital. If he worked on the basis that Stacey was one of the killers, then who was she working with? Peter couldn't be ruled out, though everything pointed to him being a victim. What if French and/or Ure had been the other killer, the one with the penchant for drowning? Maybe Stacey had grown weary of the killings, or the pair had overstepped their position and Stacey had been instructed from higher up the group to put things right? At the moment, the only person who possibly had any answers had just come out of surgery and wasn't in a position to speak to anyone.

Liam was allowed into the intensive care unit but not into the room where Ure was being looked after. He was forced to stare through the glass, towards the man who may hold the key to everything, who at present was connected to so many tubes and monitors that he looked like a futuristic nightmare.

'When will I be able to speak to him?' Liam asked the consultant in charge.

'He's going to be under for some time. It is a marvel he's still alive considering the amount of blood he lost. He went into cardiac arrest on two occasions and suffered a number of mini strokes. At present, we don't know what the result will be on his brain function. I'm sorry I can't offer any more than that, but I doubt very much that he'll be able to coherently speak to you within the next few days.'

Liam felt like he'd been punched in the stomach. He didn't know for sure if Ure had the answers he wanted, but it was a cruel blow not being able to question him when he could possibly unravel everything for them.

He considered waiting for the doctor to leave, so he could make his own direct check on Ure's wellbeing and see if he could force some words from the stricken man. Unfortunately, that was the sort of recklessness that could only happen on television. His career would be in jeopardy the second he opened the door into his room.

Instead, he instructed the pair of uniformed officers at the scene to take turns keeping watch over him. 'Make sure we have a rota in place so he's never left alone,' he told them, before calling Maya with this latest negative update.

Aside from DCI Hargreaves, who hadn't been able to make it in, CID was as busy as any weekday. Grace, Maya and DI Whitfield were coordinating efforts, the focus of which was now centred on finding out more about Stacey Smith and locating her.

Liam scrolled through the CCTV images they had of the blacked-out van from the scene. The last footage was from a petrol station, showing the van turning off the A30 in Canon's Town twenty minutes after it had left the crime scene, and though they had numerous patrol cars out in the region it hadn't been spotted since.

Liam hadn't taken a photograph of Stacey, so finding a match on the criminal database was at best a struggle. He'd created an e-fit as best as he could but there were no matches. One thing was clear, if her name really was Stacey Smith then she didn't have a criminal record, and none of Grace's contacts within the Met knew of her, at least not in her current incarnation.

'Not many of them left now,' said DI Whitfield later as the three sections got together. 'Looks like that particular OCG attempt to get a foothold in Cornwall has failed.'

'Yes, but what is left in its place?' asked Grace.

'As a reminder, we have a member of the public who is missing, who most likely was abducted early this morning,' said Liam, receiving a curt smile from Whitfield.

'You're the only one to have met this Stacey Smith, am I right?' said the DI, sharing a knowing look with a couple of his colleagues.

'Maya and I have both seen her,' said Liam, who wanted nothing more at that moment than to reach over and knock the condescending smirk from the DI's face.

Tasks were issued, and the meeting was ended. Liam decided to go back to the beginning of the investigation, which for him had started with Marlon Tomlinson's murder.

He looked through the images of the young man's corpse, recalling the night the lifeboat team had been called out to retrieve his body. As he'd done countless times before, he compared the ropes tied around Marlon's wrists and ankles to those found on Eleanor Cooper. He noted how despite their different ages, they had the same mottled skin after being dragged from the sea.

Adding Peter Britten to the equation, it was clear they had three atypical victims of the county lines. A lone woman with learning difficulties, a deprived youth looking for somewhere to belong, and in Peter Britten, another senior citizen with a large property whose life was controlled by his addictions. He understood why they had chosen the victims, but why had they killed two of them?

'I'm finishing for the day,' said Grace, who had made her way over to his desk from out of nowhere.

Liam checked his watch, surprised that it was after 7 p.m. 'I still have a lot to go through.'

'You can't work all the time. You know it can have a negative impact.' She was standing over him, and he could smell the same perfume she used to wear when they were together. Had she put it on especially for him, or was he getting ahead of himself? 'Come for a drink with me?'

Liam looked up from the images on his screen at his ex-girlfriend. It was bizarre enough that she was working at the station, but this sudden interest in him coinciding with him dating Millie was a coincidence he could do without.

The sensible thing would be to tell her about Millie, but he didn't want to come across as being presumptuous about her motives. 'A drink?' he asked.

Grace shrugged, and in the simple gesture the passion that had seen them through the nine months of their relationship rushed him. 'I'm seeing someone,' he said, blurting it out before he made a mistake he was sure he would regret.

Surprise flashed in Grace's eyes, disappearing in a split second. 'You still fancy yourself I see,' she said, though the words weren't cold.

'Bad timing,' he said.

'Bad timing,' said Grace, walking away.

Chapter Thirty-One

It had started raining by the time Liam reached the care home on Monday morning. The recent good weather had come to an end on Sunday. After seeing George play cricket in the afternoon, he'd been sitting in a beer garden in Sennen with Millie that evening when the heavens opened, and it had been raining intermittently ever since.

The gloom of the world outside was reflected in the dark wallpaper and coldness he always felt visiting his mother. He sat by her bed wondering what she would think of Millie – and, more importantly, what Millie would think of her.

He wasn't sure if he came here out of a sense of loyalty, or if there was a part of him that still needed a parent, no matter how empty that relationship was. He had memories of the time before his dad had died, even if they had been overshadowed by the tragedy of his death, and the subsequent misery of living without him. But if he tried hard enough, he could still remember who his mother had been before she changed. He recalled picture postcard moments at the beach, his mother and father hand in hand, watching him with such delight. He could see his mother in the water, hurtling through the waves, as his dad surfed further out.

He didn't know how accurate the memories were. He knew all too well from his work how memory was such a malleable thing, subject to an individual's moods and wants. It was more than likely he was putting a positive spin on that time, but he supposed if he didn't have that he would never come here at all.

Having done his duty, he left his mother and drove to Bodmin. Despite the intricacies of the current investigation, he found his thoughts preoccupied with Millie. After meeting with Fischer and the rest of the lifeboat committee in the early evening to discuss what would be happening with Wayne 'Mouse' Mainwood, he'd met Millie in Sennen for dinner last night. Although he'd enjoyed the evening, things had been a little more tense than the last time they'd got together. Maybe he'd imagined it, but Millie had seemed a little stand-offish.

He'd apologised again for having to leave so early on Saturday morning, which she'd dismissed out of hand, but things hadn't flowed as well as their date on the Friday, and he still wasn't sure why.

Arriving at headquarters, he was just about to text her when there was a knock on his car window. 'Jesus Christ, Maya, you gave me a heart attack,' he said, putting his phone away.

'Love keeping you on your toes,' said Maya, as he opened the door and got out of the car. 'Better hurry, or we're both going to be late. Hargreaves has called another briefing.'

They both sprinted through the torrential rain to the main entrance. 'Move to Cornwall, they said. Weather is glorious,' she said, shaking the water from her hair as they took the lift to CID.

'Do you mind?' said Liam, wiping water from his coat.

'Look at you. You're like the proverbial cat.'

'What the hell are you talking about?'

'If you hadn't noticed, you've been smiling ever since I knocked on your window.'

'Just pleased to see you.'

The lift opened, Maya shaking her head and blocking his path. 'No, no, it isn't that. Can it be that the hunky DS Kilshaw is in love?'

Liam couldn't help but laugh, thinking about last night. 'Here I was thinking you were a good detective.'

'The lady doth protest too much. I know what I know.'

'Whatever you say,' said Liam, ceremonially moving her arm out of the way, thinking to himself that his colleague might be an even better detective than he'd appreciated.

◆ ◆ ◆

The current focus for their investigation was finding Edward Turnbull and the woman who had claimed to be Peter Britten's niece, Stacey.

Duties assigned for the day, Liam started work on trying to track the man who had once gone by the name of Connor Adams: Edward Turnbull. After visiting the last address they had for him on Friday, Liam had been trying to piece together Turnbull's movements after he'd left the address in Looe. Despite telling people he was going to London, he seemed to have gone completely off grid. The last time anyone appeared to have known him was through his volunteering at the rugby club. Although Grace had passed on his details to her colleagues in the Met, there was no mention of him on the electoral roll or any of the various databases they had at their disposal.

Before leaving headquarters on the Saturday, Liam had put in a file request with the army regarding Turnbull and followed it up with a call to the Provost Marshal's office. Getting detailed files from the armed forces was never an easy thing, and the call had confirmed his doubts. He was told his request was being processed, and it was only when he reminded the officer they were dealing with a multiple murder case that he got any reaction at all. He left the call with a promise that his request would be put at the top of the pile.

'While you're there, perhaps you could kill two birds with one stone? I'm also looking at another former soldier. Like Turnbull, though, his record is from some time ago.' Before he'd even finished speaking, he heard a sigh on the other end of the line.

'You'll have to put through another request.'

'There is a chance that the two are linked.'

Liam heard the sigh again, and was about to say something when the officer said, 'Send the request through to my personal email. I'll work both of them at the same time.'

'Thank you, you're a star,' said Liam, already typing as he hung up.

With the file sent, Liam tried to take a look at the bigger picture of the investigation but doing so made everything seem too far out of reach. With all the deaths and missing people, it looked too chaotic, and instead he returned his focus to the things he could control, knowing that all it would take would be one break, one piece of vital information that could turn everything around.

As if fate were listening, his phone rang. It was the hospital. Malcolm Ure was awake.

Liam shared the news with the team before leaving with Maya for Truro. Numerous procedures had to be met when it came to situations like this and Liam knew they would have limited time, if any, to speak to Ure alone.

'So, is all this to do with the schoolteacher you've been seeing?' asked Maya, as Liam drove.

'What do you mean "all this"?'

'This sunnier disposition.'

'I feel anything but sunny, Maya. This investigation is driving me crazy.'

'Does Grace know?'

'About my feelings regarding the investigation? I imagine so.'

'You can keep fooling yourself, but I see the way she looks at you. I think she realises the mistake she made.'

'I think this constant questioning over my love life constitutes some kind of harassment,' said Liam.

'I'm just a colleague looking out for her subordinate.'

'Yeah, sure. Well, loose lips sink ships.'

'You learnt that in the navy, did you?'

'Amongst other things.'

Despite the gentle teasing, Maya had a way about her that made Liam want to confide in her. He almost wanted to tell her how Grace had asked him to go out for a drink again – but as this gossip involved one of their colleagues, he decided to keep it to himself for the time being. He also refrained from telling her how things hadn't gone well last night with Millie. He wondered if a combination of his tiredness and his focus on the investigation was making him overly sensitive.

As they got nearer to Penzance, they concentrated on what lay ahead of them. Liam ran through a number of approaches they might take with Malcolm Ure. They knew he was awake and responding but had no idea what form that responsiveness took. They decided the best approach was to ask short questions, and to get the most from him while they had the time.

Liam thought back to the scene at the estate – the sight of the two bodies and their multitude of wounds. It was a wonder that Ure was alive, let alone responsive. Now he had to hope that the man would be willing to talk, or if fear of retribution would stop him from telling them who was responsible for the attack.

It was a different medical team in ICU to Saturday, a stressed-looking doctor, a woman with heavy bags beneath her eyes, explaining to them that Ure was responding well but the maximum she could allow them was five minutes, stipulating that any change in his vitals would result in an immediate cessation of the interview.

Liam and Maya nodded, Maya stepping into Ure's room first and making the introductions. Ure was lying back, his bed slightly elevated. He blinked in response when Maya asked if they could ask some questions.

'Who did this to you?' said Liam, getting straight to the point.

He half expected the man to clam up and was surprised when Ure mouthed the word, 'Stacey', his voice coarse and dry.

'What is Stacey's surname, Malcolm?'

Ure shrugged, the gesture so slight that Liam nearly missed it. 'Is she really Peter Britten's niece, or was that a lie?'

Ure's lips moved as if he were trying to form a smile. 'Don't know what you're talking about,' he said, his voice almost inaudible.

Liam's body tensed. The man on the bed may have suffered a terrible attack, but it was still hard to muster any sympathy for him. 'Where is Peter Britten?' he asked.

Ure shrugged, and despite his perilous state Liam wanted to knock the truth out of him. 'We know you took over his house. Just do yourself a favour and tell me where he is.'

Ure sat with his mouth hanging open. Liam wasn't sure if the man was thinking or had lost all train of thought.

'Gary is dead, Malcolm. Whoever did this to you is not on your side,' said Maya.

'We can offer you protection. Just tell us where Peter is.'

Liam glanced at the machines attached to the man, noting the pulse rate that was getting higher.

'Thought she was one of us,' said Ure, wincing as if every word pained him.

'Who? Stacey? Who is she, Malcolm? Who could she be working for, if not your organisation?'

Ure squinted, as if the pain was increasing, his pulse going up by 10 bpm. 'They're killing all of us.'

'Who are?'

'I don't know. I thought Stacey was with us.'

His pulse was close to 100 bpm, and Liam could see the doctor outside the ICU window watching on with concern. 'Who could she be working with, Malcolm? Tell us and we can help you.'

'I don't know,' said Ure, lowering his eyes. 'Ask Appleton.'

'Appleton?' said Maya, as the doctor opened the door.

'That's enough now,' said the doctor, checking over Ure, whose pulse had lowered.

Liam ignored the doctor. He needed to know who Appleton was, and more importantly what had happened to Peter. 'Just tell me where Peter is,' he asked once more, but Ure was asleep, and the doctor silently pointed to the door.

Chapter Thirty-Two

Maya called headquarters as they drove back to Bodmin, where she was put through to Grace. She put the call on speaker phone, raising her eyebrows at Liam as if she found the situation between her two colleagues hilarious.

Liam ignored her and informed Grace of their brief interaction with Malcolm Ure. 'He mentioned the name Appleton, if that means anything?'

'You're sure he said the name Appleton?' said Grace, after a slight pause.

'Definitely Appleton.'

'Christopher Appleton is a known gangster in south-east London. From what we understand, he was close to Gregory Moore. We've yet to prove his link to the OCG but this could be it. How does this Stacey person fit in with this though?'

'Ure avoided the question. I got the impression that Appleton had vouched for her in some way. Do you have someone who could pay him a visit?' asked Liam.

'I know two people driving in a car at the moment,' said Grace.

'No way,' mouthed Maya, shaking her head furiously.

'Bit out of our jurisdiction,' said Liam.

'I'd do it, but I'm needed here. It would be good to get fresh faces on the matter, and it could take him off guard.'

'What is it, five, six hours to London?' asked Maya, still shaking her head.

'Yes, but it's a lovely drive,' said Grace, hanging up before they could put up a fight.

'See, I told you she was pissed at you. Now you're getting me involved,' said Maya, as Liam headed on to the A30.

'I can drop you off at the station if spending time with me bothers you that much, Inspector.'

'Oh, don't do me any favours, DS Kilshaw. I'll come with you so long as you promise to buy me lunch.'

'I think there's a Burger King at Exeter services,' said Liam. 'Done.'

But they only got as far north as Bodmin before they were called back to headquarters. 'My boss has Appleton's place under surveillance. Sorry, I should have known,' said Grace, sounding anything but apologetic.

'How does that help us with locating Stacey?' asked Maya, looking as pissed off as Liam felt.

'We may have some intelligence on that. Seems that Stacey popped up on the scene couple of years back. From what we understand, she started dating Appleton. I say dating, he is married, but you know what I mean.'

'How are we only finding out about this now?'

'Our UCO had been in contact. They were under the impression that Stacey was just a bit player, and these latest developments have come as a shock to the OCG. It wasn't supposed to happen.'

Liam hung up, and pulled off at the next exit so he could return to Bodmin.

'All sounds very convenient,' said Maya.

They both knew that contact with undercover officers was kept as confidential as possible to protect those involved, but it still felt like an oversight. It suggested that if Stacey had killed Gary French, and tried to kill Malcolm Ure, as appeared to be the case, that she'd done so of her own volition. It meant she could have switched sides. But Liam still didn't know what that might mean for Peter Britten.

Maya's anger had intensified by the time they returned to Bodmin. A meeting had been called in Hargreaves' office for the three SIOs and Liam. Grace muttered a half-baked apology for sending them to London. Liam could see Maya was having to rein herself in.

'Four more arrests for fentanyl possession,' said DI Whitfield, as Maya continued staring at Grace.

Whitfield glanced at Liam, searching for an explanation for the tension in the room. 'Where have the arrests taken place?' asked Liam, delaying the moment when questions would be asked about the UCO.

'St Austell, Padstow, and two more in Camborne. They are claiming they were given the drugs for free,' said Whitfield.

'They're not wasting any time,' said Liam.

'Maybe the UCO knows something about this?' said Maya, still staring intently at Grace.

Grace held her hands up. 'Look, I've apologised for sending you to London.'

'That's fine, but don't you think it would have been prudent to share the information that you had a UCO working? Just the fact that this Stacey is one of Appleton's squeezes would have saved us a lot of time and effort.'

'You know how these things are,' said Hargreaves.

'No, I don't. We agreed that we would have three SIOs working on the three strands of the investigation. And that we would fully cooperate with one another,' said Maya, emphasising the end of her sentence as she glared at Grace.

'It was out of my hands. I was told not to share,' said Grace, unrepentant.

'Did you know, sir?' asked Liam.

'It's neither here nor there,' said Hargreaves. 'We have the intelligence now, and that's a breakthrough.'

'What else does your UCO have for us?' asked Maya, the consternation evident in the furrowed line in her forehead not easing.

Grace twirled her hair – a habit Liam recalled from their time together, and one that usually meant she needed time to think. 'I'm not in charge of them. The UCO has been around long before this operation. They report to one of the senior officers on the international side of things.'

'You don't know their identity?' asked Liam.

Grace shook her head. 'All I know is that they popped their head up to give us this information, which was made by a burner phone, and that they've had to cut connection for the time being,' she said, after an over-long pause.

'So they just came out to tell you who Stacey was?' asked Liam.

'That was a by-product. They report directly to Appleton, who apparently fears for his life.'

'Who is he scared of?' said Liam.

'Everyone, from the sound of it. The OCG are closing ranks, and our officer can't risk continued contact with us. Obviously, we're watching the situation very closely.'

Hargreaves ended the meeting a few minutes later though nothing felt resolved. A divide had occurred, and Maya wasn't ready to forgive and forget. 'I knew they were withholding something from us,' she said to Liam, back in CID.

Liam wasn't as convinced as she was but began to wonder if Grace had been trying to manipulate him somehow. 'I guess they have a slightly different agenda,' he said.

'We all want the same result, but you think we'll get any credit when this is all wrapped up?'

'So what do we do?'

'We can continue doing what we've been doing. We'll solve this with or without their help,' said Maya, as DC Lawson entered the office.

'Liam, call came in for you. A Captain Fraser Baker. Army?' he said.

Maya nodded, and Liam answered the call from his desk. 'Captain Baker, DS Kilshaw, thank you for getting back to me so quickly.'

'No problem. I have the file on Edward Turnbull. I can send it over to you but be warned there are a few hoops we may have to go through. At this stage, I can answer any questions.'

'What sort of hoops are we talking about? I'm ex-forces if that helps?'

'Ah, right, well, you'll know all about the Official Secrets Act then. Some of Sergeant Turnbull's file is redacted, and I need to get the file itself signed off before I can forward it. Left on a full pension after enlisting as a teen. The odd reprimand always after one too many drinks.'

'As I mentioned in my email, we're investigating a multiple murder case at present and we are unable to locate Turnbull. Anything in the report that could help us?'

'He is still getting his pension payments. His bank would have an address for that. Aside from that, I imagine your information is more up to date than ours.'

They had already checked all the accounts associated with Turnbull, and each had his address as the house Liam had already visited in Looe. 'If Turnbull is involved in this, then we believe he could be working with a much larger team. Could you give me a list of his colleagues during his time?'

Baker sighed. 'More red tape, I'm afraid, and due to the nature of his work, Sergeant Turnbull would have worked with hundreds of colleagues.'

'You've heard about our investigation? Ten dead bodies, the threat of fentanyl on the streets?'

'And while I sympathise, DS Kilshaw, there is little I can do. I will forward Sergeant Turnbull's file as soon as I am able.'

Liam stood, raising his voice. 'They've killed two civilians, and one more is missing. If I don't get to speak to Turnbull, then they will kill this man. You want to live with that? Because I don't.'

Baker didn't answer, and Liam regretted losing his temper with him. 'Please, there must be something you can do?' Liam had dealt with the police sections of the armed forces before, and while they were very protective of their respective organisations, they usually had the same goals and aspirations of any police officer.

Baker sighed again, sounding as if he were weighing up his options. 'You have the date Turnbull left. Have a look for major arrests within a six-month period of that in the Aldershot area. Might give you some of the names you're interested in.'

Liam was already typing as he thanked the officer. The result was instant. A major drug bust involving a group of five former soldiers had taken place within six months of Turnbull leaving the army. Turnbull himself wasn't arrested, but Liam now had the names of the five that had, each having served between one and eight years for drug offences.

He told Maya about the conversation, and together they ran the names through the various databases. Two of the five were still behind bars for other offences, but the other three were at large.

'Bingo,' said Liam, showing Maya details of James Summers – a former member of Looe Rugby Club. The same club where Turnbull had once coached. An address was on file for him in Camborne, where there had been a number of arrests for possession of fentanyl.

'It's on my way home. I could pay him a visit,' said Liam.

'I'll come with you, though we'll have to take separate cars,' said Maya.

It started raining again as soon as they left the building. Liam was soaked as he sprinted to the car.

It was too soon to get excited, but he couldn't deny the thrill of possibility that Turnbull was somehow linked to the five ex-soldiers who'd been arrested in Aldershot, and that the same firm was connected to recent events.

The A30 was jammed in both directions, and as Liam inched along the road it gave him time to dwell on his aborted journey to see Chris Appleton. The emergence of the UCO within the group had started a rift between the divisions which threatened to deepen. He'd seen it happen before, competing departments jeopardising the greater operation for personal glory. Liam's immediate priority was still finding Peter Britten, and uncovering who was behind the spate of killings, and although he believed Grace and her Met colleagues wanted the same, he knew it wasn't their priority, more a means to an end for them. Maybe it wasn't too late to stop the division, but everything had felt off-kilter lately, and seemed to be getting worse on a daily basis.

The house in Camborne was a thirty-minute drive. The small property was close to a large supermarket on the outskirts of town. Liam expected a similar outcome as when he'd attended Turnbull's address in Looe, so he was surprised when a man matching James Summers' description answered the door.

Summers had been a young man when he was arrested, and had served six years as part of the arrests. Time had not been kind to him. He was heavyset, his considerable bulk now more fat than muscle. His pallid skin glistened with sweat as he answered the door, a flicker of indecision reaching his eyes as Liam and Maya displayed their warrant cards.

'Can we come in?' asked Liam.

Summers looked up and down the road. 'No, you bloody can't. What do you want?' he said.

'We're investigating a set of multiple murders we believe are related to a county lines drug operation here,' said Maya.

An incredulous smile formed on Summers' bloated features. 'Is that so? And what – cos I was once wrongly banged up, you think I have something to do with it?'

'You know this man?' asked Liam, showing him a picture of Edward Turnbull.

Summers barely glanced at the image. 'No.'

'Edward Turnbull. He was in the army, the same time as you. Same regiment, I believe.'

Summers pursed his lips. 'Rings a bell, but can't say I remember the fella.'

There were probably a few people Liam had forgotten over the years, but he could recall the name and face of every comrade he'd worked with. He'd put his life in the hands of those men and women and wouldn't forget their names so lightly. He didn't think Summers had seen the same kind of action as he had, but that wouldn't make a difference. 'Don't bullshit us, Summers. I know full well you know who Edward Turnbull is. I'm sure you also know he's been distributing fentanyl around Camborne as well. Have you been helping with that?'

Summers stared at him hard, confirming to Liam that he knew Turnbull. 'If you want to speak to me, arrest me. Otherwise, leave,' he said, close to snarling.

'You're making a mistake, Mr Summers. I don't know how you're involved, but you risk being an accessory to murder. You happy with that?'

'Leave,' said Summers, the sound of a dog barking coming from within the house.

With only such a vague connection to go on, they were forced to watch as the smiling James Summers closed the door on them, and their phones went off in unison, each receiving the same message – Malcolm Ure had been pronounced dead at RCH Treliske.

Chapter Thirty-Three

It wasn't technically a murder scene, but the corpse was a murder victim. Malcolm 'Midge' Ure had suffered a cardiac arrest, a complication from his emergency surgery and the initial attack they believed was carried out by Stacey Smith.

Liam nodded and the sheet was pulled over the man's face. His last words had pointed them to Christopher Appleton, and despite the Met's reticence, Liam hoped something good could come from that, ideally finding Peter Britten.

There would be a full autopsy in the coming days to confirm the cause of death and to ensure there was medical proof of a link between the attacks and Ure's death. After a brief interview with the doctor who had called the time of death, Liam headed towards the car park, deciding he would order a takeaway as he lacked the energy to prepare anything himself.

'Excuse me.'

Liam turned to see a nurse moving towards him. He smiled and noted the woman blush. 'You're the detective, aren't you?' she said, smiling back.

'DS Kilshaw,' said Liam, with a slight nod.

'I'm not sure if you were aware, but Mr Ure had a visitor not long before he died.'

'That can't be. Mr Ure wasn't allowed any visitors, and I have spoken to my colleague who hasn't left ICU all day.'

'No, no, the gentlemen in question came to the main reception area. I told him the exact same thing. I've been rushed off my feet so haven't been able to inform anyone, and I only just found out about Mr Ure, and I just saw you again . . .'

The nurse was getting ahead of herself. Liam lifted his hand to ask her to stop. 'Who came to visit him?' he asked.

'Well, he didn't ask to visit as such. He wanted to know where Mr Ure was being looked after.'

'Who?' said Liam.

'He didn't give his name. Young man, very tall, messy brown hair.'

'This him?' asked Liam, showing her a picture of Wayne 'Mouse' Mainwood.

'Yes, I'm sorry I didn't tell anyone sooner.'

'What time was this?'

'About 5.40 p.m.'

'You have cameras at main reception?'

'We do, yes.'

'Can you get video footage of him arriving for me?' asked Liam, giving the nurse his most winning smile.

'Of course,' she said, blushing again as Liam headed towards his car.

Wayne Mainwood hadn't been present at the last lifeboat committee meeting and Liam had been glad of the fact. It was already too much of a conflict of interest, and he hadn't wanted to see the man again. Liam had made his point very clear in a private meeting with Fischer that he would have to leave if the young man was ever reinstated as a volunteer. But if what the nurse had said was true, that was the least of Mainwood's problems.

Liam bought a dubious takeaway from a local kebab shop before heading out towards Mainwood's house near St Erth. He'd decided there was no point going in guns blazing and arresting Mainwood again. For now, it was enough that he knew there was more of a connection between his ex-volunteer colleague and the OCG. That gave him an advantage, and he hoped to use it to find out who was behind all of this.

He parked further out and took a back route into the woods. He recalled the last time he'd been here, finding Sloan in the house with Mainwood. It came as no surprise that Sloan was involved in this somehow. What did puzzle him was why Mainwood had gone to the hospital. He had no doubt that the young man was well down the food chain in whatever organisation he'd fallen into. It could have been that Sloan had sent him in to check on a fallen comrade, but it wasn't beyond the scope of possibility that he'd been sent there to finish the job on Ure.

In a perfect world, Liam would have found the blacked-out van that had collected Peter Britten and Stacey Smith from the Carnewas Estate parked up outside Mainwood's house. But he wasn't surprised when that turned out not to be the case.

It was possibly foolish to be here without calling it in, but he wanted to make a quick reccy of the place before he took it any further. There could be a simple explanation for why Mainwood had wanted to see Ure. For all Liam knew, they could simply be drinking buddies, so there was little point getting anyone else involved at present.

The air felt dense as he took the back route through the woodland, battling along a makeshift path, the ground sodden from the recent downpour, until he could see the back of the house.

What he had expected to find? Mainwood, Sloan and Stacey Smith conducting a drug empire in the back garden? Peter Britten bound and gagged awaiting his watery execution? If the current investigation had proved anything, it was nothing was ever that easy.

A light was on downstairs in the kitchen. The light trickled through the gloom on to the patio. From his vantage point, propped up against an old oak tree, Liam couldn't see any movement from inside the house.

What he really wanted was a clear view of Stacey Smith, or maybe even Peter Britten. That would be enough to call for backup. But he had no idea if Stacey was involved with Mainwood, and it was beginning to feel like a wasted journey. But he was here now, and although he'd much rather have been home in bed, he decided to wait it out.

The light went off just after midnight, the first sign that anyone was in the house. Liam was relieved for a chance to move, scurrying down the bank outside the rear of the property and crawling along the fence until he reached the front. He was in two minds. He wanted to speak to Mainwood, to find out why he'd been at the hospital asking after Malcolm Ure, but knew the situation had to be handled carefully. For now, the advantage was in knowing something Mainwood, and possibly Sloan, didn't know.

Reluctantly, he returned to his car. His clothes were damp, his skin tingling from the bugs and dirt he'd spent the last few hours with. His mind was awhirl with possibilities. But for now, there were so many intangibles that he was just hypothesising.

Yet, as he climbed into his car, he couldn't deny a second of optimism. Things were chaotic, with many different tangents he could only guess at, but he sensed they were getting nearer. Maybe it was blind optimism, but he was sure they were on the cusp of something and couldn't wait for tomorrow to come so he could find out exactly what that would entail.

◆ ◆ ◆

His earlier optimism was failing by the time he reached headquarters the following day. Sleep had been fitful, and his body ached from the hours spent cramped in the woodlands looking down on the house.

When he was on his third coffee of the day, he took Maya aside and told her what he'd discovered at the hospital.

Maya also looked tired, the exhaustion of such an active and ongoing investigation taking its toll on everyone. 'You think Mainwood and Stacey are working together?'

'I don't know what to think, but it can't be a coincidence he was at the hospital asking after Malcolm Ure.'

'How well do you know this guy? Sounds like a dumb move to me, going to the hospital like that.'

'He was just a kid as far as I was concerned, until the day he was brought in. I saw a different side to him then, one I would never have expected, but a lot of it was an act. I could still see the scared little kid trying to be brave. As to his involvement, I don't know. If I was to hazard a guess, I would suggest he is a patsy for Sloan. As for Sloan's involvement . . .' Liam threw his arms in the air.

'Shall we pay Sloan another visit, put some pressure on him? We could go back to Mainwood's house. Who knows, if he is connected with Stacey, she could be there.'

'I don't think Stacey would be that stupid. I get the impression that she might be much more deeply involved than we first thought.

There was something about her that time I saw her at Peter Britten's. She had the type of confidence that you knew wasn't an act. I was sort of impressed with her. I knew I should have pushed it.'

'No time for ifs and buts now, DS Kilshaw. Your call.'

'I think we put someone on Mainwood's house. Watch the comings and goings.'

Maya nodded.

'As long as it's not me,' added Liam, walking off to the kitchen to get some more coffee, his skin still itchy, his head beating in pain.

After a couple of ibuprofen and another coffee, Liam returned to his desk in time to receive an email from Captain Fraser Baker containing an encrypted file on Edward Turnbull. After going through a laborious process online, Liam was finally able to look at something approaching a file for the man they suspected of distributing fentanyl, though as Baker had warned, much of it was blanked out.

They already knew Turnbull was a Gulf War veteran, deployed in Operation Granby with the 1st Battalion of the Light Infantry. However, most of the information about Turnbull's deployment was obscured by thick black lines. He wondered what was so important that he wasn't allowed to read it, and how much of his own military file would look exactly the same. His own signing of the Official Secrets Act meant that he couldn't divulge any details of his operations with the SBS, so he imagined it would look pretty similar.

Nothing in the file, beyond the names of Turnbull's commanding officers, gave links to other personnel. Liam ran checks on what he had but it proved fruitless.

With no other leads, Liam cross-checked all the names he had from the major players in the investigation – many now dead – along with those of bit players such as Jason Mills and Wayne Mainwood. What he hoped to achieve he wasn't sure, but he stopped when he came to Martin Sloan's name, recalling the first time he'd spoken to the man during the investigation. Sloan had been boastful about his career in the military, stinging Liam with his remarks about Liam's parents.

It took a bit of searching – and another call to Captain Fraser Baker – but he finally got what he was looking for. It could have been another coincidence but there were now too many of them.

Baker confirmed his suspicions. Not only had Edward Turnbull served for the 1st Battalion of the Light Infantry, so had James Summers. As had – possibly more importantly – Martin Sloan.

Chapter Thirty-Four

It seemed that death was nothing new to Stacey. Her attack on the two men may have appeared frenzied but even in his drunken state, Peter had seen the precision in the way she'd moved – albeit a precision that had been mixed with a good dose of retribution.

He'd had plenty of time to dwell on that as he'd slowly sobered up. Stacey hadn't killed the two men because of the way Gary had spoken to her on her return. It had been a planned attack, something Peter imagined had been in the works for a long time.

Things were different now. Although he was mainly left alone like last time, there were no boxes of vodka to help take his mind off things. Just a cold, dusty room, with an adjacent toilet. Not the healthiest of places to endure a hangover years in the making.

Stacey was different too. She looked in on him from time to time, gave him food, but the compassion he thought he'd seen in her before had dissipated. He couldn't tell if she'd been putting on an act all these months, or if she was acting now; her cold demeanour a protective measure to align with her new comrades.

These new men were a breed apart from the wannabe gangsters Stacey had dispatched. They were ruthless and precise, discussing killing and the smuggling of drugs in cold, direct sentences, their words rarely wasted, their tone never jocular and boisterous in the way Gary and Midge had behaved. Peter heard them through the wall, their accents mainly local, the voices changing every now and then as different members of their group came and went.

Unlike his previous captors, they never used their own names. They favoured code-names which all appeared to be military in nature – Captain, Colonel, Admiral, among others. Stacey was known as Wren, which seemed wrong to Peter, but she didn't seem to mind.

He listened as they talked of a drop that was taking place soon, though it wasn't this that Peter was most interested in. What concerned him was his own fate, which even in these painful stages of withdrawal he still cared about. They called him the Stowaway, which was ironic considering he was here under duress.

With his ear to the wall, Peter heard one of their number, a young lad who went by the name of Corporal, ask, 'What are we going to do with the Stowaway?'

Silence followed, Peter imagining the collective staring at the door of his makeshift prison.

'He will soon be collateral. For now, we need him alive,' said another of the men, their boss with his deep Cornish accent.

'That cop has a hard-on to find him,' said Corporal.

'That's why we need to keep him alive. He's a bargaining tool. When the drop is complete, he's collateral. Until then, he stays here.'

Peter scurried back against the opposite wall as he heard footsteps coming his way. The door opened, and Stacey stuck her head with its spiky dyed hair through the opening. Was that sadness in her face as she looked his way, or pity?

'Get ready,' she said. 'We'll be moving soon.'

Chapter Thirty-Five

Liam shared his findings about Sloan, Summers and Turnbull – all former members of the Light Infantry, 1st brigade – with the three SIOs and DCI Hargreaves.

'Do we know if that is unusual? They're all from Cornwall, maybe that is a common regiment for them to end up?' asked Hargreaves.

Liam had anticipated the question. 'Army recruits from Cornwall often joined the Duke of Cornwall's Light Infantry, which became part of the overall light infantry in the sixties. But it's just one of many paths into the armed forces. And yes, it could be coincidence, but there is something here which links three suspects. It has to be worth investigating further.'

'I can't see Sloan being involved in something as large as this. He's a bit player, always has been,' said DI Whitfield.

'As you say, always has been. I agree that it is unlikely he is the mastermind behind this, but with the OCG on the way out, he would need someone to supply him with drugs to sell. One thing I know about Sloan is that he shouldn't be underestimated.'

'You're thinking a Cornish OCG?' said Grace.

Liam thought he detected a hint of amusement in her tone. 'Either that, or a smaller gang down here are in bed with a bigger firm upcountry. You said yourself there are competing groups.'

DCI Hargreaves looked at Grace for a response. 'I guess it's not out of the realms of possibility, but the three players you mention are all small time.'

'Turnbull, under his guise as Connor Adams, appears to be single-handedly responsible for the influx of fentanyl into the county. He must be working with someone – why not Summers and Sloan? Get people like Wayne Mainwood on board, and then the Justin Blakes and Jason Millses of the world and it becomes the start of something.'

'For argument's sake, let's say this is a possibility. What do you want to do next?' asked Hargreaves.

'We put round-the-clock surveillance on Wayne Mainwood's house, where Martin Sloan was last seen, as well as Summers' place in Camborne. In the meantime, I'll try to make contact with Sloan again if I can find him. If he is low down in this pecking order, we could lean on him.'

'We would need some extra manpower,' Maya said, looking over at DI Whitfield.

'Fine by me,' said Whitfield.

Liam tried to ignore his own internal negativity as he walked up North Terrace to Sloan's house. It mocked him, suggesting he was back to square one – calling on the local drug dealer with little to no proof or knowledge of the man's involvement, just as he had at the beginning of the investigation.

Focusing on the positives, he knocked on Sloan's door. So much had happened since that day, and he had to cling on to the hope that things were coming together. Something clearly linked Sloan, Mouse, Turnbull and Summers.

'You're like a dog with a bone,' said Sloan, opening the door, his long greasy hair falling on to his shoulders as his ancient rottweiler moped to the door and collapsed at his feet.

'I have some questions to ask, Mr Sloan. We do this here or at the station. Your choice.'

Sloan held firm. 'I think this may constitute harassment.'

'Think again.'

'Last time you arrested me, you had nothing. Why do you think anything's different this time?'

'Answer my questions, and we may not have to find out.'

Sloan shook his head, his dog getting to his feet as he stepped back into the house, the front door left open for Liam to follow inside.

The interior came as a surprise to Liam. The house was decorated to a high standard: the wallpapered hallway adorned with two original oil paintings, the living room clean and modern, with a top-end television taking centre stage on the wall above a marble fireplace. Sloan sat, not gesturing for Liam to do the same.

'May I?' said Liam, taking a seat opposite on a soft leather armchair.

'What is it this time?'

'Where's your buddy, Mainwood?'

'He's your buddy, isn't he? Or he was. Hear you had him kicked off the lifeboat crew?'

'Where is he?'

'I'm not his keeper. At home, I guess.'

'You heard about the two deaths recently in Penzance?'

Sloan shrugged. 'Not really,' he said.

'Not really, OK. Two members of a county lines gang from London were stabbed at a flat in Penzance. One died at the scene, one in hospital yesterday.'

'That is a tragedy.'

'Your mate Mainwood was asking after the one in hospital last night. Now why would he do something like that?'

'You tell me, DS Kilshaw.'

'My guess is he was desperate to know if the gang member was alive or not. Maybe because he was in part responsible for the situation he was in?'

'Why go to the hospital though? Sounds risky to me.'

Liam could see Sloan was taking delight in the situation and decided to change tack. 'It's not too late, Martin. Whatever path you're on, it can be changed. Tell me what you know about those involved in all this madness and I'll make sure you're treated well.'

'I'm sure I have no idea what you're talking about,' said Sloan, with a mocking smile.

'That time we met before, the first time I spoke to you, you mentioned you used to be in the armed forces.'

'That's right, just like your daddy.'

'But he was a marine. You were just an army grunt.'

Sloan laughed. 'I'd expect nothing else from you, quite right.'

'You know who else is ex-military? James Summers and Edward Turnbull. You know who those guys are, don't you?'

'No idea what you're talking about.'

'Edward Turnbull is the man we believe has been distributing fentanyl in Cornwall. Summers is a former colleague of his. The pair both did time for drug-related offences in the past. They're also former members of the 1st Brigade of the Light Infantry. Starting to ring any bells?'

'You know how big the light infantry is, don't you?' said Sloan, the grin fading a little.

'You ever come across them during your time?' asked Liam, trying to catch the man out.

'I don't even know who you're talking about. Now, if you haven't got any pertinent questions to ask me . . .'

'Everyone deserves a chance, Martin. I came here to give you an opportunity. I know you're involved in this one way or another. You come clean now, tell me who is behind all of this, and I'll make sure you have an easy ride.'

'Trying to recruit me as a grass? How does that usually work out?'

Liam wondered if he was referencing Justin Blake – Liam's sometime CHIS, currently under house arrest. 'Once-in-a-lifetime offer, Sloan. You know this is all unravelling.'

Sloan got to his feet, his dog lifting his head up as if asking, do we have to go through this again?

'Don't say I didn't warn you,' said Liam, standing.

'And don't say I didn't do the same thing for you.'

'You're giving me a warning?' asked Liam, taking a step closer to Sloan, invading his private space.

'No, no, I would never consider it. Just some friendly advice. I have no idea what is going on but from what I can see only bad things happen to those who get involved. That's why I'm keeping myself out of it.'

Liam stood his ground. Up close, he towered over Sloan and wanted the man to feel his presence. 'I don't take kindly to threats, Sloan,' he said. 'One last chance before I leave.'

Sloan inched a little closer. 'Give my regards to your mother,' he said, his face contorted into a snarl.

And there it finally was: Sloan's real face.

Liam matched the man's stare, like he would an angry dog's, before eventually turning his back. It was clear Sloan was trying to provoke a response, to make Liam lose his temper. Liam took the fact he was so riled as a positive, but as he opened the front door, the next words to leave Sloan's mouth almost made him lose his control.

'Oh, and give my regards to that pretty little schoolteacher friend of yours.'

Liam spun around, his composure lost. Heat surged from his cheeks and he was about to rush back to Sloan when he saw the man had his phone out.

'Smile for the camera,' said Sloan.

Liam took deep breaths. 'When this is all over, remember this was where it went wrong for you.' He walked out, slamming the front door behind him before he did something he would regret.

Chapter Thirty-Six

Liam was about to call Millie as he left Sloan's place before he realised she would still be at school. Instead, he headed for the front, thinking about what Sloan had said.

St Ives was a small town, and Liam had been out with Millie two or three times, but he didn't like the way Sloan had mentioned her as if it were some kind of threat.

If he'd any doubts that Sloan was involved in all of this, their confrontation had evaporated them. Sloan purposely tried to provoke him, and Liam took that as a sign he was worried and wanted Liam out of the way.

He walked along the wharf, the water lapping at the sea wall, adrenaline still raging through his body as he wondered what he should do next. Speaking to Mainwood would be the logical call, though he imagined Sloan was warning the young man as he spoke.

Time felt as if it were at a premium. It was inevitable that sooner or later the call would come telling them that Peter Britten's body had been discovered, drowned. The other deaths – Eleanor Cooper, Marlon Tomlinson, the members of the OCG – had seemed out of his hands, but with Peter he felt a direct responsibility. Every time he thought about him, he was taken back to his time in the Indian Ocean. He couldn't bear the thought of someone else drowning in those horrific circumstances.

He'd seen up close where the man had lived, and what had subsequently become of him. Like Liam's mother, Peter was a victim of his addictions. But unlike her, Liam had the chance to save Peter. Worse, he'd already had the opportunity to save him. Even now, he pictured Peter cowering within the house in Gwithian, as Liam spoke to Stacey outside. If only he'd been more forceful, then Peter would be home and safe.

Liam passed the lifeboat station, walking on autopilot through Pednolva Walk towards the railway station where he'd parked. He felt that he'd gone back to the beginning in speaking to Sloan, so decided he would retrace his steps from the start, meaning his next stop was out towards Praa Sands and another meeting with Justin Blake.

He tried to turn his doubts about the investigation on their head as he drove towards Blake's home prison. The electric tag on Blake's ankle prevented him from being beyond a fifty-foot radius of the house. Any further, and the authorities would be notified. Sloan's mention of Millie still lingered in Liam's mind, as did the lurid grin on the drug dealer's face when he'd pointed his phone camera at him. It was hard not to fixate, and Liam glanced at the clock on his car dashboard again, annoyed that it wasn't yet time for school to end so he could speak to Millie.

Praa Sands was somewhere Liam had frequented as a boy, though the surf was hit and miss and he'd only visited when positive reports came in. Blake lived further inland, the roads pleasingly deserted as Liam made good time to the isolated wooden shack close to the disused farm.

Differing scenarios played through Liam's mind as he left the car. Blake had been found carrying the fentanyl and had admitted to meeting the man they now knew as Edward Turnbull. It was feasible that Blake had a greater role to play – he'd been in St Ives looking for Sloan – and at the very least, Liam was sure the man still had some secrets he'd yet to share.

'What now?' said Blake, his face falling as he answered the door. He was dressed in boxer shorts and T-shirt, and the electric tag was visible, snug against his left ankle.

'Just your friendly police visit. May I come in?'

Blake knew better than to put up a protest, turning and wordlessly heading inside the darkened house.

'Jesus Christ, Blake, let's crack a window, shall we?' said Liam, holding his breath as he opened the curtains in the living room and jimmied open the window. The room stank of body odour and weed. 'You alone this time?'

'Yes.'

'Are you holding anything, Justin?'

'I'm not stupid, DS Kilshaw.'

'Our understanding of stupid must differ. You absolutely reek of the stuff. If I find any, it's a breach of your terms. Your next stop will be at His Majesty's pleasure, and there'll be no PlayStations there.' Liam glanced at the television, where animated characters were playing football against one another.

Blake collapsed on a battered black sofa, rifling inside a box to his side. For one incredible second, Liam thought he was about to light up a spliff only for the man to produce some tissues which he proceeded to blow his nose into. 'Hay fever,' said Blake.

'Is that so. Even with you all safely locked up inside?'

'I can get about ten yards into the back garden.'

'For now,' said Liam, letting the threat sink in. 'I need your help, Justin.'

'I've already given you my help.'

'And that is why you're here and not inside. But I have people dying left, right and centre, and I've yet to find Peter Britten. You heard what happened in Penzance.'

'I heard about those murders,' said Blake, wiping his nose.

'You know the victims, Gary French, and Malcolm Ure?'

Blake shook his head, but there was no conviction in the gesture.

'How about this woman?' asked Liam, showing Blake the e-fit of Stacey Smith.

'Sorry, can't help you.'

Liam nodded. 'I think we could be in for a long day, Justin. Sit back, we're going through this from day one.'

'When was day one?'

'You tell me.'

Liam had learnt during the time Blake had been his informant that the best approach was to wait and let him talk. That was always easier said than done, as his last few encounters with him had proven. But they were alone now, Blake unable to leave the house, and if it took the rest of the day, then Liam was prepared to wait.

It took some time, but Blake came to understand. He fidgeted as the silence between them grew, and eventually, he started to speak.

In another life, Blake could have made a success of his talents. He was a people person, and from what he was telling Liam there didn't seem to be anyone in Cornwall's grubby underworld he didn't know. He relayed to Liam many of things he already knew, but Liam could tell he was holding something back.

'How long have you known Turnbull for?' asked Liam.

'I had heard of him. Knew he'd done a stretch. But it was like he appeared on the scene out of nowhere.'

'Yet, you took his bag of fentanyl without question?'

'A man's got to eat, Mr Kilshaw. Anyway, he knew who I was.'

'He sought you out?'

'My reputation precedes me.'

'So who do you think he was working for?'

'I don't know, and I don't care.'

'How did Sloan take to all this?'

'What does he care? I buy hash off him. It's not as if I was trying to set up a rival business or anything.'

Blake sounded defensive and Liam decided to push him harder. 'That day I saw you, by Sloan's place, that's when it started for you. Did Sloan give you the fentanyl?'

There was panic in Blake's voice. 'No, I already told you.'

'But Sloan introduced you. Told Turnbull you were the sort of guy who could help shift the gear.'

Blake shook his head.

'That you could help start an epidemic.'

'Come on, Mr Kilshaw.'

'You come on, Justin. You more than anyone know what this shit can do.'

'I'm a fucking addict. What do you expect me to do?'

'These people don't care about you, Justin. The fact that there are so many dead bodies to contend with should alert you to that fact.'

'I'm paying the price now, so what does it matter?'

'I need to know who is behind all of this. I know Sloan and obviously Turnbull are involved, but who is in charge? Who is behind all these killings?'

'I don't know, Mr Kilshaw, I promise.'

'I can make this all disappear,' said Liam, pointing to the electric tag. 'You know that. You help me, and we can put this to rest. You're still young, Justin, you can turn your life around.'

Blake snorted. 'Honestly, I don't know any more. All I say is that I got the impression that there are a lot of them. I heard Sloan talking one day on the phone, and he kept using these code-names. It was like he was in the army or something.'

Liam rubbed his hands through his hair. 'What names, Justin?' he asked, the mention of the army alerting him.

'I don't know, he was mentioning names like Sergeant, Corporal, Captain, that sort of thing.'

'Those were the names he was using. Or did they have other names? Sergeant Kilshaw, that sort of thing?'

'No, just singular names. Sergeant, Captain. The only one I heard that was different was the Commander. Sloan said the name as if he was in awe. Or scared. Or both. I noted it because he didn't just say Commander. He said *the* Commander.'

Liam collapsed back in the chair in disbelief, recalling when he'd heard that name before.

Chapter Thirty-Seven

Liam was glad to see a text message from Millie when he left Blake's house. He'd warned Blake not to make contact with anyone, and was still reeling from what he'd been told.

Coincidences happened all of the time. In the past, Liam had been sent down the wrong line of enquiry because of them. He knew the same could happen here.

He had a hollow feeling in his chest. He hoped he wasn't right, but as he headed back inland towards Penzance, he felt that there was an air of an inevitability to events. He cursed himself for having missed something that now seemed obvious.

It was Billy Rowson who had called Miles Fischer 'Commander' instead of coxswain the night they had found Marlon Tomlinson's body. Both Liam and Fischer had laughed the comment off, putting it down to the excitement and inexperience of the young man's first proper voyage with the lifeboat. Maybe if it had been Wayne Mainwood who had made the mistake that evening, Liam would have picked up on it before and made the connection. As it was, it still felt incredible. He'd known Fischer ever since he'd returned to Cornwall. They'd bonded over their connections to the navy and it was painful, and embarrassing, to think all that had been a lie.

But worse, Liam had shared confidences with the man. Fischer was the one who had encouraged Liam to enlist with the RNLI, to take baby steps on the boats and water as a form of exposure therapy. More than anyone, Fischer knew the full extent of Liam's fears. The thought that he had a role to play in all of this sickened Liam to his stomach.

'Don't get ahead of yourself,' said Liam, out loud, as he took the Newtown roundabout towards Hayle. It was 9.30 p.m. His first instinct had been to go and see Fischer, but if his colleague from the lifeboat was involved, was in fact the Commander, then that could be a perilous mistake.

Instead, he drove back home, needing time to think before he shared his thoughts with Maya and the rest of the team. He kept telling himself that coincidences happened, and he didn't want to look foolish following up on one without something a little more concrete.

He drove the back roads to St Ives in a fugue as his mind played with the idea of Fischer being behind everything that had happened. Like Sloan, Summers and Turnbull, he was ex-military, though not from the light infantry like the other three. He had an exemplary knowledge of the sea which would have aided him in the drownings, and the murder of the six OCG members. But why would he do this? And why had he drowned Eleanor Cooper and Marlon Tomlinson – two apparently innocent bystanders?

The rain returned as he parked up, then took the steps to his flat, rubbing the rain from his scalp as he opened the front door. He made himself tea, and sat on his sofa switching on the late-night local news as he played through his mind every interaction he'd ever had with Fischer, trying to recall something he may have missed at the time, anything that would suggest Fischer was involved. The only thing that came to mind was the other week when Fischer had warned him off Sloan. At the time, Liam had thought how vehement Fischer had sounded, but now it seemed more than feasible that he had simply been protecting one of his subordinates.

Had the clues been there all along?

Liam couldn't recall anything that had seemed out of the ordinary. He had to wonder if that was because Fischer had hidden them so well, or if Liam hadn't wanted to see what was in front of his eyes.

Fischer had been a tough but fair leader at the lifeboat station. The work they did had always been a source of great pride to the man. Liam had been with him on numerous occasions when they'd saved lives and had seen the relief and happiness it had given him. Did that mean he couldn't also be running some kind of competing drug ring? No. Did it mean Fischer couldn't also be responsible for the cold and prolonged deaths of so many people? That, Liam wasn't so sure about. He'd met killers before, both in conflict and during his time in the police. Some of those had killed because of circumstances, others from various pathologies unique to them. Liam didn't want to believe that Fischer had such tendencies for various reasons. One, he didn't want to admit that Fischer had hoodwinked him from the beginning. But more importantly, Fischer was his friend and he didn't want that friendship to have been a lie.

But that was a concern for a different time. It was late, but there was still work he could do. He booted up his laptop and accessed the police database.

A quick search on Miles Fischer came up blank for any criminal record, though he was on the electoral roll showing him at the same address for the last fifteen years, prior to which he'd lived in Bognor Regis.

If it had been office hours, Liam would have called one of his contacts in the navy for Fischer's record but that was for tomorrow. There were other ways of finding out details of someone, though those avenues were soon exhausted when he found out Fischer had no social media accounts beyond his occasional admin role for the lifeboat centre.

Liam stared at the laptop, resting his chin on his hand. His stomach was empty, and his throat felt dry.

What was he really looking for here? Evidence that Fischer was guilty? Or evidence that his long-time friend was innocent?

The only real way to find out was to bring Fischer in, and Liam knew whatever happened subsequently would drive a wedge between them which they would never recover from. But that couldn't be helped.

He ran more searches on Fischer, adding various terms – navy, armed forces, drugs, fentanyl, drowning – to the filters. When nothing was apparent, he turned his attention to online newspaper archives. Matters were not helped by another man named Nathaniel Fischer, a minor celebrity who had worked on a TV drama as a member of the SAS, who dominated the majority of the search results.

Having exhausted all the searches, Liam ran two more. One with the addition of Cornwall, and the other Bognor Regis.

It was the second of the two that revealed the story Liam had been half hoping not to find:

Mother and Daughter Drown off Coast

The story was from fifty-five years ago. Fischer would have been ten years old.

Liam wouldn't have found it if he hadn't scrolled through pages of text to an old article in the *Bognor Times*. Now he had the basics, he extended the search to find more details.

Lilly-May Fischer, aged thirty-five, and Mabel Fischer, aged three, had died during a freak storm when they'd been out on the family dinghy off the coast of Bognor. They had been with Gerald

Fischer, who at the time of the story was in intensive care, and Miles Fischer, aged nine, who was injured but had survived.

Further results, focused on the local paper database, revealed that Gerald had subsequently died, meaning Miles Fischer had survived his whole family dying at sea; a connection between him and Fischer that Liam was unable to ignore.

Fischer had always been cagey about his family. He'd told Liam he was an only child and that his parents had passed on, and nothing about it had sounded out of the ordinary. Fischer was in his sixties, and the story had rung true.

Liam sat back and practised his breathing exercises.

As his heart rate slowed, and the tightness in his chest eased, he thought back to the times he'd shared his own personal tragedy with Fischer. It seemed unbelievable that the man had looked him straight in the eye, full of empathy, as Liam had told him about almost drowning in the Indian Ocean, and the comrades he'd lost, when Fischer himself had endured something so similar. Was this why Fischer had taken him under his wing, had insisted he continue with the lifeboat station despite Liam's terror of the open water? Was it comradeship from a shared sense of tragedy, or was there something more sinister at play?

Liam was no psychologist, but it seemed the deaths of Fischer's family had triggered something in the man. It was possible the trauma had lain dormant all these years, or may have manifested during his career in the navy, but it appeared Fischer had most likely witnessed his mother and sister drown, and it seemed he had in his own disturbed way begun to recreate that memory with victims of his own.

Liam checked the time, surprised to see it was after 1 a.m. Fischer's troubled history, combined with the revelation about his code-name, the Commander, were both strong indicators that he was involved in the drownings and the drug activity in the county.

But they were both circumstantial pieces of evidence, and although it was enough to bring Fischer in for questioning, it probably wasn't sufficient justification to go to his house in the middle of the night.

But if Fischer had killed Eleanor and Marlon, then what did that mean for Peter? By tomorrow morning it could all be too late. Liam wanted to be wrong, but he couldn't square Fischer's involvement and decided he had to pay a visit to the man he'd thought was his friend.

Chapter Thirty-Eight

Peter had been asleep, but now the commotion from inside the house woke him. It had been a pleasant dream, the one of him and his parents from so many years ago. He tried to focus on the image of himself as a child, walking hand in hand with his mum and dad. The remembrance filled him with such a deep melancholy that he couldn't think about it any more, his attention turning to the noises from the other rooms.

There were so many people shouting that he couldn't make any sense of the noise. He was disorientated from his sleep and had no idea what time it was, though it was still dark outside. Eventually, a single voice broke through the mayhem, shouting out, 'Quiet.'

It was enough for the whole building to fall silent. The speaker was the same voice he'd heard before. Who it belonged to, he wasn't sure. It was a rich baritone; even in the one word 'quiet', Peter heard the lilt of the man's Cornish accent. The eerie silence was proof, if any were needed, that the man had complete control over the gang, and therefore over Peter's future.

Part of him just wanted it finished. All he feared was the pain. Peter had experienced pain before. He'd been bullied as a child and bullied as an adult, suffering the occasional kicking, usually from young men after closing time with nothing better to do. That he could deal with, but the merciless way he'd seen Stacey dispatch the two men filled him with such dread that it made him want to cling to what was left of his life.

He came close to screaming as the door was flung open and Stacey appeared in the doorway, as if she could hear his thoughts. 'We need to go,' she said.

'Go where?'

'Get up.'

Peter tried to do as he was told but his legs were unsteady. His enforced sobriety was having a negative impact on him. Mentally, it made everything feel a little too real. Physically, he knew his body was going through some kind of detox process. The ache in his muscles and joints, the flash of pain in his kidneys, suggested to Peter that his body missed the poison he was used to pumping through it. And as punishment, it didn't want him to stand up straight.

'I don't have time for this,' said Stacey, hauling him to his feet. She kept her hands on him for a few seconds, holding him in place as if she feared he would topple over.

Peter tried to make eye contact, but she avoided his gaze. Had her kindness been an act? He understood she'd been playing a part from the beginning in order to gain access to his home and life, but Peter was sure he had seen some compassion in her. He'd thought she liked him, even after she had violently dispatched them, but the compassion seemed to have gone as she led him out of his prison.

Peter recognised some of the people in the outer room – Martin Sloan in particular. He was a low-level criminal type who liked to sell drugs to teenagers.

Everyone was busy, carrying bags and cleaning surfaces.

'On the boat.'

Peter looked over at the source of the voice, the thick accent the same as the one he'd heard a minute ago telling everyone to be quiet. The man looked familiar but Peter couldn't place him. Tall and stocky, he had a presence that was unsettling.

'Won't be long now, Peter,' said the man, his face unreadable as he left the house.

◆ ◆ ◆

Whatever Liam's relationship was with the man, if Fischer was truly linked to – or even the brains behind – the OCG, then he had to be considered dangerous.

Liam emailed links to the articles he'd found online to Maya, and made a call to the night shift in Bodmin telling them of his plans. A young officer answered, and asked if he needed backup, which Liam declined. He would request it if needed, but for now he just wanted to see where Fischer was holed up and what, if anything, was happening.

He stopped at an all-night petrol station before setting off to the address he had for Fischer in Lelant. He didn't know what to expect – most likely a house with its lights switched off – but wanted to be prepared in case he decided to stake the place out for the night. The man at the station barely acknowledged him as he placed his snacks and drinks on the counter, and Liam completed the transaction in silence before stepping out into the lukewarm night.

As he drove to Fischer's house, he thought back to the newspaper reports of Fischer's family dying out to sea. As well as the incident with the SBS, he acknowledged the parallels with his own father's death, albeit that had been during conflict and not a freak accident. He still felt a sharp pain as he recalled the day he'd been told by his mother. He'd smelt something sweet on her breath then as she'd sat him down and told him what had happened. She'd been sure to tell him that his father was a hero, and had died protecting them, but even then, before the drinking had taken hold and eventually destroyed her, he'd seen something in her eyes suggesting she didn't quite believe, or at least accept, that his death was anything but meaningless.

Was it any wonder Fischer had turned out the way he had? Liam still hadn't come to terms with his own father's death, and his mother had been ruined by it. But they hadn't been there to witness it.

Fischer had watched his mother and sister die, had seen his father almost drown before eventually losing him too. How that had affected the young Fischer, Liam could only imagine. Had he joined the navy as a means to make sense of what had happened? The newspaper reports hadn't gone into detail about the events of that day, but it made some kind of sense that Fischer had enlisted to face his fears, to expunge the tragedy that had destroyed his life. Was it in the navy he'd developed the desire to kill? Or had that seed been planted the day his family were thrown overboard?

There but for the grace of God, thought Liam. He'd been angry after the accident with the SBS. Angry with the organisation he felt had let him down, and angry with himself for his own perceived inadequacies, for his newfound fear of the one thing that had always made him happy. He'd been fortunate he'd had the right help, had got himself on the right mental path where he was able to channel his frustration and fears into doing something good.

But he was getting ahead of himself – making presumptions that were unforgivable in his line of work. Yet, he still couldn't shift the thought of the young Miles Fischer on the boat, watching his family drown.

He blinked away another memory that threatened to return as he reached Lelant. His chest tightened as he thought back to the night he'd been trapped underwater, and he could swear he could taste salt on his lips as from nowhere a large object bounced on the bonnet of his car.

Liam's advanced driving training kicked in as he applied the brakes rather than coming to an emergency stop and risk losing control. When the car came to a stop, he switched off the engine, letting out a deep breath which morphed into a laugh as the adrenaline surged through his bloodstream.

The object must have been a deer; he'd heard of such encounters before. He left the car to see if there was any sign of the animal. His heart was rocketing as he walked back to the corner where the collision had taken place. He crossed the road, walking thirty or so feet into the woodland, but there was no sign of a deer. It was as if it had used his car as a trampoline to cross the road, and Liam hoped it hadn't damaged itself in the process.

He returned to the car, shining his torch over the small dents in the bonnet, shaking his head at his luck. Had he been going at a different speed, the deer could have gone straight through the windscreen, which would have changed matters dramatically. Maybe he should have taken it as a sign, but he was only minutes from Fischer's address now, so he started the car again and continued, slowing as he approached the turning for the property.

Fischer had always been a great organiser. He held a number of fundraising events for the lifeboat centre, and was always the first to get involved when there were any social events. But Liam – now he thought about it – had never visited the man's house. He couldn't think of anyone who had. The satnav showed the property was another four hundred yards down the isolated lane. It was difficult to make out on his phone, but it was possible the house led down to the sea or estuary, a proximity to the water Fischer had never alluded to before.

He parked further along the road, taking another quick look at the dents on the bonnet, before walking the darkened lane towards

Fischer's house. He'd put on his utility belt before leaving, the essentials of torch, pepper spray and extendable baton, which felt inadequate in comparison to the firearms he'd carried as a marine and in the SBS.

It was lightly raining but warm. He kept close to the hedges barricading the lane, the only light from the moon and stars. Halfway down, he risked a look at his phone which showed Fischer's house to be a further two hundred yards along. The lane was narrower by this point, barely wide enough to fit a vehicle down it. Liam trod carefully, as if the sound of his feet on the loose gravel could alert Fischer to his presence.

He stopped at a small wooden gate with the name Seaview Cottage painted on it. A tight pathway led to a bungalow-styled cottage. Liam peered around the corner so he could get a better look. The cottage was swamped in darkness but he could make out the shape of a light sensor on the back of the building that he risked triggering should he walk nearer.

It didn't feel like that much of a risk. He imagined wildlife triggered the device all the time, and it seemed unlikely that Fischer would come to the window every time the light went on. Still, there didn't seem the need to risk it now and instead he continued down the lane.

The sound of the sea accompanied him through the darkness. It was at once comforting and unnerving, as if a giant wall of water awaited him at the end of the lane. Soon he was walking on sprinkles of sand as the gravel lane gave way to a small sand dune and the water became visible, in the distance the sight of a large powerboat tied to a jetty, with people moving silently on board.

Liam retreated up the lane and took out his phone. He was about to call headquarters when he heard movement behind him. 'I'd drop that if I were you,' said a familiar voice.

Chapter Thirty-Nine

The voice belonged to Billy Rowson, the young lad who had called Fischer 'Commander' on the night they'd fished Marlon Tomlinson from the water. He was standing fifteen yards away from Liam, a gun in his right hand pointed directly at Liam's chest.

Liam had faced guns before, and it was clear from his stance that Rowson either had experience or had been practising. His body was balanced, the gun steady in his hand. Liam had only known the lad a few months, but was disappointed he hadn't uncovered this side to him before. He'd seen him in conversation with Mainwood in the past but hadn't thought much of it. They were of similar age and outlook. Liam wondered how many other members of the crew were involved.

He lifted his hands in the air.

'Throw your phone over here. Slowly,' said Rowson.

Liam took a deep breath, the sea air filling his lungs, before reaching into his pocket. Rowson was too far away for the pepper spray to reach him, and the extendable baton was no match for a firearm. For now, he had no choice. He took out the phone and slid it across the ground.

It landed five yards away from Rowson, who didn't take his eyes off Liam as he took out a hand-held radio and requested backup.

'What the hell are you playing at, Billy?' said Liam, his hands still in the air.

'You shouldn't have come here.'

'Fischer is a troubled man. He manipulates people,' said Liam, thinking about how he too had been duped. 'Drop the gun and we can get out of here. You're young. Help me now and we will work something out.'

'What the hell?'

Liam lowered his eyes as Wayne Mainwood appeared, also carrying a firearm. 'Liam . . . I mean, DS Kilshaw. What brings you here?' he said.

Of the two, Mainwood appeared the more belligerent. Maybe it was his recent run-in with the law, or because of some perceived sense of seniority within his organisation, but he appeared more relaxed, amused even, by Liam being there.

'We need to cuff him,' said Rowson.

'Hear that, policeman? On your knees.'

During an operation in Afghanistan, Liam had been detained by a small militia group, who had stripped and cuffed him as part of their interrogation. He'd spent many hours training for such an event, enduring a similar ordeal albeit under controlled circumstances, but the actuality of it had been something different. Although he'd thought he was likely to die at the time, the training had eventually kicked in, and thirty-six hours later he'd been rescued. This was child's play in comparison, but he knew he wasn't any safer. If anything, Fischer and his gang were less predictable and they were more than capable of killing him.

He dropped to his knees, Rowson swivelling to the side so the gun was still pointed to his chest, as Mainwood put his knee into Liam's back and forced him to the ground, sand grinding into his cheek.

'There you go,' said Mainwood, pulling the zip-ties tight against Liam's wrists and hauling him to his feet. 'Better take him to the Commander.'

Liam put up no struggle as the pair dragged him towards the jetty, noting that Rowson had left his mobile phone where Liam had thrown it.

He heard the engines start as the boat came into view. In the darkness, he could make out the vague outlines of three other people, a fourth materialising as he reached the boat – a motor yacht with a dinghy attached to the rear – a bearded man carrying an automatic rifle over his shoulder, who didn't even glance over as Liam was ushered to the rear of the vessel.

'Loosen these,' he said to Mainwood. Rowson opened a small hatch to the rear of the boat.

'Can't loosen zip-ties, DS Kilshaw, you know that. Probably won't make any difference soon,' said Mainwood, shoving him through the opening.

Liam staggered forward, his head careering towards the side of the boat, when a hand was held out to stop him. 'Peter?' said Liam, glancing at the man with his back to the wall.

'You know my name?'

'Believe it or not, I'm here to save you.'

The boat began to move a few minutes after the policeman had been restrained beside him. They were both crouched down in a sitting position. Peter's hands were bound in front of him; the policeman's behind his back.

The policeman had introduced himself as DS Kilshaw, but he told Peter to call him Liam.

Liam was a strapping lad with a gleaming, hairless skull. He was clearly cramped in the small space but didn't appear to let their situation get him down. He kept issuing positive messages, assuring Peter that things would be all right. Which, considering their current situation, seemed optimistic at best.

'I came to your house recently,' said Liam. 'You heard about the young lad who was found at sea? Marlon Tomlinson?'

'No,' said Peter. 'But I think I remember you. Stacey answered the door. Things went a bit strange after that.'

'That's right. Stacey Smith. She said she was your niece.'

'Some niece,' said Peter, explaining as best he could the circumstances that had led to Gary French, Malcolm Ure and Stacey taking over his life.

'They call it cuckooing,' said Liam, after he'd finished.

Peter nodded, understanding the comparison with the predatory birds who would lay their eggs in other birds' nests. 'Of all of them, she was the kindest.'

'Stacey?'

'Yes, until . . .'

'You were there that night, I think. In Penzance. I saw you leave with her in the black van.'

'That's right.'

'You saw what happened to Gary and Malcolm?'

Peter closed his eyes, surprised to feel they were damp. 'She killed them. Brutal, relentless, like nothing I've seen before.'

'This is a tough question, but why do you think she kept you alive?'

Peter shrugged. 'Those men were not nice. To me or her. At the time, I thought she'd just had enough of them. But now . . . I've been hearing things. I don't know what it all means but it sounds to me like they think they're all in the army. My dad was in the army. Second World War.'

'Is that so, Peter. What things did you hear?'

'They talked about me. Said something about me being a bargaining chip. They call me the Stowaway.'

The boat jostled, shaking from side from side.

'Exiting the estuary,' said Liam, by way of explanation.

'Where do you think we are going?'

Liam let out a sigh. 'Nowhere good,' he said.

Peter was more responsive as a companion than Liam had anticipated. From all his discussions with those who knew the man, he had expected someone monosyllabic who wouldn't make eye contact. But Peter was quite eloquent when he wanted to be. And although he occasionally drifted to his internal thoughts, in particular following references to his departed parents, Liam had been able to gleam some information from his fellow captive.

Peter had confirmed they were dealing with a group with military links, repeating some of the ranks – Corporal, Sergeant – Blake had mentioned. He'd seen the Commander, and described a man similar in looks to Fischer, with a deep, guttural Cornish accent.

The journey was relatively smooth, the boat's engines not being tested to their limits. Liam called on his years of training as he waited for the boat to come to a halt, and for the door to their hatch to open. He tried not to focus on what could happen, the watery grave that was possibly waiting for him, and tried to formulate some sort of plan. The back of his mind kept showing him images of George, and Millie, and though it pained him to do so he was able to rationalise that at least George would have a father figure in his life in Mark, should Liam die, and that although Millie would be upset, they were very early into their relationship.

He shook the thoughts away, focusing again on the matter in hand. He'd searched every inch of their little hellhole during the voyage but hadn't found anything to use as a weapon, not that it would have made any difference with his hands tied behind his back.

None of it really mattered. It would all come down to Fischer, and what, if any, compassion he had for Liam.

They had been travelling for over an hour when the boat began to slow. Being within the hold had stalled most of Liam's fears about being out in the open water, as had Peter's proximity. He was here to save the man, and focusing on that goal helped him, but as the boat slowed further, the familiar pain in his chest returned and he struggle to breathe.

'Everything OK?' asked Peter.

Liam nodded. He deployed his breathing exercises as he tried to banish the thoughts of what Fischer might have in store for him. The engine of the boat was still idling when they both caught the sound of another engine in the distance.

'Does anyone know you're here?' Peter asked, his voice light with momentary optimism.

Liam thought back to his phone that had been left back by the dunes. It felt unlikely, given how early it was, that anyone had tried contacting him in the last hour or so, but it couldn't be ruled out. But even if a police boat had tracked them, they wouldn't be armed, and it appeared that Fischer had a small militia in support of him.

Peter started rocking as they heard voices on deck. The man was holding up surprisingly well considering what he'd endured. He appeared to be sober, and Liam wondered how long that had been the case, as from what he'd been told it wasn't something anyone could remember happening in the past.

Again, Liam's mind travelled to unwanted territory. He thought about what his mother would have been like had she not succumbed to her addictions, his mind going to that distant memory of the three of them by the sea when his father had been alive, when his mother was smiling and loving.

More raised voices roused him from his reverie. Even with the rumble of the two engines, he heard the urgency in the voices. In his mind's eye, he pictured Wayne Mainwood and Billy Rowson pointing their guns at unarmed officers. If it was the police on the other boat, it would most likely be the same ones who had taken him to Ralph's Cupboard the other day, and he could only hope that Fischer didn't do something stupid.

He snuck a glance at Peter who was still rocking himself when the voices stopped and everything went silent beyond the hum of the engines and the lapping of the water against the hull of the ship.

Liam barely had time to think about the lull before the storm, when one of the two groups above them began firing.

Chapter Forty

The sound of guns firing stopped Peter rocking. He'd been focusing on better times, fearful of what was to come. Liam had shuffled over to him, pushing his head down, as a second round of bullets rang out from above.

Could it be too much to hope that this was a rescue attempt? Peter knew sometimes police were allowed guns. Maybe they'd worked out where Liam was and had come to his rescue.

'Are we going to be OK?' he asked the policeman.

'Whatever you do, try to follow my lead,' said Liam, being far too cryptic as silence descended once more.

◆ ◆ ◆

The engines from both boats had been cut. Liam listened for movement on deck but could hear little beyond the occasional shuffled conversation. Peter was in a trance. The rocking had stopped but it was as if he were staring right through Liam. He told Peter to follow his lead, but the words seemed to drift over him.

He looked desperately around the room, searching for something sharp to try to cut the zip-ties, but nothing was going to work. All he could hope for now was time. In a few hours, Maya would get his message and hopefully call or text. Sooner or later they would work out he was missing, and would track the phone to the area next to the jetty at Fischer's house. It wasn't the longest of shots, but there were a number of variables – the phone still having signal and power, Maya calling or texting as soon as she got up – not to mention the next stage which would be trying to locate them this far out to sea.

Peter murmured, shaking his head as if returning from a daze.

'You OK?' asked Liam.

'Yes, what's going on?' said Peter, as the hatch opened.

Wayne Mainwood shoved his head through the opening, waving a handgun towards them. 'Right, you need to get out,' he said.

Liam did his best to help Peter get to his feet, Mainwood grabbing hold of the old man and yanking him through the hatched opening, hitting his head in the process. 'Watch it,' said Liam. He'd half considered charging Mainwood at that point, but even if he'd been able to knock him over it wouldn't have done any good with his hands all but useless behind him.

Stay calm and a situation will present itself, Liam said to himself. But his resolution was fading as he was dragged to the deck, passing a number of other hatches within the hull.

It was still dark, but he could see the second boat hadn't arrived to rescue them. Lights from Fischer's boat shone on the craft opposite whose deck was decorated with the corpses of four men. Liam wondered if the bodies belonged to the remaining members of the OCG or if they were part of another element Liam hadn't considered.

Martin Sloan was waiting for them on the deck of their boat. 'Much better meeting under these circumstances, don't you think, DS Kilshaw?' he said, an MP5 sub-machine gun strapped to his chest.

'Bit of a change from selling pot to kids, Sloan,' said Liam, noting the smiles of Sloan's colleagues. As well as Sloan there was Mainwood, who was standing behind him, Billy Rowson, also holding an MP5, and an unknown fourth person who had crossed to the boat opposite.

'You should have left well alone,' said Sloan, trying to retain his authority.

'When do I get to speak to the organ grinder?' said Liam, eliciting further smiles.

Mainwood pushed him forward towards the front of the boat where Liam caught sight of movement within the bridge. 'Sit.'

Liam helped ease Peter on to the deck floor. 'It's OK,' Liam said, as he waited for the door to the cockpit to open. If there was to be a chance for them, it would be then, and a few minutes later, two people emerged.

Stacey Smith followed by Miles Fischer.

Fischer approached, his face stern as he bent on his haunches so he was face to face with Liam. 'You worked it out then?' he said, a slight curl to his lips.

'It took some time, but I got there.'

Fischer groaned and sat down opposite. 'What gave it away?'

Liam kept his eyes focused on Fischer, resisting the urge to look over at Billy Rowson, fearing that the revelation that Rowson calling Fischer 'Commander' was the clue would not end well for the young man. 'What can I say, I'm a great detective.'

'Not from where I'm looking.'

'They'll be coming for me, Fischer. Do yourself a favour and let us go. They know you're behind it.'

'I have no doubt but surely you don't think I haven't planned for such an eventuality. Everything is in place now,' said Fischer, nodding over to Mainwood and Rowson who were collecting bags from the unknown fourth crew member, as Sloan looked down at him smiling.

'Then you can let us go. We've gone through a lot together, Miles.' This close, Liam could see the streaks of grey in the man's beard. The last time he'd seen him, he was being questioned by Maya and Grace, so it wasn't only Liam that he'd fooled. The thought was of little comfort as the boat swayed in the water, Liam focusing on Fischer to avoid thinking about the depths beneath them.

'You've seen conflict, Liam. You know how this goes down.'

'This isn't conflict, and I've never killed innocent people before. It looks like you have the drugs, the money, and are competition free. You don't need us.'

'One less copper isn't going to hurt,' said Fischer with a grin, as he pushed himself to his feet.

Despite what was happening, it felt incongruous that the man who'd been his friend these last few years could be such a chameleon. Liam wasn't sure if it was the betrayal or the stupidity he felt for being duped that bothered him the most, but he knew he was running out of time. 'I lost my father at sea,' he said.

'Tell me something I don't know.'

'And I told you how that messed me up.'

'It certainly messed your mother up,' said Sloan, who'd been watching events unfold with a stupid grin on his face.

Fischer frowned at the interjection. 'And it was a very sad story, Liam.'

'It makes us the same,' said Liam, taking one final risk.

Fischer bent down to his haunches again, closer than before, close enough that Liam could smell the staleness of his breath, could have leant forward and rammed his forehead into the man's nose and done some lasting damage. Fischer's upper lip was quivering, the tendons on his neck pushing at his skin like miniature daggers. 'What did you say?'

'I know what happened to your family, Miles. The accident at sea, and what happened to your father afterwards. You should have told me. We could have helped each other.'

Fischer continued staring at him, nodding sarcastically. 'Oh right, is that so? One thing though . . .' he said, getting to his feet again.

He paused, looking around at his group of assembled soldiers who were now all listening, Stacey included. He pulled the handgun from his holster and pointed it at Liam, before turning quickly and shooting Martin Sloan in the stomach. 'It wasn't an accident.'

Chapter Forty-One

If the crew were shocked by what had just happened, they were hiding it well. It was obvious they were used to killing – as the corpses on the boat opposite proved – but Sloan was supposedly one of their own; a point the fallen drug dealer was trying to make with his pleading eyes, as he slumped to the ground, clutching his stomach.

'It's a shame really. He's probably not going to last long. Get him ready,' said Fischer.

Although there was a sense of inevitability about what was to happen next, Liam wanted answers. He needed to know what Fischer had meant about the deaths of his parents and sister not being an accident. But the more immediate concern was Sloan.

'Why did you do that, Fischer?' Liam asked, as Mainwood and Rowson ignored Sloan's pleas and bound his wrists and ankles, before strapping a metallic harness around his body.

'Mr Sloan can answer that, can't you, Martin? Why have I done this?'

Blood was pooling around Sloan, and his skin was now a deathly white. He didn't even try to answer. Probably hadn't heard the question.

'Quick,' said Fischer to the crew, sounding agitated.

Mainwood and Rowson wasted no time, attaching the harness to the anchor winch and holding Sloan over the side of the boat and letting go. Sloan dangled in the air, his body flapping like a fish. He locked eyes with Liam. He was shivering but he tried to speak, as if he were signalling to him.

'It came to my attention recently that Mr Sloan has been doing some very bad things,' said Fischer, without irony. He looked over to Stacey, who had been watching the scene unfold dispassionately. 'Come, see.'

Liam's stomach felt hollow, his quads groaning from effort as he pushed himself up until he was in a standing position. He ignored the periphery of his mind which threatened to return him to that time in deployment when he'd almost drowned. He stumbled to the side of the boat as Fischer pressed the button on the winch, Sloan flipped on to his front as he was lowered face down into the water.

Liam took in a deep breath but his attempts to overcome his panic weren't working. The pain in his chest was excruciating, as if he were in some kind of vice, the breath being squeezed out of him. It was taking all his strength to remain upright. He began the 54321 method, trying first to focus on five things he could see to help contain his mounting panic. But nothing was calming about what he could see: the sea, the boat opposite, Peter, the bright orange life ring, the dying Sloan being dangled into the water.

'He needs to get on his back, obviously, but this will be a small mercy for him,' said Fischer, watching with glee.

Was Sloan aware of what he was going through? thought Liam as he tried to latch on to four things he could hear. The sound of the lapping sea and Sloan's muffled screams weren't exactly comforting but the focus was helping him regain his composure. 'Is this what this is all about, Fischer? Some sick affinity with the sea? For drowning people?' said Liam, trying to ignore the thought that he was likely to be next as he thought of three things he could touch: the skin on his back, the rough material of the zip-ties, his smooth fingernails.

'You know, I've never really thought about it. Sends out a great message though, doesn't it? You always hear that saying that drowning is a peaceful way to die, but we both know the truth. And for those who doubt it, they soon find out.'

'But Eleanor Cooper and Marlon Tomlinson? What did that prove?'

'War always has its casualties, you know that, Liam. They were collateral damage. Diversionary tactics. Warnings to rivals,' said Fischer matter-of-factly, as if what he was saying wasn't as mad as hell.

How Fischer had hidden this side of himself was a mystery to Liam. He was a completely different person to the man Liam had known.

He guessed Fischer had the classic psychopathic traits of intelligence, manipulation and charisma. He'd hidden in plain sight – rescuing countless people from the sea when he obviously took great pleasure in watching people drown.

'Now,' said Fischer, nodding to Mainwood and Rowson, who winched Sloan back up from the water, until he was dangling in front of them once more.

Liam looked at the two young men, wondering how Fischer had brainwashed them, and what they thought about what was happening. He gestured over at the young woman called Stacey, who'd remained silent throughout, and Liam wondered what her role was in all of this.

Sloan made a strange, muted noise, his long black hair matted to his face. Again he looked mainly at Liam, either trying to tell him something, or pleading with him to help.

Two things to smell: the sea air, diesel fumes from the boat.

'Well done, Martin,' said Fischer, nodding to the two men who submerged Sloan once more.

'What are you trying to prove?' asked Liam.

Fischer was grinning again, watching Sloan floundering with ecstatic intensity. 'I guess that's for my biographer, or psychiatrist, to unravel.'

'And your mother and sister?'

Fischer lifted his hand up, as if he didn't want the moment to be disturbed. 'Lift him up again. I'll level with you, Liam,' he said, switching his attention back. 'That was opportunistic. Can't say I hadn't thought about it before. Can't say I hadn't done some very bad things up to that point. But it wasn't planned. At least not to begin with. We hit some rough sea, and the opportunity presented itself. To be fair, I just wanted to see what would happen. Again,' he bellowed.

One thing you can taste, thought Liam, his tongue rolling around in his mouth as he focused on his salt-tinged saliva.

This was the last time. Sloan stopped struggling for a few seconds after hitting the water. The two young men waited until Fischer gave them the nod before winching Sloan on to the deck and removing the harness.

'All over too quickly, don't you agree?' said Fischer, motioning that Mainwood and Rowson should dispose of the body.

Liam knew there was no point trying to reason with the man. 'What about her?' he asked, glancing over at Stacey, who was expressionless.

'Stacey is my very good business partner. She came to me with an offer I couldn't refuse. Unfortunately, that knowledge won't be much use to you where you're going.'

Liam felt his chest tighten in anticipation of what would soon happen. He sat back down with Peter who was staring blankly into the distance, as Mainwood and Rowson threw Sloan's body overboard before jumping over on to the second boat.

Peter looked away as the two men disposed of the bodies on board, the four corpses joining Sloan's in the sea, before starting the engines and motoring away.

The sun was rising, a fiery glow stretching across the surface of the water.

'Now, remember there are rules,' said Fischer, hauling first Peter then Liam up to their feet. 'Neither of you are directly involved in this, so I will show you both the same courtesy I showed the others.' He led them to the side of the boat, and produced a hunting knife from his pocket. Again his actions were so fast that Liam didn't have time to react as he cut the zip-ties on Peter's wrists, while Stacey powered up the boat.

'I'll be thinking about you,' he said, lifting Peter into the air and throwing him overboard.

'No,' screamed Liam, hovering over the side of the boat as Stacey began manoeuvring it away.

'And I'll be thinking about you,' said Fischer, placing the muzzle of a gun into Liam's back before snapping the zip-ties off with his other hand. 'Go get him then,' he said.

If the gun hadn't been in his back, Liam would have turned and fought, but already the boat was making distance between him and Peter. Liam stared at the water and forced his fears to the back of his mind, his focus on Peter, as he took a deep breath and slipped over the side into the icy water.

Chapter Forty-Two

The cold of the water momentarily jolted Peter out of his stupor. A pain spread in his chest and he couldn't breathe. He'd tried not to watch as the crew had drowned the drug dealer. He had focused on the darkness out in the water where he swore he could hear his parents calling him. He'd heard the man's pleas, the terrible sounds of Sloan sinking into the water, only to be retrieved, fished out like a strange sea creature, and then dunked again until he'd drowned.

Peter had guessed he would be next, but in many ways this was worse. He wasn't tied and bound like the drug dealer had been, and with the two boats disappearing from sight it meant his death would be delayed, that he would be given more time both to dwell on what was about to happen to him, and the mess he'd made of his life.

He held his breath and stuck his head beneath the water. The sun was rising but he couldn't see anything in the murky depths. He let out a breath and willed himself to sink. If he could drop far enough down then he could end all of this now.

The sea rushed his ears, the sound of his parents whispering to him, urging him on. He was an able swimmer though it had been many years since he'd last been in the sea.

He swivelled into a diving position and began to kick when something grabbed on to his ankle.

◆ ◆ ◆

Liam tried the 54321 technique again but all he could see, hear, feel, taste and smell was the rippling seawater.

He'd forgotten how to swim, how to move his limbs. This is what he'd been so scared about these last few years, this was what his subconscious had been warning about. He was flailing against the water, his panic greater than the time at the SBS. He wasn't even sinking, but he knew what lay in wait for him below the surface, the incredible pressure and impotent terror, the terrible darkness that would swallow him whole.

You are not sinking.

The thought eased his crazy movements for a second, and it was time enough to catch sight of Peter. In his own personal delirium, the man appeared to have manoeuvred himself into a diving position and had begun kicking, his body disappearing from sight.

Liam tried to rationalise his position. He was out here now and the only way to deal with the situation was face it head on. He thought about George, about his own childhood living with a father who had died at sea. It didn't rid him of his fear, but it gave him the courage to put his head into the murky water and swim towards the area where Peter had disappeared.

The thing he'd always loved about the sea was the way it cleared the mind. He used to go surfing so he could think about the next wave, and nothing else. But now his mind was awhirl with thoughts. He knew if he latched on to the wrong ones he would lose his sanity so he focused solely on rescuing Peter.

As part of his marine and SBS training, Liam had completed countless free-diving exercises. That had been several years ago now, but it was a muscle memory he would never forget. But he was still on the verge of panic, and was finding it difficult to compose himself, to ensure his breathing was right before he submerged.

A man is dying.

Liam accessed his years of training and experience. He focused on the moment, getting his breathing right, before launching himself downwards, his even breathing helping him sink, his body loose, dividing the water as he headed towards Peter.

The man must have been something of a swimmer in the past, as Liam could make out his figure below, dart like, still kicking as if diving for pearls. Liam ignored the recesses of his mind, telling him this was like last time. He fought against the pressure building in his chest, knowing that the merest acceptance of his panic would stop his descent. He had a duty to save Peter, and he would do that or die trying. Fear had to be an irrelevance.

He maintained his breathing, his movements that much stronger until he caught up with Peter and grabbed on to his ankle.

Liam was surprised as the man fought, kicking him away. It hadn't crossed his mind that Peter might be doing this on purpose, and he had to dive further until he could get a better hold on the man's torso. The movement had stopped both their momentums, and for a second it was as if they were stuck in position, caught in the directionless water.

And Liam was back in the Indian Ocean, his breathing apparatus failing. He kicked for the surface, only dimly aware that this time he had hold of someone else. Peter resisted to begin with but Liam had a firm hold of him now, using all the strength in his legs and his spare arm to push against the water.

The panic took hold of every part of his body, the water exerting an unbearable pressure. It was like wading through mud, his panicked mind informing him that he was going in the wrong direction, that his breath was about to run out.

The tightness became so acute around his chest that he was forced to let go of Peter. Liam propelled the man upwards, freeing himself so he could use his whole body to attack the water. He pulled at the sea – savage, desperate movements, that saw him jet upwards until he was level with Peter, who thankfully was now swimming towards the surface.

Liam could see the sunlight above and told himself that they would make it. He swam past Peter, desperate to breach the surface before his lungs gave out. Closing his eyes, he concentrated on his breathing, and with his last ounce of strength pulled himself through the water, his body on fire, as with a rush of cold air he broke through the surface.

He gasped, filling his lungs, making sense of the situation, before turning back towards the depths. He took another deep breath and returned into the sea, his lungs bursting as he grabbed on to Peter and guided him up.

They were both coughing and spluttering, making desperate breaths for air. Liam couldn't talk, putting his hands behind his head to help fill his lungs with air as his legs kept him afloat. Peter was still panicking, thrashing in the water. Liam went to him, his breathing approaching normal. 'You need to control your breathing, Peter. I've got you,' he said.

It wasn't the first time Liam had been dumped out at sea without any support. He and six other trainees had gone through a similar ordeal as part of SBS selection. Liam had spent hours out at sea then, only the vague hope that the instructors had to be close by helping him to survive the ordeal. He'd been the only one to complete that trial, and knew he could do so again, but not if Peter kept panicking.

'I've got you,' he said, pulling Peter on to his back. 'Stop fighting it. Let me keep you afloat for now, concentrate on your breathing.'

Liam was thankful that the man was like a bag of bones. He couldn't support him for ever, but had enough energy that he could keep them both afloat until Peter regained his composure and regular breathing.

Above them, the sun was getting stronger and mercifully the sea was still calm. Liam looked around but there was no sign of land in either direction, though the occasional seagull did hover into view.

'You can let go,' said Peter, after some time, surprising Liam by floating on his back. 'One thing I can do is swim.'

Liam floated away from him, and moved on to his back as well. 'As little movement as possible,' he said.

'I know.'

A dark part of Liam wondered if this was what he'd needed all along. He'd started with the lifeboat crew as a means of exposure therapy, but nothing had worked as well as the last few minutes. He was still scared, but something had changed since he'd rescued Peter. For now, Liam accepted his situation. He had Peter to think about, and that was enough to keep him focused.

Peter appeared calm which, considering recent events, was no mean feat. Liam watched him floating, impressed by the easy way he remained buoyant. His movements were minimal, effective. He clearly had an affinity with the water which would help them for now.

A greater concern was Peter's energy reserves, and – more acutely – the risk of hypothermia. It was early morning so the water temperature was a degree or two colder than it would be in the afternoon. Although their bodies had adjusted, Liam thought the temperature was between 14 and 16 degrees centigrade. There were no exact milestones for succumbing to hypothermia, but given his age and physical state, Liam doubted Peter would last the hour without suffering some symptoms. That was if he could remain afloat for that long.

It wasn't something he wanted to dwell on, but if nothing changed then he would have to face the possibility of hypothermia taking Peter. He felt well in himself for now, but he would have to contend with it himself at some point.

Unlike during the training exercises for the SBS, there were no deep-sea divers waiting out of reach to rescue them.

Was anyone out there to rescue them? They were at least an hour out to sea, but Liam couldn't work out where they were exactly. If he was to guess, he imagined they were west of Hayle in the Celtic Sea, part of the Atlantic Ocean. There were shipping lanes out that way, but it was a huge stretch of water, and even if they did see a vessel there would be no guarantee they would be spotted and saved.

At least they were alive for now. Fischer had left in a rush. He could have shot both of them. Liam had his theories for why that hadn't happened, and they didn't involve compassion. He'd only known this new side of the lifeboat director for the last few hours, but he was sure that wherever he was, he was getting some visceral pleasure from knowing Peter and Liam were out here alone in the watery wilderness, moments away from succumbing to the depths. No doubt that pleasure had been multiplied by knowing this was Liam's greatest fear. Liam wondered if that had been the plan all along; if Fischer had been waiting for the moment, to utilise everything he knew about Liam and maximise his suffering.

Liam shook the thought away. He focused on everything that mattered most in his life, finding that came down to two people: George, and – he was surprised to realise – Millie. There were others in his life – Kim, and Maya in particular who was a good friend – but it was George and Millie he held on to as he floated in the undulating water.

He hoped George would remember him fondly. He'd tried his best not to have messed the relationship up but knew he could have handled things differently, despite the outside influences. It was hard not to think that he'd been as much of an absentee father as his dad, and in truth he was really only George's dad in name. Mark had all but raised the boy, and George no doubt saw him as his true dad. Liam had mixed feelings about that, but was glad the boy would still have someone there for him.

As for Kim, she would continue to be there for George. Maybe if Liam had met her a decade later things would have worked out, but he wouldn't have wanted anyone else to be in charge of the boy's future.

He thought of his own mother as his head bobbed down into the water. His real wish was that George didn't come to resent him in the way Liam resented his mother. If Liam drowned now, the boy would no doubt suffer, but he hoped he would remember the good in him, and not dwell on the years he'd been absent.

'Peter, are you OK?' he asked, his head slipping into the water once more, the salt stinging his lips.

Peter was floating near to him, but Liam couldn't hear his response. Liam eased his legs into the sea and drifted over to the man who had started shivering. 'I can't feel my body,' said Peter, who was still managing to keep afloat.

Liam took some deep breaths, keeping his panic at bay. He'd known this moment was coming, but it had arrived too soon. Beyond supporting him when the hypothermia fully kicked in, there was nothing he could do for Peter. He wanted to scream out at the injustice, the weeks he'd spent trying to find him only for it to end like this, in the middle of the sea waiting to be swallowed up.

'Stay on your back, Peter, you'll be OK.'

'I don't know how much longer I can last.'

Liam floated around the man, watching his body become gripped by the cold, as if he were a puzzle he could unravel. On his SBS training, he'd done his best to support those who had been failing. But they'd all been hardened marines, not men in their seventies who'd had their lives ruined by addiction.

It changed without warning, Peter's shivering intensifying, the sound of his teeth chattering audible above the squawking of the seagulls, as he lost the ability to stay afloat. Liam grabbed hold of him, told him to go loose, and he held on to the rags of the man's body.

Again, it was something he'd done numerous times before in training. As long as hypothermia didn't come for him, then he could continue doing this for hours. But Peter didn't have that long.

Liam controlled his breathing, warding off the negativity in his head. He couldn't entertain any fears of slipping beneath the surface again. He refused to allow negative thoughts to take over, focusing on one second after the other, not giving into fears about what would happen when Peter finally succumbed to the hypothermia ripping through his body. He let the monotony wash over him, his ears attuned to Peter's breathing as he waited for the potential rescue.

The waves had started to pick up over these last few minutes which didn't make the job of keeping Peter afloat any easier. 'Keep still, retain your body heat,' he said, but he may as well have been talking to himself. Peter was in his own little world now, and if something didn't come for them soon, he would be forever.

Peter looked out to the horizon. He saw his parents. They hovered above the water, illuminated by the glow of the sun. Even though they were so far away, Peter could see them in perfect clarity. He laughed, thinking how young they looked – much younger than Peter himself – and how happy they appeared. They weren't so much beckoning him as patiently waiting. They looked so serene, so happy, that he couldn't wait any more. He began swimming towards them, the water dream-like as he cut through it like hot water on ice, only stopping when he heard his name being called out again and again.

It happened in a matter of seconds, Peter's shivering intensifying to a crescendo after he stopped moving. 'Peter, Peter,' called Liam, relieved to feel the weakest of pulses on the man's neck. 'Stay with me, Peter. Just a little longer,' he pleaded, as the sound of helicopter blades cutting the air reached his ears.

Chapter Forty-Three

Liam looked up to see the coastguard helicopter hovering into view. He knew there was no point waving – they could see his location and likely had binoculars set on them at that very moment. Liam had one job: keep Peter alive until he could be lifted to safety.

Exhaustion was setting in, though he imagined that was more a result of rescue being at hand than anything else. 'Peter, they're here, hold on,' he called into the man's ear, as one of the helicopter crew was lowered from the chopper.

He checked Peter's pulse again. It was weak but still there. Peter felt so cold, so insubstantial. He was shivering, the sensation otherworldly, as if every part of him was trembling all at once. 'Stay with me, Peter,' he demanded, as the line from the helicopter drew nearer.

It was an almost perfect day. The waves were a little bigger than before, but there wasn't much wind to distract the pilot or the rescuer, who was soon in sight.

Liam held on to Peter and, still on his back, swam to where the rescuer was hovering. 'DS Liam Kilshaw,' he called out, his words lost beneath the deafening roar of the propeller blades.

The rescuer signalled to Peter and the harness. Liam understood what was needed. He had done this countless times in training.

Within seconds he had Peter secured and was indicating for the crew to begin winching him to safety.

The rescuer pointed at him, but Liam shook his head. 'Take him up. Possible cardiac arrest,' he screamed, pointing to his chest.

The operative said something into his radio headset and began ascending, Peter connected to him by the harness.

Liam returned to his back, gently moving the water to keep himself afloat. He could feel the coldness now the adrenaline had left his body. His body tensing, he fought the urge to shiver in case it set him off. Instead, he started a light backstroke to maintain his body temperature. He could only imagine what it looked like from the pilot's perspective: two men ascending to the chopper while another was doing backstroke in the sea.

'Come on, Peter,' he mouthed, as he saw the pair reach the lip of the helicopter. He hoped it wasn't too late, that the team on the chopper could revive him.

As he waited for the operative to come to his rescue, he began to process everything that had just happened, from his kidnap at Fischer's house to the barbaric drowning of Martin Sloan. He tried not to dwell on how easily he had been duped by Fischer, searching for clues in their previous interactions that would have suggested a different side to his character. The only real indication he could come up with was Fischer's propensity to keep to himself when away from the lifeboat, but the same could be said about Liam. Sometimes the best way to hide was in plain sight, and although Fischer had fooled Liam all this time, Liam wasn't the only one to have fallen for his deception.

The cold was starting to take hold of him, and he increased the pace of his backstrokes. The excessive movement would have been a mistake were it not for the helicopter hovering above him. It made him realise how different his level of fitness was now compared to when he was in the SBS, and he promised himself he would increase his training when this was all over.

The line from the helicopter was released, the operative descending. Liam swam to meet him, his teeth chattering as a large wave lifted and dropped him back down, causing his head to slip under the surface.

'How is he?' he asked, shouting over the roar of the blades, but the operative either didn't hear or didn't want to answer.

Liam slipped inside the harness and secured himself before giving the thumbs up to the operative. Another wave pushed him into the air, and this time he kept going, the winch pulling him towards the chopper, the operative next to him in communication with the rest of the team, as Liam gazed down on the blanket of water, searching for the remains of Martin Sloan, and the four murdered men who'd been dispatched from the second boat.

He was pulled inside, the noise deafening as he looked over at Peter, who appeared to be alive, strapped to a gurney with an air mask over his mouth and nose, the on-board paramedic working on him.

Liam felt a warm hand on his scalp and turned to see the beaming smile of Maya.

'I think you dropped this,' she mouthed, holding out his phone.

◆ ◆ ◆

Liam hadn't realised how much he'd been shivering until Maya helped with his sodden clothes. The crew had towels and spare clothing, and wrapped Liam in a foil blanket as he waited for the heat to return to his body, Maya putting a headset on for him so he could speak. 'How is he?' said Liam, looking over at Peter.

'Weak pulse. But he was conscious when we got him on board. We're flying direct to Truro now,' said Maya.

Liam pulled the foil blanket tighter to him, willing heat back into this body. Below them St Michael's Mount came into view, surrounded by glistening turquoise sea. 'How far out were we?' he asked, having lost track of time.

'Four nautical miles from Hayle estuary. Only, we didn't know which direction you went in. Would have been handy if you'd kept your phone.'

'Martin Sloan,' said Liam, only now remembering to tell Maya what had happened. He explained briefly the events since late last night when he'd arrived at Fischer's house.

'You definitely saw Sloan die?' asked Maya.

'He shot him, then repeatedly drowned him. The body must be near where you collected me. And there will be four others.'

The helicopter was preparing for descent into the heliport next to the hospital. Liam reiterated that Fischer and Stacey had taken one boat with one unknown person, Mainwood and Billy Rowson the other.

'Were there any other people on board?'

'I'm sure of it. I didn't see the gunfight, but there had to have been others on board.'

'Turnbull and Summers?'

'Didn't see them. Have you . . .'

'We went to Summers' house this morning but he hasn't been seen since yesterday.'

'Have you checked on our friend, Justin Blake?'

Maya nodded. 'A team was sent over there,' she said, her voice distorted with static.

They landed, paramedics taking Peter from the helicopter. 'You too,' said Maya.

'I'm fine,' said Liam.

'You're blue.'

'We need to find Fischer.'

'Not until you've been looked over at the hospital. And that's an order, in case you were wondering.'

Liam left the helicopter with Maya, crouching to avoid the blades as he made his way opposite to the accident and emergency department where Peter was being looked after. The relative silence as the sound of the helicopter faded was a respite, Liam's ears ringing as he entered the hospital.

'What about Fischer?' asked Liam.

'Coastguard is aware. We have helicopters and boats out searching for him,' said Maya.

Liam wondered what was next for the man. A return to Cornwall was never going to work. Could Fischer run things from afar? It wasn't out of the realm of possibility. Fischer had created a mini militia which must have taken months, if not years, to bring to fruition. At that moment, they had no idea who the dead people from the second boat were, but it was more than likely they were the last of the OCG Fischer had seemingly been trying to purge from the county. 'You need to speak to Grace. Stacey Smith could be key to all of this. She was the one who infiltrated the OCG from London.'

'Let's get you checked first, shall we?' said Maya.

Liam was admitted as a priority. The doctors examined him for signs of hypothermia. Bloods were taken and he was wheeled into a private room to rest.

'This isn't necessary,' he said to Maya, from his bed.

'You've gone through a lot, Liam. You saved Peter, now rest up.'

'Keep me updated,' said Liam, feeling his eyelids drooping as he stifled a yawn.

'You've got it,' said Maya, smiling and fading out of sight as Liam fell asleep.

◆ ◆ ◆

He woke with a jolt an indeterminate time later, momentarily confused as to his location. His body ached, his limbs tight. Checking his watch, he was surprised to see he'd been asleep for hours, and more surprised that all he wanted to do was go back to sleep. He resisted that particular urge, and left the room to find the nearest toilet where he freshened up, only to find a uniformed officer waiting in the corridor for him.

'Has Maya got you watching me?' he asked the young officer.

'With everything that is happening, sir . . .'

'She tell you to inform her if I leave?'

'Sir. But I'm not here for that. You have a visitor. Wanted to check if you're up for seeing her,' said the officer.

'Her?'

'Rebecca Watson. Says you might know her as Becca.'

'Oh, OK, sure,' said Liam, wondering what Millie's friend was doing here, his curiosity soon turning to fear as he recalled Sloan mentioning Millie the other day. 'Send her through, quickly,' said Liam, going back to his room where he put on a spare set of clothes someone had left for him.

The door knocked, Liam opening it to see the worried face of Millie's teaching assistant. 'Where's Millie?' said Liam, bypassing any pleasantries.

'What? That's why I'm here.'

'You've lost me, Becca, what's going on? Where is Millie?'

'I thought you knew, Liam. You were the one who called the school to inform them she wasn't feeling well.'

Chapter Forty-Four

It was only as Liam left the hospital that he realised he didn't have his car, which presumably was still parked somewhere near Fischer's house in Lelant. 'You drove here?' asked Liam.

'Yes,' said Becca. 'It's over here.'

'Take me to Millie's house,' said Liam as, hand shaking, Becca started the car.

'What do you think has happened to her?'

Liam took a deep breath, fighting the resentment he felt towards Becca who'd been at the party in Penzance where the fentanyl had been discovered. It wasn't Becca's fault, but he needed somewhere to channel his frustration. 'I don't know. Can I borrow your phone?' he asked.

'Sure,' said Becca, glancing at the screen of the phone to unlock it before handing it over.

'Do you have a charger for this?' he said, waving his phone in the air.

Becca shook her head. 'Sorry.'

'You've tried calling Millie?' he asked.

'Countless times.'

Liam checked the list of recent calls, and saw the name Millie with the number 23 in brackets at the top of the list. He scrolled down, looking for any suspicious names before calling Millie.

The sound of her voicemail stopped him dead and he felt a cold shiver run through his body. He recalled Maya's number from memory, something he'd done for the majority of numbers on his phone. 'Maya, it's Liam, calling from Rebecca Watson's phone.'

'You haven't left the hospital, have you?' said Maya, the line distorted as if she were in the middle of a storm.

Liam told her about Millie's absence from the school. 'Someone pretending to be me must have called in this morning. Sloan knew about her, and Fischer had hinted that he suspected I was on to him. He could be using Millie as protection,' he said, his mind taunting him with images of Millie being dunked in and out of the sea.

'I'm out at sea with the boat service. We're trying to locate Martin Sloan and the others.'

'It's Fischer we should be trying to find,' snapped Liam.

'I told you, we have teams on the case. I'll call Hargreaves. I'll look into what's happened to Millie for you.'

'I can do that myself. I'm heading over to her place.'

'Liam, I'll send a team over now. You need to rest.'

'What if he's taken her?'

There was a pause, and for a second Liam thought he'd lost the signal. 'If you're on your way, I guess there's nothing I can do, but you should rest. I'll speak to headquarters now,' said Maya, waiting for a few seconds before finally hanging up.

Becca could barely look at him as she drove towards Millie's house. 'When was the last time you spoke to her?' asked Liam, trying to soften his tone.

'Yesterday at school. She talked about you. Said how well things were going between you. How it was becoming a bit weird teaching George.'

'She hasn't mentioned that to me,' said Liam.

'I shouldn't have said anything, sorry.'

'No, that's fine. So she seemed happy? Nothing worrying her at all.'

Becca shook her head. 'Definitely not. She was looking forward to seeing you this weekend.'

Though it was nice that Millie was feeling that way, it wasn't something he wanted to hear now. He kept picturing her in place of Martin Sloan in the metal harness being lowered into the sea for Fischer's sick pleasure, and knew he would never forgive himself if something happened to her.

'Tell me everything again from the beginning.'

Becca snuck a quick sideways glance at him before speaking. 'I was already in the classroom setting up when the receptionist came in and told me Millie wouldn't be in today. She said her boyfriend had called in and said she wasn't feeling well.'

'She used the word boyfriend?'

'Yes. I was a little surprised too as Millie had said yesterday that she wasn't seeing you until the weekend. I just thought you two had, you know, hooked up last night.'

'Millie doesn't often miss work, does she?'

'Never since I've been here.'

'That not ring any alarm bells?'

'No, there is a horrible bug going through the school. Loads of absences the last two weeks, staff included.'

Liam called Kim as they entered St Ives. His ex sounded surprised to hear from him. 'Everything OK?' she asked. 'This isn't your number.'

'All good. I just wanted to check in on George as I heard Millie wasn't in today. Some kind of bug going around?'

The line went silent, as if Kim was gathering her thoughts. 'Yes, that's right. George is fine, though. How do you know that, Liam? Did the school contact you?'

Liam had yet to tell her how well things seemed to be going with him and Millie. It was way too early into their relationship, and wasn't something he would offer to share unless it started affecting George's education. 'Just police business, nothing to worry about. Give my love to him, won't you?'

'Of course. Is everything OK, Liam? You sound . . . different.'

'I think I'm probably catching that bug. Is Mark with you?'

'Yes, why?'

'Look, there's nothing to worry about but all three of you stay in tonight, OK?'

'You're scaring me, Liam, what's going on?'

'It's probably nothing, but make sure Mark stays in with you, OK?'

'OK.'

'I'll speak to you later.' Liam hung up before he scared her any more.

Becca pulled up outside Millie's house. Liam looked up and down the road but couldn't see any sign of Millie's car. He wanted to believe she was waiting for him inside, that this had all been a mistake, but every time he thought of her he was either taken back to the cubbyhole on the boat, or the sight of Sloan being lowered into the water. 'Do you have keys?' he asked.

Becca shook her head. 'I thought . . .' she said, her voice trailing off.

Liam peered through the windows, before knocking on the next-door neighbour's door. A woman answered. 'Can I help?' she said, with a faint Italian accent.

'DS Kilshaw. I need to access Millie Foster's house and was wondering if you had a spare key?' said Liam, displaying his warrant card, as he tried to contain his frustration.

'Millie, is she OK?'

'The key?'

'Sure, I have one. She has one of mine,' said the neighbour, rushing back inside and retrieving the key.

'I need you both to wait outside,' said Liam, opening Millie's front door and stepping inside. Nothing immediately felt out of place. 'Millie,' he said, walking from room to room, looking for any sign of disturbance but not finding anything.

'I didn't get your name,' said Liam, returning outside and speaking to the neighbour.

'Juliet Haddon.'

'Juliet, when was the last time you saw Millie?'

Juliet glanced upwards to her right. 'Yesterday, I think. We were both leaving for work at the same time.'

'She was driving?'

'Yes.'

'Did you happen to know if she returned that evening?'

'Sorry,' said Juliet, looking down the road. 'Her car isn't here. What's happening?'

Under any other circumstances, Liam wouldn't have considered Millie to be missing. She could easily have asked someone to call in ill for her, having decided to take a day off, but with everything that was happening it seemed too coincidental. 'You saw her leave school yesterday?' he asked Becca.

'Yes, she dropped me off. We car pool – it was her turn to drive.'

Liam nodded, knocking on the door of the house to the other side of Millie's. When there was no answer, he began canvassing the street. It would have been easier to call for uniform to help but there was no time. Five doors down, he got lucky, speaking to Mrs Milner who had a Neighbourhood Watch sticker in her window.

'I saw her when she came back,' said Mrs Milner. 'She parked directly outside.'

'This was yesterday?'

'Yes, about 5 p.m. I'm not a busybody, if that's what you think, but I remember because almost as she soon as she parked, I heard her engine start again.'

'She left?'

'Yes. And forgive me, I do have a curious nature, so I had a quick peek through the blinds.'

'Millie was in the car?'

'She was. But she wasn't alone.'

Chapter Forty-Five

It didn't take long to work out the identity of the person who'd been in the car with Millie. For all of Mrs Milner's protestations that she'd only had a quick peek, her description of Martin Sloan was very detailed.

'Stay here. Look through Millie's things to see if there is anything that can help us,' Liam said to Becca. 'Can I borrow your car and phone?'

Becca nodded, mouth wide open, and handed him the keys.

He had no time to call Maya as he drove through the town like an unruly civilian, weaving past traffic, blaring his horn at anyone who got in his way. Deep down he knew it was unprofessional, but all his focus was on finding Millie.

He pulled up outside Martin Sloan's house. He didn't bother knocking before entering. Sloan's ravaged body and dead eyes were all too recent in his mind's eye; he didn't care if he scared anyone inside.

He kicked at the lock, his knee shuddering as it struck against the immovable door.

Screaming obscenities into air, he tried once more but the door was reinforced and he risked doing more damage to himself.

With his knee vibrating in pain, Liam took a hoodie from the back of Becca's car and wrapped it around his elbow before smashing a downstairs window. The glass gave in one hit, Liam kicking the rest out before gingerly stepping through the opening, more attention coming his way from outside. Technically, he should have called it in but he had enough reason to suspect Millie's life was in danger, and as Sloan was the last person she'd been seen with, it was reasonable to believe she could be inside.

'Please be inside,' he mumbled to himself as he moved from room to room, checking every door and cupboard of the immaculately ordered house. The last room was Sloan's bedroom, the last chance the small en suite, but she wasn't there either.

Liam sat on the dead man's bed, and put his head in his hands. Taking a deep breath and re-centring himself, he called DCI Hargreaves' mobile and tried to make some sense of the situation.

'You're supposed to be in hospital,' said Hargreaves, after he'd gone through a lengthy explanation.

'I'm fine. I could do with backup here. We need to search through his stuff. Has Maya been able to find his body?'

'Not yet. Could be the sharks got to him,' said Hargreaves, a poor attempt at lightening the situation.

'Sir, I am worried about Millie Foster. I think Sloan may have been signalling to me when he was dying. A last good act.'

'We have everyone looking for those boats,' said Hargreaves. 'Wait until backup arrives then go home and get some rest. Everyone is working, overtime no question. We'll find them.'

Liam appreciated the sentiment, but he knew he didn't have time to wait for backup. He pulled on some protective gloves and began searching the house for anything that might help him find Millie.

It soon became apparent that Sloan was anything but a hoarder. His gauche taste was matched by a minimalistic approach to objects. His clothes were colour coordinated, every item the same colour and brand, from Levi's blue denim to Calvin Klein black underwear. The only thing Liam found of sentimental value was a framed set of medals from the man's time in the army with a photograph from his section. Liam wondered what the seven brothers in arms would think about what had happened to Sloan as he took the frame apart and reached behind the mount, his hand alighting on something stuck to the cardboard behind the photograph.

He wasted no time. He pulled the mount away to reveal a set of Polaroid photographs. His first thought was that the photographs must have been from the time Sloan had served, but that was dispelled when he saw the naked figure of Stacey Smith staring back at him; a cobra tattoo winding up the side of her body. There were ten photos in total, each of Stacey in a different pose.

So was this what had got Sloan killed? It seemed incongruous that Sloan and Stacey had been lovers, such was the age gap and – in Liam's opinion, at least – the gulf in their attractiveness. But when had such things necessarily mattered?

Stacey was still something of an enigma. It already looked like she'd been working against the OCG from London, so it seemed feasible that she may have been aligning her loyalties beyond Fischer as well.

Liam pocketed the Polaroids. 'What was wrong with a phone camera?' he said to the photograph of Sloan with his unit, as the first of the uniform search teams arrived. 'Not sure you're going to find much,' he said to them, heading towards the wharf as he called Grace and told her what he'd found.

'She's a hard one to place. How are you, Liam? I thought you were supposed to be resting?' asked Grace, as an afterthought.

'Do we have any more information on Stacey Smith?' asked Liam, ignoring her question, as he arrived at the front.

There was the slightest of pauses before Grace answered, long enough for Liam to have noticed. 'Only what we already know.'

Liam thought about the frenetic slaying of Gary French and Malcolm Ure, and wondered what Stacey had in store for everyone else. The thought triggered more fears for Millie. 'Any news on Sloan's body? Or any of the others?'

'Maya is still out on the high seas. Listen, everything is in order here. We have teams at Fischer's place, we're interviewing all your lifeboat colleagues. We will find them, Liam. You should rest.'

'Have you been talking to Hargreaves?'

'Jesus, I care about you, Liam. When will you let that sink in?'

Liam was taken aback. With everything that had been happening between him and Millie, he hadn't been giving that much thought about what had gone down between him and Grace in the past. He thought the times she'd asked him out recently had been because she was lonely, or that he was an option for her during her time in Cornwall, but what if he'd got that wrong?

'Thanks, Grace, I mean it; I'll take your advice,' he said, saying goodbye as he arrived at the lifeboat station.

There were no signs to indicate the lifeboat was out of commission. No clues that its director was a psychopath who enjoyed watching people drown. From the outside, everything seemed to be as normal; the boats were waiting for their next call. But nothing would ever be normal again for the lifeboat house, or the town itself.

At the rear of the house was a key safe. Liam entered the secure code, and retrieved a set of keys to the station. The sky was darkening outside, and he felt a drop of rain as he unlocked the door and stepped inside.

He wasn't sure why he had come here. Maybe because this had been the scene of the great deception, the place where Fischer had masterminded his operations, had even recruited a pair of his killers. Could there also be an answer here as to where the man was now? And would Millie even be with him?

The smell of seawater filled the air as he stepped inside, as if the boats hadn't been hosed down properly since their last callouts. He touched the outside of the smaller boat. The Charlotte Mae, her surface dry and rubbery. Although he'd been on a boat earlier that morning, it felt like an age since he'd been out with the crew, another life since they'd been called to find the body of Marlon Tomlinson.

That had been the night of his first date with Millie, as if he needed reminding. He tried to recall any sign he may have missed at the time hinting at what Fischer, Mainwood and Rowson were up to, but beyond Rowson's verbal slip-up where he had called Fischer Commander, there was nothing he could latch on to. It seemed Fischer had been fooling him for years. He'd lived a double life for so long that he had the ability to fully transfer into another character, much like an undercover officer.

Rain hammered the outside of the building as he entered the office and loaded the computer. He searched all the records, starting with Mainwood and Rowson, and moving on to Fischer and the rest of the crew. At this precise moment, there wasn't one member he could fully trust, although he doubted anyone beyond those three was involved. The thought filled him with a profound sadness. These were people he would have given his life for a few days ago, much like his former brothers in the marines, and now three of them were wanted for murder.

He had no idea what he'd hoped to find, but he knew it wasn't there on the computer. He shouted in frustration, the noise reverberating around the cavernous room accompanied by the steady beat of rain on glass.

Liam slumped next to the larger boat – the Annie Wilkinson – feeling helpless. He tried to ignore the nagging thoughts telling him it was all too late. If Sloan had taken Millie, it had almost definitely been because of Fischer; and if Fischer had her, he doubted he would see Millie again.

Think, think, he told himself, working through the investigation from beginning to end. If the circumstances hadn't been so hideous, he would have had to admit he begrudgingly admired Fischer for having brought the OCG to its knees. From what Grace had told them, the police had been trying to do the same for the best part of a decade. Somehow, Fischer had managed to infiltrate the group, and once inside had destroyed it from within. And how had he done that?

Stacey Smith. It all came down to her. Again, he tried not to dwell on missed chances, thinking about the confident young woman who'd claimed to be Peter Britten's niece. He shook his head, distraught as to where following police procedure had taken him.

He looked at the Polaroids and tried to understand them. The images were overtly sexual, but there was nothing erotic about them. If Stacey had wanted to be there, she hadn't told her eyes. She was posing but he couldn't rule out the possibility that she was under duress at the time.

Had Sloan been blackmailing her somehow? Is that why he'd paid the ultimate price this morning out at sea? But that didn't explain why she had killed French and Ure in such a horrific manner. Either way, there was no denying she was at the centre of everything.

Liam thought back to the vessel he'd been held captive on last night, Fischer's expensive motor yacht with its little cubbyhole prison. Obviously, the man had never mentioned the boat before but had he ever taken it out on the water? He must have done at some point, most likely when he'd killed the six OCG members in Ralph's Cupboard. But that didn't help Liam. The only tracking data Liam had here was for the lifeboat, and even if Fischer had been stupid enough to have used it, he would never have been able to do so without being noticed.

Tiredness crept over him but Millie needed him, and every second he delayed meant more time for Fischer to get away.

Once more, he tried to think straight, tried to organise and rationalise everything that had happened. He took a pen and paper from the desk, and listed events from beginning to end, but he couldn't concentrate. His mind kept drifting back to the Polaroid photographs of Stacey Smith he'd found at Sloan's house. Was there something he'd missed?

He sighed as he stared at the photos once more, switching on the lamp next to the sofa so he could get a better look. He tried to blot out the images of the young woman, focusing only on her surroundings. There was something there, he was sure, something in the background that kept him returning.

The shots had been taken from different angles in the same room. In most, the background was blurry, a haze of chipped greys and brown walls. On a couple he could see clearer and he studied them closer. Stacey appeared to be lying on a concrete floor, the walls surrounding her papered with a dated pattern from the seventies, all browns and oranges in a zigzag design he was sure he'd seen somewhere before.

It hadn't been at Sloan's house, and he hadn't got a good look at Fischer's, and anyway teams were there, or had been. No, this was somewhere else. Somewhere from a long time ago.

The memory was just out of reach. Like the times he couldn't remember the name of a famous actor, or a film he'd seen in the past.

How to will it back? Where would he have seen such dated surroundings?

He thought back to Peter's house which hadn't been decorated in a long time, but he'd seen enough of that place to know it wasn't there. He paced the lifeboat centre, walking to the end of the centre facing the sea, the tide out, the rain now gentle against the glass. Even in these extremes, it was impossible to ignore the beauty of the glittering sea, the silhouetted land masses opposite, and by ignoring the investigation for the briefest of seconds, he realised where he'd seen that wallpaper before, the answer straight in front of him.

Chapter Forty-Six

It was the glow of the lighthouse on Godrevy Island that had prompted his memory. The lifeboat team had completed numerous training exercises near and on the island. The island hadn't been manned in years, the light currently swooping the water controlled remotely, but it was still accessible, as was the lighthouse itself.

That must have been three years ago, when four of them – Liam, Fischer and two now retired volunteers – had taken a small RIB to navigate the rocks around the island. Fischer had been given keys to the lighthouse by the organisation who controlled the lights, and the four of them had gone from room to room, making sure everything was in working order.

It had been like going back in time, the dust-strewn rooms like exhibits in a museum. He remembered now why he'd recalled the wallpaper. One of the ex-volunteers had said the wallpaper reminded her of the old family sofa they'd had growing up, and Fischer had joked about how awful that must have been.

He did a quick search online, but couldn't find any photographs to match his theory. But it made perfect sense. The island was treacherous to reach, but navigable for those who knew how. What better place to smuggle drugs, and to hide boats. Sure, it was possible Fischer and the rest had already fled, but if they were anywhere it must be there, and that meant Millie could be there too.

Dismayed to see Becca's phone was now dead, he used the office phone to call Maya. She answered after the fourth ring.

How much to tell her? It was only a theory but unless she had some news to share, Godrevy Island was the most plausible place for them to find Millie. 'It's Liam. I'm calling from the lifeboat station.'

'OK, Liam from the lifeboat station.'

'Listen to me, Maya. I think I know where Fischer is,' said Liam, telling her everything from Becca turning up at the hospital to the photographs he'd found of Stacey Smith in Martin Sloan's house.

Maya listened patiently. He knew what she must be thinking, that in his desperation to find Millie he was reaching for things that weren't there, but she heard him out. 'You're sure the photos are from the island?'

'Ninety-nine-point-nine.'

'Maybe that was why Fischer killed Sloan,' said Maya softly, as if she were thinking out loud. 'The boat service are on a callout in Falmouth at the moment. We're going to have to wait until tomorrow.'

'That's going to be too late. Where are you?'

'On my way home. Why?'

Liam sucked in a deep breath. At best she was forty minutes away. 'I can get over there.'

'Absolutely no way. You're supposed to be resting and it's way too dangerous. It may have escaped your attention but Fischer has a thing for drowning people.'

'Listen, I know the water out there better than anyone. I know what I'm doing. I can approach undetected.'

'And then what? You're going to take them out one by one? You're not in the marines any more.'

That last part was true enough. He'd been carrying a weapon on every mission he'd completed for the marines or the SBS. He'd already witnessed first-hand the mini militia Fischer had on his side, but it didn't mean that it couldn't be done.

'You get the choppers on standby. We must have at least one boat in Penzance.'

'If Fischer is there, then we'll need an armed response unit.'

'Then get them ready, Maya, I'm going.'

'Fuck,' said Maya, realising she had lost the battle. 'How?'

Liam looked over to the lifeboats. 'Leave that to me,' he said.

It was a risk taking the Charlotte Mae out alone, but he had no choice. He wasted no time getting changed, pulling on thermal layers from the changing room over which he placed his drysuit, followed by his wetsuit boots and helmet with its headlamp, his floatation device and gloves. From the secured equipment locker, he pulled out the station's only pair of night vision goggles, the NVG a gift from one of Liam's former colleagues. Finally, he took out two of the multi-tools that included a knife, and connected them to the suit.

Despite his desperation to get to Millie, he made all the necessary checks to the boat. Opening the doors to the slipway, he climbed aboard and started the engine, the guttural sound reassuring in the darkness as he checked the on-board systems and navigation lights.

He stood at the controls, and looked over the sides at the water which now lapped against the runway. He knew he was being foolhardy, but that didn't bother him. All he cared about now was finding Millie. He let out a breath and released the securing mechanisms, the boat sliding down the slipway into the water,

Liam applying the throttle as he manoeuvred the boat out into the open sea.

Usually, he would be in contact with the coastguard but for now he decided on radio silence. It was enough Maya knew where he was going, and he wanted to minimise the chances of Fischer and his crew finding out he was on his way.

He set course for Godrevy, and motored out over the breaking waves. The island was only three miles away and he had to be careful how he approached. Further out to sea he cut the lights, using the on-board navigation system and the guiding light from the island's lighthouse as a beacon.

If Fischer was there, his boat would be moored on the western side of the island towards the open sea. That would give him a better chance of remaining undiscovered. It also meant Liam would have to move in from the south-east where he would be better shielded. He would have to leave the boat behind, but that was something he had more experience of than most.

As the island approached, he placed on the NVGs, the world turning various shades of green, and switched off the engine, the boat easing down through the water until it was at the mercy of the tide. Checking he had everything he needed, he dropped anchor before adjusting the seals on his drysuit, ensuring they were tight and secure.

This time yesterday, the very thought of being out at sea would have terrified him. But he had a greater concern now, and something had shifted in him since escaping the fate Fischer had devised for him.

His respect for the sea remained – he still feared it. But that fear was more balanced than it had been for the last few years. He could rationalise his strengths in comparison to the risks, and with only a few seconds' hesitation was able to slip off the side of the boat into the water. The drysuit was less than ideal for mobility, but at least he was buoyant and warm. He released some air from the valves, finding a balance that allowed him to swim.

Adrenaline kept him going, this morning's tribulations put to the back of his mind as he moved through the open water. He'd been in this situation before, had trained for stealth attacks, and had been part of them during conflict for the SBS, many times carrying a modified MP5 sub-machine gun over his shoulder; for now, he had to put out of his mind the fact that this time he would be unarmed, and could be coming up against opponents who weren't.

His legs struck rock as he approached the side of the island and he used his torch to manoeuvre around the land mass. It was risky work, and he was thankful the sea was relatively calm. Still the pull of the island created waves he had to navigate and threatened to slam him into the hidden rocks.

As he paddled to the western side of the island, he spotted a crop of dry land and made his way towards it, a wave lifting him in the air. For a second he was on the crest, high above the sea. If it crashed down now, he risked being dashed across the rocks and he fought back against the water, his drysuit keeping him afloat as the wave bounced off the rocks and returned the way it had come. Liam wasted no time, swimming as hard as he could before the next wave and dragging himself to shore, his suit catching on a jagged outcrop of rock but not tearing.

He crawled up the embankment until he was away from the water that was illuminated every few seconds from the lighthouse. He took off the NVGs. A secondary light from Fischer's boat a hundred yards or so away from him gave enough light to see by.

He'd been right about Fischer using the island, but it gave him no comfort. Fischer would be caught eventually, and his only concern right now was finding Millie. He took off his drysuit so he could move better, and watched the scene below through his binoculars.

The boat was being loaded with black leather holdalls. Liam wondered why this hadn't been done before, why Fischer had felt it necessary to return to his base, but he guessed Liam's appearance earlier that morning must have come as a surprise and that they had been waiting for darkness to move on.

From his vantage point, he could see Fischer, two operatives he couldn't identify, and Stacey Smith, who was watching events unfold. He couldn't see the boat that had belonged to the other gang, which hopefully meant Mainwood and Rowson had taken it someplace else, meaning he had two less people to contend with.

But what could he do in this situation? The two operatives were armed, and he had to presume both Fischer and Stacey were too. All he could do for now was wait and observe, hope that Maya was on the case and that reinforcements would be coming their way soon.

Knowing he had to be ready for that eventuality, he began creeping nearer the makeshift harbour when a figure came into view, aiming an assault rifle towards him.

Chapter Forty-Seven

Liam had no weapon to surrender. What he did have was a lot more experience of these types of situations than the unsteady twenty-year-old pointing the gun at him.

'I'm unarmed, Billy,' he said, taking small steps towards the man.

'Stay where you are,' said Rowson, his voice more confident than when he had called Fischer Commander a few weeks back. But it still betrayed a hint of fear.

Liam kept moving forwards. He'd seen enough from Rowson to know he was capable of shooting but not if he was undecided. 'It's over now, Billy. We know everything. There is a team of armed officers just waiting for that boat to leave, and we have two helicopters in the air. No one is getting off this island.'

Billy glanced at the radio on his waist and back to the gun. 'Stay where you are.' His voice went up an octave.

'It's not you we want,' Liam said. 'You're as much a victim here as everyone else. Fischer has been using you, and don't think he wouldn't have disposed of you like the others if he'd had to. Just look at what he did to Sloan.'

Even in the faint light, Liam could see realisation dawn on the young man's face. 'Just lower that gun, and I'll say you cooperated. I'll be honest with you, Billy, you'll be going to prison but not for as long as you will do if you use that.'

Liam took another step forward, waiting for the right moment.

'Stop,' said Rowson, reaching for the radio.

It was only a second of indecision, but that was all Liam needed. He stepped in, moved the rifle to the side and punched Rowson in the throat, and continued moving in, punching, headbutting and kicking until Rowson had dropped the gun and fallen to the ground. He slipped the man on to his back, finding a set of zip-ties on the man's belt.

Rowson's breathing was shallow, blood pouring from his mouth and nose. Liam zip-tied his wrists, his arms positioned behind him, and did the same to his ankles. 'Doesn't feel great, does it?' he said, placing the man in the recovery position, wedging his back against a loose rock. 'Do they know I'm here?' asked Liam.

Rowson's mouth opened, wordlessly. Blood-tinged spit drooled from his mouth.

'I need to know,' said Liam, kneeling next to him.

'No,' said the man, closing his eyes as if he'd used up all his strength.

It was all Liam was going to get.

Taking Rowson's gun and radio, he edged down the incline. He risked a glance at the glow of the lighthouse, which was still making sweeps along the surface of the sea as if nothing of import was happening on the island. He could hear static from the radio but no one had called, and so he had to hope that Rowson hadn't managed to alert his colleagues.

He considered leaving the gun behind. Despite the current situation, he was on dicey legal ground carrying the automatic rifle, let alone using it. He had to remind himself he was on police business, not in the middle of a conflict, though maybe it was too late for that.

Crawling along the ground, he got within fifty yards of the motor yacht. He kept imagining Millie on board, stuck in one of the cubbyholes. He could only see four people. If he was quick, he was sure he could fire off four shots before they all had time to retreat but that was never going to happen. He had no authorisation to be holding a firearm, let alone to send out shots without warning, and that was before taking into consideration that only two of them were demonstrably armed.

The radio buzzed, and he had to place it under his body to dampen the noise. 'Corporal, come in,' said the female voice.

Liam focused his binoculars on Stacey, a radio to her mouth. 'Come in,' she said again, before calling over to Fischer.

Fischer stopped what he was doing and looked in Liam's direction. Liam had already slipped his head to the ground, but it was as if the man were looking straight at him. Fischer stayed that way for an improbable length of time, as if he were trying to make out shapes from the undergrowth, before turning and making a signal with his hand.

Within seconds, the engine of the boat had started. 'Last chance, Billy,' came Stacey's muffled voice, through the radio.

Liam crawled forward, keeping his head low, fighting the frustration that any second the boat could disappear from sight, possibly with Millie on board. But what else could he do? His only other option was to run to the boat and try his luck against, at best, two armed civilians, when he wasn't even supposed to be carrying a firearm. Maybe he could fire a warning shot. That might give Maya and his other colleagues time to come to Millie's rescue.

He checked the magazine of the rifle, which was full, determining the cost-benefit probabilities of discharging the weapon, when he heard the sound of rumbling in the distance. His first thought was thunder – it had just that second started raining again – but this was a more familiar sound.

Fischer and the others had clocked it too, a helicopter moving into view – one of the police's Bell 206 JetRangers, two bright Nightsun spotlights working in direct competition with the beam of the lighthouse, scanning the water, the lights getting closer to the island and the boat.

Before Fischer and Stacey had a chance to step aboard the motor yacht, the helicopter was hovering above the island, the Nightsun spotlights illuminating the boat and surrounding areas.

'Attention, this is the police. Lay down your weapons, and switch off the engine of the boat. Cease all attempts to leave the island. Lie down on the ground with your hands above your head. Armed officers have you in their sights, and we have boats surrounding the island. I repeat, put down your guns and lie down on the ground, hands above your head.'

Liam had never been happier to hear the PA system of a helicopter in his life, though Fischer and his group had yet to do as they were told. He moved forward, deciding to jettison the weapon he had taken from Rowson. The helicopter had arrived quickly, but there had been time enough for an armed response unit team to be put together. It was likely at least one of the crew would be armed, and he didn't wish to be mistaken for one of Fischer's gang.

The helicopter PA system repeated its demand as Fischer began gesticulating. A bag was thrown from the large boat towards him, the boat proceeding to motor slowly away.

'Cease your movement immediately,' came the sound from the helicopter, but whoever was now on board had disappeared from sight, the boat making careful movements away from the island as Fischer and Stacey sprinted in different directions.

By the time Liam made his way to the quay area, he could see Fischer on board an RIB, similar to the one they'd discovered in Ralph's Cupboard, already breaking out of the waves towards St Ives, back the way Liam had come.

Further in the distance, Liam saw two police boats creating a barrier, stopping the motor yacht escaping, as a second Bell helicopter came into view.

'Stop,' screamed Liam, catching up with Stacey, who was running towards a second RIB.

It was clear now that Fischer had devised a backup plan. If Stacey boarded the RIB it would give her a chance to reach land. Liam didn't fancy either her or Fischer's chances of escape with two helicopters watching them but he couldn't let Stacey get into that boat.

'Thank God,' said Stacey, as Liam edged nearer. She looked at the speedboat which was about ten metres away, moored to the makeshift quay by rope, before smiling at him.

She didn't appear to be armed, but Liam wasn't about to risk anything. 'You remember me, Stacey, don't you? We met at Peter Britten's house – oh, and then again a few hours back when I was thrown into the sea and nearly drowned.'

'Thank God, you're alive. If there was anything I could have done, I would have. Obviously, I don't have my identification but my name is DS Emma Hamilton. I have been working undercover for the Met the last five years. Call DCI Simon Turner and he will confirm everything.'

Chapter Forty-Eight

If it was a ruse, it was an inspired one. Grace had told them there was a UCO working with the OCG, but it couldn't be this woman. For one, she'd been present when Sloan was killed, had allowed Liam and Peter to be thrown overboard with no floatation device. He appreciated that revealing her identity at that point would have put her life in danger, in addition to his and Peter's, but there was no way she should have got herself in that position in the first place.

But more than that was Peter's testimony that she had killed Gary French and Malcolm Ure. Coupled with the fact that she'd been the last one to leave the house in the Carnewas Estate on the night the two had been killed.

The police boats were still blocking the path of Fischer's powerboat, the first Bell helicopter hovering above them making it difficult to be heard. Hopefully they'd worked out it was him facing off with Stacey Smith, or whatever her name might be. 'If that is the case, you still need to get on the ground and put your hands behind your head.'

'There's no need for that,' said Stacey, taking another step closer.

Liam had his extendable baton in his hand. Whether she was an undercover officer or not, she was dangerous – and a murder suspect. 'You know the procedure. Do not take another step towards me.'

Stacey let out a breath, walking backwards towards the boat. 'You don't know what they made me do,' she said, stepping into the water, and pulling on the rope.

Liam moved towards her, stopping as she reached into the RIB and pulled out a flare gun. 'I know all about you, marine boy. I know you understand what this could do to you from such a close range,' she said, dropping any pretence that she was on his side, undercover officer or not.

'You're really police?' asked Liam, his mind racing, wondering if Grace and Hargreaves had known of Stacey's identity from the beginning. Surely they couldn't have been aware all this time?

'Five years I've lived this life,' said Stacey, starting the on-board motor. 'The things I've had to do.'

'You didn't have to do anything. You certainly didn't need to kill those two men.'

Stacey snarled, throwing the rope into the water. 'They were rapists and murderers. They got what they deserved.'

'I understand that. Just come back in. People will understand.'

Stacey gave him a weak smile as she untied the rope on the boat, opened the throttle, and uttered something indecipherable before turning the flare gun towards him and firing.

Liam dropped to the rocky ground. He smashed his nose and scraped his face against the jagged rocks. He didn't think Stacey had aimed to hit him but that didn't matter. She didn't know the water surrounding the island as well as Liam and Fischer and was making slow progress through the natural harbour of the island. It was doubtful she could get very far, but with the police craft trying to hold the motorboat in place, and Fischer himself being followed by the second of the two helicopters towards the shore in Gwithian, he wasn't taking any chances.

He eased into the water, the cold and salt stinging his face. With the drysuit jettisoned, he was able to make much quicker progress and was soon close to Stacey's boat, the propeller sending a rush of water towards him.

Years of training meant he barely had to think. Beneath him, he could see the low-level rocks. Stacey was doing a good job of avoiding them but it was taking precious time away from her. Liam swam to the side of the RIB, and prepared himself to board the boat. It had to be quick. He reached for the side ropes and launched himself up, only to see a metallic oar coming for his head.

Stacey must have noticed him following her. She was standing now, jabbing the oar at the water, as she tried to reload her flare gun. The oar was easier to avoid, but Liam was stuck in the sea now. Treading water, he watched the movements of the oar, and more importantly Stacey's eyes, which kept darting between him and the flare gun in her hand. He counted the seconds of each swipe from the oar, and as it swooped past him once more, he leaped up and grabbed it and yanked it back with all the propulsion he could muster from his position.

It was enough. Stacey dropped the gun, keeping hold of the oar. Liam had her in his sights now and he used the momentum of the water to reach up and haul her into it.

Stacey hadn't spent the day in and out of the cold sea, and the shock of entering the sea made her breathless. Liam used this opportunity, and grabbed her by the neck. He wanted to tell her to relax, but couldn't risk her getting her strength back. She was panicking but he kept his grip firm around her neck as he swam back towards the shore, the speedboat making its own way out to sea.

Swimming backwards, Liam careered into rock but he was mindful to keep hold of Stacey as he reached shallow water and used the zip-ties he'd taken from Rowson to bind the undercover officer's wrists.

'Try to keep calm,' he said, as she struggled for breath, and gun shots rang out into the air.

Chapter Forty-Nine

Liam dragged Stacey further back on to the island. The helicopter that had been hovering above them moved to where the two police boats were facing Fischer's motor yacht. The shots had come from that direction.

Liam's thoughts immediately went to Millie.

'She's not in there, if that's what you're worried about,' said Stacey, who was sitting ten yards away from him, her hands behind her back as if she were one of Fischer's victims waiting for her time in the sea.

The police boats were too far away for Liam to swim towards, as was the lifeboat on the other side of the island. 'What are you talking about?'

'That schoolteacher you're so enamoured with, navy boy. Christ, you get about, don't you? I know all about you.'

'You know where Millie is?' asked Liam.

'No, but she's not on that boat. That was never the plan. The Commander had long suspected you would work out what was going on, and he decided to take her as leverage if needed.'

'Fischer?'

'Who else?'

'Where is she, Stacey? If you have any good in you, you need to tell me,' said Liam, realising too late how naive his words sounded, how he was trying to bargain with someone who'd long since put the concerns of others behind her.

'I want a lawyer,' said Stacey.

The Bell helicopter had its spotlight on the motor yacht, and Liam could just make out the sight of the boat being boarded. 'It's over now. Talk to me. Do yourself a favour.'

'I don't know where she is, honest truth,' said Stacey, not making eye contact, as she rocked on the spot.

'I saw the photos,' said Liam.

Stacey turned towards him. 'Photos?'

'It's how I found this place. Sloane had them. I remembered the interior of the lighthouse. I'd been here before.'

Stacey shrugged. 'All part of the initiation. Fischer said he needed to take them so he could trust me. Would have probably killed me if I'd said no.'

Liam lowered his eyes. He'd never been involved in undercover work, but understood the emotional toll it could take. It wasn't like other police work. He'd heard stories of how former UCOs could never return to usual police work afterwards.

'I'm very sorry that happened to you, Stacey,' he said. 'But I need to know where Millie is.'

'I may have fucked things up here, but I wouldn't hurt an innocent person if I could help it. I swear, I don't know where she is. Sloan took her, and that sick fuck could have taken her anywhere.'

Liam stood as he saw a small craft navigating to the rocky shore. 'Stay there,' he said, moving towards the police boat which was carrying a number of armed officers. He helped them off, delighted and surprised that behind them, the last to leave, was Maya.

'You OK?' she said, stumbling over the rocks and taking his hand until she was safely on the island. She seemed distressed and reached out to touch his face, making him wince.

'I was until you did that,' said Liam. 'Millie?'

Maya shook her head. 'We've searched the boat, nothing. But we've got Fischer. We had teams posted on the coast.' She frowned as she looked at the injuries on his face and scalp. 'Stacey Smith?' she asked, glancing over to the woman who was still rocking on the ground.

'She claims she's the UCO. Calls herself DS Emma Hamilton,' said Liam, studying Maya for a reaction.

'What? No, she can't be. She killed those two men.'

'She didn't quite deny that. Someone knew, Maya. Possibly Grace, possibly Hargreaves, maybe both.'

'I didn't know, Liam, I promise you that.'

'I need to speak to Fischer. He knows where Millie is.'

'I understand, but we need to be careful how we do this.'

'I speak him to first, Maya, it's the least they can do.'

Maya nodded and said, 'I'll see what I can do.'

A team was organised to search the lighthouse buildings as Billy Rowson was brought down from the hills and taken away, Liam calling DCI Hargreaves on Maya's phone.

'Where's Grace?' Liam asked Hargreaves.

'London. She's on her way now.'

Liam had never considered him the strongest of senior officers although in the main he'd been a competent boss, but if he knew Stacey was the UCO then Liam wasn't sure he would ever be able to trust him. 'Did you know, sir?'

'What's that?'

'That Stacey Smith was the Met's UCO?'

Hargreaves paused before answering, Liam wishing he was face to face with the DCI so he could see his facial features as he spoke. 'DS Kilshaw, you have my word that I had no idea she was the UCO, if she actually is. That has yet to be confirmed. But mark my words, heads will roll if that's true. Believe you me.'

'Where's Fischer?'

'On his way to Bodmin.'

'I need to speak to him about Millie.'

Hargreaves sucked in a breath. 'You've done well here, Liam – even if it's been a bit off book. You can speak to him, but DI Trent will need to be present.'

'Thank you, sir,' said Liam, signalling to Maya that he was ready to go.

◆ ◆ ◆

'Try to get some sleep,' said Maya, as she drove him to Bodmin.

Liam lay back in the passenger seat and closed his eyes. Aside from his enforced sleep at the hospital, he'd been awake for nearly twenty-four hours and they'd been some of the toughest hours of his life. If he hadn't gone through first marine training, then SBS selection, he doubted he'd have survived the ordeal. This time yesterday morning, he was watching Martin Sloan being lifted by a winch and dumped in the sea, and so much had happened since then.

He felt removed from himself, as if his body wasn't his. Every time he closed his eyes, it felt like he was on water, and when he came close to falling asleep he was back beneath the surface. For now that wasn't somewhere his subconscious wanted to be.

But he must have dozed for a bit, because they were arriving at the station before he knew it, and Maya said, 'You know you snore in your sleep,' as she parked up.

Liam blinked, his face red raw and tender to the touch.

'You need to shower and change before you speak to anyone. I'll make sure everything is ready. We're searching everywhere we can think of for Millie,' said Maya, stopping short of promising Liam that they would find her.

He wasted no time. As he showered the sea and blood from his body, he took some small comfort in knowing that everyone involved was in custody, and he no longer had to track down Fischer and his boat; at the same time, he refused to give any credence to the voice telling him Millie had gone the way of the others.

Maya was waiting for him outside the interview room. 'Any news?' he asked.

'None yet.'

'When's Grace getting here?'

'That I don't know. You sure you're ready for this?'

'It's just nice to be on land,' said Liam, opening the door.

Fischer was sitting inside next to a solicitor Liam had never met before. Liam took a seat opposite, Fischer studying the injuries on his face as Maya sat down. She went through the preliminaries, introducing everyone present, and listing the charges they currently had on Fischer.

Liam wanted to know every last detail of Fischer's involvement, how he'd assembled his team and seemingly overthrown the OCG, but that was for another time. 'Only weeks ago we were on the lifeboat together, Fischer. You remember? Marlon Tomlinson's corpse? Funny, I never suspected that you were responsible,' said Liam.

Fischer glanced at his lawyer. 'No comment.'

'Listen, that's for another time. I'm sure you've got a lot you want to get off your chest. But for now, I want to know where Millie is.'

'Millie?' said Fischer, tilting his head as if he'd never heard the name before.

'How long have I known you, Miles? How many shouts have we done together? I'm sure you've got your reasons for doing what you did, but you don't need to add Millie to that number.'

'I don't know what you're talking about, I'm sure.'

Liam looked at Maya. There was little they could offer the man in exchange for the information beyond a favourable word regarding cooperation when it came to sentencing him. Either way, it was more than likely that Fischer would spend the rest of his life behind bars, which put Liam in a weak bargaining position, something Fischer had evidently cottoned on to. 'We never had any issue, did we? I understand why you took her, but you're here now. She doesn't need to suffer.'

Fischer shook his head. 'You know, I was surprised when I found out you were ex-SBS. Never thought you had that type of instinct to you. You're too nice, Kilshaw. Too trusting. For argument's sake, let's say what I would do if I knew where your little schoolteacher friend was. Do you know what that is? That's right, nothing, because I don't care. I don't care about her, or you. Now, offer me something worthwhile or end this charade.'

Fischer was only inches away. Liam was sure that within seconds he could land fatal blows on the man, and had to access every memory from his training to stop him succumbing to such a violent response. 'What has Stacey to do with all this?'

'Who?'

Liam laughed, wondering if Fischer knew she was police, albeit a police officer who was about to spend a long time in prison. 'Think about it, Fischer. This is your chance. Change your narrative. It doesn't need to be you who takes all the blame. We know what Stacey did to French and Ure. You tell me where Millie is now, and this could work in your favour.'

Liam saw the slightest flicker of indecision in Fischer's eyes, the man exchanging another quick look with his solicitor before responding. 'Have you spoken to her?'

Liam nodded.

'You ask her where your girlfriend is?'

'She said she didn't know,' said Liam.

'Well, that's a lie. It was Stacey who came up with the perfect spot to hold her.'

◆ ◆ ◆

Speaking to Stacey Smith – aka DS Emma Hamilton – was a different proposition to interviewing Fischer. Liam was just one of many detectives who wanted to speak to her, including some from the Met's Professional Standards. The fallout from a serving officer being involved in a murder spree and drug operation was going to be huge, and already people way beyond Liam's pay grade were discussing the best way to handle it.

'I need to speak to her now,' said Liam, who had suspended the interview with Fischer and was currently in DCI Hargreaves' office with Maya.

'I'm waiting on permission,' said Hargreaves, flustered.

'Come on, Tom, this is ridiculous. Fischer has just told us she knows where Millie is being held.'

'And you believe that nut-job?'

It was taking all of Liam's willpower not to react. Exhaustion had reached every part of his body, and he risked saying or doing something he would regret. 'What harm can it do?' he said.

Hargreaves pursed his lips, clearly not appreciating Liam's tone. He was about to reply when Grace arrived in the outer office.

Liam was the first out of his seat, adrenaline fuelling his movement and anger. 'Did you know?' he shouted to Grace, who had arrived with two other detectives, presumably from Professional Standards.

'Can we do this somewhere else?' said Grace, under her breath.

'No, we can't. When did you know Stacey was a UCO?'

'The same time as you. I swear, Liam. Only her handler and a couple of very senior officers knew her identity.'

'And they didn't think to bring her in when she killed two people?'

'It's never that easy. You know that, Liam.'

He wasn't sure if he believed her, didn't think he would ever take her word for anything again. 'I need to speak to her, Grace. Before you get into whatever internal bullshit you have planned. She knows where Millie is.'

'And do you think you're the best person to be speaking to her?' said one of the two colleagues who'd arrived with her.

Liam felt Maya's hand on his shoulder. 'And you are?' he said, forcing the anger down.

'DI Graham, Professional Standards,' said the man, meeting Liam with a steely gaze which Liam was seconds from smacking away.

Rescue came from an unlikely source in the form of DCI Hargreaves, who'd decided to take charge of the situation. 'I think we need a few minutes to regain our composure. It is an emotive time. But I agree with DS Kilshaw. If Stacey Smith/DS Hamilton knows where Millie is being kept, that has to be our number one priority. Let's reconvene, and we can determine who is best suited to speak to her,' he said.

Liam allowed Maya to guide him away as Hargreaves spoke to Grace and the two officers from Professional Standards.

In the end, Maya and DI Graham were chosen to interview Stacey. Liam was forced to watch behind the two-way mirror with Hargreaves, Grace and the second officer from the Met. He understood that procedures had to be maintained, and there were certain methods that needed to be utilised to get Stacey to talk, but he just wanted Maya to ask the question.

Grace was within touching distance but Liam had barely looked at her, let alone spoken to her, since his outburst in the outer office. The previous time they'd spoken, he'd been feeling guilty about not fully considering her feelings, and now her very presence was aggravating him. The simple truth was he didn't trust her.

The undercover officer he knew as Stacey looked as punch-drunk as he felt. He wondered if she'd spent the last couple of hours questioning her own decisions. The attack on French and Ure appeared to have been premediated, and whatever the extraneous circumstances were, there was going to be no excusing her actions. And that was before they got into her complicity in Martin Sloan's death, and possibly many others. She may have been in danger herself, but she had a duty to act, something she also failed to do, when Liam and Peter had been left to drown.

'It sounds like you've had a terrible ordeal, Emma, but you're still a police officer,' said Maya.

'Am I?'

'Tell us where Millie is. You have nothing to gain from letting her die.'

Stacey frowned and although she was manipulative and duplicitous, Liam was sure at the moment that she didn't know where Millie was being held. 'I don't know. What, did he tell you that? The man's a monster. Of course, he would say that. I'm really sorry, if I knew I would tell you.'

'If he's such a monster, why did you side with him?' asked DI Graham.

'Time for my solicitor now,' the officer who had gone by the name Stacey Smith said, sitting back in her chair, folding her arms.

◆ ◆ ◆

Liam didn't want to go home. He managed to get an hour's sleep in the welfare room.

'Don't,' he said, when he returned to the office and saw Maya looking like she was about to tell him how terrible he appeared.

Most of Fischer's gang had been arrested, but James Summers and Edward Turnbull were still at large, neither man having been at Godrevy Island or on Fischer's boat. Liam tagged along as Maya drove to the address they had in Camborne for Summers, but the house had already been raided that morning and Summers was nowhere in sight.

Liam was still in and out of reality. The hour's sleep had done little other than to remind him how much he needed to sleep.

'Where next?' asked Maya, after they'd re-questioned Summers' wife. 'I could take you home.'

Liam shook his head, too tired to answer. All possible avenues were being investigated, and he knew he wouldn't be missed, but he couldn't give up on Millie. 'Let's go and see Peter Britten, see if he has any ideas.'

He hadn't seen Peter since the man had been taken to A&E, so was pleased to find him sitting up in his bed. He even managed a smile as Liam and Maya walked over.

'Thank you,' said Peter, as Liam sat on the chair next to him.

'This is my colleague, Maya. She was in the helicopter that came to our rescue.'

'Thank you as well, then,' said Peter.

'We won't keep you long, Peter. We wanted to let you know that Fischer, the man on the boat, and his crew have been arrested.'

'Thank goodness. And Stacey?'

'Her too.'

Peter nodded, allowing the information to settle in.

'You'll be questioned later, but can you confirm who killed Gary French and Malcolm Ure?'

'It was her, Stacey. They were horrible men if that makes any difference.'

Liam glanced at Maya, who had taken a note of the conversation. 'A friend of mine, Millie, has gone missing, Peter. We believe Fischer has taken her but he won't talk to us. I'm worried about her. Can you think of anywhere she could be? Maybe somewhere you were taken?'

Peter looked crestfallen, the wrinkled skin beneath his eyes quivering. 'I take it you've looked at my house.'

Liam nodded. 'And the place where French and Ure were killed. Is there anywhere else they may have taken you at some point?'

Peter shook his head.

'OK, thanks, you get some rest.'

'Wait,' said Peter, as they stood to leave. 'Before they took me to the boat, they stopped somewhere. I couldn't tell which way they had travelled as the windows were blacked out. But when they stopped they slid the side doors of the van open. I couldn't see much but I was sure I could hear the sea in the distance, and I caught sight of something that made me rather nostalgic.'

'What was that, Peter?'

'I'm not sure if I imagined it, but it looked like an old petrol pump. Like one of the ones they used to have when I was a child.'

Liam searched online for images of the old petrol pump he'd seen on the way to Justin Blake's the other day. Peter couldn't confirm that was the one he'd seen but the similarity was enough for Liam to instruct Maya to drive them to Blake's place in Praa Sands.

'He's under home detention, isn't he?'

'I've seen the tag myself.'

'You really think Millie will be there?'

'I think Blake knows a lot more about all of this than he is letting on. Why else make a stop there before going to Fischer's boat?'

'Call for backup,' said Maya, activating the integrated lights as she sped out of the hospital, past the helicopter port, towards Praa Sands.

Liam kept focused, as if sheer belief could make his theory come true. He refused to believe Millie wasn't at Blake's house, refused to even think that she hadn't survived.

The car had barely stopped outside Blake's before Liam leapt from the passenger seat. He ran to the front door, his extendable baton ready by his side as Maya moved to the rear of the property. There were no niceties this time. Liam rang the bell and as soon as it inched open he kicked at the lock, sending the door into Blake. 'Where is she?' said Liam as he burst through. Blake stumbled and fell on to his backside.

'I don't know what—'

'Stop,' said Liam, close to screaming at his one-time informant – all of his frustrations threatening to come out at once.

He hovered over the fallen man, baton in his hand. He had no intention of using it but he needed Blake to know he was serious.

'I know Fischer left her here.'

Blake went to protest. Liam lifted the baton higher into the air.

'Tell me.'

'OK, OK. This has nothing to do with me. There is a wastewater manhole at the end of the garden. Fischer knew all about it. He left her there, I think. I don't know, do I, I can't leave,' said Blake, pointing to the electric tag on his ankle.

'Show me.'

'I just told you, I can't.'

'I think breaking your home detention conditions is the least of your problems. Now get to your feet.'

Blake gingerly stood up. Liam grabbed the back of his oversized T-shirt and hauled him out through the kitchen door into the morning sunshine. The alarm on his tag went off as they came face to face with Maya, and a man – taller than Liam, and twice as wide – who had her in a neck lock.

Liam dropped Blake to the ground. 'Edward Turnbull?' He recognised the man from his official photographs.

'I don't want any trouble. Give me your keys and I'll be gone.'

Liam looked at Maya. She was managing to breathe but Turnbull's arm looked huge in comparison to her slender neck, and Liam feared if he squeezed any harder he would snap it clean. 'We're not here for you, we're here for Millie.'

'You best be quick then, cos that water's rising.'

'The keys are in the car, take it.'

'You must think I was born yesterday.'

'I swear,' said Liam.

'You can drop that for starters,' said Turnbull, glancing at the baton.

Liam threw it to the ground, exchanging a glance with Blake. 'Let her go,' he said, noting that Maya was also looking at Blake, who was on his knees.

'Not that simple. I need to make sure you're all safely put away first,' said the man, as Blake got to his feet and threw the handful of gravel he'd been collecting directly into Turnbull's eyes.

Turnbull couldn't fight his instincts. He instinctively tried to protect his eyes, losing his grip on Maya. She stepped down hard on his foot and drove her head back into the man's face before scrambling free, leaving room for Liam to charge him down.

The attack was quick and brutal, Liam repeating the movements that had disarmed Billy Rowson back in Godrevy, this time having to land twice as many impacts before he could flip

Turnbull, Maya thrusting her knee into his back as they managed to get cuffs on him.

'Where?' screamed Liam.

'Here,' said Blake, hobbling down the barren garden and beyond a faded hedge to a manhole cover.

'Help me,' said Liam, bending down and removing the large metal disc where he found Millie up to her neck in water.

She was shivering, her hair matted with blood and grime. 'My hands and ankles are tied to the ladder,' she managed to say.

Liam dropped into the stagnant water next to her, the knife from his utility belt in his hand. He snipped the ties binding her hands before slipping beneath the repugnant surface, doing the same to the ties on her ankles. 'You're safe now,' he said, spluttering as he eased her out of the prison.

Epilogue

Liam watched his mother sleep. Recent events had made him re-evaluate some things about his life. He thought all this time he'd been visiting his mother out of some sort of misguided loyalty, but he'd come to realise that despite the conflicted way he felt towards her, he had come here out of love.

Not necessarily for the person she'd become after his dad had died, nor for the old woman lying on the bed now, but for the mother she'd once been. The one who'd given birth to him, raised him, helped fight off the bullies, and loved him.

He was sure she was still there now, beneath the cocoon she'd built around herself – the shell she'd formed once the addictions had taken over and age had now hardened. He liked to think of that young woman listening to him now as he told her about everything that had happened, and how eventually he'd once more survived.

He hoped she was proud of him, and understood the real reason he came to visit her. 'See you next week,' he said, kissing her goodbye before heading out into the July sunshine.

The schools had broken up. Within the next couple of hours, the roads around St Ives would be horrendous. He walked along the wharf and past the lifeboat station, the boats gleaming inside, the place still on lockdown as it dealt with recent events. The RNLI had already been in contact with Liam about taking over as operations director, but he simply didn't have the time. He'd agreed to continue volunteering, and to help with the selection process. What he really wanted to do was get out there again, put Fischer's terrible legacy behind him.

The case against Fischer and the rest of his makeshift militia would likely be months in the making. During interrogation, it was discovered that Fischer and Christopher Appleton, the gangster from London who'd been having the affair with Stacey Smith, had been in the marines together decades ago. That was how it all started. Whether or not Appleton knew about Fischer's appetite for drowning people at the time was still unclear, but what wasn't unclear was the fact that a lot of people would be going away for a very long time, including the former police officer Emma Hamilton, Stacey Smith's alter ego, who was being prosecuted for the murders of Gary French and Malcolm Ure, among other charges.

As for Grace, she was back in London facing an internal investigation. It was still unclear who knew about the UCO's involvement in the county lines gangs, but from what Liam had heard her whole department was being disbanded as the investigations continued.

Liam collected his car from the train station car park and made the short journey to George's house. It wasn't his weekend to see the boy but Kim and Mark had agreed to be a bit more flexible in the times he was allowed to see his son, and George was waiting for him by the front door, boogie board by his side.

They drove to Gwithian where Liam had been spending a lot of time of late. Peter Britten had survived hypothermia and was discharged from hospital a week later. Liam had been helping him get back on his feet, a carer appointed to visit him three days a week, and Peter was attending addiction counselling.

'Tide's in,' said Liam, as they parked up and made their way to the beach, neither of them wasting much time getting into the water.

A delicious shiver ran through Liam, as he fought through the waves with George. Despite everything he'd faced out in the sea, there was nowhere he'd rather be at that moment.

The pair of them held on to their boards, floating in the swell as they waited for the next set of breakers to come in. 'We're meeting someone for lunch,' he said to George.

George looked at him as he drifted over a wave, water splashing on to him. He looked at Liam with his mouth open. 'No way,' he said, a half-grin forming on his face.

'Technically she isn't your teacher any more. She said you can call her Millie out of school.'

Millie was still coming to terms with what had happened. She was seeing a counsellor, and had even joked with Liam that she was now having the same nightmares he did.

Liam would have done anything to be able to turn time back, to stop her having to face that trauma, but as she'd said to him, they were both safe now, and the most important thing was that they'd found each other. 'Though she did mention she was interested in teaching Year Five next year . . .' said Liam, as the waves began to build.

'No way,' said George, the pair of them giggling as a huge wave rolled towards them.

'Race you,' said Liam, pointing his board forwards so he could ride the wave into shore.

'Easy,' said George.

The pair of them caught the wave with perfect timing, the crest lifting them into the air as if they were flying before hurtling them towards shore in perfect lines dissecting the water.

They both fell off their boards laughing, before heading back out to sea to do it all again.

ACKNOWLEDGEMENTS

It has been a great pleasure to set a novel in Cornwall, and I would like to thank the following for helping make this book the best it could be:

To my development editor, Russel McLean, who always knows how to push me and the story to reach its potential. *The Lines* wouldn't be the same without his input, and I am, as always, grateful for his insight.

To my publishing editor, Sammia Hamer, for her continued support and enthusiasm in starting this new series, and to the entire Amazon Publishing team for their amazing work behind the scenes.

A special thank you to Alexia Capsomidis for her early read and thoughtful suggestions that helped shape the story.

My Cornwall family for all their input. Special thanks to Michael Brolly for his vague answer about the lifeboat station in St Ives.

And, last but not least, Alison, Freya, Hamish, Snuffy, and Herbie, for their continued love and support.

AUTHOR'S NOTE

Please finish reading the novel before reading this as there are spoilers ahead!

Finished? Good.

I first visited Cornwall sometime in the early eighties and have been in love with the place ever since. My parents and siblings decided to move to the county the year I went to university, and it has been a second home to me ever since. Many of the places in the novel are very well known to me, especially Hayle, St Ives and Penzance, though certain locations have been fictionalised for the story.

When I sat down to write *The Lines*, I only had a vague idea of what would happen in the story. I knew there were going to be a few baddies, but I hadn't realised they would mainly turn out to be volunteers from the lifeboat station in St Ives! It goes without saying that none of the characters in the novel are based on real-life people.

I want to take a moment to emphasise my deep admiration for the incredible work done by the RNLI (Royal National Lifeboat Institution). As a registered charity, they save lives at sea and depend entirely on donations to continue their vital operations. If this story has sparked your interest, or if you simply want to support an extraordinary cause, please visit their website at www.RNLI.org and contribute in any way you can.

Thank you for reading, and I hope you enjoyed your journey through *The Lines.*

The second in the series will be with you soon . . .

ABOUT THE AUTHOR

Photo © 2019 Lisa Visser

Following his law degree, where he developed an interest in criminal law, Matt Brolly completed his Masters in Creative Writing at Glasgow University. He is the *Wall Street Journal* and Amazon bestselling author of the DI Blackwell novels, the DCI Lambert crime novels, the Lynch and Rose thrillers *The Controller* and *The Railroad*, and the standalone thrillers *Zero*, *The Running Girls* and *The Alliance*. *The Lines* is the first in a new series set in Cornwall, featuring DS Kilshaw. Matt lives in London with his wife and their two children. You can find out more about him at www.mattbrolly.com or by following him on X: @MattBrollyUK.

Follow the Author on Amazon

If you enjoyed this book, follow Matt Brolly on Amazon to be notified when the author releases a new book!
To do this, please follow these instructions:

Desktop:

1) Search for the author's name on Amazon or in the Amazon App.
2) Click on the author's name to arrive on their Amazon page.
3) Click the 'Follow' button.

Mobile and Tablet:

1) Search for the author's name on Amazon or in the Amazon App.
2) Click on one of the author's books.
3) Click on the author's name to arrive on their Amazon page.
4) Click the 'Follow' button.

Kindle eReader and Kindle App:

If you enjoyed this book on a Kindle eReader or in the Kindle App, you will find the author 'Follow' button after the last page.